The PEN/O. Henry Prize Stories 2011

The PEN/O. Henry Prize Stories 2011

Chosen and with an Introduction by
Laura Furman

With Essays on the Stories They Admire Most by Jurors
A. M. Homes
Manuel Muñoz
Christine Schutt

ANCHOR BOOKS
A Division of Random House, Inc.
New York

AN ANCHOR BOOKS ORIGINAL, MAY 2011

Permissions appear at the end of the book.

Cataloging-in-Publication Data for *The Pen/O. Henry Prize Stories 2011* is
available at the Library of Congress.

ISBN 978-0-307-47237-3

Book design by Debbie Glasserman

www.anchorbooks.com

Printed in the United States of America
10 9 8 7 6 5 4

For FJK and WW, again and always

The series editor wishes to thank the staff of Anchor Books for making each new collection a pleasure to work on and to read, and to the staff of PEN American Center for the work they do for writers all over the world and for our collection.

Jessica Becht and Benjamin Healy read, wrote, thought, talked, and made this collection one deserving of their intelligence and talent. The series editor thanks them more than they can imagine.

Publisher's Note

A BRIEF HISTORY OF THE PEN/O. HENRY PRIZE STORIES

Many readers have come to love the short story through the simple characters, easy narrative voice and humor, and compelling plotting in the work of William Sydney Porter (1862–1910), best known as O. Henry. His surprise endings entertain readers, even those back for a second, third, or fourth look. Even now one can say, " 'Gift of the Magi,' " in a conversation about a love affair or marriage, and almost any literate person will know what is meant. It's hard to think of many other American writers whose work has been so incorporated into our national shorthand.

O. Henry was a newspaperman, skilled at hiding from his editors at deadline. A prolific writer, he wrote to make a living and to make sense of his life. He spent his childhood in Greensboro, North Carolina, his adolescence and young manhood in Texas, and his mature years in New York City. In between Texas and New York, he served out a prison sentence for bank fraud in Columbus, Ohio. Accounts of the origin of his pen name vary: one story dates from his days in Austin, where he was said to call the wandering family cat "Oh! Henry!"; another states that the name was inspired by the captain of the guard in the Ohio State Penitentiary, Orrin Henry.

Porter had devoted friends, and it's not hard to see why. He was charming and had an attractively gallant attitude. He drank too much and neglected his health, which caused his friends concern. He was often short of money; in a letter to a friend asking for a loan of $15 (his banker was out of town, he wrote), Porter added a postscript: "If it isn't convenient, I'll love you just the same." The banker was unavailable most of Porter's life. His sense of humor was always with him.

Reportedly, Porter's last words were from a popular song: "Turn up the light, for I don't want to go home in the dark."

Eight years after O. Henry's death, in April 1918, the Twilight Club (founded in 1883 and later known as the Society of Arts and Letters) held a dinner in his honor at the Hotel McAlpin in New York City. His friends remembered him so enthusiastically that a group of them met at the Biltmore Hotel in December of that year to establish some kind of memorial to him. They decided to award annual prizes in his name for short-story writers, and formed a Committee of Award to read the short stories published in a year and to pick the winners. In the words of Blanche Colton Williams (1879–1944), the first of the nine series editors, the memorial was intended to "strengthen the art of the short story and to stimulate younger authors."

Doubleday, Page & Company was chosen to publish the first volume, *O. Henry Memorial Award Prize Stories 1919.* In 1927, the society sold all rights to the annual collection to Doubleday, Doran & Company. Doubleday published *The O. Henry Prize Stories,* as it came to be known, in hardcover, and from 1984 to 1996 its subsidiary, Anchor Books, published it simultaneously in paperback. Since 1997 *The O. Henry Prize Stories* has been published as an original Anchor Books paperback, retitled *The PEN/O. Henry Prize Stories* in 2009.

HOW THE STORIES ARE CHOSEN

All stories originally written in the English language and published in an American or Canadian periodical are eligible for consideration. Individual stories may not be nominated; magazines must submit the year's issues in their entirety by May 1. Only stories appearing in a printed periodical are considered. No online-only publications are eligible for inclusion.

As of 2003, the series editor chooses the twenty PEN/O. Henry Prize Stories, and each year three writers distinguished for their fiction are asked to evaluate the entire collection and to write an appreciation of the story they most admire. These three writers read the twenty prize stories in manuscript form with no identification of author or publication. They make their choices independent of each other and the series editor.

The goal of *The PEN/O. Henry Prize Stories* remains to strengthen the art of the short story.

To William Trevor

In the past seven *PEN/O. Henry Prize Stories,* work by William Trevor has appeared five times; this dedication comes in a year when we are Trevor-less.

Trevor was born in Ireland and his work is identified with the literature of that country. Trevor's greatest gift sometimes seems to be distance. He can write as heartbreakingly about young love as he can about the weight of political troubles on obscure individual lives. He is capable of creating a character both unattractive and despicable, such as Mr. Hilditch in *Felicia's Journey,* side by side with Felicia herself, an incorrigibly gullible young woman who becomes, by the end of that excellent novel, nearly saintly in her martyrdom and humility. Painful and involving as the novel is to read, the most disturbing moment comes when the reader begins to feel for the horrible Mr. Hilditch. Often Trevor's deep intelligence and unobtrusively beautiful prose works coercively. In his many novels and short stories, Trevor pulls his reader out of the comfortable complacency of not being someone like Mr. Hilditch. In exchange for our discomfort, we gain insight into the criminal and unlikable, and we feel compassion, whether we want to or not. In a collection of essays, *Excursions in the Real World,* Trevor wrote that a writer "needs space and cool; sentiment is suspect. Awkward questions, posed to himself, are his stock-in-trade. . . . he has to stand back—so far that he finds himself beyond the pale, outside the society he comments upon in order to get a better view of it. Time, simply by passing, does not supply that distance. . . ."

We can rejoice that however far William Trevor ventures beyond the pale to create his fictional world, he still returns to tell us the tale.

Contents

Introduction

Every year, after the long process ends of choosing the twenty PEN/O. Henry Prize stories from the many submitted, friends ask me what trends were revealed by all that reading and deliberation. The question doesn't have to do with aesthetics or literary technique but with subject matter: What do this year's stories show about our world?

Those who pose the question seem to believe that short-story writers are prophets or seers, or at the very least mirrors reflecting the joys and horrors of our time. It's a common notion that writers are society's canaries in the coal mine, sensitive and intelligent canaries who bring us news about the way we live now. Many are known for doing exactly that; Charles Dickens springs to mind, and so many other writers with a social vision such as Upton Sinclair, John Dos Passos, Margaret Atwood. And who could have done a better job than Herman Melville of portraying the multiracial, multiethnic mix that was his America and is ours?

But for many writers, an explicit social agenda and social commentary—even contemporary life itself—are of limited interest. The relevance of a good writer transcends time and place. We continue to read Charles Dickens even though we don't live in Victorian England. Fyodor Dostoyevsky thrills us not because we recognize czarist Russia but because we recognize the struggle of our own souls.

Literature—writing that lasts because of its superior quality—does have a way of seeming both predictive and definitive. When we see a suburb of a certain type, we see Cheever Country or the Land of Yates; literature over time defines life. When we reread the best short stories, we recognize both their technical power and the true-to-life human crises embedded in them.

Of course, one practical obstacle to the idea that stories have something to tell us about our moment is that often they are written long before they are published. The moment they arrive in print before the reader's eyes might make a writer seem prescient, but the excellent timing is more often than not a happenstance. There have always been apocalyptic stories, but one published on September 10, 2001, would have a predictive power unavailable to the same story if published much earlier or later.

That said, it's hard to deny that some stories capture the zeitgeist perfectly, and in *The PEN/O. Henry Prize Stories 2011* the mood is a savage fierceness, which seems apt at the moment. Many of the stories are laden with a convincing sense of doom and intimations of what civilization looks like minus the civilization. All of this year's stories are written with end-of-the-world honesty.

One example of such intensity is Lynn Freed's "Sunshine." Because the author is a native of South Africa, her brilliant, rock-hard prose might seem to be expressing metaphorically the horrors of that nation's past, but "Sunshine" is larger than recent political history. Its true subject is evil. Its world is an eternal, almost mythic, struggle of Master and Slave. The story's drama is about the breaking of a wild spirit by a spoiled creature too used to getting his way. The manner in which the struggle ends is haunting and frightening—and rings true. Our juror A. M. Homes was also struck by these strengths, and she chose "Sunshine" as her favorite.

Helen Simpson's "Diary of an Interesting Year" brings the reader into a postapocalyptic world that seems at first familiar from screen incarnations. Yet the quotidian, middle-class voice of the narrator is in powerful contrast to the dramatic privations of a society's collapse. The story is funny until it is distinctly not, and then it is powerful and unnerving.

"The Black Square" by Chris Adrian is about the limits of love of all kinds, except the love of death. Its central conceit—a black square one can enter but never return from—is an invention of brooding, Rothko-like minimalism, and suggests a different world from ours, one in which suicide is accepted, perhaps even respectable. This is the way the world ends—through a small black square, one person at a time.

In "Melinda" by Judy Doenges the violence, as well as the melancholic monotony of a degrading world, is supplied by methamphetamine, to which Melinda has devoted her young life and what's left of her mind. The cool, matter-of-fact tone of Melinda's narrative is perfect for the destruction she describes: her world that will end before she knows it, as she loses her sense of time and her capacity to care about anything but the drug and what it takes to get it.

The stories of David Means are not unacquainted with destruction. (A previous Means story was included in *The PEN/O. Henry Prize Stories 2006*.) In "The Junction" Means layers two narratives of hobo life in the American Midwest: one is the tale Lockjaw tells one freezing night to a bunch of cynical kibitzers permanently down on their luck—a tale about hot cherry pie, fresh-baked bread, and home; the other is the story of Lockjaw's audience of fellow hobos and his relationship to them. Lockjaw is a talker because "you had to spin out a yarn and keep spinning until the food was in your belly and you were out the door." But Lockjaw's peers are way beyond home, fresh cherry pie, and Lockjaw's gift of gab.

In "Ice" by Lily Tuck, we're in the Antarctic. On a cruise ship the quiet drama of a frozen marriage acts as a diversion to the real iciness to come, the coldness of death. Tuck's characteristic compression and elegant brevity shape a dangerous world that has shrunk to one element—the ice that surrounds the boat and defines the characters' lives.

Another kind of isolation overwhelms a young couple in Lori Ostlund's "Bed Death." Two American women arrive in Malaysia to find work and to be together. In the end, they are alienated both from the place and from each other, separated not just by the "bed death" of the title—the end of their lovemaking—but by the end of their mutual tolerance.

In what might be the sweetest story in the collection, "Nightblooming" by Kenneth Calhoun, a young musician, filled with doubts and condescension, plays a gig with the Nightblooming Jazzmen, a band of elderly musicians who are "marching the saints and balling the jack." The illusions crushed by the end of the night are those of the youth, who loses a new home he's surprised to find he wanted.

Three other stories in the collection revolve around varieties of love, or rather its impossibility, power, and elusiveness: *"Pole, Pole"* by Susan Minot, "Nothing of Consequence" by Jane Delury, and "The Rules Are the Rules" by Adam Foulds.

Susan Minot's story is set in Kenya and centers on the accidental, sexually heated meeting of a young woman, newly arrived, and a man whose elusiveness is soon made plain, as is the tenuousness of the woman's reason for being in Africa. The story begins with a passionate coupling of strangers and ends in isolation.

In Jane Delury's "Nothing of Consequence" a widowed French schoolteacher goes to Madagascar and meets a young man. The important transformation in the story comes, surprisingly, to the young man. The encounter allows him to understand his own story, and gives the Frenchwoman a measure of justice for a grave wound in her past. The story reveals with delicacy and humor how incidentally yet significantly the lovers touch each other's lives.

In Adam Foulds's "The Rules Are the Rules" the life of Reverend Peter and his congregation in suburban London is complicated by his closeted homosexuality and his loss of faith. "Off the grid. That was how Peter thought of himself when he lost contact with God, when Jesus was a dead man and he was alone. Then the world was vast and contained nothing, nothing real, only his loneliness between hard surfaces." He finds refuge in anger and in petty cruelty to those smaller than he, and despair at what he sees as the coming loss of his lover, Steve, who is free to go to bars and clubs for casual sex. The story conveys without sentimentality Peter's aching imprisonment. The intensity in the story derives from the awful sense that there is no escape from the rules because they are the only ones Peter accepts.

The energy and music of "How to Leave Hialeah" by Jennine Capó Crucet lie in the voice of the narrator. She begins with sassy happiness at her successful escape from Florida, her mother, her extended Cuban American family, and what appears to be a sadly restricted existence. As she moves along an outwardly successful path toward another kind of restriction within an academic life built on the corrupting exploitation of her ethnic identity, our narrator crosses from authenticity to falseness, from a world with flaws and joys to one in which success means compromising self-definition and petty internecine triumphs. The story ends with a new and opposite desire, perhaps unattainable.

Mark Slouka's "Crossing" works both as an engrossing, involving tale of a man trying not to screw up again and as a metaphor for all parenting. Has there ever been a parent who hasn't felt the terror and responsibility this father faces? Slouka's story is a vivid portrait of the love of a helpless parent for his child, one that leaves us caught in midstream, holding our breath.

Helplessness, irresponsibility, mistaken identities—these are also elements in Elizabeth Tallent's rich story "Never Come Back," about a man who, in the middle of his life, finds frustration and disintegration in his family and his rural California community, and internally in his sense of his own manhood. His grandson seems to offer him a fresh start, but the child, like everything else in the story's world, isn't his to have. Tallent's prose is dense and involving; her characters and their place are believable and heartbreaking.

A story by Brian Evenson was included in *The PEN/O. Henry Prize Stories 2007;* that story, "Mudder Tongue," was about a father whose language was failing him. "Windeye" is a child's story about belief in make-believe. Evenson blurs the distinction between being dead and not being alive, between pretending and not knowing what is real. The boy's need for his sister's affirmation of his feelings and perceptions spells lasting trouble for him, but his fidelity to his young, fearless sister pulls the reader through the story.

Another exploration of childhood comes in Brad Watson's "Alamo Plaza," about a family's vacation in Gulfport, Mississippi. Brad Watson's previous PEN/O. Henry story appeared in the 2010 collection and also took place in a motel. The pleasure of the current story lies in the narrator's exploration of memory tainted by knowledge. The characters are both who they are in the present of the story and who they will be when their fates, announced early in the story, catch up with them. For the moment, though, there's an uneasy truce between remembered unhappiness and the web of details that the narrator illuminates with a survivor's skepticism and uneasy affection.

Four of our stories reach into the historical past with a present-day intensity; nothing will do now but to tell the truth.

Jim Shepard, a master storyteller, sets "Your Fate Hurtles

Down at You" in 1939 Switzerland, a time of fateful political tran-
sition. Four volunteers—Die Harschblödeln, the Frozen Idiots—
are spending the winter "in a little hut perched on a wind-blasted
slope . . . nine thousand feet above Davos." They are avalanche
researchers, which is to say that their fates will hurtle down at
them with impersonal destructiveness. The high-spirited young
scientists court disaster as the narrator's courtship of an old
acquaintance turns into another kind of disaster. The narrative
tone is commemorative yet hardly solemn; between gallows
humor and the perils of the quartet's scientific research, there's an
almost jaunty quality to the story's beginning. As the story devel-
ops, the reader's sense of doom and sorrow grows until the final
surprising and satisfying ending. Our juror Christine Schutt
chose "Your Fate Hurtles Down at You" as her favorite.

Tamas Dobozy's "The Restoration of the Villa Where Tíbor
Kálmán Once Lived" takes place in Hungary in the last years of
World War II and during the Soviet occupation. To László, a survivor of conscription into the German army and then of the
Soviet bureaucracy, restoring the villa where a Hungarian hero
once lived becomes both his raison d'être and his excuse for
behavior exemplifying what the philosopher Hannah Arendt
termed "the banality of evil."

"The Vanishing American," Leslie Parry's story of early Hollywood, World War I, and lost love, is full of feeling, intelligence,
and narrative confidence and skill. A silent film is being shot in
California, and illusion reigns. The protagonist is a mute actor
playing Indian #9. The buffalo are imported and Indian #9 is not
Native American. He is a veteran of the all-too-real Argonne Forest, haunted by the war's losses and his own uncertain future, and
he moves through the film's shooting both present and absent.
The story fascinates the reader, who will gradually put together
Indian #9's identity, where he has been, and where he is going.

Matthew Neill Null's West Virginia tale "Something You Can't
Live Without" is a terrific story about a con man who is himself

conned in a particularly horrible way. Our juror Manuel Muñoz chose the story as his favorite. What gives "Something You Can't Live Without" its heft and glory is the deep authenticity of the narrative. There are no caricatures here, no researched settings. Everything in the story feels true to life—as gruesome and glorious, in fact, as life itself.

It's possible, of course, that the apocalyptic ferocity of *The PEN/O. Henry Prize Stories 2011* is in the eye of the beholder. The hope is that each of the stories will outlast the original time and place that inspired it. That's the best news about the latest incarnation of our annual collection of twenty stories—each of them displays a vigor and intensity that suggest that the end-time of the short story as an art form is nowhere in sight.

Laura Furman
Austin, Texas

The PEN/O. Henry Prize Stories 2011

Jim Shepard

Your Fate Hurtles Down at You

WE CALL OURSELVES Die Harschblödeln: the Frozen Idiots. There are four of us who've volunteered to spend the coldest winter in recent memory in a little hut perched on a wind-blasted slope of the Weissfluhjoch nine thousand feet above Davos. We're doing research. The hut, we like to say, is naturally refrigerated from the outside and a good starting point for all sorts of adventures, nearly all of them lethal.

It's been seven years since the federal government in Bern appointed its commission to develop a study program for avalanche defense measures. Five sites were established in the high Alps, and, as Bader likes to say, we drew the short straw. Bader, Bucher, Haefeli, and I wrap ourselves in blanket layers and spend hours at a time given over to our tasks. The cold has already caused Haefeli to report kidney complaints.

He's our unofficial leader. They found him working on a dam-building project in Spain, the commission having concluded correctly that his groundbreaking work on soil mechanics would translate usefully into this new field of endeavor. Bucher's an engineer who inherited his interest in snow and ice from his father, a meteorologist who in 1909 led the second expedition across Greenland. Bader was Professor Niggli's star pupil, so he's our resident crystallographer. And I'm considered the touchingly passionate amateur and porter, having charmed my way into the group through the adroit use of my mother's journals.

It might be 1939 but this high up we have no heat and only kerosene lanterns for light. Our facilities are not good. Our budget is laughable. We're engaged in a kind of research for which there are few precedents. But as Bader also likes to say, a spirit of discovery and a saving capacity for brandy in the early afternoon drives us on.

We encounter more than our share of mockery down in Davos, since your average burgher is only somewhat impressed by the notion of the complexities of snow. But together we're now approaching the completion of a monumental work of three years: our *Snow and Its Metamorphism,* with its sections on crystallography, snow mechanics, and variations in snow cover. My mother has written that the instant it appears, she must have a copy. I've told her I'll deliver it myself.

Like all pioneers we've endured our share of embarrassment. Bader for a time insisted on measuring the hardness of any snowpack by firing a revolver into it, and his method was only discredited after we'd wasted an afternoon hunting for his test rounds in the snow. And on All Hallows' Eve we shoveled the accumulation from our roof and started an avalanche that all the way down in Davos destroyed the church on the outskirts of town.

I'm hardly the only one excessively invested in our success. Haefeli at the age of eighteen lost his father in what he calls a Scale Five avalanche. As to be distinguished from, say, his Scale One or Two type, which obliterates the odd house each winter but otherwise goes unnoticed.

His Scale Five was an airborne avalanche in Glärnisch that dropped down the steeper slopes above his town with its blast clouds mushrooming out on both sides. His father had sent him to check their rabbit traps on a higher forested slope and had stayed behind to start the cooking pot. The avalanche dropped five thousand vertical feet in under a mile and crossed the valley floor with such velocity that it exploded upward two hundred feet on the opposite hillside, uprooting spruces and alders there with such force that they pinwheeled through the air. The snow cloud afterward obscured the sun. It took ten minutes to settle while Haefeli skied frantically down into the debris. Throughout the next days' search for survivors, there were still atmospheric effects from the amount of snow concussed into the upper atmosphere.

The rescuers found that even concrete-reinforced buildings had been pile driven flat. When he finally located a neighbor's three-story stone house, he mistook it for a terrazzo floor.

Fifty-two homes were gone. Seventeen people were dug out of a meetinghouse the following spring, huddled together in a circle facing inward. Four hundred yards from the path of the snow, the air blast had blown the cupola off a convent tower.

But I had my own problems when it came to a good night's sleep.

When I was a child it was general practice for Swiss schools around the Christmas holidays to have a Sport Week, during which we all hiked to mountain huts to ski. My brother, Willi, and I were nothing but agony for our harried teachers every step up the mountains and back. He was a devotee of whanging the rope tows once the class hit an especially steep and slippery part of the hillside. I did creative things with graupel or whatever other sorts of ice pellets I could collect from under roof eaves or along creek beds.

We were both in secondary school and sixteen. I'd selected the science stream and was groping my way into physics and chemistry, while he'd chosen the literary life and went about fracturing Latin and Greek. Even then, he'd surprised me: When had he become interested in Latin and Greek? But given the kind of brothers we were, the question never arose.

I claimed to be interested in university; he didn't. We had a father to whom such things mattered: he called us his happy imbeciles, took pride in our skiing, and liked to say with a kind of amiability during family meals that we could do what we pleased as long as it reflected well on him.

He styled himself an Alpine guide, though considering how he dressed when in town, he might as well have been the village mayor. He wore a watch fob and a homburg. He always spoke as though a stroke of fate had left him in the business of helping Englishmen scale ice cliffs, and claimed to be content only at altitudes over eleven thousand feet, but we knew him to be unhappy even there. The sole thing that seemed to please him was his weakness for homemade medicines. Willi considered him reproachful but carried on with whatever he wished, secure in our mother's support. I followed his moods minutely, even as disinterest emanated from him like a vapor. We had one elder sister who found all of this distasteful and whose response was to do her chores but otherwise keep to her room, awaiting romances that arrived every few months via subscription.

His self-absorption left Willi impatient with experts. On our summer trek on the Eiger glacier the year before, we'd been matched for International Brotherhood Week with a hiking group from Chamonix. They spoke no German and we spoke no French, so only the teachers could converse. The French teacher at one point brought the group to a halt by cautioning us that any noise where we stood could topple the ice seracs looming above us.

Willi and I had been on glaciers since we were eight. While everyone watched, he scaled the most dangerous-looking of the seracs and, having established his balance at the top, shouted loud enough to have brought down the Eiger's north face. "What's

French for 'You don't know what you're talking about'?" he called to our teacher as he climbed back down.

We were to base our day around one of the ski huts above Kleine Scheidegg. The village itself, on a high pass, consists of three hotels for skiers and climbers and the train station and some maintenance buildings serving the Jungfraubahn, but our group managed to lose one of our classmates there anyway—one of those boys from the remote highlands where a cowherd might spend the entire summer in a hut, with his cows and family separated only by a waist-high divider—and by the time he was located we were already an hour behind schedule. We were led by one of the schoolmistresses who held a ski instructor's certificate and her assistant, a twenty-year-old engineering student named Jenny. They had as their responsibility fourteen boys and ten girls.

The ski run to which we were headed was, in summer, a steep climb along the edge of a dark forest broken by occasional sunlit clearings, before the trees thinned out and there were meadows where miniature butterflies wavered on willow herbs and moss campion. Above those meadows sheep and goats found their upland pastures. Above that were only rocks and the occasional ibex. There was an escarpment above the rocks that was ideal for wind-sheltered forts. We'd discovered it on our ninth birthday. Willi said it was one of those rare places where nothing could be grown or sold: one of those places the world had produced exclusively for someone's happiness. In winter storms the wind piled snow onto it, the cornices overhanging the mountain's flanks below. And the night before our Sport Week outing, there'd been strong westerly winds and heavy accumulation on the eastern slopes. Avalanche warning bulletins had been sent to the hotels an hour after our departure.

We spread ourselves out around the bowl of the main slope. Some of us had climbed in chaps for greater waterproofing and were still shedding them and checking our bindings when our schoolmistress led the others down into the bowl. The postmaster's daughter, Ruth Lindner, of whom Willi and I both retained fantasies, waited behind with us while we horsed about, setting her hands atop her poles in a counterfeit of patience. She had red hair and pale smooth skin and a habit, when laughing with us, of lowering her eyes to our mouths in a way that we found impossibly stirring.

The skiers who'd set off were already slaloming a hundred yards below. We'd been taught from the cradle that in winter, however much we thought we knew, there were always places where our ignorance and bad luck could destroy us. A heavy new snow mass above and an unstable bowl below: this was the sort of circumstance in which our father would have said: If you're uncertain, back away.

"Race you," I said. "*Race* me?" Willi answered. And he nosed his ski tips out over the bowl edge. "See if you can stay on your feet," I teased, above him, and flumphed my uphill ski down into a drift.

There was a deep cutting sound like shears through heavy fabric. The snowfield split all the way across the bowl, and the entire slab, a quarter of a mile across, broke free, taking Willi with it. He was enveloped immediately. Ruth shrieked. I helped her pole herself farther back out of the bowl. The tons of snow roaring down caught the skiers below and carried them all away. One little girl managed to remain upright on a cascading wave but then she too was upended and buried, the clouds of snowdust obscuring everything else.

Guides climbing up from the hotels spread the alarm and already had the rescue under way when Ruth and I reached the debris field. The digging went on for thirty-six hours and fifteen of our classmates, including Willi and the schoolmistress, were uncovered alive. The young assistant, Jenny, and seven others were dug out as corpses. Two were still missing when the last of their family members stopped digging three weeks later.

My brother had been fifteen feet deep at the very back edge of the run-out. They found him with the sounding rod used for locating the road after heavy snowfalls. He'd managed to get his arm over his face and survived because of the resulting air pocket. A shattered ski tip near the surface had aided in his location. One of the rescuers who dug him out kept using the old saying "Such a terrible child!" for the difficulties they were encountering with the shocking density of the snow mass once it had packed in on itself. We called for Willi to not lose heart, not even sure if he was down there. Ruth dug beside me and I was taken aback by the grandeur of her panic and misery. "*Help* us," she cried at one point, as if I weren't digging as furiously as the rest.

He was under the snow for two hours. When his face was finally cleared, it was blue and he was unconscious but the guides revived him with a breathing tube even as he still lay trapped. And when someone covered his face with a hat to keep the snow from falling into his mouth and eyes, he shouted for it to be taken away, that he wanted air and light.

He was hurried home on a litter and spent the next two days recovering. I fed him oxtail soup, his favorite. His injuries seemed slight. He asked about Ruth. He answered our questions about how he felt but related nothing of the experience. When I questioned him in private he peered at me strangely and looked away. On the third night when we put out the lamp he seemed suddenly upset and asked not to be left alone. I said, "You're not alone; I'm right here." He cried out for our mother and began a horrible rattling in his throat, at which he clawed. I flew down the stair-steps to get her. By the time we returned he was dead.

The doctor called in another doctor, who called in a third. Each tramped slush through our house and drank coffee while he hypothesized and my mother trailed from room to room in his wake, tidying and weeping until she could barely stand. Their final opinion was contentious but two of the three favored delayed shock as the cause of death. The third held forth on the keys to survival in such a situation, one being the moral and physical strength of the victim. He was thrown bodily out of the house by my father.

How should our mother have survived such a thing? The inquiry into the tragedy held that the group leaders—the schoolmistress and dead Jenny—were blameless, but the parents of the children swept away decided otherwise, and within a year the miserable and ostracized schoolmistress was forced to resign her post.

Our mother had always seemed to carry within herself some quality of calm against which adverse circumstances contended in vain, but in this case she couldn't purge her rage at the selfishness of those whose blitheness had put the less foolhardy at risk. She received little support from my father, who refused to assign blame, so she took to calling our home "our miserable little kingdom," and mounting what questions she could at the dinner table as if blank with fatigue.

By May, scraps from the two missing children poked through the spring melt like budding plants, and in the course of a day or two a glove, a scarf, and a ski pole turned up. Renewed digging recovered one of the little girls, her body facedown, her arms extended downhill, her back broken, and her legs splayed up and over it.

Our mother talked to everyone she considered knowledgeable about the nature of what had happened, and why. From as early as we could remember, she'd always gathered information of one kind or another. I'd never known anyone with a more hospitable mind. My sister often complained that no one could spend any time in our mother's company without learning something. She was the sort of woman who recorded items of interest in a journal kept in her bedroom, and she joked to our father when teased about it that it represented a store of observations that would someday be more systematically confirmed as scientific research. Why did one snowfall of a given depth produce avalanches when another did not? Why was the period of maximum danger those few hours immediately following the storm? Why might any number of people cross a slope in safety only to have some other member of their party set the disaster in motion? She remembered from childhood a horrible avalanche in her grandmother's village: a bridge and four houses had been destroyed and a nine-year-old boy entombed in his bed, still clutching his cherished stuffed horse.

She spent more time with me as her preoccupation intensified. There was no one else. Her daughter had grown into a long, thin adult with a glum capacity for overwork and no interest in the business of the world. We had few visitors, but if one overstayed his welcome my sister would twist her hair and wonder audibly, as if interrogating herself, "Why doesn't he leave? Why doesn't he leave?"

One early morning I found my mother on my bed. When she saw I was awake, she remarked that Willi's shoulders had been so broad that it made him appear shorter than he was. "And mine, too," I said. "And yours, too," she smiled. Somewhere far away a dog was barking as if beside itself with alarm.

I told her I thought I might have started the avalanche. She said, "You didn't start the avalanche." I told her I might have, though I hadn't yet explained how. She reminded me of the farmers' old saying that *they* didn't make the hay; the sun made the hay.

"I think *I* made the avalanche," she finally suggested. When I asked what she was talking about, she wondered if I remembered the Oberlanders' tale of the cowherd whose mother thought he'd gone astray and, in a rage at having been offered only spoiled milk by his new wife, called on ice from the mountain above to come bury her son and his wife and all of their cows.

How old was I then? Seventeen. But even someone that young could be shocked by his own paralysis in the face of need. My mother sat on my bed picking her heart to pieces and I suffered at the spectacle and accepted her caresses and wept along with her and fell asleep comforted, and failed to offer my own account of what might have happened, whether it would have helped or not. The subject was dropped. And that morning more than any other is what's driven me to avalanche research.

Bucher's a good Christian but even he gave up the long ski down to services after a few weeks, and instead we spend our Sabbaths admiring the calm of early morning in the mountains. The sun peeps over the sentinel peaks behind us and the entire snow-covered world becomes a radiance thrown back at the sky. The only sounds are those we make. On our trips to Davos for supplies, Bader and I for a few months held a mock competition for the affections of an Alsatian widow who negotiated the burden of her sexual magnetism with an appealing modesty. Then in February I slipped on an ice sheet outside a bakery and bounced down two flights of steps. "So much for the surviving Eckel brother," Ruth Lindner said in response from across the street.

What was she doing in Davos? She'd been reassigned to a new school district. How did she like teaching? She hoped the change of scene would help. What did her parents make of the move? They'd been against it. But lately she'd started to feel more in prison than at home. We arranged to meet for coffee the following weekend, and the group, back at the hut, made much of my announcement of my withdrawal from the Alsatian sweepstakes.

I'd lost track of Ruth after Willi's service had concluded. My last words to her had been "I blame myself," and her response had been "I blame everyone." Then she'd gone on holiday to her maternal grandparents' farm near Merligen. That holiday had extended itself and my two letters to that address had been returned unopened. When I'd pressed her father for an explanation, he'd assumed that the postmaster must have found them undeliverable. When I'd protested that he was the postmaster, he lost his temper. My parents had been no more help. Her few friends claimed to be equally mystified.

Over coffee she asked how I was finding Davos and then moved on to Willi: his poor grades and how he liked to present himself as indisposed to exertion indoors, and the way outside he had no time for anything except his skis. She became misty-eyed. She asked if he'd ever told me that the high summits were like giants at their windows looking down at us.

"No," I said. She wore a beeswax and aloe mixture on her lips to protect them, and the effect was like a ceramic glaze I longed to test with my finger.

"He told me that," she said, pleased.

She asked if I remembered a winter camping trip some of our classmates had taken a month before the Sport Week outing. I told her I remembered it better than she imagined. I had worked up the courage to ask if she was going and she had said no, so I had dropped out. Later I discovered that both she and Willi had gone.

"Had that always been the plan?" I wanted to know, pained even after all these years.

"I need you to listen," she told me.

"What do you suppose I'm doing?" I answered.

"This is not easy for me," she went on to say.

"Does it seem so for me?" I asked.

She told me that that first afternoon they'd pitched camp in a little squall of butterflies blown above the snow line by an updraft. That night a full moon had risen above their tents and their breath vapor had frozen onto the canvas above them. It had broken off in a sheet when in the predawn stillness she'd lifted the flap to slip into Willi's tent.

"I don't need to hear this," I told her. But it was as if I'd said I did. She said that once they'd shed their clothes and embraced inside his sleeping sack, she'd felt the way she had years earlier during an electrical storm when her hair had lifted itself into the air and her hands, holding a rake, had sung like a kettle with the discharge.

We sat across from each other and our coffees. Why does anyone choose one brother and not another? I wanted to ask.

"You have his facial expressions," she said, instead.

"Twins are like that," I answered.

"He told your mother when he got back," she added, by way of addressing my silence. That part of the story seemed to affect her most of all.

"Told her what?" I asked.

"That we were in love," she said.

A truck outside the window ground its gears. "And you got pregnant," I told her.

"And I got pregnant," she said. She seemed to be considering our hands.

Carousers clattering skis and poles came and went. "Did my mother find out?" I wanted to know.

"I assume she guessed," Ruth said.

"I have to get back," I told her.

At the door while I bundled against the weather she said she was sorry. She said she had so much more to tell me. She asked if I would see her again. When I didn't respond at first, she removed one of my mittens and placed my hand against her cheek. But she already knew what I wanted. She already knew what I felt. It was as if there'd never been any point in pretending otherwise.

The position in which she left me brought to mind the subject that Haefeli insists should be absorbing our every waking moment. The American W. A. Bentley was the first to have photographed snow crystals, having recorded over six thousand different forms before conceding that he'd only scratched the surface, in terms of the number of types that must exist. Such crystals are formed when water vapor in the cooling air condenses onto particulate matter in the atmosphere and then freezes, the ice particles growing as more vapor attaches itself in a process called sublimation: that small miracle, Bader reminds us, as we dig cores, in which a substance transforms itself from gas to solid without having passed through its liquid state. The variations in design are as infinite as the conditions that govern the crystals' development, but each as it reaches the ground is subject to a change of environment: from having been a separate entity, it becomes a minute part of the mass and begins to undergo a series of changes in its nature, all of which will reflect on the stability of the area of which it's a part. When new snow alights, its crystals interlock by means of their fine branches and spikes, but the strength of this cohesion is undermined by destructive metamorphism as the branches and spikes regress under the pressure of rising temperatures or the snow's weight. It was Professor Paulcke of Innsbruck who first observed a particular kind of degraded crystal that because of its shape constituted a noncohesive mass in the snow cover: such crystals were excessively fragile and ran like loose pebbles; they formed, wherever they were found, a hugely unstable base for the other layers above. He called them "depth hoar" or "swim snow." My mother recorded the same phenomenon in her journals and called it "sugar snow" because it refused to bond even when squeezed tightly in the hand. Haefeli loved the term. A stratum of such crystals is like a layer of ball bearings under the tons of more recently fallen snow on a slope, requiring only the slightest jar to set the mass in motion.

We spend the afternoon, after my coffee with Ruth, cutting blocks of snow out of various slopes and tapping the tops to test the frequency of layer fracture and collapse. Bader wears an outsize dinner jacket over his cardigan, claiming it's the only material he's discovered to which snow doesn't cling. He looks as young as I do, in his beardlessness reminding everyone of a cleric or a shepherd. Before Professor Niggli found him, he'd lived a life circumscribed by the peaks on both ends of his valley.

I'm teased for being love-struck because of my silence, then teased further for failing to react. But throughout the day, my heart roams in and out of my chest as though tethered to its own misery. Of course my mother knew—that was the source of her Oberlander remark—and in my newly reconfigured map of that time, everyone knew everything, except Willi's endlessly oblivious brother. Had she had the baby? Of course she'd had the baby. How had I left without asking if she'd had the baby?

"I need to go back down," I finally told Haefeli as we hiked back from a northeastern ice wall. We'd been sampling under a twenty-five-foot cornice.

"Not right now you don't," Haefeli answered.

"Now he's pouting," Bucher informed the group, half an hour later.

"What are you going to settle today?" Haefeli wants to know once we're all back in the hut for the night. The sun's a vermilion line along the western ridge. "Are you going to go down there and profess your undying love? Haul her back up here for your wedding night?"

He's working by lantern light on what he calls a penetrometer: a pointed steel tube a meter long for measuring the firmness of strata. He has perhaps the two virtues most important to such a place as this: presence of mind and affability. In his own casual way he combines for us the functions of priest, guide, and hotelier. Once, during a rockfall in a narrow gully, he stepped between me and a head-size stone that appeared out of the snow cloud and deflected it with the handle of his shovel the way a cricketer bats a ball.

"Go if you have to," he finally tells me later that night, in exasperation, into the frigid darkness above our hammocks and blankets. "Go. Go. Go. God knows we don't need you up here."

Of course it occurs to me only as I finally reach Davos the next morning that she's in school, and that she'll be in school for most of the day. I have little money to spare but waste some of it anyway on coffee and a sweet roll to get in out of the cold. The lunch rush comes and goes. I man the chair farthest from the door, a nose to the window with the unsettled vacancy of an old dog left home alone.

At the awaited hour I'm outside her school, the dismissal bell ringing, and shouting and happy children stream past, looking no different than we did. "What are you doing here?" she wants to know. Somehow she's come out another door and come up to me from behind.

"So you had the baby?" I ask.

"This is my supervisor, Frau Döring," she tells me.

Frau Döring and I exchange greetings. Frau Döring appears to be hoping that whatever I'd just asked will be repeated.

"This is the brother of my late fiancé," Ruth informs her. It's as if the world's been filled with unexpectedly painful things.

Once back at the coffee shop she asks, "Why do you think you're so in love with me? What is it that you think you love?"

"You never answered about the baby," I tell her.

She looks at me, gauging my reaction. She makes a let's-get-on-with-it face.

"You gave it to an orphanage," I tell her. "Some convent or other. The Sisters of Perpetual Help."

She continues to consider me. I'm not weeping, but I might as well be.

"What is it you want?" she finally asks. "You want me to say that you're as nice a boy as Willi?"

She adds after a silence, "I always thought of you as the sort of boy who pinned the periodic table over his bed, instead of pictures of girls from magazines." An older couple at an adjacent table has grown quiet, eavesdropping.

"I thought about you more than Willi did," I finally tell her. "That camping trip when you were *with* him, I thought about you more than he did."

It angers her, and that's at least something between us.

The eavesdropping couple resumes its conversation.

She talks a little about her work. She notes the way her loneli-

ness has been exacerbated by her fondness for children. At least
here she slept better, though. Maybe that's what relocation was: a
balm for the fainthearted.

"You said you had more to tell me," I remind her.

She puts a hand around my coffee cup. "I've always liked you,"
she says. "I'll put the question to you. Do *you* think you were
Willi's equal?"

She's sympathetic and tender and would sleep with me if she
weren't sure it would lead to further tediousness. She'd like to help
but she's also sure of the justice of this injustice, the way the
English believe the poor to be poor and the rich rich because God
has decreed it so.

"You're not really still unable to get over this, are you?" she asks.

"What we're doing on the mountain is more important than
any of this," I tell her, and she's relieved to hear it.

"How's your mother?" she wants to know.

Outside she turns and steps close and presses her mouth to my
cheek and then lets it drift across my lips. "There's no reason for
us to stay angry with one another," she says, as though confiding
with my mouth. The couple from the adjacent table emerge, fixing their collars and hats, and excuse themselves to get by.

My mother and I had both dealt with our devastation in the
months after Willi's death by devoting our free time to the library
at Lauterbrunnen. We seemed to have arrived at this attempted
solution independently. We went mostly after chores on Satur-
days. Sometimes I'd take the bus and discover, having arrived, that
my father had driven my mother in the car. Sometimes I'd search
for a book in the card catalog and discover that she'd already
signed it out and was leafing through it on the other side of the
reading room. There was very little written, then, about the prop-
erties of snow, and we were continually driven back to geographies
and histories of the high Alps, there to glean what we could. We
encountered Strabo's accounts of passes subject to the collapse of

whole snow mountains above them that swept his companions into abysmal chasms: passes he listed as "places beyond remedy." We found Polybius's account of Hannibal's having had to witness the eruption of a slope that took with it his entire vanguard. Saint Bernard's of having stepped out of a chapel to relieve himself when his fellow pilgrims inside were scoured away by a roaring river of snow, and his prayer, having been saved downslope in the branches of a pine, that the Lord restore him to his brethren so he might instruct them not to venture into this place of torment. One rain-swept early evening my mother set before me a memoir of one of Napoleon's generals relating an anecdote of a drummer boy swept into a gorge who drummed for several days in the hope of attracting rescue before he finally fell silent. The librarians, intrigued by our industry and single-mindedness, helped out with sources. We read how in ancient days avalanches were so omnipotent and incontestable that they were understood to be diabolic weapons of the powers of darkness. How else to explain an entire village smashed flat while a china cupboard with its contents remained undamaged? A single pine left upright on the roof of a pastor's house, as if it had grown there? A house so shattered that one of the children had been found in a meadow three miles away, tucked up into her bed as if by human hands? Each of these stories caused my mother pain. Each of them drove us on.

If one house was spared and others were destroyed, it was because that house had been favored by the spirits: when I first came across that claim, I closed the book and circled the library before returning to it. And those spirits rode astride such calamities as they thundered down the slope. Erstfeld's town history recorded a spinster blown from her house who, still in her rocking chair, negotiated a wave of snow into the center of her village, and who, as she was giving thanks to Providence for her life, was carried to a clearing by her enraged neighbors, surrounded by a pyre, and burned alive.

How was my mother? I answered Ruth before I left to return to my hut mates. My mother wasn't doing so well. My mother, like everyone else in this drama, seemed determined to blame herself. My mother used to believe that we all could call the thunder down onto anyone's head whenever we wanted.

"You're just like Willi," Ruth said in response, after a moment. And it was the first time that I saw something in her look like the admiration he must have enjoyed.

Those were the sorts of histories, reiterated for Haefeli and Bucher, that went a long way toward ensuring my success when I interviewed to join the group. Haefeli believes there's much to be learned from such narratives, particularly when the phenomena described seem confirmed elsewhere. He collects his own and recounts them for us when he's in the mood, once we're swinging in our hammocks in the dark. They're especially compelling when we reflect that we're hearing them in an area that's itself an avalanche zone. "I think our friend Eckel *wants* to be blown out of his hammock," Bader complains about my appetite for them.

As a compromise, Haefeli promises us just one more for the time being. A sixteenth-century avalanche in Davos, just below us, was recorded to have generated such force that it smashed through the ice of the lake—measured at two feet in thickness—and scattered an abundance of fish killed by the concussion out onto the snow. But then he can't resist adding two more: one of a porter he knew, an Austrian, who stepped momentarily off his line of ascent to adjust a shoulder harness and saw his three companions blasted out of their skis by a snow cloud moving with such velocity that its sound seemed to follow it. And another of an infamous pass called Drostobel, above Klosters, that came to be known as a death trap because of an extraordinarily large and steep catchment area that fed into a single gully. Drostobel, the French liked to say, was German for "your fate hurtles down at you."

The following weekend we all ski down to Davos to resupply. I'm responsible for the sausage, bread, lemons, raisins, prunes, sugar, and raspberry syrup. The entire way down I'm determined not to call on Ruth, and the instant I hit the valley floor I go to the rooming-house address she provided. I'm ushered into the breakfast room and watch her butter both sides of a biscuit before she glances toward me.

The breakfast room has a view of the Jakobshorn. Filaments of snow and vapor stream from its summit in the wind. It's foreshortened here, as opposed to how it appears from nine thousand feet. Under overcast conditions the peak splits the clouds that pass over as though tearing fabric.

"I was always jealous of your mother," Ruth remarks, once I've settled into my chair. The wicker seat's seen better days and every movement occasions fusillades of pops and cracks.

"She and Willi had this tradition of summer walks," I tell her, though she probably knows. "She called them revivifying. She told me a neighbor said to her once, 'You have twin sons, yet I always see you with only the one.' "

"It was kind of your mother to have passed that along to you," Ruth responds. No one's come out of the kitchen to see if there's anything I require.

"When I've dreamed of him, he's always been with your mother and you," she adds. She says that in the last one, he had a hold of her ear.

"Been with us in what way?" I want to know. She smiles as though at the practicality of my question. "Could you be any more Swiss?" she asks.

"You think I'm not forthcoming," I tell her.

"I think some people don't seem to *want* information," she tells me. She's crimping the lacework under the creamer and it reminds me how, even back at school, her brain and fingers were always at work.

"So do you know where the baby is now?" I ask.

"I should hope so," she says, and more comes into focus with a jolt.

"You didn't give it away," I tell her.

"Her," she says. "Marguerite. Why would I give her away? She's with her grandmother. Probably napping."

We both take a few moments to absorb the news. The housemistress brings a filled coffeepot.

"Are you bringing the baby here?" I ask.

"I'm going to try my hand at homemaking," she tells me. "Don't the French have a word for a cow that at the end of the day just gives up on its own desires and returns, without being herded, to the stable?"

"A little girl," I say to myself.

"Maybe I'll end up as one of those women you see tossing hay in the upper fields," she jokes.

"Willi's little girl," I say.

"Your mother and father both have met her," she tells me.

"Of course they have," I tell her back. One of Haefeli's most insistent bromides concerning snow safety has to do with the way, at certain altitudes, nothing might be less like a particular location than that same location under different conditions.

Everyone's all bustle and efficiency in the hut when I finally labor up to it in midafternoon. While I unpack the provisions, Bader informs me that we're going on a rescue. Down in town the group discovered that a pair of Germans had gotten themselves in a fix on the south face of the Rinerhorn, just over the ridge. From below it was apparent that they were in some sort of distress and that the easiest route to them was from our hut. Haefeli and Bucher's silence while he relates all of this is unsettling.

Once we're ready we set out. Haefeli straps on to each of us one of his innovations: what he calls avalanche cords, thin red ropes eight meters long that will trail behind us like long tails. Each has a fisherman's float on the end and the hope is that those, at least, would be visible on the surface should the slope let go. They've never been tested. He still hasn't spoken and now he's taken the lead. Bader, who tends to chatter when frightened, is behind me in the column and tells me more than I want to know. The south face is a vast bowl that catches the sun from all angles and channels avalanches from each side into its middle. Climbing that bowl in heavy snow will be like climbing up into a funnel. Haefeli has in Bader's presence called that face "self-cleaning" because it avalanches so often. In the summer smashed trees and boulders spread out from its base like a river delta. Bader's from the flatlands and not one to panic easily—for some weeks he thought the White Death the villagers referred to was a local cheese—but even his eyes are glittery with apprehension. And the sudden rise of temperature around midday will have softened the snow.

We follow Haefeli's thigh-deep track through the heavy drifts and enter from our ridge halfway up the bowl. The Germans are lodged on the face only a couple of hundred meters above us. One waves and the other has perhaps broken his leg. None of us speak. Who knows why the Germans do what they do.

We keep a gap of fifteen meters between each of us. We put our boots only in one another's tracks. With each step we listen for the sound that indicates our weight has broken the layer between strata and that the ball bearings of the depth hoar are about to start into motion. It never comes. Haefeli has us traverse laterally, once we've reached the Germans, across the face to get out of the bowl as quickly as possible. Bucher and I take the injured boy's shoulders and Bader his good leg. His broken one we bind with his snowshoe.

The sun is setting by the time we return from having guided them down to a part of the slope from which a sled can carry them to Davos. We'd traded off hauling the boy but we're all still exhausted, and fall into our hammocks after barely stripping off our outer garments. No one's even lit the lamp.

"We should have stayed down in the village," Haefeli says out of the darkness, thinking of the slopes around and above us. Eight inches have fallen in snowstorms in the last three days, and temperatures have dipped and climbed with a kind of cheerful incoherence. Bader was the last one in, and on almost his last step before regaining the hut, triggered a slab release that carried away below us a piece of the slope the breadth of a city block. It swept off an outcropping to the southwest and then was lost to sight.

Now everything has settled into a quiet. The night is windless and no one stirs in their hammocks. There's no sound of snoring.

Eventually I hear Bader's breathing, and then Bucher's. A hammock eyelet creaks. The mountain makes subtle, low-frequency sounds, like freight shifting.

I ask Haefeli if he's awake. He responds so as not to disturb the others. He says that an avalanche's release depends on a system of factors so complicated that prediction involves as much divination as science. I offer as rebuttal that we do know some things, and he says of course: we know that gravity and temperature fluctuations together propel the settling and creep that create the stress within the layers. And that those stresses are greater or smaller depending on the slope's steepness and the snowpack's weight and viscosity. And that the snow's ability to resist that stress is measured by its cohesion, or the friction between its crystals.

"Shhh," he instructs, though I haven't made a sound.

For an avalanche to occur, then, he murmurs, something has to either increase the stress or decrease the cohesion. The process by which the ratio changes can be gradual, or some kind of incident.

And then we're silent. Does he know I'm weeping? I do my best to remain discreet, and he makes no indication that he's heard.

A boy makes a happy gesture in the snow: a gesture meant to signal *We're so close*. Fractures streak away from his ski at the speed of sound, find the stress lines beneath the surface, and generate the ruptures that cause the release.

I once refused to sit still for one of my mother and brother's walks. I was twelve. He explained I wasn't invited. I'd been once again baffled and once again unwilling to explain that I was upset.

"Leave him alone," my father counseled, indicating me. He felt as left out of my mother's plans as I was. In his last letter to me, after I arrived at the hut, he wrote *My memory is going! I'll devote the rest of my energies to digging potatoes and other pursuits suitable to a second childhood.* My sister wrote soon after *Your mother now has nothing to do with him, or with me. I've always been the one ignored. You always were the one who shed suffering and went off to your life.* I wanted to write back that in our family the most exacting labor had been required to obtain the bleakest of essentials. I wanted to confide to her my devotion to Ruth. I wanted to ask her what it meant when women did the sorts of things Ruth had done outside the coffee shop. I wanted to tell her the story our father had told us about how old Balmat, having conducted the empress Eugénie around a glacier, kept for the rest of his life the piece of chocolate that, upon their return, she'd broken in half to share with him. I wanted to tell her that I was like the man who after a cataclysm tethered his horse in the snow to an odd little hitching post that revealed itself the next morning to be the top of a church steeple.

But in the end I wrote nothing. Because mostly I wanted to write to Ruth. Because my sister was right: I had what I thought I required. I had my resentments, and my work, and I made my choices with even more ruthlessness than the rest of my family.

Haefeli is asleep now, as well, his breathing uncertain, as though awaiting that offstage tremor. We've learned more than any who've come before us what to expect, and it will do us less good than if we'd learned nothing at all. Tonight, or tomorrow night, or some night thereafter, the slopes above us will lose their patience and sound their release. We'll be overwhelmed with snow as if in a flume of water, the sensation of speed fantastic. We'll none of us cry out, for our leader has instructed us, in or out of an avalanche, to keep our mouths shut, whatever our impulses to open ourselves to the snow's power. We'll be uncovered, months later, gingerly, because no one likes to touch the faces when recovering the bodies. Bucher will appear as though he's come to rest in midsomersault, Bader as though he were still swimming free-style, downhill. Haefeli will have his arms extended, as if having embraced what the mountain would bring. And I'll be discovered petrified as though lunging forward, flung far from my companions' resting place, my eyes open, my shoulders back, my expression that familiar one of perpetual astonishment.

Helen Simpson

Diary of an Interesting Year

February 12, 2040. My thirtieth birthday. G. gave me this little spiral-bound notebook and a Biro. It's a good present, hardly any rust on the spiral and no water damage to the paper. I'm going to start a diary. I'll keep my handwriting tiny to make the paper go further.

February 15th. G. is really getting me down. He's in his element. They should carve it on his tombstone: I WAS RIGHT.

February 23rd. Glad we don't live in London. The Hatchwells have got cousins staying with them—they trekked up from Peckham (three days). Went round this afternoon and the cousins were saying the thing that finally drove them out was the sewage system—when the drains backed up, it overflowed everywhere. They said the smell was unbelievable. The pavements were swimming in it, and of course the hospitals are down, so there's nothing to be done about the cholera. Didn't get too close to them in case they were carrying it. They lost their two sons like that last year.

"You see," G. said to me on the way home, "capitalism cared

more about its children as accessories and demonstrations of earning power than for their future."

"Oh, shut up," I said.

March 2nd. Can't sleep. I'm writing this instead of staring at the ceiling. There's a mosquito in the room, I can hear it whining close to my ear. Very humid, air like filthy soup, plus we're supposed to wear our face masks in bed, too, but I was running with sweat, so I ripped mine off just now. Got up and looked at myself in the mirror on the landing—ribs like a fence, hair in greasy rats' tails. Yesterday the rats in the kitchen were busy gnawing away at the bread bin, they didn't even look up when I came in.

March 6th. Another quarrel with G. OK, yes, he was right, but why crow about it? That's what you get when you marry your tutor from Uni—wall-to-wall pontificating from an older man. "I saw it coming, any fool could see it coming, especially after the Big Melt," he brags. "Thresholds crossed, cascade effect, hopelessly optimistic to assume we had till 2060, blahdy blahdy blah, the plutonomy as lemming, democracy's massive own goal." No wonder we haven't got any friends.

He cheered when rationing came in. He's the one who volunteered first as car-share warden for our road; one piddling little Peugeot for the entire road. He gets a real kick out of the camaraderie round the standpipe.

—I'll swap my big tin of chickpeas for your little tin of sardines.

—No, no, my sardines are protein.

—Chickpeas are protein, too, plus they fill you up more. Anyway, I thought you still had some tuna.

—No, I swapped that with Violet Huggins for a tin of tomato soup.

Really sick of bartering, but hard to know how to earn money since the Internet went down. "Also, money's no use unless you've got shedloads of it," as I said to him in bed last night. "The top layer hanging on inside their plastic bubbles of filtered air while the rest of us shuffle about with goiters and tumors and bits of old sheet tied over our mouths. Plus, we're soaking wet the whole time. We've given up on umbrellas, we just go round permanently drenched." I stopped ranting only when I heard a snore and clocked that he was asleep.

April 8th. Boring morning washing out rags. No wood for hot water, so had to use ashes and lye again. Hands very sore, even though I put plastic bags over them. Did the face masks first, then the rags from my period. Took forever. At least I haven't got to do nappies, like Lexi or Esmé—that would send me right over the edge.

April 27th. Just back from Maia's. Seven months. She's very frightened. I don't blame her. She tried to make me promise I'd take care of the baby if anything happens to her. I havered (mostly at the thought of coming between her and that throwback Martin—she had a new black eye, I didn't ask). I suppose there's no harm in promising if it makes her feel better. After all, it wouldn't exactly be taking on a responsibility—I give a new baby three months max in these conditions. Diarrhea, basically.

May 14th. Can't sleep. Bites itching, trying not to scratch. Heavy thumps and squeaks just above, in the ceiling. Think of something nice. Soap and hot water. Fresh air. Condoms! Sick of being permanently on knife edge re pregnancy.

Start again. Wandering round a supermarket—warm, gorgeously lit—corridors of open fridges full of tiger prawns and fillet steak. Gliding off down the fast lane in a sports car, stopping to fill up with thirty liters of petrol. Online, booking tickets for *The Mousetrap, click,* ordering a crate of wine, *click,* a vacation home, *click,* a pair of patent-leather boots, *click,* a gap year, *click.* I go to iTunes and download *The Marriage of Figaro,* then I chat face-to-face in real time with G.'s parents in Sydney. No, don't think about what happened to them. Horrible. Go to sleep.

May 21st. Another row with G. He blew my second candle out, he said one was enough. It wasn't, though. I couldn't see to read anymore. He drives me mad—it's like living with a policeman. It always was, even before the Collapse. "The earth has enough for everyone's need, but not for everyone's greed" was his favorite. Nobody likes being labeled greedy. I called him Killjoy and he didn't like that. "Every one of us takes about twenty-five thousand breaths a day," he told me. "Each breath removes oxygen from the atmosphere and replaces it with carbon dioxide." Well, pardon me for breathing! What was I supposed to do—turn into a tree?

June 6th. Went round to the Lumleys' for the news last night. Whole road there squashed into front room, straining to listen to radio—batteries very low (no new ones in the last government delivery). Big news, though: compulsory billeting imminent. The Shorthouses were up in arms, Kai shouting and red in the face, Lexi in tears. "You work all your life," etc., etc. What planet is he on? None of us too keen, but nothing to be done about it. When we got back, G. checked our stash of tins under the bedroom floorboards. A big rat shot out and I screamed my head off. G. held me till I stopped crying, then we had sex. Woke in the night and prayed not to be pregnant, though God knows who I was praying to.

June 12th. Visited Maia this afternoon. She was in bed, her legs have swollen up like balloons. On at me again to promise about the baby, and this time I said yes. She said Violet Huggins was going to help her when it started—Violet was a nurse once, apparently, not really the hands-on sort but better than nothing. Nobody else on the road will have a clue what to do now that we

can't Google it. "All I remember from old films is that you're supposed to boil a kettle," I said. We started to laugh, we got a bit
hysterical. Knuckle-dragger Martin put his head round the door
and growled at us to shut up.

July 1st. First billet arrived today by army truck. We've got a Spanish group of eight, including one old lady, her daughter, and twin
toddler grandsons (all pretty feral), plus four unsmiling men of
fighting age. A bit much, since we have only two bedrooms.
G. and I tried to show them round but they ignored us. The
grandmother bagged our bedroom straight off. We're under the
kitchen table tonight. I might try to sleep on top of it because of
the rats. We couldn't think of anything to say—the only Spanish
we could remember was *"muchas gracias,"* and, as G. snapped,
we're certainly not saying that.

July 2nd. Fell off the table in my sleep. Bashed my elbow. Covered
in bruises.

July 3rd. G. depressed. The four Spaniards are bigger than him,
and he's worried that the biggest one, Miguel, has his eye on me
(with reason, I have to say).

July 4th. G. depressed. The grandmother found our tins under
the floorboards and all but danced a flamenco. Miguel punched
G. when he tried to reclaim a tin of sardines and since then his
nose won't stop bleeding.

July 6th. Last night under the table G. came up with a plan. He
thinks we should head north. Now that this lot are in the flat and
a new group from Tehran promised next week, we might as well
cut and run. Scotland's heaving—everyone else has already had
the same idea—so he thinks we should get on one of the ferries to
Stavanger, then aim for Russia.

"I don't know," I said. "Where would we stay?"

"I've got the pop-up tent packed in a rucksack behind the shed," he said. "Plus our sleeping bags and my windup radio."

"Camping in the mud," I said.

"Look on the bright side," he said. "We have a huge mortgage and we're just going to walk away from it."

"Oh, shut up," I said.

July 17th. Maia died yesterday. It was horrible. The baby got stuck two weeks ago, it died inside her. Violet Huggins was useless, she didn't have a clue. Martin started waving his Swiss Army knife around on the second day and yelling about a cesarean—he had to be dragged off her. He's round at ours now drinking the last of our precious brandy with the Spaniards. That's it. We've got to go. Now, says G. Yes.

August 1st. Somewhere in Shropshire, or possibly Cheshire. We're staying off the beaten track. Heavy rain. This notebook's pages have gone all wavy. At least Biro doesn't run. I'm lying inside the tent now. G. is out foraging. We got away in the middle of the night. G. slung our two rucksacks across the bike. We took turns wheeling it, then on the fourth morning we woke up and looked outside the tent flap and it was gone, even though we'd covered it with leaves the night before.

"Could be worse," G. said. "We could have had our throats cut while we slept."

"Oh, shut up," I said.

August 3rd. Rivers and streams all toxic—fertilizers, typhoid, etc. So we're following G.'s DIY system. Dip billycan into stream or river. Add three drops of bleach. Boil up on camping stove with T-shirt stretched over billycan. Only moisture squeezed from the T-shirt is safe to drink; nothing else. "You're joking," I said, when G. first showed me how to do this. But no.

. . .

August 9th. Radio news in muddy sleeping bags—skeleton government obviously struggling, they keep playing the Enigma Variations. Last night they announced the end of fuel for civilian use and the compulsory disabling of all remaining civilian cars. From now on we must all stay at home, they said, and not travel without permission. There's talk of martial law. We're going cross-country as much as possible—less chance of being arrested or mugged—trying to cover ten miles a day, but the weather slows us down. Torrential rain, often horizontal in gusting winds.

August 16th. Rare dry afternoon. Black lace clouds over yellow sky. Brown grass, frowsty gray mold, fungal frills. Dead trees come crashing down without warning—one nearly got us today, it made us jump. G. was hoping we'd find stuff growing in the fields, but all the farmland round here is surrounded by razor wire and armed guards. He says he knows how to grow vegetables from his gardening days, but so what. They take too long. We're hungry now—we can't wait till March for some old carrots to get ripe.

August 22nd. G. broke a front crown cracking a beechnut, there's a black hole and he whistles when he talks. "Damsons, blackberries, young green nettles for soup," he said at the start of all this, smacking his lips. He's not so keen now. No damsons or blackberries, of course—only chickweed and ivy.

He's just caught a lame squirrel, so I suppose I'll have to do something with it. No creatures left except squirrels, rats, and pigeons, unless you count the insects. The news says they're full of protein—you're meant to grind them into a paste—but so far we haven't been able to face that.

August 24th. We met a pig this morning. It was a bit thin for a pig, and it didn't look well. G. said, "Quick! We've got to kill it."

"Why?" I said. "How?"

"With a knife," he said. "Bacon. Sausages."

I pointed out that even if we managed to stab it to death with our old kitchen knife, which seemed unlikely, we wouldn't be able just to open it up and find bacon and sausages inside.

"Milk, then!" G. said wildly. "It's a mammal, isn't it?"

Meanwhile, the pig walked off.

August 25th. Ravenous. We've both got streaming colds. Jumping with fleas, itching like crazy. Weeping sores on hands and faces—unfortunate side effects from cloud seeding, the news says. What with all this and his toothache (back molar, swollen jaw) and the malaria, G. is in a bad way.

August 27th. Found a dead hedgehog. Tried to peel off its spines and barbecue it over the last briquette. Disgusting. Both sick as dogs. Why did I moan about the barter system? Foraging is MUCH MUCH worse.

August 29th. Dreamed of Maia and the Swiss Army knife and woke up crying. G. held me in his shaky arms and talked about Russia, how it's the new land of milk and honey since the Big Melt. "Some really good farming opportunities opening up in Siberia," he said through chattering teeth. "We're like in *Three Sisters*," I said. " 'If only we could get to Moscow.' Do you remember that production at the National? We walked by the river afterward, we stood and listened to Big Ben chime midnight." Hugged each other and carried on like this until sleep came.

August 31st. G. woke up crying. I held him and hushed him and asked what was the matter. "I wish I had a gun," he said.

September 15th. Can't believe this notebook was still at the bottom of the rucksack. And the Biro. Murderer wasn't interested in them. He's turned everything else inside out (including me). G. didn't have a gun. This one has a gun.

September 19th. M. speaks another language. Norwegian? Dutch? Croatian? We can't talk, so he hits me instead. He smells like an abandoned fridge, his breath stinks of rot. What he does to me is horrible. I don't want to think about it. I won't think about it. There's a tent and cooking stuff on the ground, but half the time we're up a tree with the gun. There's a big plank platform and a tarpaulin roped to the branches above. At night he pulls the rope ladder up after us. It's quite high—you can see for miles. He uses the platform for storing stuff he brings back from his mugging expeditions. I'm surrounded by tins of baked beans.

October 3rd. M. can't seem to get through the day without at least two blow jobs. I'm always sick afterward (sometimes during).

October 8th. M. beat me up yesterday. I'd tried to escape. I shan't do that again, he's too fast.

October 14th. If we run out of beans I think he might kill me for food. There were warnings about it on the news a while back. This one wouldn't think twice. I'm just meat on legs to him. He bit me all over last night, hard. I'm covered in bite marks. I was literally licking my wounds afterward when I remembered how nice the taste of blood is, how I miss it. Strength. Calves' liver for iron. How I haven't had a period for ages. When that thought popped out I missed a beat. Then my blood ran cold.

October 15th. Wasn't it juniper berries they used to use? As in gin? Even if it was, I wouldn't know what they looked like—I remember only mint and basil. I can't be pregnant. I won't be pregnant.

. . .

October 17th. Very sick after drinking rank juice off random stewed herbs. Nothing else, though, worse luck.

October 20th. Can't sleep. Dreamed of G. I was moving against him, it started to go up a little way, so I thought he wasn't really dead. Dreadful waking to find M. there instead.

October 23rd. Can't sleep. Very bruised and scratched after today. They used to throw themselves downstairs to get rid of it. The trouble is the gravel pit just wasn't deep enough, plus the bramble bushes kept breaking my fall. There was some sort of body down there, too, seething with white vermin. Maybe it was a goat or a pig or something, but I don't think it was. I keep thinking it might have been G.

October 31st. This baby will be the death of me. Would have been. Let's make that a subjunctive. "Would have been," not "will."

November 7th. It's all over. I'm still here. Too tired to

November 8th. Slept for hours. Stronger. I've got all the food and drink, and the gun. There's still some shouting from down there but it's weaker now. I think he's almost finished.

November 9th. Slept for hours. Fever gone. Baked beans for breakfast. More groans started up just now. Never mind. I can wait.

November 10th. It's over. I got stuck into his bottle of vodka—it was the demon drink that saved me. He was out mugging—left me up the tree as usual—I drank just enough to raise my courage. Nothing else had worked, so I thought I'd get him to beat me up. When he came back and saw me waving the bottle he was beside himself. I pretended to be drunker than I was and I lay down on the wooden platform with my arms round my head while he got the boot in. It worked. Not right away but that night.

Meanwhile, M. decided he fancied a drink himself, and very soon he'd polished off the rest of it—more than three-quarters of a bottle. He was singing and sobbing and carrying on, out of his tree with alcohol, and then, when he was standing pissing off the side of the platform, I crept along and gave him a gigantic shove and he really was out of his tree. Crash.

November 13th. I've wrapped your remains in my good blue shirt; sorry I couldn't let you stay on board, but there's no future now for any baby aboveground. I'm the end of the line!

This is the last page of my thirtieth-birthday present. When I've finished it I'll wrap the notebook up in six plastic bags, sealing each one with duct tape against the rain, then I'll bury it in a hole on top of the blue shirt. I don't know why, as I'm not mad enough to think anybody will ever read it. After that I'm going to buckle on this rucksack of provisions and head north with my gun. Wish me luck. Last line: Good luck, good luck, good luck, good luck, good luck.

Judy Doenges

Melinda

WHEN I first met James, he was a meth chef. This year he doesn't need to cook because he has another guy to do it. The chef has runners—guys who take the city bus from drugstore to drugstore to get antihistamine for our special ingredient, one legal box at a time. Now James is our punisher, our savior, our iron-and-brass man. He gives us our worktable and our tools: pens, tape, change of address cards, Mountain Dew, cell phones, shards, and pipe.

When he's not cleaning and cleaning, RJ Dumpster dives and rifles through cans and recycling bins for credit-card bills and bank statements, sometimes just feathers of paper, and then he dumps the pile on our worktable. Ripped to the winds, no problem, James says today, his hand heavy on Little Fry's neck. She bows her head and starts sifting. There's nothing a tweaker can't do if she sets her mind to it, James says. Right, Fritzie? he asks me.

It's blue-snow December outside and it stinks of cigarettes inside. Little Fry needs a shower. I need to get busy, James says to me. He tries to put his hand on my neck, but I shrug him off.

When I first met James, I was Melinda Renée von Muehldorfer

and I lived at 145 South Poplar. My grandma told me once that *von* means my ancestors were German royalty. James says, You're out of your castle now, babe. After I graduated, ruined my parents' credit rating, sold everything except my ice skates, and moved in with James at the farm, I was Fritzie, no last name, just a girl good at asking for things.

Little Fry tapes strip to strip until she finds a number or a name or both. Today she looks like a cartoon of someone concentrating, the tip of her tongue working around her lips, her hands shaking. She's not very good with numbers and names, so she turns her creations over to me.

Look at this, Fritzie, Little Fry says. Here's one like yours.

She hands me a taped library overdue notice, all of the ragged corners perfectly matched, even the split letters lined up and repaired. Richard von Behren, it says, 653 Oak. Four streets away from my old house. I picture Richard von Behren with one of those regal profiles, a sharp face like a statue's. He's clearly in a hurry, so impatient with his pile of mail and bills that he doesn't save and shred.

Break time. Little Fry always lights up first because she's the hungriest. She passes to me as we slump on the couch. James walks in to retrieve me and air comes punching into the room. He carries his own weather, RJ said one time when he was gakked.

In bed is where reputation gets iffy. It's only as good as who's on top of you, a girl named Share, who is no longer with us, used to say. I wonder what that means vis-à-vis James.

Oh, but James goes down, unlike most guys. When you're made of iron and brass, I think, sliding up on the pillow, you're not afraid of anything.

Sex is as selfish as drugs, I think, my nerves undulating inside my arms and legs like earthworms, and I like to be selfish, at least that's what my parents used to say, screaming outside my bedroom door. James doesn't have to work hard or long. He just breathes on me, just shivers me, until I answer back and then James disappears in a suck of air. I don't open my eyes until he's in and over me. Then I come again while he watches. The sun sets over his shoulder, a red blazing that seems to start the cornstalks on fire, while the last of the light slides off the side of the barn. James always leaves me gasping. From the bed, I grab his ankles. He puts on his jeans anyway.

I get dressed and go out to the living room. RJ has turned on the light over the barn door, so we know he's out there with the chef. Little Fry is back at the table, guzzling Mountain Dew. She solves the puzzle of the paper strips. The house shakes with James's absence, every atom chiding us.

Merilee, she of the cheery name, is James's wife. She lives elsewhere. Sometime in the morning she comes in her TrailBlazer with Riley, the boy she has with James. Merilee lets Riley lay on the horn until James comes out, pulling cash from his back pocket. She does all right—the bitch, James always says after she leaves. Then he laughs. Today Merilee and James talk at the car window, while Riley pulls at the ends of James's long hair.

Fritzie, keep going, RJ says. I'm sweeping in front of his mop: double-team double-clean, RJ calls it. He'd lick the floor if he could. Little Fry continues her Good Work at the table, selfless and tireless, like a nun. James sometimes calls her Holy One, she does her one thing so pure.

Oh, Merilee, I think, how have you kept your narrow waist, your big boobs, and your auburn hair to the ripe age of thirty-five? Oh, Merilee, how do you hold on to a husband/boyfriend/father/sugar daddy/fucker like James? Merilee, how? Neither James nor Merilee use anymore. Because of Riley, Merilee says, which James claims too. But I know it's really because James is CEO. You can't run a business and do its work at the same time.

Riley cries in the window of the TrailBlazer as it turns around in the yard slush. James comes into the living room, tracking. Get it, get it, RJ yells, pushing me and my broom along.

RJ, James says, you and Fritzie go to town. He gives us a card and the keys to the old Ninety-Eight.

I'm not done here! RJ yells.

James puts his hand on RJ's neck and he calms down. I'll keep an eye on it, James says. Get going.

RJ holds the steering wheel as if it's made of eggs. If you let me drive, I say, we'll get there lickety-split. Cops, RJ says.

They'll think something is really wrong with you, you go like this, I say.

RJ ignores me and starts on the list of his DUIs, DWIs, driving while fucked up, short stints in the pokey, and I mention that these incidents always center on a wayward girl. Correct, RJ says. Women are the bane of my existence. Were.

RJ and I have this same conversation every time we go to town. Everything is always the same, right down to the number and kind of transgressions. I just go with it. RJ has been with James for a few years, so his stories and his thoughts run in the same tight circle. The cornfields finally give out and then we're chugging through the outskirts of the city so slowly that I have plenty of time to read NO SOLICITING on at least five doors.

I make RJ go to the Hy-Vee on our side of the city proper so I won't see anyone I know. We do a foilie in the car for courage and strength, RJ says, as if there's going to be heavy lifting. He's right about the possibilities, though. One day, when he was gakked and ergo superhuman, RJ sawed down a whole tree and cut it into perfect logs even though our fireplace is broken. But here, well. The city is full of people we've never seen and expectations that have passed us by, and we're never sure how we're presenting ourselves. To us, we're just fine.

Inside the store, RJ grabs a cart; I stand on the back and he pushes me. We have a list. We like lists and tasks, but we're never very hungry. Uck, RJ says too loudly, looking around at all the food. I know, I say, but whisper, man. What's first?

When Little Fry eats, it's always bananas and milk because she heard somewhere that it's the perfect combination of food. I point out that there's no protein there, but my opinions on diet don't carry much weight anymore. So RJ and I load up on bananas and the kiwi James likes, then fruit leather for RJ. We tour meat for James's chicken parts, then zoom to dairy for Little Fry's milk and RJ's string cheese, then over to cereal for Cheerios. I've eaten them since I was a baby; my parents have a picture of me sitting in my high chair, those little oaty lifesavers on the tray. Now I like them in a red bowl, one by one, while I work. The last thing for the cart is cigarettes, different brands to please everyone. On the way up to check out we swing by the drug section, and even though I didn't plan it, I grab some cold medicine and head back to the bath-room. A surprise for James. I put the foil sheets of pills in my pocket and bury the box under paper towels in the trash. RJ rolls us up to the registers. The checker slides our stuff over the reader, but she also takes some time to look us over. She's seen photos on billboards of guys like RJ, all skinny and snuffly and with that new kind of acne, teeth sprung. I can feel her thinking about call-ing the manager, but for what? We haven't done a thing but ride the cart. RJ hasn't noticed any of this; he's just holding out the shaking card. I sign in the swiper window—Jacqueline Zingle—and then, thank God, we're out in the parking lot loading bags. We progress at grandma speed back to James's.

When we get there, the football players' Jeep is in the yard. The team is going to a bowl game, and everyone in the city is in a fever. Part of the proceeds from the sale of RJ's string cheese goes to a fund for the new stadium.

Four huge men stand around the living room, slushing up RJ's clean floor. Hey, he shouts, and drops the bag he's carrying.

Let's keep it moving, James says, hustling RJ and me into the kitchen. I go back out, though, just to get a gander at all that healthy flesh. The players are ruddy, thick. Veins pop out on their hands. They fill out their team jackets, and their feet are as big as oars in their matching shoes. One of them looks in my direction, but he stops at my hair and frowns. Little Fry couldn't keep her hands still one night, so I gave her a pair of scissors and closed my eyes. Now my hair is like little blonde eruptions all over my head.

There's a new guy this time, the biggest one of the group, wearing a hemp necklace and a small gold cross. You take checks? he asks James.

RJ, James, me, even Little Fry crack up. What? the guy asks, looking around.

Don't be a dipshit, the one black player says. He's the only gentleman of color, as RJ always calls him, who ever comes around, and he tries hard not to look at anything.

The player who looks like an oversize cowboy, down to the Resistol covering his crew cut, pulls out the cash.

They turn to leave, but Player #4, a mammoth redheaded sad sack, looks at me again, this time giving me a morose stare. I gasp. It's Jorge, my conversation partner from junior year Spanish. I can't remember his real name. *Buenas noches,* Marita, he says, before heading toward the door.

Shit, James says, looking first at me and then at the wide back of Jorge.

Marita, Little Fry says after they go. Marita! Marita! she calls, picking up the pipe. RJ, Little Fry, and I retire to the sofa. James goes into his room and slams his door.

When I first moved in, James said, No way do you go upstairs. Of course I go.

There are four freezing bedrooms and an old bathroom with the sink torn out and a shower that drips. The bedrooms are all the same size, one in each corner, but in each one the windows look out on something different: barnyard, road, clump of trees, pasture. You can go from room to room, as I have, and get a 360-degree view of where you are. It's the opposite of how all of us downstairs live, in our closed fist of work, and that's why James doesn't want us up here.

I figured I'd find old stuff up here like newspapers from World War II or tickets to a county fair or receipts for horses and cows, but the place looks as if RJ's been at it. Not a nail or a shoelace, but I did find a honey-colored curl of hair in a closet once. If I were a different kind of girl, I would have kept it.

I'm up here during a day sometime after the football players' visit, after break time. *Dormitorio,* I say to each bedroom; *ventana* to each window; *árboles,* I say out one window, then *camino* out another one, *pasto* where the cows would be. Translate "barnyard," Marita, *por favor.*

Around dawn, James jumped out of bed, crouching and feeling for cigarettes. Fritzie, he barked, how long have you been here? Quick!

I closed my eyes. Six months, I said. No, eight.

Wrong, babe! James said. Ten months, two weeks. You've got to work on memorization, James said, and he sounded just like my Spanish teacher, Señorita O'Connor. You've got to keep as much in your head as you can, James said. You don't want to end up like RJ, like a CD you can't turn off. Or Little Fry, like all you can do is play with paper.

I didn't say that we were working to his specifications, working for James his very self. I also didn't say that when you don't sleep, like Little Fry, RJ, and I don't, you live in one long hour and that hour takes place during that last minute you're in a class, when you're waiting for the big IBM clock on the wall to make its final click. So why not run on like RJ does? Why not cut and paste like Little Fry?

I'm moving you into a supervisory position, James said, shocking me. I can't afford to hemorrhage any personnel, he says. So you're in charge of Little Fry and RJ. Make sure they don't fly away.

Fly away like past chefs and runners, like girls he diddled, like everyone who passes through a business like this.

You're here for the duration, James said at dawn.

When I go downstairs, everything's the same. Little Fry: table, soda, tape. RJ: trying to do some speedy old-school break dancing on the living room floor. My work is done.

You're not going to break anything but your head, I say. I'm going for a walk. Where's James?

Out, RJ says. Who's he doing? I wonder before I can stop myself. RJ's upright now, doing a silly big skip, slide, and sway, like some guy in a boy band.

Little Fry looks up from the table. Take a hat, she says.

Outside the sun is high. It's colder than a tweaker's lungs, as RJ always says, but I've got my old red down jacket with matching mittens and hat. When I get to the end of the driveway, I stick out my thumb and start walking in the direction of the city, even though no one is coming yet on this dinky road. I haven't mailed the change of address card yet. It's in my pocket: Richard von Behren, 653 Oak. I haven't planned what I'm going to do or say.

Pretty soon, an old car pulls up. It's an Impala, lumpy with Bondo, and there's a guy I almost know behind the wheel. Cody, he says when I get in, and I know he's a local. There were probably thirty Codys in my high school.

I'm Merilee, I say. Are you going all the way in?

Sure are, he says. What side do you want?

North, I say, Stratford Acres, by the river.

He gives a low whistle. Then there's a long silence. Horses crowd together in the pastures. I see a farmer close by the road, checking a fence post.

Cody clears his throat. I think I seen you before, he says.

Where? I ask quickly. I look to make sure the Impala has door handles that work from the inside.

You're at James's place, yeah? I'm a friend of Tommy's, Cody says.

Tommy's the best chef in three counties, even James says so. People compete for product, not territory, so there're no fights, no shootouts on rural routes. Just admiration and awe. Ah, Tommy, James always says when he hears the name. He kisses the air. Ah, Tommy.

I should have guessed anyway. Cody's got one knuckle rapping the steering wheel and his nondriving foot is pumping up and down. You can see the sinews in his cheeks.

That would be me, I say with a little laugh. I can't remember the last time I was alone, or with a stranger, someone I had to say new things to.

Who're you going to visit? Cody asks. We stop at a four-way and he sits there too long.

Just a guy, I say. He owes me some money.

Cody snorts. Don't I know it, he says. Then he launches in, telling me all about life at Tommy's place, which he should definitely not do to anyone outside. For miles, he talks about their new satellite dish, his bust last year and how Tommy bailed him, how much product Tommy's putting out, then, inevitably, there's the story of some girl who he has the hots for, this one being Tommy's old lady. Blabbady, blab, blab, blab, goes Cody, as only a meth head can. We get to the city. What will be, will be, Cody the philosopher finally says about life and love at Tommy's.

That's fatalistic, I say, pulling out the word from someplace. You can't do a thing about a life like that, man. Stop here.

Cody pulls into the parking lot at the playground I used to go to when I was a kid. It's too cold for anyone to be on the swings, and the slide would catch even the tiniest piece of skin. I turn and smile at Cody.

Duck down, he says, pulling the pipe out of the glove box. We laugh.

. . .

I race the five blocks to Oak on foot, keeping my head down. I practically do the two-step. I rub my fingers together inside my mittens. On Oak, all of the houses are bigger than my old one. They're huge blocks of brick—brown, red, cream, with the sun hitting their front windows so the glass glows like porcelain. Richard von Behren at 653 Oak is at the end of the block. The house is two-story, red and brown in alternating groups of bricks, and there are two tall windows in the front, both of them with fake little wrought-iron balconies.

From the skinny window next to the front door I can see back into one of those kitchens that flows into a dining room. Richard von Behren is getting a plate down from a high shelf. When he answers the door and sees it's me, he scrunches his eyebrows together and purses his lips.

Sorry, he says, but we're not buying anything. I could have put my son through college on what I've paid for candy and magazine subscriptions. A dog snorts and sticks its black muzzle between the man's leg and the doorjamb.

I'm lost, I say, for lack of something else. My car broke down, I add.

What? Richard von Behren asks. Where's your car? He sticks his head out and looks up and down the block.

It's up on the big street, I say, pointing with my mitten. My hand is shaking. I'm sorry to discover that I'm hopping up and down on the front mat.

Jesus, it's cold, Richard von B. says. Get in here, and we'll figure this out.

I walk in and the dog immediately puts its big paws on my shoulders. Batman, down, Richard von B. says.

My boots drip water onto the Oriental rug in the hallway. To my right is the flowing dining room and kitchen, everything gleaming; to my left is the living room with deep red walls, bookcases and pictures, and a huge piano. Oriental rugs all the places my parents have carpeting. Richard von Behren is skinny and has the same thick blond hair and pink cheeks as my dad. A blonde woman comes down the stairs with an empty laundry basket. Her hand squeaks along the banister.

Dick, Richard von B. says to me, holding out his hand. And that's my wife, Sherry. Hi, Sherry says, making the same face her husband did.

This young lady is lost, Mr. von B. says. Oh, no, Mrs. von B. says.

Share, I say. I'm Sharon. My car broke down a few blocks back. I wave my hand behind my head. I'm stamping my feet, but quietly.

And you came all the way down here? Sherry von Behren asks.

Where are you trying to go? Dick asks, interrupting her.

I thought I went to school with somebody who lives on this street, but I was wrong, I say. I was coming home from band practice, I say, and my car broke down.

It's Saturday, Sherry von B. says. She makes that face again.

Sherry, where's the map? Dick asks, heading for the kitchen. Where did you say you were going? he calls back to me.

My car broke down, I say again. But I'm lost too. And I need to tell my brother where to meet me. Somewhere up by my car, maybe.

Here, Sherry says, following Dick into the kitchen. You're no good at finding anything.

So, wait, you're not from around here? Richard calls from the kitchen. I can hear him going through a cupboard and Sherry whispering.

No, I say. I moved here two weeks ago. On a shelf in the living room next to a set of old books are coins in a frame. I take three steps to my left, lift the frame off the shelf, and slide it down inside my jacket. Then I'm back in the hall on the rug, waiting. Batman wags his tail.

What am I thinking? Dick says. He's coming out of the kitchen with a phone in his hand. We need this more than a map. Here, call your brother.

I dial RJ's cell. My car broke down, I say when he answers. What? he asks. Meet me at—, I say. Where should I meet him? I ask Sherry, who is now back in the hall with her arms crossed. What's on the big street? I ask.

Go to Carl's, Dick says. It's a restaurant two blocks west of Oak on Grover. Grover's the big street, he says laughing.

Meet me at Carl's, *Brad*, I say into the phone. It's on Grover. Who is this? RJ asks. What the fuck?

I hang up and say thanks about twenty times. The dog sticks his nose in my crotch. Dick stretches out a leg and pushes the dog back, all the time saying good luck with band, he played trumpet in high school and college, forcing me to say I play glockenspiel, which is the only instrument I can think of at the spur of the moment.

You know, I say, *von* in a name means your family were princes or something in Germany. Way back. I've got it too.

You told her our last name? Sherry asks, her voice high.

Dick just frowns. He's not sure, I think. Royalty, he says. He laughs. Tell it to my accountant.

It's hard to start school in the middle of the term, isn't it, Sherry von B. says. She holds herself tight.

Really hard. Unless you get pretty good grades and have extracurricular activities that keep you busy and confident, I say. This last was what the guidance counselor suggested to my parents.

Good for you, Dick von B. says.

I had a horse, I say quickly. But the truth is that my parents decided not to buy me one once everything caught up with me, and once my total lack of concern for the welfare of others required a second mortgage. *Have* a horse, I tell the von Bs. His name is Star. He looks like Black Beauty. Dick's face is starting to freeze, but I can't stop myself. I say, When Brad picks me up we're going out to the stable to see Star. I have some carrots in my trunk. Does your son like sports? I ask.

Well, Richard says.

I was in soccer when I was little, I say. It's suddenly way too noisy under my hat so I take it off, which is not good because the von Bs can see my scalp and all its tufts. There's a big bell clanging inside my head. Goalie, the hardest position, I say. We won city for our age group one year. I fought off a lot of balls that season. Then there was gymnastics, five years.

Whose life am I telling? This one belongs to another kid—the kind of kid I never talked to.

Senior play I was Eliza Doolittle, I say, the bell inside me ringing. They put a notice in the paper. Math was my favorite subject, which is not usual for girls. It's like I'm sure you've said to your kid, find something you're passionate about. All the teachers at school said goals were important. Achieve has an *I* in it, I say.

I stop talking. My brain is clanging like a church bell. All of this was before, I say. Before I moved here from Illinois two weeks ago. We stand there looking, even the pictures on the walls. That does it for Richard and Sherry von Behren, their son, and my old neighborhood.

Know where you are now? Sherry asks me. She herds me toward the door. Dick manages to get a hand on my shoulder, so I look back. Take care, he says, but he glances away at the end like I hurt his eyes.

I practically knock myself out saying thanks some more, and then I'm out of the house and the door is closed and I'm trying to catch my breath. I bend down and pretend to tie my boots for a minute, and then I check the mailbox. I take what's there and walk quickly down the street. When I'm a few houses away, I take a sharp left and crunch through a snowy yard until I'm on the next street. Back on Grover I take the first guy that stops, an old farmer in a pickup. He's silent the whole way to James's, as if I'm just some stock he has to transport.

RJ loves the coins. This one's from 1903 Germany, he says. That's their kaiser on it. He strokes the glass. Man, you know you have a lot of money when it just sits out on display, he says. I'll take that, James says, pulling the frame from RJ's hand. RJ goes back to chasing Riley around the house.

Riley and Merilee are here, picking up money and giving Riley a chance to see his dad not framed in a car window. Little Fry finds a bank statement in the last delivery of mail Richard von Behren will receive for a while, so James gets me on the phone immediately to 24-Hour Customer Service.

This is Sherry von Behren of 653 Oak, I say. How are you?

Wonderful! the helpful person says. What can I do for you?

I'd like to get your credit card but I lost the offer, I say. I give the checking account number.

Password? the helpful person asks.

Batman, I say, and then I'm in.

A while later, Riley wants to go outside. The sun is low again, this time striped with clouds. James makes us all go with Riley, even Little Fry. RJ, Little Fry, and I have a foilie in the pantry before we venture forth. Home, again. The chef stands by the barn with a cigarette, carefully flicking his ash into a tin can.

There's a big cow pond behind the barn that's frozen solid. RJ takes off and slides on his stomach like he's stealing a base. Riley cracks up.

I took Richard von Behren's change of address card down to the box myself and put up the flag. The mail truck comes late here, we're so far out. Dick and Sherry are going to visit their own mail-box over and over—nothing there. Every day will be like pressing on a bruise to test the pain. Those two will figure it out quick, but by the time they do, Little Fry, RJ, me, and James will have their finances in a snarl and then James will sell everything about Richard von Behren to someone else. People get passed around that way. They get lost.

Everyone's standing at the side of the cow pond watching RJ go crazy on the ice. All of that's going to hurt later. Riley is pulling on Merilee's hand. I go inside. My skates are in James's room.

Everyone is slipping and sliding on the pond when I come back out, so no one notices when I sit on a stump and put on my skates. The leather is like soft hands holding my feet. I took lessons until I was fourteen, and when I get on the ice everything comes back. I do an arabesque and a single Axel.

Wow, Fritzie, Merilee says. That's amazing. Do it again! Riley says. A girl of many talents, James says, but he looks mad.

Everyone gets in a crowd trying to do my moves, but they can't. This pond is all mine, I want to say. James starts sliding after me. Right away everyone follows, yelling and laughing. I take off, floating from side to side until my wheezy lungs smooth out. Marita, come back! Little Fry calls.

I skate faster and faster toward the snowbank at the other end of this glassy ground, so fast I can't feel the surface or hear a voice, so strong I could part the clouds over the sun. The wind is wicked.

Kenneth Calhoun

Nightblooming

I WAS TOLD they found themselves retired and so they said,
Now's finally the time to form a band! You should see the
instruments they fished out of attics and basements. Not so much
the instruments themselves—horns haven't changed much over
the years—but the cases. Some are covered with flesh-tone leather,
boxes made of wood with rusty hinges, lined with red velvet.
When they crack them open, it looks like they're pulling metal
bones from the insides of a body.

The dudes are severely elderly, these Nightblooming Jazzmen.
They wear white belts and bow ties, polyester pants pulled up
high. Our angle is we're old, they say. So you have to dress the part
if you're going to be our pulse, drumbo. They got me wearing
plaid pants and bowling shoes. A couple of them have mustaches
and they're serious about them. I paste one on for the big gig just
to fit in around the face. Bleach my eyebrows and stick that silvery
fringe under the nostrils, pop on a straw hat.

They have the coolest names. There's Clyde and Chet and
Wally and Ernie and Horace. Do you believe that? When I first
met up with them, when I told them my name was Tristan, they

said, Ho, ho, what kind of name is that? Some of them thought I said Christian. I said I didn't know what kind of name it was, how should I know? I wasn't there when I was named.

They said, Where are your people from?

My people? Sounded like they were talking about tribes. But I didn't have an answer for them. I'm from nowhere, around, all over.

You can't use a name like that, they told me. We'll think of a new one.

After my audition, Clyde and Horace came over to my car when I was packing up my drums. They told me I got the gig but from now on they were calling me Stanley and if I didn't like it I could take my twenty-two years of living and go sit on a dick.

They were grinning when they said it.

The big gig is under the elms in a lonely old park. The bandstand is covered with graffiti and the tennis courts have tattered nets and faded lines. A crowd of old people and a few of their grandkids look on from folding chairs. Everyone's eating. I watch them bite at deviled eggs and salted watermelon from behind my cymbals. The fans of the Nightblooming Jazzmen drink wine from Styrofoam cups. They eat cheese logs and grapes resting atop green Coleman coolers. Seeds are spat into the grass.

Clyde puffs into the mic and says, Good afternoon, ladies and germs. Then we're off and running. We cook up a carousel of sound with our hands, with the wind in our chests. Me and a gang of senior citizens just tearing up the place.

We're marching the saints and balling the jack. And, damn, these Nightblooming Jazzmen can bring it. Chet is coaxing sad wah-wahs out of his t-bone, muting with a toilet plunger. Clyde noodles out golden lassos on the clarinet and Wally burps wetly along on the tuba. I buzz the rolls and grab the crash. I stir the soup with brushes. I do all the stuff I never get to do—that no one plays anymore. Stuff I learned from my dad.

We play the Charleston and people are grabbing at their knees and head dancing. We stir up a flock of jazz hands.

The sun tilts through the trees and everywhere are shafts of dust. We're just a speck in the grand whirling scheme, but at least we're making noise.

We close the set like landing a plane, bouncing along a little then rolling to a stop. The guys are breathing heavy. They empty their spit valves into the lawn.

People applaud, then stand and fold up their chairs.

I'm tearing down my set and a kid comes over, starts asking me questions. How come there's a Rush sticker on my snare case? How come I'm not old but I play old music?

How do you know I'm not old? I ask.

Your elbows, he says. Too smooth.

I'm waiting for Clyde to cut the checks, sitting in my car smoking some reefer. I can see some of the guys standing by their van, arguing about something. Me? I'm mellow. It was just as good a gig as any. Better in some ways because there's nowhere to hide in this kind of sound. No smoke screens of distortion or feathered edges of reverb. You have to give these guys their due. They put it down precisely where they want it, dotted notes and all. I thought they were going to be a drag. I figured I'd play this one time and score the check, then ditch them. But I don't know. That gig was pretty sweet.

Clyde and Horace come over. I stash the nub of weed and step out. Great job, they tell me. You can swing, by God. How'd you learn it?

My dad, I explain. He loved Krupa.

Did he play?

Yeah. That's all I say, recalling his old Ludwig drum kit. His traps, he would call them. The shells were as thin as lampshades and the cymbals were brown and dull. I pawned it all a few years after he died, after I changed the skin on the floor tom and found some blood down in the crease under the ring. He threw up his guts during a gig once. He shouldn't have been playing in that state. They carried him home and put him to bed in his bloody T-shirt. He was a welder by profession. Health insurance was like a Rolls-Royce—both things he knew he'd never have.

Clyde gives me my check. His hand's all shaky when he signs his name.

Horace says, I tell you what, we met some nice old ladies and they've invited us over for a visit. Up for joining us?

What the hell, I say. It's not like I have anywhere else to go.

Horace rides with me as we caravan over. He tells me more about the band. What happened was that they used to be a big band, all Glenn Miller, Tommy Dorsey, Benny Goodman. They had a good run for a while, playing locally. You can't tour with a big band unless you have serious, Sinatra-size bank. Costs too much to put all those guys in hotel rooms. But they did their thing often enough around town. Fellas started dying though, Horace says. Not because they whooped it up or got in car wrecks—the way the young bands die. These guys just died from staying in the world too long. Cancer mostly. Heart attacks and strokes. One after another.

So much for the big band. They tried to roll with it, calling themselves the littlest big band, but they couldn't draw a crowd. So Clyde, who's basically the leader, said they were going Dixieland and did anyone have a problem with that. Horace tells me one guy walked out, kicked over a music stand, and flipped them the bird, grumbling that Dixieland was for Disneyland. Everyone else stayed put, even though Wally and Chet are starting to get flaky, Horace says.

He looks out at the yards sliding by. It's a crazy thing to say you're going to stick with something until you die, Horace tells me. You pick two or three things you feel that way about and life organizes itself for you.

He winks and it's a little spooky how he's talking right into me, how his words are driving into my head like pennies dropped from eight miles up.

The ladies are sisters, widows, some of them twice over. Three of our guys are widowers. Chet and Ernie are married, but Ernie's wife is an invalid. Doesn't give me an excuse to fool around, he says glumly.

What about you, they ask me before we go in.

We're standing in the street of some shady neighborhood— shady meaning it's leafy, not ghetto. The sidewalks are old and broken where the roots of oak trees push up. There's a dove cooing somewhere. A sprinkler hisses a few houses down. I see the blue haze of mist in the evening light.

They're waiting for an answer and I don't know how much to say. You can't tell people about your loneliness without adding to it. No one wants to hear how you're somewhere between the beat with people, never finding the count.

I'm in between, I say.

A pair of legs? Clyde asks, grinning. He has a square jaw and a Charlie Brown curl of gray hair on his big, blotchy forehead.

Between girlfriends.

Oh! Ménage à twat, Horace says.

Not like that, I say.

Now they're all grinning.

You guys are some dirty grandpas, I tell them.

They laugh. Good band name, they say. They slap me on the back. Clyde makes like he's strangling me. His hands are rough at my throat. You're a good kid, he says. He pulls me aside. You're not a cockblocker are you?

I shake my head. Me? I'm thinking.

No one likes a cockblocker, Clyde says. He's patting me hard on the back, like he's burping a baby.

. . .

The women are waiting. They've laid out a happy-hour spread. There's a green ceramic serving dish with pretzels and Ritz crackers. The dish has a built-in bowl that they have filled with some kind of white creamy dip. There's another plate of cheese and grapes and a can of roasted peanuts. I start attacking the snacks, standing over the low table, raining down crumbs.

Horace says, Easy, Stanley.

The women laugh. Someone's hungry!

They say, You boys should take a seat, waving us over to the long, avocado-colored couch. I sit down with a handful of crackers and line up cubes of cheese on my leg and start the assembly line. As I cram it all in my mouth, I take in my surroundings. The colors are green and yellow. A massive organ sits in the corner, its wooden pedals like a rib cage on the floor. There are plastic plants in the corners and hook rugs on the wall—shag tapestries of trees with red leaves, clouds over an island, an owl with furry eyes clutching a real piece of driftwood. There are shelves lined with little owl statues made from glass and clay. Someone likes owls. This is an owl house.

The women gather up and introduce themselves. They have cotton-candy hair and foggy eyes. There's more than one brooch and bracelets all around, so they jangle when they move. Shiny pants and small knitted vests; clown collars, nurse shoes. I have to say, these are some good-looking old ladies. The Jazzmen really scored. The ladies smell nice, too. I can smell them from across the room: it's all baby powder and flowers. They deliver their names like they're performing a song. Ruth and Ethel and Nancy are sisters, we learn, and Betty is an old friend from the neighborhood. Great names, I say. Some cracker crumbs fly from my mouth and Clyde gives me a look.

The women tell us how much they loved the music.

Ethel says her fingers are sore from snapping. The guys chuckle at this.

I hit the peanuts, throwing a handful in my mouth. I watch their lips move through the grinding in my head. When I swallow, I hear Betty say, So many of the summer concerts are such disappointments.

Ruth recalls a terrible rap act and they all shudder.

Wally says, That's not poetry, what they're doing. I don't buy it.

They look to me, expecting an opinion, I guess. Rap sucks, I say as I reach for some more cheese.

You have the most unusual eyebrows, Nancy says.

I don't understand, then I remember that I had bleached them.

Goes better with the mustache, I say.

Everyone laughs because, at the moment, my mustache is curled up on the dashboard of my car.

How's that for commitment? Clyde says. The kid lands a gig and he goes the extra mile to fit in. You didn't tattoo our name on your backside, did you?

I shake my head, because my mouth is full.

Stan the man can swing, Clyde says, reminding me of my new name. His smile has something like pride in it. They all look at me, smiling warmly.

I feel like I'm eight years old—a little kid with a whole army of grandparents. I never knew my real grandparents. My dad was already old when I was born and my mom never told her parents about me. One day she told me her father had finally died. That was all I had ever heard about them.

Wally slaps his thighs. Say, how about some drinks?

Clyde says to Chet, You bring in your kit?

Chet says, Get yours.

The way he says it is kind of harsh. Clyde looks at him and there's a quiet little stare-down before Clyde whistles through his teeth and heads out.

When Clyde comes back he has a small black box with a handle. It's like a square suitcase. He puts it on the dining room table and opens it up. I go over to check it out and he tells me not to get crumbs all over the place. I peer inside the case and see its shimmering contents. The inside is lined with black velvet. Held in places cut into the walls of the box are stainless-steel tools—shaker cups, some tongs and long spoons, a strange coil of spring, and, behind a secret panel, he shows me that it holds a blue bottle of gin and another bottle of tonic water. It's an incredible thing. I like cases and gear and kits. That's one reason I love the drums. I like how everything collapses, folds up, and has its place to go. It looks professional, just like Clyde's kit looks professional, even a little religious.

Would you ladies like to try a fine gin and tonic? Clyde asks. When they seem to hesitate, Clyde reminds them that the gin and tonic was invented as a health drink. Everything about it is designed to keep you alive. British troops in India came up with it, he explains. The tonic water has quinine, which cures malaria. Add gin for its cleansing quality and a lime to fight scurvy and you have yourself a good glass of medicine.

No, insists Betty. You're pulling our leg.

Nancy says, It's true, Betty. I heard that somewhere before.

Ethel and Nancy head to the kitchen to get glasses and ice while Clyde goes to work. Not everyone wants gin and tonics, but the ladies also have scotch and rum. There's no wine or beer, just hard liquor.

The party chugs forward, with the ladies pumping on the organ and some of the guys playing along on their horns, with stories of wars and coming west to pick citrus, more nuts being poured, more cheese being cubed and tossed like dice.

In the kitchen, a roast sits smoldering like a meteorite in the old car-size oven. Nancy is sitting in the breakfast nook, telling a story about how she was the only sister brave enough to go barnstorming with a crazy carnival pilot, spinning low over the long-gone orchards and vineyards and looping over the fairgrounds, so close to clipping the Ferris wheel she could hear the riders scream.

She's staring into space as she tells about it, like she's watching it happen on an invisible screen.

After the dishes are done, they start dancing to records. Ethel's on the turntable, spinning Rosemary Clooney and Louis Armstrong. Horace thumbs through a dead husband's stacks and finds Bob Wills and His Texas Playboys. He insists on "Sittin' on Top of the World" and it calls for pushing back the coffee table and pairing up. I watch, still hitting the crackers and nuts, even though Nancy had served up roast beef and potatoes, hot buttered rolls and Jell-O salad, cottage cheese on a leaf of lettuce. Wally sits next to me, watching Clyde dancing with Betty.

Wally hums along. His ears are big and floppy. Hair creeps out of them.

He turns to me and says, Why don't you cut in?

Cut in?

You never cut in?

I don't know what you're talking about, Wally.

Cutting in? You know, you just go up to a fella who is dancing with the gal you want to dance with and you tap him on the shoulder and say, I'd like to cut in. Then he has to stand aside and let you take over.

Why?

It's just that way.

What if he doesn't want to give up the girl?

He won't want to, but he has to.

Who says?

No one says, it's just the way it is. Go on and see.

I can't dance to this kind of music.

Sure you can. It's just a box step. Go cut in.

I look over the dancing couples. The lady who catches my eye is Nancy. I notice the way her hands rub at the back of the guy she's dancing with. She just keeps them moving in slow circles on his back. She's doing it to Chet now. He has his head bowed and

I can see the age spots on his neck. That looks like it would feel pretty good, just to have her rubbing that way. So I stand up and a bunch of nuts fall from the folds of my shirt. I'm a little buzzed from Clyde's gin and tonics, so I knock into Horace as I make my way to Nancy and Chet. Clyde sees me and frowns over Betty's shoulder, but lightens up when I move past him. I tap Chet on the shoulder and tell him I want to cut in. It works just like Wally said it would. Chet kind of puts Nancy's hand in mine with a little bow. Up close it's a small hand with swollen knuckles and purple veins, but it's warm and softer than it looks. Nancy smiles and even looks a little flattered. She moves in close as Chet stands back with his arms crossed.

I don't know how to dance to this music, I say.

Just follow my lead, Nancy says. She starts pushing me around the floor. I step on her foot once and she winces, but her smile climbs right back onto her face. She has waxy skin and bright red lips. Her hair is a cake of white curls. Her face sits behind a veil of wrinkles and creases, but the smile shines through it. She's light in my arms and I take care not to crush her. She's saying, Step and step and step and step. I smell the gin on her breath and I like it.

When I finally get the step, she says, Atta boy!

Her hands are rubbing at my back. I feel it in my chest, this feeling of almost burning warmth. It's been a long time since I felt it. It's how my body responds to kindness. I used to feel it at school, when a teacher would lean over me and show me how to draw cursive letters. Or when an older kid showed me how to fly a kite. I thought I had outgrown the ability to have that feeling. I had forgotten about it. But here I am, feeling it again as Nancy rubs my back.

I'm lost in these thoughts when Chet taps me on the shoulder and asks to cut in. I surrender Nancy like a real gentleman, transferring her hand like it's a parakeet that has to hop from my finger to his. He says, Thank you kindly, sir, and pretends to tip a hat.

No problem, sir, I say.

What a classy bunch of fellas, Nancy says, eyes rolling.

Looking out from the haze trapped in my car, I can see them, silhouettes jitterbugging in the rosy window. The music is faint, but I tap along on the steering wheel. Maybe it's sad to say, but it's been just about the best party I've ever attended. Through the window they look like a movie flashed on a wall, hanging in space with no connection to time. It seems impossible that I stepped out from it, or that I could get back in. It's like a soap bubble you try to put in your pocket.

I pick up the mustache, which has curled up from the heat, and I smooth it under my nose. It still has some stick. From across the street, I hear a song end and everyone shouts out, More!

That's all I need to be called back. I cross the dark street and walk up the curvy brick path. I finish the joint leaning against a massive pepper tree, listening as I press at the mustache.

They're laughing in waves, singing harmonies. Someone's mixing drinks, shaking ice like a maraca. Someone's slicing meat with an electric knife. Why couldn't I have met them a long time ago, and played their music and eaten their cheese and crackers and drank their gin? But they didn't exist a long time ago, I know. Not as they are now. They only exist now and not much into later.

My dad didn't talk much. In the time I knew him, he only said one religious thing. He said, You know why people like beats? Because they tell you what's going to happen next. I've thought about that a lot. I think he was talking about patterns, about loops. And it's true that once you hear a measure or two of the beat, you know what's going to happen next and what to do when it happens. And the part that makes me think everything still has a chance—always has a chance—to work out is that you never know when the beat has completed a full cycle. This means everything in life that seems so random could actually be part of a beat. We just don't know yet. The full measure hasn't been played.

The door opens and one of the ladies peers out. It's Nancy.

There you are, Stanley! she says when her eyes lock in on me.

I wave, thinking I should probably tell her my real name.

Don't think I don't recognize you behind those handlebars.

I touch the mustache and smile.

She shuffles toward me and I offer my arm.

Got you right where I want you, she says.

She slowly leads me around to the other side of the pepper tree.

Whoops. Tipsy, she says when she trips on a root.

We step out on the lawn under the massive dark canopy. I can see a rope slicing down from a high branch, catching light from the house. I follow it down with my eyes and see that it is weighted on the end with a tire swing. Nancy pulls me to it.

We have this here for the grandkids, but they've outgrown it, she explains. It needs a muscle man to get it going and here you are. Lift me?

Before I know it, she has both her arms around my neck and she's hanging off me like a human necklace. I scoop up her legs and slide her into the tire. All I can say is, Really? You want to swing?

Swing, baby, swing, she says. Be-dap bap bap!

I look up at the rope. It looks solid, but it's dark so who can tell. I stand back. There's a buzzed eighty-year-old woman hanging a couple feet off the ground in front of me, jewelry jangling, white hair slightly aglow.

Come fly with me, she sings, Come fly, we'll fly away!

I'll swing her a little, I think. Why not?

I push her gently forward again. She's shaking her head.

Come on now, she says. Put some muscle into it! We're not going to get off the ground if that's your idea of swinging.

I give her a good push and she swings out over some of the yard. That's better!

She swings back into me and I grab on to the tire and throw it out into the darkness. She goes with it, saying, Atta boy. Now really put your back into it!

She comes back at me and I sidestep her like a bullfighter, but as she passes by again, I throw my weight into a push that drops me to my knees. I watch her sail up and away, then reach the top of her arc, ease to a point, then fall back at me. She's yelling, Woohoo!

I roll out of the way and get to my feet in time to add to her momentum as she swings by. I watch her flying upward, now higher than the roof of the house. So high, her feet are up above her and her head aimed at the ground. The rope is creaking. The tree is moaning, shuddering when she hits the end of some slack.

All the way, honey! Loop-the-loop! Loop-the-loop!

I stand back and watch her moving past me like the arm of a metronome. She's keeping time but losing the beat with every pass, slowing more and more, until I come in and use everything I have to get her back on the beat, to hold the time steady. It will only slow down if I let it. I step in after her as she jangles by and try to send her over the top.

Glorious! she shouts as she sails up into the darkness.

Then I hear the guys yelling inside. Something crashes and someone screams. Be right back, I tell Nancy, giving her another shove into space.

Inside, I find the living room a mess. The coffee table has been knocked over and crackers and peanuts cover the ground. The guys are trying to pull Wally and Clyde apart as they grapple on the floor. I push in and pick up Wally.

Clyde comes with him, then lets go and falls to the ground with a grunt. The others pull Wally away as Horace helps Clyde to his feet. Clyde makes a big show of dusting himself off.

Hey, guys, I say. Chill out!

You're lucky this kid came along, Clyde says. I was close to murdering you.

You see what you did, you son of a bitch! Chet is yelling at Clyde. You see?

Chet points at Wally's ear, which is ripped a little by the lobe.

Blood runs down into his collar. Wally dabs it and looks at his fingers. He rushes at Clyde but I push him back and he falls onto the couch.

You're all a bunch of assholes, Horace says, swatting at the air. You're all bent on ruining a good thing.

What's going on? I say.

Everything has to end, Wally says. It's the way of the world. You think you can escape that?

At first, I think they're talking about the party, the ladies. But what I soon realize is that they're talking about the band. They're talking about breaking up the band.

I sit down on the couch. Well, goddamn.

You said it was over when Abe died, Wally tells Clyde.

Then they're all shouting about Abe, who I learn was the drummer who just died. Abe was their meter man, their beat. It seems that Clyde promised Abe on his deathbed the band was kaput.

But you just got to keep going with the charade, Chet says. Look at us, for Christ's sake, we're down from fifteen guys to just the five of us.

I count the guys and it's clear that Chet isn't counting me. I'm six. If they want me, I'm six.

You think anyone cares about what we're doing? Chet yells.

They argue on, shouting in each other's faces. Ruth comes in and says if they don't leave she's calling the police, but they ignore her as they bring up old complaints about each other: Horace is losing his ear and he's hitting a lot of clinkers. Wally's lip is shot. Chet can't make it through a song without getting dizzy.

It's DOA, Wally is saying. It's DOA.

I reach up and pull off the mustache and smooth it out on my thigh, then crumple it up in my hand and stuff it in my pocket. Outside, I can hear a woman's frail voice, calling for someone named Stanley.

Tamas Dobozy

The Restoration of the Villa Where Tíbor Kálmán Once Lived

TÍBOR KÁLMÁN. Tíbor Kálmán's villa." That's what Györgyi told László the night they went AWOL from the camp, the two of them huddled in the barracks amid the other conscripts, boys like them, but asleep, some as young as sixteen, called on in the last hours of the war in a futile effort to salvage a regime already fallen, a country and people already defeated. "We need to get to Mátyásföld," Györgyi said, "that's where the villa is. Tíbor Kálmán will give us papers." But Györgyi didn't make it far, only to the end of the barracks, to the loose board and through the fence, frantically trying to keep up to László, who always seemed to run faster, to climb better, to see in the dark. László was already waiting on the other side of the ditch, hidden in the thicket, when the guard shouted, when they heard the first crack of bullets being fired, Györgyi screaming where he'd fallen, "My leg! I've been shot! Laci help me," and László looked back at his friend for a second, calculating the odds of getting to him in time, the two of them managing to elude the guards, limping along at whatever speed Györgyi's leg would allow. They'd be caught, charged with desertion, executed—both of them. And then László turned in the direction he was headed, Györgyi's cries fading in the distance.

It was the end of December 1944, and that night, running from the makeshift encampment and its marshaling yard, running and running long after the military police had given up, not wanting to risk their own lives by following him east, László realized it was hopeless, there was a wall of refugees coming at him, and behind it, the Russian guns, already so loud he felt as if they were sounding beside his ears. Budapest was streaming with people fleeing from the suburbs—Rákospalota, Pestszentlörinc, Soroksár, Mátyásföld—because the Red Army had not only arrived to these places already and taken control, but was advancing on Budapest itself.

So László became part of the human tide flowing from one death trap to another during the siege, and the things he'd seen would live on, unspoken, beneath everything he was to think and say from that point forward. Civilians used as human shields by the Red Army. Nazis exploding bridges over the Danube while there were still families and soldiers streaming across. Men and women forced to carry ammunition across the frozen river to German soldiers stationed on Margit Island while Soviet bullets and shells and bombs rained around them. He saw a soldier holding off two dozen Russians by running up and down the stairs of a devastated building, shooting from every window, making them think there were a dozen other soldiers trapped inside. Young boys crashing in gliders while attempting to fly in supplies for the fascist armies of Hitler and Szálasi, the fields littered with broken fuselages and wings and pilots contorted in positions that seemed to László the war's alphabet—untranslatable into human terms. There was a broken gas main near Vérmezö that for days shot flame through every crack and hole in the asphalt—blue, orange, yellow—dancing along the road as if fire alone were capable of celebrating what had become of Budapest.

He'd seen exhausted doctors trying to save patients from a

burning hospital, carrying them into the snow only to realize they had nothing—a blanket, a sheet, even a shirt—to keep them from freezing. He'd come across the most beautiful girl, eighteen or nineteen, in one of the ruined homes filled with those too wounded to go on, staring up, whispering from the mass of bodies, injured, starving, gripped by typhus, and as he leaned in to hear what she wanted to say—"Shoot me, please shoot me"—he noticed both her legs had been torn away.

And all that time László had been tormented by Tíbor Kálmán's villa—it was like the place was imagining him rather than the other way around—it sometimes appeared in place of what he was running from, and László had to stop himself from leaping into a burning apartment, a metro tunnel, or a garden under shelling, thinking: this is it, finally, I've made it.

After a while, László began to feel protected by the villa, as if the new life it promised was his true life, and the one he was living now only an alias, false, as if there was no one really inside, and that anything that happened was therefore not really happening to him. This is what helped László survive when he was press-ganged, along with a number of other boys and young men fleeing west, into the Vannay Battalion, and ended up doing the very thing he'd hoped to avoid: fighting for the Nazis. He would have liked to remember when it happened, but there were no dates then, the end of December, the beginning of January, sometime during those hundred days of a siege that never did end for him, being hauled out of the cellar where he was hiding by Vannay's men, him and the rest, given a gun and told what the Russians looked like, and from there the black minutes, schoolboy comrades falling around him, Vannay making radio announcements to the Soviets that they would take no prisoners, and the Soviets responding to this as Vannay had hoped, likewise killing every one of them they captured, which Vannay was only too pleased to tell László and the others, knowing it would make them fight with that much more desperation. And then the breakout attempt of

February through Russian lines, German and Hungarian soldiers cut down in the streets as they tried to escape the gutted capital to make it to the forests and then west to where the rest of Hitler's armies were stationed, running headlong into rockets, tank fire, snipers stationed in buildings along the routes the Soviets knew they would take, drowning in sewers where the water level rose with each body that climbed down the ladder until it was up to their noses, pitch-black, screaming panic. So few of them made it. Three percent, the historians would say. And the rest, the thousands, killed along Széna Square and Lövöház Street and Széll Kálmán Square, piled into doorways, ground up by tanks, swearing, pleading, sobbing, unable to fire off even the last bullet they'd saved for themselves.

But László was not there. He'd gone over to the other side by then, turning on the boys he was fighting with, aged sixteen and seventeen, shooting them dead as they stared at him dumbstruck, and then saw, over his shoulder, the approaching Russians. He thought he saw a last glimmer of envy in the boys' eyes, regret at not having thought of it first, before what light there was forever went out, and László turned, feeling something fade inside him as well, his voice cracking at the edges, soft and unwavering as radio silence. "Death to the fascists," he shouted, and was rewarded with bits of red ribbon the Russians tied around his arm, and a hat they placed on his head, before sending him back into battle.

It was László's decoration as a "war hero" by the Soviets that finally brought him to Tíbor Kálmán's villa late in 1945, to the place where it seemed all his misfortune and redemption were concentrated, where he might be absolved of his guilt for having claimed the place someone better—anyone at all—might have taken, someone worthy of survival, like that legless girl in the makeshift infirmary, for he had done what she asked that day, scrounging among the soldiers crammed wounded or dying or dead into that corridor, found a revolver, and embraced her with one arm while with the other pressed the barrel to her temple. If only he'd gotten to the villa in time, he told himself. If only he'd chosen the one other option he had: death. He knew now it was preferable to what he'd done to save himself, though it was too late by then, betrayal had become László's vocation, and the woman who met him that November day in the doorway of the villa sensed it, with the tired look of someone who has outlasted her interest in life and can't understand why she's being provoked by those who insist on living. She introduced herself as Tíbor's daughter-in-law, Karola, wary enough of László and his uniform to give only the answer he wanted and not a drop more, keeping her voice to a perfect monotone, without a single nuance he might have fastened onto had he been seeking something other than forgiveness.

"I wish I could help you," she said. "But Tíbor is dead."

László stood there with his military decorations and wondered why he'd come, given that the war was over, and with it his reason for seeking out Tíbor. "He's dead," Karola said again. "He was dead when we returned here from Budapest." And she pointed at the hole left by the bomb in the roof above the dining room, covered with a number of tarps inexpertly sewn together. She told him the story in a manner so offhand it was clear she was still in shock: Tíbor Kálmán had lost both hands when a Russian shell landed on the villa. He'd raised his arms to protect his wife, Ildikó, from the collapse of the ceiling, and a beautiful chandelier of Murano glass sheared off both hands at the wrist, though it hardly mattered to Tíbor by then because both he and Ildikó were dead, crushed by the weight of plaster, bricks, and several tons of antique furniture they'd stored in the attic overhead. Karola stood for a moment, as if waiting for László to respond, and when he didn't she said, "Anyhow," and he could see the effort it was costing her to repress a sneer as she scanned the medals on his chest, "you don't seem to be doing too badly."

There was something else, something other than scorn, in the way she said this, a quiet acknowledgment of what he'd come for, and at the same time, a dismissal of the explanation he wanted so badly to make. "Vannay sent out radio messages to the Soviets," he whispered, and immediately regretted it, as if even now, in attempting to make amends, he was still looking out for himself. "They weren't taking any prisoners. I had to make them a sign of good faith," he said. "I was only eighteen!"

"Why are you telling me this?" she asked, and he noticed that even while talking to him she was gazing elsewhere—at the orchard, the flight of birds, a fence fallen to its side—unable to keep her eyes on anything for long.

"I killed two boys," he said. "I wanted to show that I had switched sides . . ."

"I don't know anything about what you're saying."

"You do!" he shouted. "I was supposed to have come here. Tíbor was waiting for me, for boys like me. And I couldn't get across the Russian lines!"

She shrugged. "We couldn't make it either. We were trapped inside Budapest. There were many people who suffered."

"I was part of Vannay's battalion. It was during the breakout. And when I saw the Russians coming I killed two of the boys I was fighting with." He was shaking. He no longer had any control over what he was saying.

"Then you are not welcome in my house," said Karola, and for the first time since she'd opened the door, László felt her gaze rest on him, and he realized, too, that she'd been looking away not because she was disinterested in him, but because her eyes had seen too much, absorbed too much, images impossible for her to contain, which made her look elsewhere for fear of passing them on. He felt ashamed then for not being able to do what she did, keep it to himself, or expend it by shifting his gaze to where it would do no harm—the air, the fields, the sky.

"Then you do not deserve to come in here," she hissed, and slammed the door in his face.

. . .

And so began László's persecution of Tíbor Kálmán's family, using every opportunity his status in the party gave him—making false claims, denying them meaningful jobs, padding the files on Karola, her husband Boldizsár, their children István, Adél, Anikó, citing their attendance at mass, their political support for the Smallholders Party in the elections of 1945, their open criticism of the Soviet occupation and its control of the police, factories, transit system, everything. But at the time there were so many people like this the Soviets couldn't make them disappear fast enough. It wasn't until he saw what was happening to the members of the resistance, old trade union leaders, those who'd been outspoken communists prior to the arrival of the Red Army— who had paved the way for it but made the mistake of expecting Marxism in its wake—only when all of them were being arrested, sentenced in show trials, and murdered did László realize that the most dangerous thing of all, the most grievous of crimes, next to being a Nazi, was to have actively fought against Hitler in the name of communism. These men and women had had the courage to oppose the state, been brave enough to think for themselves, even at the cost of their lives. And it was because of this, exactly this, that the Soviets got rid of them. They were not the kind of citizens the Kremlin wanted, any more than Hitler had wanted them. Picking off the most loyal had the added benefit of amplifying the fear, of making everyone feel equally vulnerable, because if loyalties didn't matter, if the liquidation of men and women appeared random, then survival had nothing to do with you and everything to do with grace, which arrived from the state, as mysterious and medieval as the favor of God.

László filed report after report to the Allied Control Commission, which was controlled by the Soviets, about the activities of Tíbor Kálmán and his family during the war: how they'd sheltered political refugees from Germany, how they'd helped young men escape being drafted by a government they despised, how they'd drawn up false papers for all of these. "Conscientious objectors," he called them, and it was this, finally, that elevated the Kálmáns above the common stream of citizens complaining about the occupation. It wore the family down—visits by police, seizure of property, arrests and brief imprisonments that were hints, preludes, to the sentences yet to come—and then, in a final blow, László managed to get them evicted from the villa, and to have himself, the war hero, the decorated veteran, the loyal subject of the party, installed in their place.

That was late in 1946, the letter from the state informing the Kálmáns that their villa was being "reallocated" to "a more suitable candidate." In return, they would be given a cowshed in Csepel. The shed had held three cows and could easily fit six people, which meant that only one member of the family would have to sleep outside. And so the family finally left, driven beyond exasperation, beyond fear, beyond even the love of their country. Rumor was they escaped to the west, following their eldest son, who'd left the country six months earlier. In many ways, László was happy to have been part of their forced removal, and he was delighted to think of what it must be like for them out there, wherever they'd gone—not speaking the language, not making any money, not having their degrees and expertise recognized. At night, when he couldn't sleep, it was helpful to know that in some way they were suffering at least a fraction of what he'd suffered during the siege, at a time when he should have been with them, in Tíbor's care, being given a new identity and a new life.

But in the end, he had to admit, it was not the Kálmáns he'd been after, not really. It was the villa, the freedom to walk inside, to feel its mass around him.

He never forgot his first time crossing the threshold. There was the falling plaster, the bullet holes still in the walls, the water damage along the ceiling, the bits of furniture and possessions the family had left behind. There was the room where Tíbor Kálmán had died, its door nailed shut, the debris still inside as it had been when the family returned from the siege. But more than this was the feeling László had, walking down the hall, entering the rooms, that he was not yet inside, that he was still searching for a point of entry. "Another step and I will be there," he told himself, speaking into the emptiness of the home. And with the next movement, he said it again, "Another step and I will be inside." Eventually, he would exit the villa, stand in the courtyard bewildered, then cross the threshold again, hoping this time to get it right, haunted by how he'd dreamed of the place, hoped for it, imagined being safe inside these rooms, when in reality he was facing bullets and starvation and disease in Budapest. And killing people.

At night, unable to sleep, he would shake off nightmares of the siege by fixing up the place—the water damage, the rotten studs and joists, the plastering, the paint, the careful work of reconstructing the villa—as if by restoring the building to what it was it might finally open up to him, truly open, and he'd step inside to the life he should have had.

After the third week, he ripped off the boards covering the door to the room where Tíbor died, and a day or two later, steeling himself, went inside, staring at the mounds of rubble, the debris strewn along the floor. The Kálmán family had already exhumed and buried the bodies, touching the rubble only as much as was needed to pull it apart. After that, the family kept the door nailed shut, László had thought, because they couldn't bear to face the site where Tíbor and Ildikó died, but as he began to clear away the rubble, he discovered why they'd really left it as it was, for once the bricks and plaster and shattered beams and bits of glass were swept aside, he found the hole in the floor where Tíbor had kept his workshop, and inside, the stacks of messages he'd received during the war from the resistance, from places as far away as Cologne, and the equipment he'd used to forge identities, along with the lists of names and addresses under which Tíbor had hidden the refugees. László would use these lists to keep himself useful to the state, exposing identities one by one whenever he felt the pressure to demonstrate his loyalty. In return, they let him keep the villa. The villa with its printing press, the one they knew nothing about, his escape.

The names would run out regardless of how carefully, how slowly, he delivered them. In fact, if he delivered them too slowly the Soviets would grow impatient, demand that he tell them where he was getting his information, and then, when he refused, they'd come into the villa to find out for themselves, and his last hope would be ended.

So he went looking for someone to help with the press. He met Agi later that year, as the first wave of deportations, imprisonments, and executions took place. Her father and mother had been devoted communists dating back to Béla Kun's brief dictatorship of Hungary in 1919, and were persecuted in the white terror that followed against Jews and leftists when Admiral Horthy established control over the country for the next twenty-four years. Her father had been both—Jewish and leftist—and more than once it was only the thickness of his skull that kept him from being beaten to death, just as it was his skill with the printing press that kept all three of them alive during the period of anti-Semitic laws, ghettoization, the Holocaust. "If you wear the yellow star they will kill you," he once told Agi, tossing hers and her mother's and his into the flames, "and if you do not they will kill you." He stirred the fire. "So why bother?" But he had done more than just that, drawing up papers for many others—Jews, but also members of the resistance, fellow communists, British soldiers parachuted into the capital, others who needed to escape, for one reason or another, from the powers bearing down on them— whatever he could do to subvert the fascist cause. And therefore, like so many other communists, Agi's father was arrested after the Soviet occupation on Malinovsky's orders, not so much for his vocal criticism of the Russian "liberator"—for asking what good it had done them to await liberation when it meant free looting for the Red Army, rape, robbery, extortion, the requisitioning and hoarding of the country's food for the military while the general population starved, the ransacking of the nation in the way of reparations, mass arrests, murder—but because he wasn't afraid for his life. They were to be sent to a prison camp—one of the many the Soviets had set up—in Gödöllö, when László stepped in, saying he needed someone adept at "paperwork." Malinovsky had reported to Moscow that he had captured 110,000 fascists, but as he only had 60,000, the rest had to be made up by dragging people at random from the streets and their homes, and László was put in charge of making these substitutes look legitimate.

Naturally, Agi's father objected, and so László took him aside, reminding him that the youngest women raped by the Red Army were twelve, and the oldest ninety, which meant that both his wife and daughter were within the normative range; he spoke, too, of the sorts of venereal diseases they could expect, not to mention how long it would last, given that some women were locked up for two weeks "entertaining" as many as thirty soldiers at a time. In the end, Agi's father agreed, and to soften the blow László made sure they were provided for, keeping his promise even after Agi's parents, having done the work they were asked to do, were visited one night by the ÁVO and taken away for "unauthorized forgery of government documents," and László inherited Agi.

He made a nominal attempt to save her parents, trying to get her on his side, to make her believe he wasn't really an appa-ratchik, that he was just using the system until he could make his escape. So he made sure she was there when he made inquiries and phone calls, made sure that when they came to the villa for her as well, the agents of the ÁVO knocking on the door, he was there to bar the entrance, listing off his decorations and accomplishments and contacts to make it clear he, and by extension she, was "pro-tected," though in truth, no one was protected, no matter how high up your friends were, for the most dangerous friend of all was the highest ranking, Stalin himself.

It was an act of bravery, maybe the only act of bravery he'd ever performed, though it was only due to his hope that Agi would fix the printing press hidden beneath the villa. He knew that she could fix and operate the press with her eyes closed, the old man had said as much, boasting that she'd been more than his little helper. When her father was called away on business, she'd run the whole show.

Agi was silent through it all, absolutely quiet, the look in her eyes exactly the same as Karola's had been, too hard for a girl of nineteen—still lithe, a little boyish—meeting his gaze with one in every way its equal. The war had made them old. He saw it in the way her eyes left him isolated, a lesson on shouldering what he'd done alone rather than lessening the burden by passing it on, by turning it into a secret she had to share.

It always seemed to be winter, down in the hole, Agi squatting above the trapdoor peering at him, as if listening to the clack and whir as László tried, without expertise or success, to start up Tíbor's old machinery, the presses and lamps and generators. Nothing worked. All that happened was the clashing of parts, the tearing and spewing and grinding of paper, the flickering of lamps. The generator hummed dangerously, and charged every metal object around it so badly László was continuously cursing the jolts and shocks.

Agi would leave his dinner at the edge of the trapdoor, listening for a moment and then hammering it with the heel of her shoe, making him jump in the midst of whatever repairs he was attempting so that he would lose his grip on the screw or wire or flashlight and have to scramble after it in the dark. László sometimes felt she was transforming the villa by her presence. The smell of her cooking in the kitchen. The bedroom filled with the rustle of her turning in sleep. The shaded gallery, with its columns and ivy, unbearable for him because the only time a smile ever played across Agi's face was when she stepped out onto it and took in the smells of the garden and sunshine she and half the country had dreamed about in cellars and shelters during the siege, when all they had was the sound of bombs, the slow fog of plaster shaken from the walls and ceiling and floor with every explosion.

Instead of helping him, Agi reminded László, day after day, of the terrible things he'd done. She made love to him without flinching, without motion, the daughter of a man he'd killed, a woman unlawfully his, stolen, forced against her will, as if nurturing his hopelessness, his self-hate, his absent courage.

When he grew frustrated with the work he'd sit with her in one of the ruined rooms, Agi staring at the floor, not at all there. "What would you have done?" he asked, as if having told her about the press, his plan to create a new identity, to get away before scrutiny of his activities became too intense, he was now free to tell her *everything,* all of what that scrutiny might uncover. "What other choice was there?"

She stared at the hatch he'd left open, or the slow work of renovation he'd begun, trying to replaster the walls, to repair the hole in the ceiling, to paint over a half decade of water damage, her silence refusing him the one thing he most wanted: to hear someone, anyone, say that they too would have done what he did. But all he heard was the villa, rain on its roof, the ticking of radiators and plumbing, the wind playing on the windows, as if it was telling him it took a special person to do what he'd done, to have shot those boys. "No one but you could have done that," the villa said.

At other times he would remind her of those he'd assisted—the legless girl in the infirmary, Agi herself—and ask her to help him square this against the other things he'd done—to her parents, to the two boys. "How is it that I could do any good at all?" he asked. "Maybe I haven't gone so far. Maybe there's still something of me left," he said, waiting for her to speak, the villa answering instead.

When he grew angry with her silence, he threatened to stop protecting her from the ÁVO. Agi never raised her eyes from the floor, and he would shout that they were both going to die there, in the villa, and then go back down the hatch, kicking and beating the useless machinery. "If only you would help me!" he yelled up through the trapdoor, letting it out before he could stop the words. "We could use this machine." But it was pointless. For years now, his job had been destroying names, not creating them.

In March of 1947 László finally ran out of names—all but one. He'd done what he could, he told Agi. At first, he'd only handed in the aliases Tíbor had given to communists, to those, László knew, who were even now active in the party, and who'd enjoyed their fill of atrocity, and now it was their turn. When these were used up, László had moved down the list to those he knew were missing or sick or single. The very last names he'd handed in belonged to men who had families—wives, children, next of kin. And when those were gone—identified, questioned, arrested—when there was only the last, the one he'd picked out in advance, an address in Székesfehérvár, someone guiltier than most, susceptible to blackmail, with the means necessary to help László hide away, then he turned to Agi.

"If we're going to get away, you're going to have to help me." She made no reply. He turned, putting his hands against their bedroom wall. "I've been waiting," he said. "I thought there might be time, and that if I was patient, the names would last longer than the Soviets. We could make this place mine, or ours, whatever." He took his hands from the wall. "But they aren't leaving this country. They aren't ever leaving this country. You wait and see! And there are no names left!"

She watched him pacing back and forth, giving her a precise account of who was asking questions about him, what departments were interested, whose hands had delivered and traded memos on how he happened to know so much, on where he'd gotten the information that led to so many arrests. "The only thing that would have been worse," he hissed, "is if I'd given them no names at all."

He moved to the bed and grabbed one of her wrists. "If only I could fix the equipment Tíbor left," he said. "It would at least give me, give us, a chance to get away."

She looked at him as if she had no idea who he was.

"What's wrong with you?" he shouted. He yanked Agi out of bed then, and she stumbled after him, rounding the corner to the room where Tíbor and Ildikó had died, and down the ladder to the workshop.

He grabbed a list of names from a bench he'd built, thrusting it in her face. "Read it!" he said to her. "Read the names!"

Lazily, her eyes moved along what was written there.

"I got it from the ministry," he said, holding it up to her face, his other hand still gripping her wrist, "the names of the confirmed dead. I thought I could use it to make an alias. They'd never be looking for someone who has already died."

Her eyes moved side to side, along one of the only records that still testified, name by name, to a whole society that was one day taken out of existence so that this one could come into being. And that's how she came to it.

"Leo Kocsis," she whispered.

"Yes," he said, "exactly. How eager are you to join him? Because that's exactly what's going to happen, your name and my name, right here"—he waved the paper in front of her eyes—"if you don't get us out."

She let the paper fall. Leo Kocsis. Her father.

László would never remember whether Agi agreed with a yes or a nod, or whether she agreed at all, only that she moved forward. And he had the premonition he always had, an instinct for how betrayal might benefit him, the same instinct that had made him show Agi her father's name, knowing it was the only way to break what had formed between them. Agi worked without stopping, and was not finished before the evening of the next day. There was so much to do, so many papers, copying everything László brought to her, every sheet, without speaking.

And when it was done, days later, and László was standing in the doorway, his bags packed, it occurred to him that she had not prepared an alias for her own escape, and he quietly asked if she wasn't coming along.

She stared at him.

"I'm going to Székesfehérvár," he whispered, needing to say something, to cover up this moment, this need for an apology. "I'm going to stay there for a little while." He rubbed his head. "There's still someone . . . I might get help."

Agi said nothing, only stood there in the doorway, as if she had no intention of ever leaving Tíbor Kálmán's villa.

"What's wrong with you?" he asked. "You think they'll leave you alone when they come for me? You think you'll be spared?"

"They . . ." she began. "*They* have never left me alone." And she stepped back inside and quietly closed the door.

László was still standing in front of the villa minutes later, still there, silent, unable to step off the threshold, almost as if he was waiting for her to invite him back in, as if, after all this time, all he really wanted was to be welcomed into the place—as if it had never been about an alias at all.

And even then, László lingered, unable to turn decisively toward Székesfehérvár, moving along the sidewalk and glancing back, retracing five or six steps, eyes resting on Tíbor Kálmán's villa, long after Agi had opened the windows, brought the record player out onto the gallery, and poured herself what remained of the *pálinka.* He stood there, half hidden behind a willow, barely making out the melody of the *sláger,* watching her tilt the glass to her lips. She had the run of the place now, he realized, and he wondered if she'd known it would come to this, that for him the worst memory of all would be Agi accepted into the villa, as if his removal was all that Tíbor Kálmán's home needed to be complete, all it had needed to be finally restored.

Lily Tuck

Ice

O N BOARD the *Caledonia Star,* sailing through the Beagle Channel and past the city of Ushuaia on the way to Antarctica, Maud's husband says to her, "Those lights will probably be the last we'll see for a while."

Mountains rise stark and desolate on both sides of the channel; already there does not look to be room for people. Above, the evening sky, a sleety gray, shifts to show a little patch of the lightest blue. Standing on deck next to her husband, Maud takes it for a good omen—the ship will not founder, they will not get seasick, they will survive the journey, their marriage more or less still intact.

Also, Maud spots her first whale, another omen. She spots two.

In the morning, early, the ship's siren sounds a fire drill. Maud and Peter quickly put on waterproof pants, boots, sweaters, parkas, hats, gloves—in the event of an emergency, they have been told to wear their warmest clothes. They strap on the life jackets that are hanging from a hook on the back of their cabin door and follow their fellow passengers up the stairs. The first officer directs them to the ship's saloon; they are at Station 2, he tells them. On deck, Maud can see the lifeboats being lowered smoothly and efficiently and not, Maud can't help but think, how it must have been on board the *Andrea Doria*—a woman, who survived the ship's collision, once told Maud how undisciplined and negligent the Italian crew was. The first officer is French—the captain and most of the other officers are Norwegian—and he is darkly handsome. As he explains the drill, he looks steadily and impassively above the passengers' heads as if, Maud thinks, the passengers are cattle; in vain, she tries to catch his eye. When one of the passengers tries to interrupt with a joke, the first officer rebukes him with a sharp shake of the head and continues speaking.

When the drill is over and still wearing his life jacket, Peter leaves the saloon, saying he is going up on deck to breathe some fresh air, and Maud goes back down to the cabin.

Of the eighty or so passengers on board the *Caledonia Star*, the majority are couples; a few single women travel together; one woman is in a wheelchair. The average age, Maud guesses, is mid to late sixties and, like them—Peter was a lawyer and Maud a speech therapist (she still works three days a week at a private school)—most are retired professionals. And although Maud and Peter learned about the cruise from their college alumni magazine, none of the passengers—some of whom they assume must have attended the same college—look familiar to them. "Maybe they all took correspondence courses," Peter says. Since his retirement, Peter has been restless and morose. "No one," he complains to Maud, "answers my phone calls anymore." The trip to Antarctica was Maud's idea.

When Maud steps out on deck to look for Peter, she does not see him right away. The ship rolls from side to side—they have started to cross the Drake Passage—and already they have lost sight of land. When Maud finally finds Peter, her relief is so intense she nearly shouts as she hurries over to him. Standing at the ship's rail, looking down at the water, Peter does not appear to notice Maud. Finally, without moving his head, he says in a British-inflected, slightly nasal voice, "Did you know that the Drake Passage is a major component of the coupled ocean-atmosphere climate system and that it connects all the other major oceans and that it influences the water-mass characteristics of the deep water over a large portion of the world?"

"Of course, darling," Maud answers in the same sort of voice and takes Peter's arm. "Everyone knows that."

Peter has an almost photographic memory and is, Maud likes to say, the smartest man she has ever met. Peter claims that he would have preferred being a mathematician to being a lawyer. He is an attractive man, tall and athletic looking, although he walks with a slight limp—he broke his leg as a child and the leg did not set properly—which gives him a certain vulnerability and adds to his appeal (secretly, Maud accuses him of exaggerating the limp to elicit sympathy). And he still has a full head of hair, notwithstanding that it has turned gray, which he wears surprisingly long. Maud, too, is good-looking: slim, tall, and blonde (the blonde is no longer natural but such a constant that Maud would be hard put to say what her natural color is); her blue eyes, she claims, are still her best feature. Together, they make a handsome couple; they have been married for over forty years.

Maud knows Peter so well that she also knows that when he adopts this bantering tone with her, he is either hiding something or he is feeling depressed. Or both. Instinctively, she tightens her grip on his arm.

"Let's go in," she says to him in her normal voice. "I'm cold."

In their cabin, the books, the clock, the bottle of sleeping pills, everything that had been neatly stacked on the nightstand is, on account of the ship's motion, lying pell-mell on the floor.

Instead of a double bed, their cabin has two narrow bunks. The bunks are made up in an unusual way, a Norwegian way, Maud guesses—the sheet wrapped around the blanket as if it were a parcel and tucked in. In her bed, Maud feels as if she were lying inside a cocoon; also, she does not dislike sleeping alone for a change. As if Peter could read her mind—he has an uncanny ability to do this sometimes—he pats the side of his bunk and says, "Come here for a minute, Maud." Maud hesitates, then decides not to answer. She does not feel like making love—too much trouble and often, recently, sex does not work out, which makes her anxious and Peter anxious and angry both. Over their heads, on the wall, the public-address speaker crackles and a voice says: "Long before the poet Samuel Coleridge penned his 'Rime of the Ancient Mariner,' the albatross was a creature of reverence and superstition. The sailors believed that when their captain died, his soul took the form of an albatross. Of course I cannot speak for our excellent Captain Halvorsen, but I, for one, would not mind being reincarnated as an albatross." In the bed next to Maud, Peter snorts and says again, "Maudie, come over here." Maud pretends not to hear him. "By the way, my name is Michael," the voice continues, "and in case you have not yet met me, I am your naturalist on board." Peter says something that Maud does not quite catch although she can guess at the meaning. "The albatross has the largest wingspan—the record, I believe, is thirteen feet, three inches—and the oldest known albatross is seventy years old. When he is ten, the albatross goes back to where he was born to mate—" Maud tenses for a comment from Peter but this time he makes none. The public-address speaker crackles with static, ". . . feeds at night . . . eats luminous squid, fish, and krill." Maud looks over at Peter's bunk and sees that Peter's eyes are closed. Relieved, she reaches up to turn down the volume on the speaker as Michael says, "The albatross will fly for miles without moving its wings, or setting foot on land. Soaring and gliding over the water, the albatross's zigzag flight is determined by the wind."

. . .

The captain's cocktail party is held in the saloon—or, as Maud refers to it, Emergency Station 2. She is dressed in her best slacks and a red cashmere sweater, and Peter wears his blue blazer and a tie. The saloon is packed tight with passengers who are all talking at once. Right away, Maud orders a vodka martini at the bar while Peter has a beer.

"Take it easy," Peter says, handing her the martini.

The ship's motion is more pronounced. Maud hangs on to the edge of the bar with one hand and holds her martini glass in the other. Sometimes Maud drinks too much. She blames her age and the fact that she is thin and cannot hold her liquor the way she used to—not the actual amount she drinks. Standing in the center of the room, Captain Halvorsen is a tall man with thinning red hair; he smiles politely as he talks to the passengers. Maud guesses that he must dread this evening and the enforced sociability. Looking around the room, she does not see the darkly handsome first officer. A woman holding a golf club—which, at first, Maud thought was a cane—walks over to them and, standing next to Peter at the bar, orders a glass of white wine.

"If I am not mistaken, that's a five-iron you have in your hand," Peter says to her in his nasal voice.

"Yes, it is," the woman answers. She is dark and trim and does not smile.

"Do you always travel with a golf club?" Peter, when he wants, can be charming and act completely entranced by what the other person is saying. If that person happens to be a woman, Maud tends to resent it even though she knows that Peter's attention may not be entirely genuine. Peter continues, "By the way, my name is Peter and this is my wife, Maud."

"I'm Barbara," the woman says. "And, yes, I always travel with my golf club."

"As protection?" Maud manages to ask.

"No," Barbara frowns. "My goal is to drive a golf ball in every country of the world."

"Oh."

"And have you?" Peter asks. He does a little imitation golf swing, holding his bottle of beer in both hands. When, in the past, Maud has accused Peter of toying with people, Peter has accused Maud of misreading him.

"As a matter of fact, I have. Or nearly. Except for Antarctica, which of course is not a country but a continent, and a few African nations which are too dangerous. I began twenty years ago—"

Why? Maud is tempted to ask.

"After my husband died," Barbara says as if to answer Maud.

"Can you get me another martini?" Maud asks Peter.

That night, Maud cannot sleep. Every time she closes her eyes, she feels dizzy and nauseated and she has to open her eyes again; she tries sitting up in bed. To make matters worse, the *Caledonia Star* creaks and shudders as all night it pitches and lurches through a heavy sea. Once, after a particularly violent lurch, Maud calls out to Peter, but either he is asleep and does not hear her or, perverse, he does not answer her. To herself, Maud vows that she will never have another drink.

In the morning, at seven according to the clock that is on the floor—Maud has finally managed to sleep for a few hours—Maud and Peter are awoken by the now-familiar voice on the public-address speaker.

"Good morning, folks! It's Michael! I hope you folks were not still sleeping! For those of you who are on the starboard side of the ship—that means the right side for the landlubbers—if you look out your porthole real quick, you'll see a couple of minke whales."

When Maud looks outside, the sea is calm and it is raining.

"Do you see them?" Peter asks from his bed.

"No," Maud says. "I don't see any minke whales."

"Michael is lying to us," Peter says, rolling over on to his other side. "Be a good girl and give me a back rub. This mattress is for the birds."

In the rubber Zodiac, Maud starts to feel better. The cold air clears her head and she is looking forward to walking on land. Behind her, the *Caledonia Star* rests solidly at anchor as they make their way across to Livingston Island. The passengers in the boat are all wearing orange life jackets as well as identical red parkas— when Maud inquired about the parkas, she was told that red was easy to see and made it easier for the crew to tell whether any passenger was left behind on shore. And had a passenger ever been left behind? Maud continued. Yes, once. A woman had tried to hide. Hide? Why? Maud had asked again, but she got no reply.

Holding her golf club between her legs, Barbara sits across from them in the Zodiac. Instead of a cap, she wears a visor that has GOLFERS MAKE BETTER LOVERS printed on it. Michael, the naturalist, is young, blond, and bearded, and he drives the Zodiac with smooth expertise. Once he lands the boat, he gives each passenger a hand, cautioning them: "Careful where you walk, the ground may be slippery. And steer clear of those seals," he also says, pointing. "Especially the big fur seal, he's not friendly."

Looking like giant rubber erasers, about a dozen seals are lying close together along the shore; their beige and gray hides are mottled and scarred. Except for one seal who raises his head to look at them as they walk past—the fur seal no doubt—none of the seals moves. Maud gives them a wide berth and makes no eye contact; Peter, on the other hand, deliberately walks up closer to the seals and takes several photos of them.

A few yards inland, Maud sees Barbara lean over to tee up a golf ball. She watches as Barbara takes up her stance and takes a few practice swings. Several of the other passengers are watching her as well. One man calls out, "Make it a hole-in-one, Barbara!" The golf ball sails straight toward the brown cliffs that rise from the shore; a few people applaud. Barbara tees up and hits another golf ball, then another. Each time, the sound is a sharp crack, like ice breaking.

Michael is right—it is slippery. Wet shale and bits of snow litter the ground; also there are hundreds—no, perhaps thousands—of penguins on Livingston Island. Maud has to watch where she steps. It would not do, she thinks, to break a leg in Antarctica or to crush a penguin. Like the seals, the penguins appear oblivious to people. They are small and everywhere underfoot and Maud feels as if she is walking among dwarves.

When Peter catches up to her, he says, "You think one of these penguins is going to try to brood on a golf ball?"

"Incubate, you mean," Maud says. "You brood on a chick."

"Whatever," Peter answers, turning away from her. He does not like being corrected, and although Maud should know better by now, old habits die hard.

In the Zodiac, on the way back to the *Caledonia Star,* the wind has picked up and the sea is rougher. In spite of Michael's efforts, waves slap at the boat's sides and cold spray wets the back of the passengers' red parkas.

"Tomorrow, we will see icebergs," Captain Halvorsen promises during dinner. Maud and Peter are sitting at his table along with another couple, Philip and Janet. Philip claims to have been in the same college class with Peter and to remember him well (he alludes to an incident involving the misuse of cafeteria trays, but Peter has no recollection of it and shakes his head). Janet, a tall brunette with smooth olive skin and dark full eyebrows, is much younger; she never attended college, she tells Maud, giggling. She took up modeling instead.

"If the ice were to melt," Captain Halvorsen tells Peter, "the water would rise sixty-six meters."

"Isn't a meter like a yard?" Janet asks. "I was never any good at math."

Sitting next to Maud, Philip, who is in real estate, is describing the booming building industry in Florida, where he lives.

"The grounding line is where the ice mass begins to float," Maud overhears Captain Halvorsen say. "In Antarctica, icebergs form when ice breaks away from large flat plates called ice shelves."

"I read that the Ross Ice Shelf is the size of the state of Connecticut," Peter says.

"The size of France," Captain Halvorsen says.

Leaning over, Janet says something to Peter that Maud cannot hear, which makes him laugh. Maud watches as, still laughing, Peter puts his hand on Janet's forearm and pats it in a gesture of easy camaraderie.

"Can you pass the wine, Philip?" Maud interrupts him.

"Eighty-five percent of the ice in the world is in Antarctica," Captain Halvorsen says. Then, as an afterthought, he adds, "and six percent of the ice in the world is in Greenland."

And the rest? The 9 percent? Maud wishes to ask but does not.

For years, as a child, Maud had a recurring dream. A nightmare. In her sleep, she always knew when the nightmare was beginning but she was unable to stop it or wake herself up. The other thing, too, was that Maud could never describe it. The dream had nothing to do with people or monsters or violent situations or anything she might know or recognize. The dream could not be put into words. The closest way she could come to describing it was to say that it was about numbers (even so, that was not quite right as the numbers were not the familiar ones like 8 or 17 or 224); they were something other. (When consulted about the nightmare, the family physician suggested that Maud stop taking math for a while but, at school, math was Maud's best subject.) The numbers (if in fact they were numbers) in the dream always started out small and manageable—although, again, Maud knew that was temporary, for soon they multiplied and became so large and unmanageable and incomprehensible that Maud was swept away into a kind of terrible abyss, a kind of black hole full of numbers.

It has been years now since Maud has thought about the dream. Antarctica, the vastness, the ice, the inhospitable landscape, is what she assumes has reminded her of it. When she tries to describe the dream to Peter and mentions the math part, Peter says he knows just what she means.

"You're in good company, all sorts of people had it. The Greeks, Aristotle, Archimedes, Pascal."

"The dream?"

"No, what the dream stands for."

"Which is?" Maud is not sure whether Peter is being serious.

"The terror of the infinite.

"Interestingly, the ancient Greeks did not include zero or infinity in their mathematics," Peter continues, displaying his fondness for the arcane. "Their word for *infinity* was also their word for *mess*."

Captain Halvorsen is right. The next morning they see icebergs. The sea is filled with them. Icebergs of all shapes and sizes. Some are as tall as six-story buildings, others remind Maud of modern sculptures and are tinged with blue—a brilliant aquamarine blue. It is also snowing.

Despite the snow, Peter spends the morning on deck with his camera, taking pictures. When Maud joins him, he says, "Have you ever seen anything like those icebergs? Have you ever seen a blue like that?"

"Are you warm enough?" Maud asks. A part of her—a part she dislikes—resents seeing Peter so happy and excited about the icebergs, and she feels excluded. At the same time, she also envies his ability to be so genuinely absorbed and enchanted by nature—at home, Peter is always pointing out large, beautiful trees to her. His appreciation seems pure and unmotivated and Maud wishes she could share it but she is too self-conscious. Too self-referential, she decides. She cannot look at the stars without wishing for a falling one, or gaze at the sea without thinking "drown."

Each time the *Caledonia Star* runs into a large ice floe, there is a loud thumping noise, but since the ship's hull is made of steel, there is no need for concern. Many of the ice floes have penguins and seals on them. When the ship goes by, the penguins, alarmed, dive off like bullets; the seals, indifferent, do not move. Often, blood, looking like paint splashed on a canvas, stains the ice around the seals—the remains of their kill. In addition to fur seals, Maud is told, there are crabeater seals, Ross seals, leopard seals, elephant seals, and the Weddell seals.

"A marine mammal exhales before he dives," Michael is saying over the public-address speaker in Maud and Peter's cabin, "and oxygen is stored in his blood, not in his lungs."

This time, Maud and Peter are making love on one of the bunks.

"Shall I turn him off?" Maud starts to move away.

"No. Stay put." Peter has an erection.

"Seals collapse their lungs when they dive. Their heart rate drops and their arteries constrict. In fact, everything is shut down—"

Maud half listens.

"Except for the brain, the adrenal, and the placenta—that is, of course, if the seal is pregnant—"

Afterward, still lying pressed together on the little bunk, Maud frees her arm, which has gone to sleep, from under Peter and, as if to make up for her movement which breaks the postcoital spell, she kisses Peter lightly. Also, in spite of herself, she asks, "So what are you going to do with all the photographs you took of icebergs?"

Peter does not answer Maud right away. He shifts his body away from her a little before he says in his British-inflected, nasal voice, "Why enlarge them, naturally."

. . .

Instead of going ashore again in the Zodiac with the others, Maud decides to remain on board. Except for the woman in the wheel-chair, who appears to be asleep (her eyes are closed and she breathes heavily), Maud is alone in the saloon, and from where she is sitting reading or trying to read her book, she can watch the passengers, dressed in their red parkas, disembark at Port Lockroy, the British station. She watches as they spread out and start to climb the snow-covered hill behind the station. Some of the passengers have brought along ski poles and Maud tries to pick out which red parka belongs to Peter and which belongs to Janet, but the figures are too far away. She thinks again about the woman who tried to hide and again she wonders why. Was the woman suicidal? But freezing to death, Maud also thinks, may not be such a bad way to die. How did the Emily Dickinson poem go? "As Freezing persons, recollect the Snow—/ First—Chill—then Stupor—then the letting go—." In spite of herself, Maud shivers. Then she makes herself open her book. When next she looks up, all the figures in their red parkas have disappeared.

"You didn't miss anything," Peter tells Maud when he returns from the station. Nevertheless, he looks animated. "There was a museum that was kind of creepy—an old sled and some frying pans—but Janet bought some postcards."

"Ah, lovely Janet," Maud says.

"What do you mean by that?" Peter asks.

"What do you suppose I mean?"

"For God's sake, Maud, why must you always be suspicious of me? Why do you always attribute some underhanded motive to everything I do?" Peter turns and limps out of the saloon, leaving Maud.

The woman in the wheelchair has woken up; she gives a little embarrassed cough.

The first time, twenty or so years ago, Maud accused Peter of having an affair, the discussion had turned violent—Maud threw a plate of food at Peter and Peter picked up a glass full of wine and flung it across the table at Maud, shouting, "I can't live like this!" Then he left home for three days. When finally he returned, he did not say where he had been and Maud did not ask. Nor did they ever again discuss either the fight or the affair. What Maud remembers vividly is her panic. During the time Peter was gone, she could hardly breathe, let alone eat, and she could not sleep. She was assailed by all kinds of conflicting emotions, but the dominant one was fear: the fear that she had driven Peter to some action she would regret and the fear that she would never see him again.

When the *Caledonia Star* crosses the Antarctic Circle, all the passengers crowd onto the bridge to look. The sky is a cloudless blue and the sea calm, but the horizon is a wall of icebergs. Maud recognizes the handsome French first officer up in the crow's nest, dressed in a bright yellow slicker and waterproof pants. He is reporting back to Captain Halvorsen on the bridge by walkie-talkie. The ship's chief officer is tracing the ship's course on a sea chart with a compass and a protractor; on the radar screen, the larger tabular icebergs show up as small luminous points.

Below, on deck, Peter is looking through his binoculars.

"What do you see?" Maud asks, but she cannot hear his answer.

By then, Maud is able to recognize most of the passengers on board the ship, and she knows many of them by name. One flight below their cabin, she has discovered the gym and she exercises regularly on the treadmill. She has also become more tolerant—even of Barbara, the golfer—and has made a few friends. One is the woman in the wheelchair.

"She's from Philadelphia and she's already identified five different species of albatross," Maud tells Peter, "the gray-headed albatross, the sooty albatross, the wandering—"

"What's wrong with her?" Peter wants to know. "Why is she in a wheelchair?"

Maud shrugs. "I didn't ask."

After dinner one night, a film is shown in the saloon. The film is old and grainy and tells the true story of the perilous voyage of a ship named the *Peking*. Sailing around Cape Horn, the *Peking* encounters a terrible storm—the mast breaks, waves crash on deck—and, to make matters worse, the captain of the *Peking* has brought his dog, a vicious little terrier, on board. The terrier is seen jumping up and biting the sailors who have as yet not been swept overboard. The dog provides a kind of gruesome comic relief and makes everyone laugh, including Maud and Peter.

When the film ends, Janet tells Maud, "I once had a dog who looked just like that. His name was Pepe."

"I love dogs," Maud, expansive, answers her.

Peter moves to sit next to Janet and starts to describe a cruise he once took in the Mediterranean as a college student. "I was on deck one night after dinner—we were docked in Cannes— and my wallet, which was in my back pocket, must have fallen overboard—"

Maud has heard the story a thousand times and does not listen. Instead she strikes up a conversation with the woman in the wheelchair. "Have you always loved birds?" Maud asks.

"You can't imagine! The most extraordinary piece of luck," Peter is telling Janet as he leans in closer to her. "A fisherman caught my wallet in his net. The wallet had over a thousand dollars in cash in it—I was planning to buy a car in England, an MG—"

Looking over, Maud sees that Janet has stopped paying attention to what Peter is saying. She is looking past him toward the door of the saloon and Maud follows her gaze. She sees the handsome French first officer standing there; she sees him signal to Janet.

"Excuse me," Janet says, getting up and leaving the saloon.

"Pinned up on the wall of the Cannes police station was every last dollar—" Peter's voice trails off.

Maud looks away. She is fairly used to seeing Peter flirt, but she is not used to seeing him defeated.

A few minutes later, Peter says, "I'm tired, I'm going to bed."

Maud would like to say something that might be of comfort to him but cannot think what that might be. She merely nods.

When Maud wakes up during the night to go to the bathroom (or *head* as she knows she is supposed to call it), she sees that Peter is not in his bed. The sheets and blankets are half lying on the floor as if Peter had thrown them off in a rush.

"Peter," Maud calls out in the dark.

Turning on the light, Maud goes to the bathroom, then pulls her jeans over her nightgown, grabs her parka, a hat, and gloves.

The ship's corridor is dimly lit and empty. As Maud half runs toward the stairs, her steps echo eerily. All the cabin doors are shut and, briefly, she imagines the occupants sleeping peacefully inside. The ship's motor hums smoothly, there is an occasional thud of the hull hitting an ice floe. Her heart banging in her chest, Maud runs up to the saloon. The saloon, too, is dimly lit and empty. In the dining room, the chairs are stacked, the floor ready for cleaning. From there, she opens a door and goes out on deck. The cold air momentarily takes her breath away but the sky is unnaturally light. The ship's huge searchlights move back and forth over the sea, restlessly illuminating here an ice floe, there an iceberg. Inside the bridge house, Captain Halvorsen, holding a mug of coffee, stands next to the pilot at the wheel. The handsome first officer briefly glances up from the radar screen as Maud comes in.

"My husband—" she says.

"Is he ill?" Captain Halvorsen asks, without taking his eyes from the horizon. "Has something happened?"

"I'm looking for him," Maud answers, intimidated.

His face expressionless, the first officer continues to study the radar screen.

Every few seconds the pilot at the wheel shouts out numbers, coordinates, compass points. He, too, pays Maud no attention.

Directly in front of the ship's bow, a tabular iceberg that is taller and longer than the *Caledonia Star* appears yellowish green in the spotlight. In the bridge house all the attention is fixed on getting safely past it and not on anything that Maud says or does. For a moment longer, Maud stands motionless, not daring to speak or breathe, and watches the boat's slow, safe progress past the iceberg.

"Where were you?" Peter asks when Maud opens the cabin door and switches on the light. He is in bed, the sheet and blanket neatly tucked in around him.

"Where were *you?*" Despite the enormous relief she feels on seeing him, Maud is angry.

Peter tells her he went up on deck for a few minutes and they must have missed each other. At night, he says, the icebergs look even more amazing. "All that uninhabitable empty space. So pure, so absolute." Peter sounds euphoric, then, as if suddenly remembering something important, he says, "Maud, it's four-thirty in the morning."

Maud does not feel tired, nor does she feel any desire to sleep. Back in bed, she has switched off the light when Peter calls over to her, in his slightly inflected British voice, "Sweet dreams, darling."

Maud says nothing.

Jennine Capó Crucet

How to Leave Hialeah

IT IS IMPOSSIBLE to leave without an excuse—something must push you out, at least at first. You won't go otherwise; you are happy, the weather is bright, and you have a car. It has a sunroof (which you call a moonroof—you're so quirky) and a thunderous muffler. After fifteen years of trial and error, you have finally arranged your bedroom furniture in a way that you and your father can agree on. You have a locker you can reach at Miami High. With so much going right, it is only when you're driven out like a fly waved through a window that you'll be outside long enough to realize that, barring the occasional hurricane, you won't die.

The most reliable (and admittedly the least empowering) way to excuse yourself from Hialeah is to date Michael Cardenas Junior. He lives two houses away from you and is very handsome and smart enough to feed himself and take you on dates. Your mother will love him because he plans to marry you in three years when you turn eighteen. He is nineteen. He also goes to Miami High, where he is very popular because he plays football and makes fun of reading. You are not so cool: you have a few friends, but all their last names start with the same letter as yours because, since first grade, your teachers have used the alphabet to assign your seats. Your friends have parents just like yours, and your moms are always hoping another mother comes along as a chaperone when you all go to the movies on Saturday nights because then they can compare their husbands' demands—*put my socks on for me before I get out of bed, I hate cold floors*, or *you have to make me my lunch because only your sandwiches taste good to me*—and laugh at how much they are like babies. Michael does not like your friends, but this is normal and to be expected since your friends occasionally use polysyllabic words. Michael will repeatedly try to have sex with you because you are a virgin and somewhat Catholic and he knows if you sleep together, you'll feel too guilty to ever leave him. Sex will be tempting because your best friend Carla is dating Michael's best friend Frankie, and Michael will swear on his father's grave that they're doing it. But you must hold out—you must push him off when he surprises you on your eight-month anniversary with a room at the Executive Inn by the airport and he has sprung for an entire five hours—because only then will he break up with you. This must happen, because even though you will get back together and break up two more times, it is during those broken-up weeks that you do things like research out-of-state colleges and sign up for community college classes at night to distract you from how pissed you are. This has the side effect of boosting your GPA.

During these same break-up weeks, Michael will use his fake ID to buy beer and hang out with Frankie, who, at the advice of an ex-girlfriend he slept with twice who's now living in Tallahassee, has applied to Florida State. They will talk about college girls, who they heard have sex with you without crying for two hours afterward. Michael, because he is not in your backyard playing catch with your little brother while your mother encourages you to swoon from the kitchen window, has time to fill out an application on a whim. And lo and behold, because it is October, and because FSU has rolling admissions and various guarantees of acceptance for Florida residents who can sign their names, he is suddenly college bound.

When you get back together and he tells you he's leaving at the end of June (his admission being conditional, requiring a summer term before his freshman year), tell your mom about his impending departure, how you will miss him *so* much, how you wish you could make him stay just a year longer so you could go to college at the same time. A week later, sit through your mother's vague sex talk, which your father has forced her to give you. She may rent *The Miracle of Life;* she may not. Either way, do not let on that you know more than she does thanks to public school and health class.

—I was a virgin until my wedding night, she says.

Believe her. Ask if your dad was a virgin, too. Know exactly what she means when she says, Sort of. Try not to picture your father as a teenager, on top of some girl doing what you and Carla call a Temporary Penis Occupation. Assure yourself that TPOs are not sex, not really, because TPOs happen mostly by accident, without you wanting them to, and without any actual movement on your part. Do not ask about butt sex, even though Michael has presented this as an option to let you keep your semivirginity. Your mother will mention it briefly on her own, saying, For that men have prostitutes. Her words are enough to convince you never to try it.

Allow Michael to end things after attempting a long-distance relationship for three months. The distance has not been hard: you inherited his friends from last year who were juniors with you, and he drives down to Hialeah every weekend to see you and his mother and Frankie. Still, you're stubborn about the sex thing, and still, you can't think of your butt as anything other than an out-hole. Michael has no choice but to admit you're unreasonable and dump you.

Cry because you're genuinely hurt—you *love* him, you *do*—

and because you did not apply early decision to any colleges because you hadn't yet decided if you should follow him to FSU. When the misery melts to fury, send off the already-complete applications you'd torn from the glossy brochures stashed under your mattress and begin formulating arguments that will convince your parents to let you move far away from the city where every relative you have that's not in Cuba has lived since flying or floating into Miami; you will sell your car, you will eat cat food to save money, you are their American Dream. Get their blessing to go to the one school that accepts you by promising to come back and live down the street from them forever. Be sure to cross your fingers behind your back while making this promise, otherwise you risk being struck by lightning.

Once away at school, refuse to admit you are homesick. Pretend you are happy in your tiny dorm room with your roommate from Long Island. She has a Jeep Cherokee and you need groceries, and you have never seen snow and are nervous about walking a mile to the grocery store and back. Ask the RA what time the dorm closes for the night and try to play it off as a joke when she starts laughing. Do not tell anyone your father never finished high school. Admit to no one that you left Hialeah in large part to piss off a boy whose last name you will not remember in ten years.

Enroll in English classes because you want to meet white guys who wear V-neck sweaters and have never played football for fear of concussions. Sit behind them in lecture but decide early on that they're too distracting. You must do very well in your classes; e-mails from the school's Office of Diversity have emphasized that you are special, that you may feel like you're not cut out for this, that you should take advantage of the free tutors offered to students like you. You are important to our university community, they say. You are part of our commitment to diversity. Call your mother crying and tell her you don't fit in, and feel surprisingly better when she says, Just come home. Book a five-hundred-dollar flight to Miami for winter break.

Count down the days left until Nochebuena. Minutes after you walk off the plane, call all your old friends and tell them you're back and to get permission from their moms to stay out later than usual. Go to the beach even though it's sixty degrees and the water is freezing and full of Canadians. Laugh as your friends don their back-of-the-closet sweaters on New Year's while you're perfectly fine in a halter top. New England winters have made you tough, you think. You have earned scores of 90 or higher on every final exam. You have had sex with one and a half guys (counting TPOs) and yes, there'd been guilt, but God did not strike you dead. Ignore Michael's calls on the first of the year, and hide in your bedroom—which has not at all changed—when you see him in his Seminoles hoodie, stomping toward your house. Listen as he demands to talk to you, and your mom lies like you asked her to and says you're not home. Watch the conversation from between the blinds of the window that faces the driveway. Swallow down the wave of nausea when you catch your mother winking at him and tilting her head toward that window. Pack immediately and live out of your suitcase for the one week left in your visit.

Go play pool with Myra, one of your closest alphabetical friends, and say, Oh man, that sucks, when she tells you she's still working as a truck dispatcher for El Dorado Furniture. She will try to ignore you by making fun of your shoes, which you bought near campus, and which you didn't like at first but now appreciate for their comfort. Say, Seriously, chica, that's a high school job—you can't work there forever.

—Shut up with this chica crap like you know me, she says.

Then she slams her pool cue down on the green felt and throws the chunk of chalk at you as she charges out. Avoid embarrassment by shaking your head No as she leaves, like you regret sending her to her room with no dinner but she left you no choice. Say to the people at the table next to yours, What the fuck, huh? One guy will look down at your hippie sandals and ask, How do you know Myra? Be confused, because you and Myra always had the same friends thanks to the alphabet, but you've never in your life seen this guy before that night.

While you drive home in your mom's car, think about what happened at the pool place. Replay the sound of the cue slapping the table in your head, the clinking balls as they rolled out of its way but didn't hide in the pockets. Decide not to talk to Myra for a while, that inviting her to come visit you up north is, for now, a bad idea. Wipe your face on your sleeve before you go inside your house, and when your mom asks you why you look so upset tell her the truth: you can't believe it—Myra is jealous.

Become an RA yourself your next year so that your parents don't worry as much about money. Attend all orientation workshops and decide, after a sexual harassment prevention role-playing where Russel, another new RA, asked if tit fucking counted as rape, that you will only do this for one year. Around Rush Week, hang up the anti-binge-drinking posters the hall director put in your mailbox. On it is a group of eight grinning students; only one of them is white. You look at your residents and are confused: they are all white, except for the girl from Kenya and the girl from California. Do not worry when these two residents start spending hours hanging out in your room—letting them sit on your bed does not constitute sexual harassment. Laugh with them when they make fun of the poster. *Such Diversity in One University!* Recommend them to your hall director as potential RA candidates for next year.

When you call home to check in (you do this five times a week), ask how everyone is doing. Get used to your mom saying, Fine, fine. Appreciate the lack of detail—you have limited minutes on your phone plan and besides, your family, like you, is young and indestructible. They have floated across oceans and sucker punched sharks with their bare hands. Your father eats three pounds of beef a day and his cholesterol is fine. Each weeknight, just before crossing herself and pulling a thin sheet over her pipe-cleaner legs, your ninety-nine-year-old great-grandmother smokes a cigar while sipping a glass of whiskey and water. No one you love has ever died—just one benefit of the teenage parenthood you've magically avoided despite the family tradition. Death is far off for every Cuban—you use Castro as your example. You know everyone will still be in Hialeah when you decide to come back.

Join the Spanish Club, where you meet actual lisping Spaniards and have a hard time understanding what they say. Date the treasurer, a grad student in Spanish literature named Marco, until he mentions your preference for being on top during sex subconsciously functions as retribution for *his* people conquering *your* people. Quit the Spanish Club and check out several Latin American history books from the library to figure out what the hell he's talking about. Do not tell your mother you broke things off; she loves Spaniards, and you are twenty and not married and you refuse to settle down.

—We are not sending you so far away to come back with nothing, she says.

At the end of that semester, look at a printout of your transcript and give yourself a high five. (To anyone watching, you're just clapping.) Going home for the summer with this printout still constitutes coming back with nothing despite the good grades, so decide to spend those months working full-time at the campus movie theater, flirting with sunburned patrons.

Come senior year, decide what you need is to get back to your roots. Date a brother in Iota Delta, the campus's Latino fraternity, because one, he has a car, and two, he gives you credibility in the collegiate minority community you forgot to join because you were hiding in the library for the past three years and never saw the flyers. Tell him you've always liked Puerto Ricans (even though every racist joke your father has ever told you involved Puerto Ricans in some way). Visit his house in Cherry Hill, New Jersey, and meet his third-generation American parents who cannot speak Spanish. Do not look confused when his mother serves meat loaf and mashed potatoes and your boyfriend calls it *real home cooking*. You have only ever had meat loaf in the school dining hall, and only once. Avoid staring at his mother's multiple chins. Hold your laughter even as she claims that Che Guevara is actually still alive and living in a castle off the coast of Vieques. Scribble physical notes inside your copy of *Clarissa* (the subject of your senior thesis) detailing all the ridiculous things his mother says while you're there: taking a shower while it rains basically guarantees you'll be hit by lightning; paper cannot actually be recycled; Puerto Ricans invented the fort. Wait until you get back to campus to call your father.

After almost four years away from Hialeah, panic that you're panicking when you think about going back—you had to leave to realize you ever wanted to. You'd thank Michael for the push, but you don't know where he is. You have not spoken to Myra since the blowout by the pool table. You only know she still lives with her parents because her mom and your mom see each other every Thursday while buying groceries at Sedano's. At your Iota brother's suggestion, take a Latino studies class with him after reasoning that it will make you remember who you were in high school and get you excited about moving back home.

Start saying things like, What does it really mean to be a minority? How do we construct identity? How is the concept of race forced upon us? Say these phrases to your parents when they ask you when they should drive up to move your stuff back to your room. Dismiss your father as a lazy thinker when he answers, What the fuck are you talking about? Break up with the Iota brother after deciding he and his organization are posers buying into the Ghetto-Fabulous-Jennifer-Lopez-Loving Latino identity put forth by the media; you earned an A- in the Latino studies course. After a fancy graduation dinner where your mom used your hot plate to cook arroz imperial—your favorite—tell your family you can't come home, because you need to know what home means before you can go there. Just keep eating when your father throws his fork on the floor and yells, What the fuck are you talking about? Cross your fingers under the table after you tell them you're going to grad school and your mom says, But, mamita, you made a promise.

Move to what you learn is nicknamed the Great White North. Tell yourself, this is America! This is the heartland! Appreciate how everyone is so *nice,* but claim Hialeah fiercely since it's all people ask you about anyway. They've never seen hair so curly, so dark. You have never felt more Cuban in your life, mainly because for the first time, you are consistently being identified as *Mexican or something.* This thrills you until the beginning-of-semester party for your grad program: you are the only person in attendance who is not white, and you're the only one under five foot seven. You stand alone by an unlit floor lamp, holding a glass of cheap red wine. You wish that Iota brother were around to protect you; he was very big; people were scared he would eat them; he had PURO LATINO tattooed across his shoulders in Olde English lettering. Chug the wine and decide that everyone in the world is a poser except maybe your parents. You think, *What does that even mean—poser?* Don't admit that you are somewhat drunk. Have another glass of wine and slip Spanish words into your sentences to see if anyone asks you about them. Consider yourself very charming and the most attractive female in your year, by far—you are *exotic.* Let one of the third-year students drive you home after he says he doesn't think you're okay to take a bus. Tell him, What, puta, you think I never rode no bus in Miami? Shit, I grew up on the bus. Do not tell him it was a private bus your parents paid twenty dollars a week for you to ride, along with other neighborhood kids, because they thought the public school bus was too dangerous—*they* had actually grown up on the buses you're now claiming. Your dad told you stories about bus fights, so you feel you can wing it as the third-year clicks your seat belt on for you and says, That's fascinating—what does *puta* mean?

Spend the rest of that summer and early fall marveling at the lightning storms that you're sure are the only flashy thing about the Midwest. Take three months to figure out that the wailing sounds you sometimes hear in the air are not in your head—they are tornado sirens.

As the days grow shorter, sneak into tanning salons to maintain what you call your natural color. Justify this to yourself as healthy. You need more vitamin D than these Viking people, you have no choice. Relax when the fake sun actually does make you brown, rather than the Play-Doh orange beaming off your students—you have genuine African roots! You knew it all along! Do not think about how, just like all the other salon patrons, you reek of drying paint and burned hair every time you emerge from that ultraviolet casket.

Date the third-year because he finds you *fascinating* and asks you all sorts of questions about growing up in el barrio, and you like to talk anyway. More important, he has a car, and you need groceries, and this city is much colder than your college home—you don't plan on walking anywhere. And you are lonely. Once the weather turns brutal and your heating bill hits triple digits, start sleeping with him for warmth. When he confesses that the growth you'd felt between his legs is actually a third testicle, you'll both be silent for several seconds, then he will growl, It doesn't actually *function*. He will grimace and grind his very square teeth as if you'd just called him Tri-Balls, even though you only said it in your head. When he turns away from you on the bed and covers his moon-white legs, think that you could love this gloomy, deformed person; maybe he has always felt the loneliness sitting on you since you left home, except for him, it's because of an extra-heavy nut sack. Lean toward him and tell him you don't care—say it softly, of course—say that you would have liked some warning, but that otherwise it's just another fact about him. Do not use the word *exotic* to describe his special scrotum. You've learned since moving here that that word is used to push people into some separate, freakish category.

Break up with him when, after a department happy hour, you learn from another third-year that he's recently changed his dissertation topic to something concerning the Cuban American community in Miami. He did this a month ago—*Didn't he tell you?* On the walk to the car, accuse him of using you for research purposes.

—Maybe I did, he says, But that isn't *why* I dated you, it was a *bonus*.

Tell him that being Cuban is no more a bonus than, say, a third nut. Turn on your heel and walk home in single-digit weather while he follows you in his car and yelps from the lowered window, Can't we talk about this? Call your mother after cursing him out in front of your apartment building for half an hour while he just stood there, observing.

—Oh please, she says, her voice far away, Like anyone would want to read about Hialeah.

Do not yell at your mother for missing the point.

Change advisers several times until you find the one who does not refer to you as *the Mexican one* and does not ask you how your research applies to *regular* communities. Sit in biweekly off-campus meetings with your fellow Latinas, each of them made paler by the Great White North's conquest over their once-stubborn pigment. They face the same issues in their departments—the problem, you're learning, is system-wide. Write strongly worded joint letters to be sent at the end of the term. Think, *Is this really happening? I am part of this group?* Look at the dark greenish circles hanging under their eyes, the curly frizz poking out from their pulled-back hair and think, *Why did I think I had a choice?*

. . .

Call home less often. There is nothing good to report.

—Why can't you just *shut up* about being Cuban, your mother says after asking if you're still causing trouble for yourself. No one would even notice if you flat-ironed your hair and stopped talking.

Put your head down and plow through the years you have left there because you know you will graduate: the department can't wait for you to be gone. You snuck into the main office (someone had sent out an e-mail saying there was free pizza in the staff fridge) and while your mouth worked on a cold slice of pepperoni, you heard the program coordinator yak into her phone that they couldn't wait to get rid of the troublemaker.

—I don't know, she says seconds later. Probably about spics, that's her only angle.

You sneak back out of the office and spit the pepperoni out in a hallway trash can because you're afraid of choking—you can't stop laughing. You have not heard the word *spic* used in the past decade. Your parents were *spics. Spics* is so seventies. They would not believe someone just called you that. Crack up because even the Midwest's slurs are way behind the East Coast's. Rename the computer file of your dissertation draft "Spictacular." Make yourself laugh every time you open it.

Embrace your obvious masochism. Make it your personal mission to educate the middle of the country about Latinos by living there just a little longer. But you have to move—you can't work in a department that your protests helped to officially document as Currently Inhospitable to Blacks and Latinos, even if it is friendly to disabled people and people with three testicles.

Decide to stay in the rural Midwest partly for political reasons: you have done what no one in your family has ever done—you have voted in a state other than Florida. And you cannot stand Hialeah's politics. You monitored their poll results via the Internet. Days before the election, you received a mass e-mail from Myra urging you to vote for the candidate whose books you turn upside down when you see them in stores. Start to worry you have communist leanings—wonder if that's really so bad. Keep this to yourself; you do not want to hear the story of your grandfather eating grasshoppers while in a Cuban prison, not again.

Get an adjunct position at a junior college in southern Wisconsin, where you teach a class called the Sociology of Communities. You have seventy-six students and, unlike your previous overly polite ones, these have opinions. Several of them are from Chicago and recognize your accent for what it actually is—not Spanish, but Urban. Let this give you hope. Their questions about Miami are about the beach, or if you'd been there during a particular hurricane, or if you've ever been to the birthplace of a particular rapper. Smile and nod, answer them after class—keep them focused on the reading.

At home, listen to and delete the week's messages from your mother. She is miserable because you have abandoned her, she says. You could have been raped and dismembered, your appendages strewn about Wisconsin and Illinois, and she would have no way of knowing.

—You would call if you'd been dismembered, right? the recording says.

It has only been eight days since you last spoke to her.

The last message you do not delete. She is vague and says she needs to tell you something important. She is crying. You call back, forgetting about the time difference—it is eleven-thirty in Hialeah.

Ask, What's wrong?

—Can I tell her? she asks your father. He says, I don't care.

—Tell me what?

Tuck your feet under you on your couch and rub your eyes with your free hand.

—Your cousin Barbarita, she says, Barbarita has a brain tumor.

Say, What, and then, Is this a fucking joke?

Take your hand away from your eyes and stick your thumbnail in your mouth. Gnaw on it. Barbarita is eleven years older than you. She taught you how to spit and how to roller-skate. You cannot remember the last time you talked to her, but that is normal—you live far away. Then it comes to you. Eight months ago, at Nochebuena, last time you were home.

—It's really bad. They know it's cancer. We didn't want to tell you.

Sigh deeply, sincerely. You expected something about your centenarian great-grandmother going in her whiskey-induced sleep. You expected your father having to cut back to one pound of beef a day because of his tired heart.

Ask, Mom, you okay? Assume her silence is due to more crying. Say, Mom?

—She's been sick since February, she says.

Now you are silent. It is late August. You did not go back for your birthday this year—you had to find a job, and the market is grueling. Your mother had said she understood. Also, you adopted a rabbit in April (you've been a little lonely in Wisconsin), and your mother knows you don't like leaving the poor thing alone for too long. Push your at-the-ready excuses out of the way and say, Why didn't you tell me before?

She does not answer your question. Instead she says, You have to come home.

Tell her you will see when you can cancel class. There is a fall break coming up, you might be able to find a rabbit-sitter and get away for a week.

—No, I'm sorry I didn't tell you before. I didn't want you to worry. You couldn't do anything from up there.

Wait until she stops crying into the phone. You feel terrible—your poor cousin. She needs to get out and see the world; she has never been farther north than Orlando. When she was a teenager, she'd bragged to you that one day, she'd move to New York City and never come back. You think (but know better than to say), Maybe this is a blessing in disguise. When you see her, you will ignore the staples keeping her scalp closed over her skull. You will pretend to recognize your cousin through the disease and the bloated, hospital-gown-clad monster it's created. You will call her Barbarino like you used to, and make jokes when no one else can. Just before you leave—visiting hours end, and you are just a visitor—you'll lean in close to her face, so close your nose brushes the tiny hairs still clinging to her sideburns, and say, Tomorrow. Tomorrow I'm busting you out of here.

Your mother says, She died this morning. She went fast. The service is the day after tomorrow. Everyone else will be there, please come.

You are beyond outrage—you feel your neck burning hot. You skip right past your dead cousin and think, *I cannot believe these people. They have robbed me of my final hours with my cousin. They have robbed Barbarita of her escape.*

You will think about your reaction later, on the plane, when you try but fail to rewrite a list about the windows of your parents' house in the margins of an in-flight magazine. But right now, you are still angry at being left out. Promise your mother you'll be back in Hialeah in time and say nothing else. Hang up, and book an eight-hundred-dollar flight home after e-mailing your students that class is canceled until further notice.

Brush your teeth, put on flannel pajamas (even after all these winters, you are still always cold), tuck yourself in to bed. Try to make yourself cry. Pull out the ladybug-adorned to-do-list pad from the milk crate you still use as a nightstand and write down everything you know about your now-dead cousin.

Here's what you remember: Barbarita loved papaya and making jokes about papaya. One time, before she even knew what it meant, she called her sister a papayona in front of everyone at a family pig roast. Her mother slapped her hard enough to lay her out on the cement patio. She did not cry, but she stormed inside to her room and did not come out until she'd said the word *papay-ona* out loud and into her pillow two hundred times. Then she said it another hundred times in her head. She'd told you this story when your parents dragged you to visit Barbarita's mom and her newly busted hip while you were home during one of your college breaks. Barbarita's mother, from underneath several white blankets, said, I never understood why you even like that fruit. It tastes like a fart.

Barbarita moved back in with her parents for good after her mom fractured her hip. The family scandal became Barbarita's special lady friend, with whom she'd been living the previous eight years. You remember the lady friend's glittered fanny pack—it always seemed full of breath mints and rubber bands—how you'd guessed it did not come off even for a shower. Barbarita took you to Marlins games and let you drink stadium beer from the plastic bottle if you gave her the change in your pockets. She kept coins in a jar on her nightstand and called it her retirement fund. She made fun of you for opening a savings account when you turned sixteen and said you'd be better off stuffing the cash in a can and burying it in the backyard. She laughed and slapped her knee and said, No lie, I probably have ninety thousand dollars under my mom's papaya tree.

Look at your list. It is too short. Whose fault is that? You want to say God's; you want to say your parents'. You want to blame the ladybug imprinted on the paper. You are jealous of how she adorns yet can ignore everything you've put down. Write, *My cousin is dead and I'm blaming a ladybug.* Cross out *My cousin* and write *Barbarita.* Throw the pad back in the crate before you write, *Am I really this selfish?*

Decide not to sleep. The airport shuttle is picking you up at four a.m. anyway, and it's already one. Get out of bed, set up the automatic food dispenser in your rabbit's cage, then flat-iron your hair so that it looks nice for the funeral. Your father has cursed your frizzy head and blamed the bad genes on your mother's side since you sprouted the first tuft. Wrap the crispy ends of your hair around Velcro rollers and microwave some water in that I-don't-do-Mondays mug that you never use (the one you stole off the grad program coordinator's desk right before shoving your keys in the drop box—you couldn't help stealing it: you're a spic). Stir in the Café Bustelo instant coffee your mother sent you a few weeks ago in a box that also contained credit card offers you'd been mailed at their address and three packs of Juicy Fruit. The spoon clinks against the mug and it sounds to you like the slightest, most insignificant noise in the world.

Sit at the window seat that convinced you to sign the lease to this place even though your closest neighbor is a six-minute drive away. Listen to the gutters around the window flood with rain. Remember the canal across from your parents' house, how the rain threatened to flood it twice a week. There is a statue of San Lázaro in their front yard and a mango tree in the back. Lázaro is wedged underneath an old bathtub your dad half buried vertically in the dirt, to protect the saint from rain. The mango tree takes care of itself. But your father made sure both the mango tree and San Lázaro were well guarded behind a five-foot-high chain-link fence. The house's windows had bars—rejas—on them to protect the rest of his valuables, the ones living inside. You never noticed the rejas (every house around for blocks had them) until you left and came back. The last night of your first winter break in Hialeah, just before you went to sleep, you wasted four pages—front and back—in a notebook scribbling all the ways the rejas were a metaphor for your childhood: *a caged bird, wings clipped, never to fly free; a zoo animal on display yet up for sale to the highest-bidding boyfriend; a rare painting trapped each night after the museum closes.* Roll your eyes—these are the ones you remember now. You didn't mean it, not even as you wrote them, but you wanted to mean it, because that made your leaving an escape and not a desertion. Strain to conjure up more of them—it's got to be easier than reconciling the pilfered mug with your meager list about your cousin. But you can't come up with anything else. All you remember is your father weeding the grass around the saint every other Saturday, even in a downpour.

Peek through the blinds and think, *It will never stop raining*. Pack light—you still have clothes that fit you in your Hialeah closet. Open the blinds all the way and watch the steam from your cup play against the reflected darkness, the flashes of rain. Watch lightning careen into the flat land surrounding your tiny house, your empty, saintless yard. Wait for the thunder. You know, from growing up where it rained every afternoon from three to five, that thunder's timing tells you how far you are from the storm. You cannot remember which cousin taught you this—only that it wasn't Barbarita. When it booms just a second later, know the lightning is too close. Lean your forehead against the windowpane and feel the glass rattle, feel the vibration pass into your skull, into your teeth. Keep your head down; see the dozens of tiny flies, cap-sized and drained, dead on the sill. Only the shells of their bodies are left, along with hundreds of broken legs that still manage to point at you. If you squint hard enough, the flies blend right into the dust padding their mass grave. And when your eyes water, even these dusty pillows blur into an easy, anonymous gray smear.

Your hands feel too heavy to open the window, then the storm glass, then the screen, to sweep their corpses away. You say out loud to no one, I'll do it when I get back. But your words—your breath—rustle the burial ground, sending tiny swirls of dust toward your face. It tastes like chalk and dirt. Feel it scratch the roof of your mouth, but don't cough—you don't need to. Clear your throat if you want; it won't make the taste go away any faster.

Don't guess how long it will take for the clouds to clear up; you're always wrong about weather. The lightning comes so close to your house you're sure this time you'll at least lose power. Close your eyes, cross your fingers behind your back. Swallow hard. The windowsill's grit scrapes every cell in your throat on its way down. Let this itch convince you that the lightning won't hit—it can't, not this time—because for now, you're keeping your promise. On the flight, distract yourself with window lists and *SkyMall* magazine all you want; no matter what you try, the plane will land. Despite the traffic you find worse than you remember, you'll get to Hialeah in time for the burial—finally back, ready to mourn everything.

David Means

The Junction

AS HE HEAVES down through the weeds with a plate in his hand and a smear of jelly on his lips we watch him and stay silent, stay calm, and listen now to that high middle western bitterness in his voice as he talks about the pie cherries and the wonderfully flaky crust and the way he found it steaming on the sill, waiting for him as he'd expected. Our bellies are roaring. Not a full meal in days. Just a can of beans yesterday—while we wait out the next train, the Chicago–Detroit most likely, tomorrow around ten. He talks about how the man of the house was inside listening to a radio show, clearly visible through the front parlor window, with a shotgun at his side, the shadow of it poking up alongside his chair. Same son of a bitch who chased me out of there a while back, he explains. Then he pauses for a minute and we fear—I feel this in the way the other fellows hunch lower, bringing their heels up to the fire—he'll circle all the way back to the beginning of his story again, starting with how he left this camp, a couple of years back, and hiked several miles to a street, lined with old maples, that on first impression seemed very much like the one he'd grown up on, although he wasn't sure because years of drifting on the road had worn the details from his memory, so many miles behind him in the form of bad drink and that mind-numbing case of lockjaw he claims he had in Pittsburgh. (The antitoxin, he explained, had been administered just in time, saving him from the worst of it. A kind flophouse doctor named Williams had tended to his wound, cleaning it out and wrapping it nicely, giving him a bottle of muscle pills.) He hiked into town—that first time—to stumble upon a house that held a resemblance to whatever was left in his memory: a farmhouse with weatherworn clapboard. A side garden with rosebushes and, back beyond a fence, a vegetable patch with pole beans. Not just the same house—he explained—but the same sweet smell emanating from the garden, where far back beyond a few willow trees a brook ran, burbling and so on and so forth. He went on too long about the brook and one of the men (who, exactly, I can't recall) said, I wish you still had that case of lockjaw. (That was the night he was christened "Lockjaw Kid.") He had stood out in the road and absorbed the scene and felt an overwhelming sense that he was home; a sense so powerful it held him fast and—in his words—made him fearful that he'd find it too much to his liking if he went up to beg a meal. So he went back down to the camp with an empty belly and decided to leave well enough alone until, months later, coming through these parts again after a stint of work in Chicago (Lockjaw couched his life story in the idea of employment, using it as a tool to get his point across, whereas the rest of us had long ago given up talking of labor in any form, unless it was to say something along the lines of: Worked myself so hard I'll never work again; or, I'd work if I could find a suitable form of employment that didn't involve work), he decided to hike the six miles into town to take another look, not sure what he was searching for because by that time the initial visit—he said last time he told the story—had become only a vague memory, burned away by drink and travel; the aforesaid confession itself attesting to a hole in his story about having worked in Chicago and giving away the fact that he had, more likely, hung on and headed all the way out to the coast for the winter, whiling his time in the warmth, plucking the proverbial fruit directly from the trees and so on and so forth. We didn't give a shit. That part of his story had simply given us a chance to give him a hard time, saying, You were out in California if you were anywhere, you dumb shit. Not anywhere near Chicago looking for work. You couldn't handle Chicago winters. Only work you would've found in Chicago would've been meat work. You couldn't handle meat work. You're not strong enough to lug meat. Meat would do you in, and so on and so forth. Whatever the case, he said, shrugging us off, going on to explain how he hiked the six miles up to town again and came to the strangely familiar house: smell of the brook. (You smelled the brook the first time you went up poking around, you dumb moron, Lefty said. And he said, Let me qualify and say not just the smell but the exact way it came from—well, how shall I put this? The smell of clear, clean brook water—potable as all hell—filtered through wild myrtle and jimsonweed and the like came to me from a precise point in my past, some exact place, so to speak.) He stood outside the house again, gathering his courage for a knock at the back door, preparing a story for the lady who would appear, most likely in an apron, looking down with wary eyes at one more vagrant coming through to beg a meal. I had a whopper ready, he said, and then he paused to let us ponder our own boilerplate beg-tales of woe. Haven't eaten in a week & will work for food was the basic boilerplate, with maybe the following flourish: I suffered cancer of the blood (bone, liver, stomach, take your pick) and survived and have been looking for orchard work (blueberry, apple) but it's the off-season so I'm hungry, ma'am. That sort of thing. Of course his version included lockjaw. Hello, ma'am, I'm sorry to bother you but I'm looking for a meal & some work. (Again, always the meal & work formula. That was the covenant that had to be sealed because most surely the man of the house would show up, expecting as much.) He moved his mouth strangely and tightened his jaw. I suffered from a case of lockjaw back in Pittsburgh, he told the lady. I lost my mill job on account of it, he added. Then he drove home the particulars—he assured us—not only going into Pittsburgh itself (all that heavy industry), but also saying he had worked at Homestead, pouring hot steel, and then even deeper (maybe this was later, at the table with the entire family, he added quickly, sensing our disbelief) to explain that once a blast furnace was cooked up, it ran for months and you couldn't stop to think because the work was so hard and relentless, pouring ladles and so on and so forth. Then he gave her one or two genuine tears, because if Lockjaw had one talent it was the ability to cry on command. (He would say: I'm going to cry for you, boys, and then, one at a time, thick tears would dangle on the edges of his eyelids, hang there, and roll slowly down his cheeks. Ofttimes he'd just come back to the fire, sit, rub his hands together, and start the tears. You'll rust up tight, Lockjaw, one of the men would inevitably say.) In any case, the lady of the house—she was young, with a breadbasket face, all cheekbones and delicate eyes—looked down at him (he stayed two steps down; another technique: always look as short and stubby and nonthreatening as possible) and saw the tears and beckoned him with a gentle wave of her hand, bringing him into the kitchen, which was warm with the smell of baking bread. (Jesus, our stomachs twitched when he told this part. To think of it. The warmth of the stove and the smell of the baking! We were chewing stones! That's how hungry we were. Bark & weeds.) So there he was in the kitchen, watching the lady as she opened the stove and leaned over to poke a toothpick into a cake, pulling it out and holding it up, looking at it the way you'd examine a gemstone while all the time keeping an eye on him, nodding softly as he described—again—the way it felt to lose what you thought of as permanent employment after learning all the ropes, becoming one of the best steel pourers—not sure what the lingo was, but making it up nicely—able to pour from a ladle to a dipper to a thimble. (He'd gotten those terms from his old man. They were called thimbles, much to the amusement of the outside world. His father had done mill work in Pittsburgh. Came home stinking of taconite. He spoke of his father the way we all spoke of our old men, casually, zeroing in as much as possible on particular faults—hard drinking, a heavy hand. The old man hit like a heavyweight, quick and hard, his fist out of the blue. The old man had one up on Dempsey. You'd turn around to a fist in your face. A big ham-fisted old brute bastard. Worked like a mule and came home to the bottle. That sort of thing.) In any case, he popped a few more tears for the lady and accepted her offer of a cup of tea. At this point, he stared at the campfire and licked his lips and said, I knew the place, you see. The kitchen had a famil-iar feel, what with the same rooster clock over the stove that I remembered as a boy. Then he tapered off into silence again and we knew he was digging for details. Any case, no matter, he said. At that point I was busy laying out my story, pleading my case. (We understood that if he had let up talking he might have opened up a place for speculation on the part of the home owner. The lady of the house might—if you stopped talking, or said something off the mark—turn away and begin thinking in a gen-eral way about hoboes: the scum of the world, leaving behind civility not because of some personal anguish but rather out of a desire—*wanderlust* would be the word that came to her mind—to let one minute simply vanish behind another. You had to spin out a yarn and keep spinning until the food was in your belly and you were out the door. The story had to be just right and had to begin at your point of origin, building honestly out of a few facts of your life, maybe not the place of birth exactly but somewhere you knew so well you could draw details in a persuasive, natural way. You drew *not* from your own down-and-out-of-luck story, because your own down-and-out-of-luck story would only sound sad-sack and tawdry, but rather from an amalgamation of other tales you'd heard: a girlfriend who'd gone sour, a bad turn of luck in the grain market, a gambling debt to a Chicago bootlegger. Then you had to weave your needs into your story carefully, placing them in the proper perspective to the bad luck so that it would seem frank & honest & clean-hearted. Too much of one thing—the desire to eat a certain dish, say, goulash, or a hankering for a specific vegetable, say, lima beans—and your words would sound tainted and you'd be reduced to what you really were: a man with no exact destination trying to dupe a woman into thinking you had some kind of forward vision. A man with no plans whatsoever trying as best he could—at that particular moment—to sound like a man who knew, at least to some degree, where he might be heading in relation to his point of origin. To speak with too much honesty would be to expose a frank, scary nakedness that would send the lady of the house off—using some lame excuse to leave the room—to phone the sheriff. To earn her trust, you sat there in the kitchen and went at it and struck the right balance, turning as a last resort to the facts of railroad life, naming a particular junction, the way an interlocking mechanism worked, or how to read semaphores, for example, before swinging back wide to the general nature of your suffering.) We knew all of the above and even knew, too, that when he described, a moment later, the strange all-knowing sensation he got sitting in that kitchen, he was telling us the truth, because each of us had at one point or another seen some resemblance of home in the structure of a house, or a water silo, or a water-pump handle, or the smell of juniper bushes in combination with brook water, or the way plaster flaked, up near the ceiling, from the lathe. Even men reared in orphanages had wandered upon a particular part of their past. All of us had stood on some lonely street—nothing but summer-afternoon chaff in the air, the crickets murmuring drily off in the brush—and stared at the windows of a house to see a little boy staring back, parting the curtain with his tiny fingers.

You sit down to the table, set with the good silver, the warmth of domestic life all around, maybe a kid—most likely wide-eyed, expecting a story of adventure, looking you up and down without judgment, maybe even admiration, while you dig in and speak through the food, telling a few stories to keep the conversation on an even keel. You talk about train junctions, being as specific as possible, making mention of the big one in Hammond, Indiana, the interlocking rods stretching delicately from the tower to the switches. Then you use that location to spin the boilerplate story about the sick old coot who somehow traveled from Pittsburgh or Denver (take your pick), making a long journey, only to find himself stumbling and falling across one of the control rods, bending it down, saving the day, because the distracted and lonely switchman up in the tower had put his hand on the wrong lever (one of those stiff Armstrong leyers) only to find it jammed up somehow—ice-froze, most likely, because the story was usually set at dawn, midwinter—and then had sent a runner kid out to inspect the rod, and when the runner kid was out the switchman went to the board and spotted his error, and the runner kid (you slow down and key in on this point) found the half-dead hobo lying across the rod. You shift to the runner's point of view. You explain how during the kid's year on the job he had found a dozen or more such souls in the wee hours of dawn: young boys curled fetal in the weeds; old hoboes, gaunt and stately, staring up at the sky; men quivering from head to toe while their lips uttered inane statements to some unseen partner. You shake your head and mention God's will, fate, Providence, luck, as the idea settles across the table—hopefully, if you have spun the yarn correctly—that hoboes do indeed serve a function in God's universe. (Not believing it one whit yourself.) If the point isn't taken, you backtrack again to the fact that if the switchman had pulled the lever, two trains would've collided at top speed coming in, each one, along the lovely, well-maintained—graded with sparkling clean ballast to keep the weeds down—straightaway, baked up good and hot for the final approach, eager, wanting in that strange way to go as fast as possible before the inevitable slowdown (noting here that nothing bothers an engineer more than having to brake down for a switch array, hating the clumsy, awkward way the train rattles from one track to another). To spice it up, if the point still hasn't been taken, you fill them in on crash lore, the hotbox burnouts—overheated wheel-journal accidents of yore; crown-sheet failures—a *swhooooosh* of superheated steam producing massive disembowelments, mounds and mounds of superheater tubes bursting out of the belly of enormous engines, spilling out like so much spaghetti. All of those unbelievable catastrophic betrayals of industrial structure that result in absurd scenes: one locomotive resting atop another, rocking gently while the rescue workers, standing to the side, strike a pose for the postcard photographer. You go on to explain the different attitudes: engineers who dread head-ons, staring mutely out into the darkness while the brakeman grabs his flagging kit—fuses, track torpedoes—and runs ahead to protect the stalled train.

At the dining room table with the entire family, Lockjaw turned to the boilerplate story, personalizing it by adding that he had been given medical care in Pittsburgh (an injection of antitoxin by a kindly charity doctor, the wound cleaned out and bandaged, a bottle of muscle pills to boot) and had found himself wandering off before the cure set in, only to collapse several hundred miles away on the rods at the State Line junction. He gave all the details—about the rods, the way the tower worked—and kept the tone even and believable until the entire table was wide-eyed for a moment, with the exception of the man of the house, who, it turned out, had done a stint as a brakeman on the Nickel Plate, worked his way up to conductor, and then used his earnings to put himself through the University of Chicago Law School. The man of the house began asking questions, casually at first, not in a lawyerly voice but in a fatherly tone, one after another, each one more specific, until he did have a lawyerly tone that said, unspoken: Once you've eaten, you pack yourself up and ship out of town before I call the sheriff on you. Go back to your wanderlust and stop taking advantage of hardworking folks. Right then, Lockjaw thought he was safe and sound. Dinner & the boot. Cast off with a full belly, as simple as that. But the lawyerly voice continued. Lockjaw went into this in great detail, spelling out how it had shifted from leisurely cross-examination questions—you sure you fell across a rod hard enough to bend it? you sure now you saved the day exactly as you're saying, son?—to tighter, more exact questions: Where'd you say you're from? What kind of work did you say you did in Pittsburgh? Did you say you poured from a ladle into a thimble, or from a ladle into a scoop? You said interlocking mechanism? You sure those things aren't fail-safe? You said an eastbound and a westbound approach on the same line? (At this point, most of the men around the fire knew how the story would turn. They understood the way in which such questions pushed a man into a corner. Each answer nudged against the last. Each answer depended on a casualness, an ease and quickness of response, that began to give way to a tension in the air until the man of the house felt his suspicions confirmed when the answers came between bites, because you'd be eating in haste now, making sure your belly was full up as fast as possible, chewing and turning to the lady and, as a last ditch, making mention of a beloved mother who cooked food almost, but not quite, nearly, but not exactly, as good. These are the best biscuits I've ever had, and that's factoring in the fact that I'm so hungry. Even if I wasn't this hungry, I'd find these the best biscuits I've had in my entire life.)

When Lockjaw told this part of the story, the men by the fire nodded with appreciation because he was spinning it all out nicely, building it up, playing it out as much as he could, heading toward the inevitable chase-off. One way or another the man of the house would cast him off his property. He'd stiffen and adjust his shirt collar, clearing his throat, taking his time, finding the proper primness. A stance had to be found in which casting off the hobo would appear—to the lady of the house—to be not an act of unkindness but one of justice. Otherwise he'd have an evening of bitterness. When the man turned to God, as expected, after the cross-examination about work, employment, and the train incident, Lockjaw felt his full belly pushing against his shirt—a man could eat only so much on such a hungry gut—and had the cup to his mouth when the question was broached, in general terms, about his relationship to Christ. Have you taken Christ? the man said, holding his hands down beside his plate. Have you taken Christ as your Holy Savior and Redeemer? (I knew it. Fuck, I knew it, the men around the fire muttered. Could've set a clock to know that was coming. Can't go nowhere without being asked that one.) At that point, the man of the house listened keenly, not so much to the answer—because he'd never expect to get anything but a yes from a hobo wanting grub—but to the quickness of the response, the pace with which Lockjaw said, Yes, sir, I took Christ back in Hammond, Indiana, without pausing one minute to consider the width and breadth of his beloved Lord, as would a normal God-fearing soul, saved by Christ but still unable to believe his good grace and luck. (Gotta pause and make like you're thinking it out, Lefty muttered. Gotta let them see you think. If they don't see you thinking, you ain't thinking.) Lockjaw had given his answer just a fraction of a second too quickly, and in doing so had given his host a chance to recognize—in that lack of space between the question posed and the answer given—the flimsiness of his belief. Here Lockjaw petered off a bit, lost track of his train of thought, and slugged good and hard from the bottle in his hand, lifting it high, tossing his head back and then popping the bottle neck from his lips and shaking his head hard while looking off into the trees as if he'd find out there, in the dark weeds, a man in white robes with a kind face and a bearded chin and arms raised in blessing. Fuck, he said. All the man of the house saw was a goddamn hungry tramp trying to scare up some grub. We faced off while his wife prattled away about the weather, or some sort of thing, giving her husband a look that said: Be nice, don't throw him out until he's had a slice of my pie. But the man of the house ignored her and kept his eyes on mine until he could see right into them, Lockjaw said, pausing to stare harder into the woods and to give us time enough to consider—as we warmed our feet—that it was all part of the boilerplate: the man of the house's gaze would be long & sad & deep & lonely & full of the anguish of his position in the world, upstanding & fine & good & dandy & dusted off, no matter what he did for a living, farming or ranching or foreclosing on farms, doctoring or lawyering—no matter how much dust he had on him during his work he'd be clean & spiffy with a starched collar & watch chain & cuff links & lean, smooth, small fingers no good for anything, really, except sorting through papers, or pulling a trigger when the time came. A little dainty trigger finger itching to use an old Winchester tucked upstairs under the bed, hazy with lint but with a bullet in the chamber ready for such a moment: cocky young hobo comes in to beg a meal and wins over the little wife, only to sit at the table with utter disrespect, offering up cockamamy stories that make the son go wide-eyed and turn the heart.

As Lockjaw described the stare-down with the man of the house, his voice became softer, and he said, The man of the house excused himself for a moment. He begged my pardon and went clomping up the stairs, and I told the lady I probably should be going but she told me about her pie, said she wanted me to have a bite of it before I left, and I told her maybe I'd have to pass on the pie, and we went together to the kitchen, he said while we leaned in intently and listened to him, because the story had taken a turn we hadn't expected. For the sake of decorum, most of us would've stayed in the house until the gun appeared. Most of us would've stuck it out and held our own as long as we could, sensing how far we might push it for the chance to hear the lady give the man of the house a piece of her mind, saying, Honey, you're being hard on the poor boy. He doesn't mean any harm. Put that gun away. Even if his story was a bit far-fetched, he's just hungry, and so on and so forth, while the cold, steely eyes of the man of the house bore the kind of furtive, secretive message that could be passed only between a wandering man—a man of the road—and a man nailed to the cross of his domestic life.

Months ago, when he first told the story, Lockjaw explained that he'd gone off into the kitchen with the lady (while overhead the man of the house clomped, dragging the gun out from under the bed), who gave a delightful turn, letting her hair, golden and shiny and freshly washed, sway around her head, leaning down lightly to expose her delicate, fine neck, and then leaning a bit more so that her skirt pressed against the table while she cut him a slice of pie. Right then I felt it and knew it and was sure of it, he said. I was sure that she was my mother and had somehow forgotten me, or lost whatever she had of her ability to recognize me. I know it sounds strange, he added, pausing to look at us, going from one man to the next, waiting for one of us to make a snide remark. The rooster clock in the kitchen and the layout and the fact that the street was exactly like the one I grew up on and the way the pump handle outside the kitchen window was off balance; not to mention the willows out back, and beyond them that smell of the creek I mentioned, and the way the barn had been converted to serve as a garage for the car, and the fact that around the time I took to the road my mother was readying to have another son, and that boy would've been close to the right age by my calculation—give or take—to be the one she wanted. I would've asked her to confirm my premonition if the old man hadn't come down and chased me clean out of there before I could even have a bite.

Whatever the case, Lockjaw fooled himself into believing his own story, one way or another, and across the fire that night he dared us to put up some bit of sense in the form of a question, just one, but none of us had it in him to do so, because we were too hungry. (At least I think this is why we let him simply close his story down. He shut it down and began to weep, crying in a sniffy, real sort of way, gasping for breath, cinching his face up tight into his open palms, rubbing them up into his grief again and again. He was faking it, Hank said later. He was pulling out his usual trump card. He had me up until that point. Then his story fell apart.) None of us said a word as night closed over us and the fire went dead and we slept as much as we could, waking to stare up into the cold, flinty sky, pondering the meal he had eaten—the green beans waxy and steaming, the mashed potatoes dripping fresh butter, and of course the pork, thick with juice, waiting to be cut into and lifted to the mouth of our dreams. Then the train came the next day and we went off into another round of wander—west through Gary, through the yards, holding on, not getting off, sticking together for the most part, heading to the coast for the winter and then east again until we found ourselves at the same junction a year later, the same trees and double switch and cross tracks where the line came down out of Michigan and linked up with the Chicago track, and once again, as if for the first time, Lockjaw said he recognized the place and then, slowly, bit by bit, he remembered the last visit and said he was going back, heading up through the verge with his thumbs hooked in his pockets, turning once to say he'd try to bring us back a bit of pie. By golly, she said she'd put the pie on the sill for me, he said. She told me anytime I wanted to come back, she'd have it waiting for me. If you remember what I told you, I was running out the door with the gun behind me when she called it out to me, he added, turning one last time before he disappeared from sight. (Forgot all about that foolishness, Hank said. Guess he's home again, Lefty said. And we all had a big, overripe belly laugh at the kid's expense, going on for a few minutes with the gibes, because in Lincoln and in Carson and Mill City and from one shitting crop town to the next he had come back from whatever meal he had scrounged up with the same kind of feeling. He seemed to have an instinct for finding a lady willing to give in to his stories.) By the time he came back the jokes were dead and our hunger was acute. Like I said before, he has the pie on his face and a plate in his hand and he's already talking, speaking through the crumbs and directly to our hunger, starting in on it again, and when he comes to the smell of the brook, we interrupt only to make sure he doesn't go back over the story from the beginning again, sparking him with occasional barbs, holding back the snide comments but in doing so knowing—in that heart of hearts—that we'll make up for our kindness by leaving him behind tomorrow morning, letting him sleep the sleep of the pie, just a snoring mound up in the weeds.

Susan Minot

Pole, Pole

GOODNESS, SHE said. That was something.

You're something.

With you I am. She added under her breath, apparently.

She looked across the room of the cottage to heavy curtains, which blocked out the daylight.

That sliver of light, she said, it's totally white. You can't see the trees or grass or anything. It must be late.

The African noon, he said.

It's blinding.

Too bright to go out in. You better stay right here.

Here? she said. I don't even know where I am.

The night had ended late. It had started way back there at the engagement party she'd gone to with Bragg. Bragg was the ex-fiancé of a friend of hers in London and the bureau chief in Nairobi, who'd taken her under his wing when she'd arrived in Kenya a couple of weeks before. He seemed to know everyone in the crowd at the Muthaiga Club, which spread out into a lantern-lit interior garden. At one point he called to a tall man who walked toward them, looking at her. Here was one of his boys, Bragg had said, fresh in from Mogadishu tonight and Bragg had winked, leaving her to chat with the man. Then it was Bragg who corralled them both afterward to dinner at the restaurant in Langata. The restaurant was called the Carnivore and waiters sliced long strips of meat from spits set on carts which were wheeled from table to table so you could choose zebra, antelope, buffalo, ostrich. The side walls of the restaurant were low and open to the black night. A thatched roof towered above. She and the man sat beside each other at the long table, but chatted with everyone else, shouting above the noise. At the end of the meal the man turned to her, smiling with a presumptuous look.

Connected to the eating area by a concrete ramp was a throbbing dance floor with another bar and tables and chairs. After dinner the group flowed down the ramp and disappeared into the jumbling crowd and danced and drank more beer. They both danced till the crowd began to thin out.

In an unlit parking lot Bragg was sorting out rides. Some people were going back to somebody's house, and there was the usual indecision and stumbling and pulling of sleeves and keys stabbing at dark ignitions. She told the man she really did need to call it a night even though she wasn't working the next day and he replied he had a car. Coming out of the restaurant's driveway to the main road, the red taillights of the other cars turned to the left, floating one after another in the darkness. He and she, in a partly open Jeep, turned to the right.

There were no other cars on the road, so the only light was the dim topaz bar cast by the headlights of his rattletrap Jeep. Sometimes the road was paved, with enormous black craters bitten out of it, then it would revert to a rusty dirt, polished hard with a deep rut, like a road beside a farmer's field.

As the Jeep rounded a bend it lurched off the road. She thought he had lost control. Then he applied the brake and she saw they were in a pull-over. She looked at the man, whose face was solemn, staring ahead.

What is it? she said.

He said he needed to kiss her. He said it still looking through where the windshield was detached from the hood to the darkness beyond the headlights.

The direct statement stopped her. A direct statement often had that effect. She sat there, powerless. It was a welcome feeling. She felt the outline of herself begin to dissolve.

When they pulled back onto the road, the Jeep made a sharp U-turn and headed back toward his place.

She rode in the passenger seat on the left side, not the right. Many things here were like that. These were the sort of moments she waited for, being whisked away in the dark. It wasn't something you could do on your own. So much of what she did was on her own. Though that had its advantages, too. On your own you could pick up and leave. You could visit new lives and try them on for a while. What else was life for but to check it out?

She rode with a hand on the roll bar, taking the bumps as if riding waves. His kiss had both woken her up and made her sleepy. A warm air blew around them in the dark.

They turned onto a smaller road and drove till they came to a driveway. The Jeep stopped in front of a metal gate. A figure rose up out of the darkness. A face turned toward the headlights, squinting with an offended expression. He was one of many Masai warriors who'd left nomadic life on the savannahs to find work as *askari*, guarding houses in Nairobi's suburbs. This *askari* wore a gigantic overcoat, his black and red *shuka* showing below the hem. He lifted his spear in greeting, ducking away from the light, and went to unwind a heavy chain from the gate post. He walked the swinging gate out toward the car and stood beside it as the Jeep drove in.

Does he stay there all night? she said.

The man shrugged. He'll go back to sleep.

They drove up a short hill, rocking side to side, then stopped in a turnaround in front of a cottage. Paned French doors reflected the light back at them. Off to the right she could see the pale shape of a low building with one small window and a door. When the headlights went off everything was black. She saw nothing as he led her to the door and then inside.

Now they lay in bed with the curtains closed and the noon light slashing a blade of light across the floor. From the front room, the other room in the cottage, came the sound of something like a couch being scraped across the concrete floor.

What's that? She looked alarmed.

Nothing, he said. Just Edmond.

Who?

My man. The extent of my staff.

That's what you call him, your man?

No, I call him Edmond. Edmond takes very good care of me. He has done for a long time. He lives in that little place next door with one of his wives.

How many wives does he have?

Three, poor sod.

In the other room a radio went on, very loud, then immediately switched off.

He's in there tidying up. It's okay.

Okay, she said.

After a while she said, Doesn't anyone around here have to work? Besides Edmond.

No.

Don't we have to get to work?

Sure, he said. Let's go to work.

Really.

No, really. I'm ready. His arms wrapped around her.

I thought you said you had a story to file.

It would give Bragg a heart attack if I handed a story in on time. The man spoke with a Kenyan accent, We are not in a hurry hee-ah.

Then he said, What are you doing to me?

She gave a small laugh, unconvinced.

You're dangerous, he said.

Okay. I was wondering if you were sincere. Now I know. You're not.

From the front room a door banged shut, rattling panes.

You're brave to be here, he said.

How's that?

Usually I scare them off.

She looked at his profile. It was not unusual for a man in his late thirties to have an unlined face, but the man's skin was unusually smooth and fair. It was not a face that would scare off a woman.

Them? she said. She looked past him to the curtains. They were thick and white but looked dark in the shadows. She sat up a little.

Hey, she said, something just went by. She narrowed her eyes. A red streak.

Where?

She pointed to the window. In that sliver of light.

He lifted his head off the pillow, looked concerned for a moment, then laid it back down. Who knows, he said.

Doesn't worry you?

Can't.

You don't get worried about the attacks?

Oh, them. We've always had the attacks. They're just more newsworthy to the world at large at the moment. It's nothing new for us. He closed his eyes. If you let yourself worry here you'll go mad.

I thought everyone here was mad.

He opened one eye, interested. So she had been listening to what he'd said the night before. He peered back toward the sliver of light. Could be anyone out there. Edmond's got nine children. At last count.

Yikes. They're not all next door, are they?

No, but Cecily lets them visit. Which not all wives do. Cecily rules the roost. She also does my clothes washing.

Your staff is expanding.

He held his fist to her chin.

Where do the other wives live?

In Kibera.

People here are spoiled, she said.

Not in Kibera.

She gave him a withering look. The whites, I mean.

Did you know Kibera is one of the largest slums in the world? That's something to make us Kenyans proud.

She looked past him into the shadowy room. There was a kilim-covered hassock near a small table with an old brown dial phone on it. Clothes were gathered in small piles at the edge of the room and newspapers and books rose in loose stacks against the wall. Hanging in the doorway instead of a door was a faded purple and yellow *kikoi* with dangling tassels. On the wall beside it was a large black-and-white photograph of a Masai warrior leaping a few feet into the air above blowing dust. A heavy iron hat stand made by a local artist whose ironwork she'd noticed in other Nairobi houses held a dirt-spattered oilcloth, a few safari hats with curled brims, and balanced on top, a *rungu,* a carved wooden club with its persimmon-shaped knob. She looked at the room, but she was thinking of the Kibera slum. She'd been filming the children there at an orphanage. Most of her work before had been in nature documentaries; she'd not seen this sort of poverty up close. At first the children she was filming had watched her with an expectant stare as if she were about to burst into flame. Then gradually they became animated till they were swirling around her like a school of fish, showing the most perplexingly joyful smiles. These children had lost their parents and were living in a place made up of a jumble of lean-tos the size of armchairs and she couldn't get over how much they were smiling. The camera around her neck cost more than most of them would see in a lifetime. Most of these children had a deadly disease. She told herself, I am here to help, a weak plea of self-justification. She had an even more uneasy feeling she admitted to no one, that in some way she was worse off.

We are spoiled, said the man with his hands crossed behind his head. But there's justice. We're also miserable wrecks. What are you looking at?

You.

The man's face may have been smooth, but his eyes did not look spoiled. They looked worn out.

She turned on her back and faced the ceiling. It was painted dark blue and where it met the stucco walls you could see the undulating line of the human hand. The plaster had been smoothed by hand, too, making a soft, uneven surface.

So what are you doing here? he said.

She glanced at him to see if he meant something more. His face was placid.

The documentary, you know—

He shook his head. I mean, really. Here, on the other side of the world.

I always wanted to come here.

His eyebrows rose.

You mean, what am I running away from? She went on in a flat tone. Nothing. Getting as far away as possible from Darien, Connecticut?

Is that where you're from?

Was.

Not anymore?

It's not a place I ever really related to.

So you've come to Africa to relate?

Oh no, she said. You're not going to be one of those people.

What people?

Who give you a hard time for being in Africa.

He shrugged. I just don't have a lot of patience for the thrill-seeking tourist.

She said nothing. She thought of Babette, the German woman who ran the orphanage they were filming. Babette was not a thrill seeker. She was a good human being as far as one could tell, stern one moment, loving the next. She had a purposeful manner. The first day filming she had taken one look at Babette with her steady eyes and strong jaw and thought, Now there's the sort of person I'll never be.

After a while he said, I'm glad you're in Africa.

Can I ask you something?

Anything. He sounded relieved.

You don't happen to have . . . her voice trailed off and she sort of laughed . . . a girlfriend or a wife, do you?

Well yes, he said in the same gentle tone. I do.

You do?

Yes, I thought you knew.

Her body went still. They were both facing the ceiling and neither turned.

I thought Bragg would have told you, he said.

She shook her head. They were silent.

Which? she said.

Which what? He too seemed surprised.

Wife or girlfriend?

Wife.

They were silent again.

Children? she whispered.

Uh-huh. He cleared his throat. Two. Girls.

She turned on her side, propping herself up on an elbow. She thumped him on the chest. It hit harder than she meant it to.

Ow, he said.

Sorry. She flopped onto her stomach and smushed her face into a pillow. She reached back for the tangled sheet and pulled it up over her backside. The sheets were sort of olive brown, typical bachelor sheets, she'd thought.

That's okay, he said.

I'm an idiot, she said into the olive-brown pillow.

No you're not.

I thought you lived here. One finger tapped the olive-brown sheets near her head while the rest of her remained frozen.

I do. When I'm working in Nairobi.

She peeked out of one eye. How old are they?

Fiona's six and Emma's three.

Jesus. She sat up, holding the sheet around her. I didn't ask, she murmured. She looked at him. He looked back. Okay, so I didn't ask.

Where are you going?

Getting up. She dragged the sheet with her and stood on the thin rug. She scanned the dim floor for her clothes.

I thought you knew, he said again.

It looked like such a bachelor pad, she said under her breath. She located her bra and wisp of a shirt. I thought . . . I mean, I wasn't even . . . I mean, whatever. I didn't want to think. She found her skirt crumpled under the bed.

Are you upset? he said.

She was putting on her clothes and stopped for a moment. I don't know, she said. Then she started moving again.

He got up. He put on new clothes, different from the ones he'd worn last night. He buttoned a light blue shirt, looking at each button. He went to the window and pulled back one of the curtains. More light came into the room.

Where are they?

He looked over, worried.

Your family.

In Naivasha, at the lake. His voice was still gentle but the honey had gone out of it. We have a house there.

Oh, they're out there, she said. She sounded as if she were day-dreaming.

My wife grows flowers.

She looked at him, frowning.

No, he said, a farm. It's our business, a flower farm.

Oh. She found her sandals. That sounds nice.

He kept looking out the window. My wife's really the one who runs it.

Uh-huh. She sat on the kilim-covered hassock and began strapping on her sandals. They were well-traveled sandals with a worn-down heel.

He looked back at her. We're apart a lot, he said.

She regarded him from lowered brows.

Will I see you again? he said, watching her from the window.

Her hands were occupied buckling her sandals. She didn't roll her eyes when she looked at him, but the expression was the same.

No?

She rethreaded her sandal straps, first making them tighter, then making them looser. What for?

I don't know about you, he said. But that doesn't happen all the time. He pointed to the bed.

Oh, I think actually it does. She laughed.

He stepped toward her and stood there with his bare feet and light blue shirttails untucked. You said so yourself it was something.

She released her sandal and set her feet on the floor. Her mouth made a small puffy sound. I don't know, she said, and seemed to deflate. Her shoulders slumped.

I do, he said. He sat down beside her on the hassock. He slumped, too, but his shoulders still were above her head.

It was great, he whispered. He sounded sure.

For you, she shot back, but her heart wasn't in it. Inside she felt a flutter of panic.

He was sitting close to her and she would only have had to move her head a few inches to slump a little further against him. But she didn't. She remained in the freeze position.

Filming the wild dogs of the Kalahari Desert she'd learned about the three strategies for survival: flight, fight, or freeze.

I'm not going to say I don't love her.

God no, she murmured. And then, Sorry.

She felt how near he was. She thought, I'll just stay here one more minute then I'll stand up and smile and walk out. He'd accept that. Standing up, she could still keep a small amount of her dignity intact, maybe. She would pick up her handbag and go into the front room, find her cigarettes on the driftwood tree-stump table, get a drink of water in the bare kitchenette, and wait for him to follow with the car keys. They would get back in the Jeep and he'd drive her to the guesthouse in Karen where she was staying and where she'd stay another two weeks till they finished shooting. Then she'd check out about doing that story about the cattle vaccinations in the Sudan and go there, or would find another story to do or another project somewhere or anything as long as it was somewhere else and Nairobi was not in it.

Daisy, he said.

What? she said, impatient.

Daisy.

She wished he wouldn't do that, say her name that way. She glanced up and made the mistake of looking into his face. Oh God, she thought, or didn't think. His face was full of concern. She found herself believing it. Just for a second, she said to herself, and down her head came and collapsed on his chest.

. . .

The night before it had seemed as if she were sailing toward something warm and enveloping. Now she was being swept in a different direction. At least she was being moved, she reasoned, one way or another.

OK, though, now was the moment to stand up.

She didn't move and the moment passed. Another moment passed. She was still not standing.

Lulled by the heartbeat in her ear, she wondered, was this the moment she would look back on and think, I could have walked away, but didn't?

In the quiet they both heard something crack like two rocks hitting. It came from in front of the cottage.

Now what? he said. His head tipped forward. They heard shouts. Christ, he said. He sprang up, though his face was not alarmed. He headed for the doorway, pulled aside the purple and yellow *kikoi,* and disappeared. The soles of his feet were the last thing she saw.

She heard him rattle open the front door and yell out something in Swahili. The voice grew faint when he stepped outside and moved away from the house.

She sat on the hassock. After a while she heard people's voices coming back into the cottage. She heard the man. A voice answered in native accents. She got up and ducked past the *kikoi* into a small hallway. She peeked out from the door frame into the front room.

The man's back was to her, his hands shoved in his front pockets. A thin man stood in front of him, gesturing as he talked. He had a dark, shaved head and was wearing a cream-colored shirt with short sleeves and four pockets. That would be Edmond. He was about the same age as the man. Next to him were two boys, not quite teenagers, looking caught. The taller one wore a large red T-shirt, which came almost to his knees. He didn't look at

Edmond or at the man. The younger one had a dark T-shirt which said VOTE THE MIAMI WAY. He also faced the floor, but was watching Edmond out of the corner of his eye.

As Edmond talked, the man was nodding. He shook his head, listening. He ran his hand over his hair. At one point he lifted his arms, as if to say, Now what? Wait, Daisy thought, What had she been thinking of just now? She'd lost the thread of something . . . oh, that's right, a wife. There was a wife. She looked at the man's back. He looked different to her now.

Edmond cleared his throat. He looked away for a moment, as if not wanting to get to this part of the story, and he saw Daisy hiding by the door. Smoothly his gaze slid by her, betraying nothing of what he'd seen.

The man's hands were clasped on top of his head. Edmond looked once at the boys, then looked at no one and finished what he had to say.

Everyone stood there, silent.

The man dropped his arms. He turned a stony profile to the boys. The younger one was rolling his shirt around his fist. The man spoke to the older one in the red T-shirt, asking him a question. The boy raised his eyes, blinked slowly, and spoke. His tone of voice was defiant.

The man snapped. His screaming startled Daisy in her little hall. The boy did not look startled. He listened, unimpressed. When the man finished yelling, the boy spat on the floor near the man's feet.

Daisy watched the man's long arm swing back and come forward and smack the small face on one cheek, then with the back of his hand hit the other. The boy's head jerked a little with each blow. His feet didn't move. Edmond and the smaller boy didn't move either. After a moment the boy in the red T-shirt raised his hand to cover his cheek. Daisy thought she saw a smile hidden by his fingers.

The man turned abruptly. He made a gesture that said, This is nonsense and I'm not going to bother myself further. Then he wheeled back toward Edmond. He pointed out to the turnaround, giving him some last orders. Edmond nodded, though Daisy could see his attention was already being pulled toward the boys, though it was unclear whether he wished to check if they were okay, or to continue the punishment. Daisy ducked away from the door before the man saw her.

Her heart was pounding. She went over to the window and the parted curtain. She looked out at the backyard. The brittle grass was covered with a film of dust and at the edge of the lawn were olive bushes and thorny dwarf trees and floppy banana leaves. Half hidden by the brush was a high chain-link fence with loops of new silver barbed wire on top. Beyond the fence was a brown forest floor with spindly tree trunks and discarded, huge maroon leaves.

The man came back into the room, shaking his head with tiny shakes. Sorry about that, he said.

Daisy was looking out the window. He stood close behind her and parted the curtains wider and they both looked out.

What was that all about? she said. I heard you shouting.

He took a deep breath and exhaled. She felt his breath in the hair on the top of her head. He put his arms loosely around her. Just the usual, he said. It's not worth going into.

She thought of the slap and shivered. Maybe he really thought so. Maybe that wasn't a lie. His arms tightened around her.

But you're still here, he said. I'm glad.

I should be going. . . . Her voice trailed off.

She kept staring out at the garden. Nothing was moving in the bleached yard. She was mesmerized, trying not to think of what was behind her. She thought of the boy in the red T-shirt and his strange smile. She stared out to the garden, feeling as if *she* had been slapped. It felt eerie, as if she were right where she belonged.

...

I saw you hit that boy, she said.

The man spoke in the same full-bodied voice. He had it coming to him, he said.

That's a little harsh, isn't it?

You have to be from here to understand.

People say that a lot.

Maybe because it's true.

She heard his attention straying and turned her head. He was looking toward the other end of the lawn where a woman was hanging laundry.

Come, he said. He unclicked the lock on the tall windows. Meet Cecily.

The air was thick and warm. Daisy followed him outside as if she were in a net, still in the physical lure of him.

The woman at the clothesline wore a crimson short-sleeved dress and a green scarf knotted around her head. She was not tall and when she reached to drape the clothes over a thin rope clothesline, her orange heels lifted out of flip-flops that were thin as pancakes. Her figure was sturdy, her neck and arms thin. The man called to her.

Hello, Mistah T, she said, not turning. She clipped on clothespins made of pink plastic.

Cecily, I'd like you to meet my friend Daisy.

Karibu, Cecily said, and paused for a moment to tip her wrapped head in Daisy's direction. Then she bent down for more clothes.

Asante sana, Daisy said. This about exhausted her Swahili. Welcome. Thank you much.

Daisy's from America, the man said.

Cecily nodded. She snapped open a towel, not looking up.

Since she'd been in Kenya, Daisy had noticed that she was either being stared at as a curiosity or else pointedly ignored. Only occasionally she'd receive a look of hatred from a stranger.

The man walked over to the other side of the woven yellow plastic basket and spoke to Cecily in Swahili. Being in a place where she didn't know the language, Daisy had learned to watch people instead. Often that told her more.

Now Cecily was paying attention to the man. She stared at the towel in her hand, then flung it absently up on the line. She folded her smooth arms, took a big breath, and tucked in her chin. She looked at the man as if sizing him up. For a moment Daisy thought she was going to upbraid the man, and it filled her with an odd sort of hope.

The man mimed how he had hit the boy. Cecily nodded slowly. Yes, yes she knew. The man shrugged and winced. Cecily shook her head in agreement. She pursed her lips. Before speaking she frowned and when she finally did say something it was decisive. Daisy was transfixed. Cecily was giving the man a piece of her mind.

Then suddenly Cecily's face burst into a smile. She let her arms drop and slapped at the man's shoulder. They both laughed. Cecily kept shaking her head and the man was nodding and they laughed together at her joke. Daisy backed away from them, feeling suddenly transparent like a flame in sunlight.

She stood waiting in the driveway next to the Jeep. Through the front window of the cottage she could see the man on the telephone with his back to her, facing the wall. Talking to the wife, she figured. It was bright outside and she was without sunglasses. She strolled off to be out of sight of the man, scuffing the ground. Lots of footprints had distressed the dirt. Suddenly she felt exhausted. For a moment she was back in bed with the man. He was holding her wrist. Sex was like that, not all of you came back right away. Part of you lingered a little longer with the person though eventually that part would return.

She had come near Edmond's house. The one door was open to a turquoise-painted wall. There were only sprigs of grass in the front yard and a small circle of charred wood. Against the ocher wash of the house sat two white molded plastic chairs. A small child stood in the doorway. She was wearing a pink sleeveless dress with ruffles at the shoulders and eating a papaya. She eyed Daisy. Daisy smiled and said, *Habari*. The little girl's eyes widened and she turned back to the house for instruction, then she looked back at Daisy, saying nothing.

Cecily appeared from behind the little girl, shooing her out the door. Her arms were straining under the weight of a large gray tub. The little girl sat on a log near the burned area biting the papaya, staring at Daisy. Cecily hauled the tub to the end of the yard near some scarlet hibiscus flowers and tossed the water out. It floated in the air like a mirror then came down flat and disappeared in the dirt.

Cecily turned around and saw the white woman standing on the tan drive in her tan skirt. Daisy waved and smiled and started to step back. She rocked on her sandals. Cecily came forward a few steps and stopped. Her smooth solid face was not smiling. At first Daisy thought she was getting some version of the cold stare, the look of disapproval a girl might get stumbling out of the man's cottage, another aimless white girl. But when Cecily lifted her hand to shield her eyes from the sun, Daisy saw a different expression, and it took her breath away. She was looking at Daisy with pity.

The man locked the front door. Everyone here was always jangling keys. When she got into the Jeep she noticed a spiderweb of cracked glass on the center of the windshield. She hadn't seen it the night before, but then it had been dark and she wasn't looking.

The man got in the driver's seat. He turned the key a few times before the engine started. Where to? he said, and pulled at the steering wheel with an effort.

She didn't answer. It wasn't really a question. Back where I belong, she thought. The Jeep bounced forward. They drove out the gate, which was wide open now in the daytime. Now she saw the road they'd come on. It looked as if it had been heaped with fresh dirt and raked.

Everything okay? he said.

Fine. She didn't look at him. She wanted to start right then not looking at him. The sooner the better. Immediately she felt expanded. She thought, And I don't even need to tell him. She couldn't remember the last time she'd actually felt that way, not needing to explain herself—to him, to anyone.

The feeling was so rare she tried to think where it had come from and Cecily's face appeared.

There was a phrase Daisy had heard a number of times in Kenya: *pole, pole,* pronounced with an accent. It had a number of related meanings. It could mean, Careful now, one step at a time or, Gently does it. It could also mean Sorry and Too bad.

It was the thing people said to comfort someone with a little hardship. You'd say it to a child who'd scraped his knee or to someone whose car had broken down. *Pole.* Poor you, it means. Shame. That had been Cecily's expression: *pole, pole.* You poor thing. It was the understanding expression a mother might have, though Daisy couldn't remember ever having seen it on her own mother's face. Cecily had emphasized the look by nodding, as if to say, Don't forget this conversation we've had. Poor you. Shame. Step by step. Gentle now. How that could all be in a look, Daisy didn't know, but there it was.

When things like that came your way, you should take them. Bouncing along in the Jeep, Daisy thought if she could keep that face in mind she'd be all right. It was nearly like praying to concentrate on it. The light coming through the trees threw barred shadows over the road. She was riding through stripes.

Brad Watson

Alamo Plaza

THE ROAD to the coast was a long, steamy corridor of leaves. Narrow bridges over brush-choked creeks. Our father drove, the windows down, wind whipping his thick black hair. Our mother's hair, abundant and dark and long and wavy, she'd tried to tame beneath a pretty blue scarf. He wore a pair of black Ray-Bans. She wore prescription shades with the swept and pointed ends of the day. He whistled crooner songs and smoked Winstons, and early as it was, no one really talked. My older brother, Hal, slept sitting up, his mouth open as if he were singing silently in a dream.

This was before things changed, before Hurricane Camille, the casinos. Long before Hal's death in a car wreck at the age of twenty-one, my father's heart attacks and fatal stroke, the aneurism that took our mom, my younger brother Ray's drug addiction and long-term illness.

On this trip Ray, too young to bring along, too much trouble most of the time, had been left with our grandmother. He was just two, yet already his sharp, hawkish eyes constantly sought their prey, which was insufficient attention, which he would rip to shreds with tantrums, devour in small bloody satisfying chunks until he received either punishment or, better, mollification. I was so very glad that he was not along, not only because of his querulous nature, but also because his absence made it more possible— or so I imagined—for me to get more of Hal's and my parents' attention myself.

By noon we smelled the brine-and-fish stink of the bays. The land flattened into hazy vista, so flat you could see the curve of the earth. Downtown Gulfport steamed an old Floridian vapor from cracked sidewalks and filigreed railings, shaded storefronts—not a soul out, everyone and everything stalled in the heat, distilling. The beach highway stretched out to the east, white and hot in the sun. Our tires made slapping sounds on the melting tar dividers and the wind in the car windows was warm and salty. We passed old beach mansions with green shutters, hundred-year-old oaks in the yards. A scattering of cheap redbrick motels, slat-board restaurants, bait shops. The beach, to our right, was flat and white and the lank brown surf lapped at the sand.

East of Gulfport, the Alamo Plaza Motel Court, with its fortlike facade of white stucco, stood flanked by low regular motel rooms around a concrete courtyard. The swimming pool lay oddly naked and exposed in the middle of the motel's broad front lawn, one low diving board jutting over the deep end like a pirates' plank. No one was out.

We stopped in the breezeway beside the office and went inside, where the floor was cool Mexican tile. Lush green plants sprouted from large clay pots in the corners, and there was a color television on which we could watch programs unavailable back home. I have a vivid memory of seeing a Tarzan movie there in which Tarzan, standing in the crook of a large tree, is shot right between the eyes by a safari hunter's rifle, and doesn't even flinch. Is it possible this is a true memory, not invented or stretched? Would Hollywood in the thirties—for this was an old movie even then—have allowed Tarzan to be shot directly in the forehead with a high-power rifle, the bloody spot at the point of entry jumping out on his skin, without so much as blinking his eyes? I was, I am, as incredulous as the safari men on the jungle trail below, holding their high-power rifles and gaping at this jungle god, who just stared coolly back at them with the bullet hole in the center of his forehead.

It seemed very real and possible, however, in the moment.

We rented a bungalow in the rear of the Alamo Plaza. In the mornings we went to the beach, joining hands to cross the white concrete path of U.S. 98, the beach highway, to the concrete steps that led down to the beach on the Sound. It was not exhilarating, as Gulf beaches go, its white sand having been dredged from beyond the barrier islands twenty miles out to cover the muddy shore of the Sound, where the natural flora included exposed roots of cypress and mangrove. Huge tarpon, an almost prehistoric-looking fish, cruised here between the river and the sea.

Our father, my brother, and I waded far out, where the water was still just knee deep to a six-year-old. We turned and waved to our mother, who sat on the white sand on a towel, a pale blue scarf on her head, the cat-eyed sunglasses perched on her nose. She did not swim, and though one reason we came to Biloxi instead of the more beautiful beaches in Gulf Shores or Pensacola was the cheaper prices at motels, the other reason was her fear of the water. She felt safer sitting on the edge of the Sound, which was more like a lake, than she did near the crashing waves of the Gulf. The year before, standing near her beach towel in the sand at Gulf Shores, Alabama, as if it were her sole tentative anchor to the dry world, she had seen a young man drown in a rip current while trying to save his little boy, who somehow escaped the current on his own and survived. She'd watched as the rescue squad dragged the man's body onto the beach. A year later, and for many years after that, the terror she felt still welled up in her with a regularity as steady as the ticking minute hand on the clock, and with that same regularity she forced it back down, into her gut, where it fought with her frequent doses of paregoric.

I can still remember her in the swimming pool, at the country club they'd struggled to join and couldn't really afford, before the hard times forced us to drop out. She would step into the shallow water with a look on her face that now I understand as terror but that then I took for simple cautiousness and uncertainty. A slim hand out as if to steady herself from some unknown that could unsteady the whole deal. A cream-colored bathing cap covered her dark curls, as if she were going to plunge in with the boldness of an Olympic diver, though her pointed, blue-framed sunglasses still rested on her slim nose. And before the water reached above her waistline she would bend her knees and, holding her head up on her neck as far as she could stretch it, push herself gently forward and dog-paddle around the shallow end, her toes bumping the bottom and pushing her forward every few little strokes. I'm astonished she had the courage to get into the pool, with others there who might see her and laugh at the fact that she couldn't really swim. All those club people, who might laugh and think what a country girl she was—did you *see* that? Can't even swim! And my admiration for her swells in some proportion to my sense of her loss in the intervening years.

But there we stood, far out in the tepid brown Mississippi Sound, waving to her. She was not actually distinguishable to us as herself, that far out. She was a figure who occupied the spot where we'd last seen our mother, apparently wearing the same pale blue scarf on a head of thick dark hair, with the same pale skin, and waving back for a moment, then falling still. A figure in the light of the moment just a millisecond away, her image reaching us far out over the water, yet gone as if she'd been gone for a dozen years.

In the evenings, we went out to eat oysters on the half shell, platters of fried shrimp and fish, french fries, and hush puppies, and returned to sleep in the luxurious window-unit air-conditioning of our room. Our mother would almost never let us use the AC at home, as it cost too much on the power bill.

Mornings and late afternoons, we went over to the beach and frolicked. I so love that word. Sand castles, not such artful ones, of mounds, moats, and tunnels. A tall woman with big blonde hair and tits like pale luminescent water balloons walked by in a green two-piece bathing suit, moving so carefully she seemed to be treading along the shore through a very narrow passage only she could see. We glanced at our father, and he bobbed his eyebrows. We fell over into the sand, yipping like hyenas.

I once told my mother of being propositioned by a lascivious young country girl at a filling station in Buckatunna, Mississippi, on my way home for a visit. I'd been filling up my little Honda coupe and this woman ambled over and stood there leering at me. You sure are good-lookin', she said. I'm having a party at my house, you want to come on over?

Did you go with her? my mother asked me when I told her the story. Of course not, I said. I didn't know her from Medusa. Well, that's the difference between you and your father, she said.

At this time they had been divorced for about seven years.

My brother and I danced barefoot across the white-hot parking lot to the center of the Alamo Plaza's interior court—its *plaza,* I suppose. There beneath a small shed roof sat a humming, sweating ice-making machine. We would tip open the canted lid to the bin and scoop out handfuls of ice crushed so fine it seemed shaved. We packed it into snowballs and threw them at one another, tossed them into the crackling hot air and watched them begin to shed water even as they rose and then fell to the sizzling concrete, melting instantly into wet penumbras that shrank and evaporated into smoky wisps. We opened the bin again and wedged our heads and shoulders in there for the exquisite shock of the cold. For at least a few moments as we reeled in the white-hot courtyard on burning bare feet, our heads felt as dense and cold as ice cubes on top of our icicle necks.

We drove to a group of small cabins on a cove and a grizzled man rented us a skiff. Our father sat at the stern and gunned the motor, buzzing us out into the stinking Sound, bouncing us through the light chop, our mother holding on to her sun hat.

We drifted a half mile or so offshore, baited our hooks, and cast out. For a while there was nothing, just the little boat rocking in the gentle waves of the Sound, the hazy sky, gulls creaking by and inspecting us with cocked heads, a dispassionate black eye.

My brother pulled up the first fish. He swung it over my head and into the boat. It was a small fish, with an ugly face. As soon as it popped from the water it began to make ugly, froggish sounds. Croaker, our father said. He unhooked it and tossed it back into the chop. I asked about the strange noise it made and he said it was the sound they made trying to breathe out of water.

The truth is the Atlantic croaker makes its sound by tightening the muscles around its swim bladder, and uses the sound for general communication and to attract a mate. It's said to be a "prodigious spawner."

I reeled one in, too, the fight leaving it. Up it came, into the boat. Croak, croak. A brownish fish with a little piggish snout. A small mark on the back of its eye gave it an angry what-are-you-looking-at? kind of look. These fish looked pissed off to be interrupted in the middle of their prodigious spawning.

Soon we were all pulling in croakers. The boat floor crowded with flapping, croaking fish. A chorus of their dry frog noises rose around us. After a while, my father had had enough and started tossing them overboard. Some smacked dead on the surface and floated away. Others knifed the water with a final croak and were gone, back to their spawning and general communication with their kind.

. . .

When I was too young to remember now how young I was, I began to have a recurring dream, or nightmare. The air in the dream was electric, much like the electron-buzzing screen of our television when the station went off the air. Jumping with billions of little black dots. A charged, nervous air, the atmospheric equivalent of the feeling you get when you knock your funny bone. In the dream I felt weak and heavy, as if my mass were compounding, draining my strength. I was aware of a hellish din of angry voices, though there were never any distinct words. The room was often very small, the only exit a tiny door in the corner, little larger than a mouse hole. Other times, the dreamscape changed to one of dreadful empty vastness, all gray, in which the horizon seemed impossibly distant and I seemed very small, and the pressure of the air was heavy upon me. I suppose it was a simple dream of anxiety, though I have sometimes fancied it a latent, deeply buried, sensorial memory from the womb, and who knows but that this is possible on some level. Though I was too young to create such a memory from what little I'd heard about gestation. I probably knew nothing of that when the dream began. I may have been told where I came from—I don't remember. In any case, I have no firm idea where such anxiety in one so young could have come from—except that I'd had, from a very young age, the sense and fear that my parents would divorce and force me to choose between them. Maybe I had picked up on some general unhappiness. I don't know. I do know that, like my mother, I spent much of my time worrying that something terrible and heartbreaking would happen. For me, as with her, emotional dread of the probable was always more real and present than the moment something terrible actually occurred. It may be that my dream was just a subconscious expression of anxiety, but it seems comically apt to me to consider that even in the womb I was expecting the worst concerning my impending birth.

. . .

In our room that evening, after the fishing, we could hear people out by the pool talking loudly and laughing. We heard the splashes of people hitting the water and the thumping of the diving board, on its fulcrum, in the splashes' wake. A woman cried out, Stop! Oh, stop it! Laughter rose and drowned in the humid salty darkness, and I lay in bed and listened long into the night to the sound of cars cruising past on the cooling white-slab highway along the beach. My father snored lightly, while my mother, next to him, and Hal in the bunk above me lay in their beds as still as the dead. The Gulf breezes puffed against the windows, slipped between seams, and drifted through the chilled air of the room like coastal ghosts released from their tight invisibility, sustained for a while by the softly exhaled breath of the living.

My brother met another boy and began going off with him, around the Alamo's grounds or at the pool or, when I'd followed them to the highway, across to the beach, where I wasn't allowed without an adult. He became more of an absence, and so I drifted into the same safe quietude where I spent most of my time anyway, where most middle children spend their time.

At some point in my childhood I began to feel emotionally estranged from my family, although I loved my mother and father and tolerated my brothers as well as anyone else. I had fantasies of belonging to other families instead of my own—families of friends or even families I hardly knew, such as the missionary family from our church that spent part of every year in Pakistan. Or an imaginary family. When you are quiet, you are different, which makes everyone a little nervous and suspicious. It seems a small thing, unless you're the child who's aware of it. I was at ease if left alone in my room to read comics, comfortable alone in the large tract of woods bordering our cul-de-sac street. I loved spying on others walking in the woods when I was hidden and could see them without their seeing me. Sometimes I looked into windows at night, but only at ordinary things. People eating supper, or watching television. No undressing or showers or such. I only wanted to experience the mystery of seeing things as they were when I essentially did not exist to alter them. If you were quiet and still, it was almost as if you weren't there. It was like being a ghost, curious about the visible world and the creatures in it. As if you were dreaming it, and not a part of the dream but there somehow, unquestioned or unknown.

One day Hal asked permission to go out with his new friend's family on a charter fishing boat. They would have to leave very early, before dawn. I determined to rise then, too, and see him off. But I wasn't able to, and no one woke me, so I didn't get up until light was seeping into the sky over the Sound. I rushed outside onto the motel lawn, stood there barefoot in the dew and the cool heavy breeze, and looked out across the water. On the horizon I could see the gray silhouette of a big ship, which in my memory's surviving image appears to be a tanker of some kind, an oceangoing vessel. But at that moment, on the lawn, I thought it must be the boat Hal had gone on with his new friend and family—these people I'd never spoken to, whom I'd only watched from across the lawn, complete strangers to me and already fast friends with Hal. Watching the ghostly ship far out in the Sound, I had the strongest feeling that he'd gone away and would never return. It was something I couldn't quite grasp just yet, someone going so far out in the water on a boat that you can't see him anymore, and then coming back in. I was very sad, thinking that he was gone forever. And I have lost the memory of his returning from the fishing trip to the motel. I've often wondered why I felt so much sadder then than I did when he died. Anticipation is expansive in the imagination. Memory is reductive, selective. And any great moment must be too much to absorb in that moment, without the power of genius or mental illness. When Hal died, years later, it seemed like the completion of something I'd been watching and waiting for all that time.

His last words, as the other car tumbled toward them out of control, were a blurted "Look out!" A driver's warning to his friends in the car. I doubt that alone saved anyone, but the survivors told me they remembered him shouting this just before they blacked out.

My father's last words, as he pressed his hand to the base of his neck, were "Something's wrong."

If my mother had any last words, they are a secret, as she was old and alone. And if any words formed in her mind as she lay unconscious and slowly dying on her bedroom floor, no one will ever know what they were.

It's hard to remember Hal in very specific ways. He was a small boy, and then a small man. I did not remember him that way, since he was four years older, and so until I was into my later teens he was larger than I was. I remember how shocking it was when, a couple of years after his death, I went into his room and tried on one of his shirts. It was tight across the shoulders, too short in the sleeves. I had thought he was at least as tall as I was and stockier, but he was not. He had just always carried himself like a larger boy and man.

A second child will always feel displaced by the first. People say it's the other way around but it's not. Later in life there are the photographs you discover of your older sibling, before you were born, with one or both of your parents. It's then, after you've had children yourself and know the experience in your own life, that you understand the bond between the new, young parents and their first child. You understand how miraculous and illuminating it is. You know how the experience has remade the whole world for the parents, and how the only child's world, entirely new in the magnificent, solipsistic way only an only child's world can be, eclipses all else, and when the second child comes along it is only as if the eclipsing body has moved aside, moved along in its path. The parents' sense of wonder has passed, leaving behind a washed-out and dazed sense of deep and cathartic change, a knowledge that such an experience will never be repeated for anyone in that little world, which leaves them somehow diminished. And as the second child you realize this when you are older and your memories have been informed, in a slow infusion of understanding, by the old photographs taken before you were even conceived.

Hal was a prodigy, in many ways a typical first child in that he was precocious, gregarious, fearless, bestowed at birth with the grandest, most natural sense of entitlement. Every first child is a king or queen. A prince or princess, an enfant terrible of privilege and favor. And Hal was talented. When he was three, he learned the words to the popular song "Davy Crockett, King of the Wild Frontier" and sang it so adorably that our parents secured a recording session for him down at a downtown radio station.

He was introduced by George Shannon, a local radio and television personality. I imagine Hal wearing his cowboy outfit: a black hat, black sequined shirt, black pants, black filigreed cowboy boots, a toy six-shooter in a toy holster on his belt. He probably wasn't wearing this outfit, since it had nothing to do with Davy Crockett, but there's a framed photo of Hal at about that age, wearing that outfit, which hung for decades on our mother's living room wall, and so that's how I see him then. A musical cousin, Doc Taylor, strummed the song's tune on a guitar, and Hal sang the song in his piping voice.

> *Born on a mountaintop in Tennessee*
> *Greenest state in the land of the free*
> *Raised in the woods so's he knowed ev'ry tree*
> *Kilt him a b'ar when he was only three*
> *Davy, Daavy Crockett, king of the weeld frontier*

Weeld—that was how he pronounced "wild," like some kind of flamboyant elf.

In the background on the recording, toward the end of the song, you can hear a baby crying a little fitfully, fussing. That was me, only a few weeks old, trying, as would become usual, to assert myself, to little avail.

This recording was of course a precious possession, always, but it became all the more so after Hal's early death, when he was a young man only recently married. It disappeared after the accident, and my mother bitterly accused Hal's widow of having taken it for herself. I took this for the truth. And then, many years later, after my mother's death, I found the record beneath a stack of papers and documents in a dresser drawer in her bedroom.

Well, no, said one of my cousins. It was never lost, not that I know of.

She never told you that Sophie had taken it?

No, my cousin said. She never said that to me.

I could have sworn she'd told me the recording was missing, stolen, possibly destroyed out of spite. But even the memory of her telling me that comes from so long ago now that I can no longer be sure.

The day after Hal's fishing trip there were a few people out at the pool, a woman with two toddlers down in the shallow end, a few grown-ups in loungers along the apron. The big fat man who must have been the one jumping and doing cannonballs the night before was again on the diving board, leisurely bouncing and looking around, as if this were simply his place. He bounced easily, the board bending beneath his great weight and bringing him slow as an elevator back up again. His toes hung over the end, his arms at his sides, and he nodded to the four of us as we walked up.

Two men holding cans of beer stood on the pool's apron, watching the big man on the board, and Hal sat at the edge of the pool in front of them, his legs over the edge and his feet in the water. He, too, watched the man, with a rapt expression, as if he expected something either wondrous or entertaining to happen. Across the highway the beach was empty. The Sound lay flat and brown in the sun's glare.

Morning, the man called out to our mother. She smiled and nodded back. Morning, sir, our father said in his clear baritone sales voice. From my spot at the three-foot mark, I called good morning to the man, too, and he called back with a little salute and a wave, Morning, young man.

Standing there bouncing.

A long, big-boned woman lying flat out on a lounger, with a big broad hat over her face, called to him. The voice came from her, but you couldn't see her face. The hat didn't move. Harry, she said to the man. Don't go splashing all over creation.

The man looked at her, still bouncing, then looked at me and smiled and winked. He pivoted and walked back to the base end of the board and turned back around.

Harry, the woman said.

The big man rose on his toes. It looked comical, the action of a much lighter, fitter man. He spread his arms like a ballerina, ran tiptoeing down to the end of the board, and came down heavily. The board slowly flung him up. He descended in a cannonball, leaning in the woman's direction, and sent up a high sheet of water that drenched her pretty good. She sat up and adjusted the wet floppy hat on her head. Harry swam to the pool's edge, turned, and grinned at Hal and me. I turned around and looked at our mother. She was staring at the man and woman, her mouth cocked into a curious smile. She saw me looking and picked up a magazine and started reading it. Our father sat in a deck chair in his swim trunks, his elbows on his knees like a man watching a baseball game. A can of Jax beer rested on the concrete apron between his white feet.

I heard the board bend, release, and bounce against its fulcrum, and a broad shapeless shadow darted onto the dimpled surface of the pool. There again was Harry suspended in all his bulk high in the air, a diving mule pushed off the circus platform. At the last second he tucked his head and rolled over onto his shoulders, sending an arc of water toward the mother with her two toddlers in the shallow end. They screwed up their faces, cringing. When the water settled they all three turned, dripping, to stare at Harry, the mother annoyed, the children bewildered.

That's enough, Harry, the woman said. She'd snatched her hat off and I saw she was wearing a man's heavy black sunglasses, like our father's, and her wide mouth was painted bright red, her hair frizzled and graying.

All right, sorry, Harry said.

But as soon as the woman had pulled the hat brim back down over her eyes, Harry was up and tiptoeing back to the diving board. He made shushing gestures to all of us, a finger to his lips. At the shallow end, the mother hustled her toddlers from the pool, grabbed up their things, and headed for their room.

Harry was poised at the base of the board. He spread his arms, rose on his toes, and pranced down its length. He swung his arms above his head, scrunched his big body down like a compressed spring. The board bent almost to the surface of the water, seemed to hesitate there, then cracked and split down its length and tossed Harry awkwardly into the air.

He hit the water with a loud, flat smack. The fissured board bounced a couple of clackity times and lay still. Harry floated motionless as the rocking water lapped the edges of the pool. A little scarlet cloud bloomed around him. Then he jerked into a flurry of motion. His head rose up and he bellowed, then sank down again.

The big woman shouted and stood up from her lounger, her hat tumbling into the grass. The two men standing poolside leaped into the water. They managed to subdue Harry and pull him to the pool's edge. The woman stood rigid, watching them, her mouth hanging open. Then she closed it with a clap and her face took on what looked like a long-practiced expression of disgust. Other people came and helped drag Harry out onto the concrete apron. He made a groaning, desperate sound. Blood leaked from a wound on his foot. One of the men who'd helped rescue him pulled a car around, and he and the other man helped Harry into it. The woman got into the backseat beside Harry and they drove away, to the hospital, I suppose.

I walked over to the diving board, leaned down low, and looked at the split board, its two pieces splayed, blond splinters sticking out like bleached porcupine quills. Hanging there jammed tight in the divide was a small blunt wedge drained of color. It appeared to be Harry's little toe.

It was fantastic. It made the whole trip.

Our mother was horrified, of course. One year, a drowning. The next, a dismembered toe. Not so disturbing as a death, but awful in its own way. I think it settled deeply into her subconscious, one more augury of vague misfortune looming.

For our father, who was her opposite in terms of being able to live in each present moment without a terrible awareness of the past and a foreboding sense of the future, the accident had a different effect. He would remember it with a kind of morbid humor, closing his eyes and pursing his lips and shaking with silent, wincing laughter. Ooo, shit, that had to hurt, he'd say. I still remember the time, riding with him in the car when I was a boy, and I had my arm out the passenger's side window. He glanced over and told me to keep my arm in the car, that he'd heard about a man riding along with his arm out the window who was sideswiped by another car that took his arm right off at the shoulder. Ever since, I've never been able to leave my arm out a car window if there are other cars present within anything close to striking distance. I live with a combination of my mother's morbid fear of danger and my father's irreverent appreciation of it.

Years later, long after my parents had divorced, I wasn't even sure if the incident with the poor man's toe had really happened. It had been so long ago and I had been so young and I hadn't thought about it in some time. But I was remembering it and trying to recall the details, when I had the disturbing thought that I may have invented it all. I asked my mother if she remembered it. She was eating a piece of toast at the breakfast table, so I suppose my timing wasn't good. She stopped chewing, as if stomach acid had suddenly boiled into her esophagus, and her eyes took on that vaguely alarmed and unfocused look she got when she was presented with something horrible. But then it passed, and she swallowed.

It was his big toe, she said.

I found that hard to believe and said so. I asked was she certain.

I'm certain, she said. That's what made it so horrible.

I saw my father a couple of weeks later, though, and put the question to him. I told him what my mother had said.

He scoffed. It wasn't his big toe, he said. That would've been impossible. It was his little toe.

I didn't say anything.

It's just like your mother to make it into something worse than it actually was, he said.

We went back home that very afternoon of the accident, and a storm had passed through. A tornado had hopped right over our neighborhood, which was in a low area between two modest ridges, and had snapped off the tops of several tall pines. One of the pine tops lay in our backyard, another in the street in front of our house. The air was gray and you could smell the spent, burnt residue of destructive energy in the air, feel it prickling the skin, as if we were inside a big discharged gun barrel. Green leaves and small limbs were strewn across yards and in the street and on rooftops. A telephone pole leaned toward the ground, the wires on one side taut, those on the other side loose and hanging low toward the damp grass. Everything was wet and smoking.

Some incredible violence had occurred, and yet almost everything remained intact. There sat our little brick ranch-style house. There, the pair of mimosas in the yard where I crouched concealed in the fernlike leaves, dreaming of Tarzan. There, the azaleas beneath my and Ray's bedroom window, where every year our mother took an Easter photo of her boys, our bow ties and vests and hair flipped up in front. There, the picture window of the living room we used only at Christmas or when she and our father hosted their supper club. There, the inexplicable everyday, the oddness of being, the senseless belonging to this and not that. I was barely able to contain myself. Something in me wished it had all been blown to smithereens.

Chris Adrian

The Black Square

HENRY TRIED to pick out the other people on the ferry who were going to the island for the same reason he was. He wasn't sure what to look for: black Bermuda shorts, an absence of baggage, too-thoughtful gazing at the horizon? Or just a terminal, hangdog look, a mask that revealed instead of hiding the gnarled little soul behind the face? But no one was wearing black, or staring forlornly over the rail. In fact, everyone was smiling. Henry looked pretty normal himself, a man in the last part of his young middle age dressed in plaid shorts and a T-shirt, a dog between his legs and a duffel bag big enough to hold a week's clothes at his side.

The dog was Bobby's, a black Lab named Hobart, borrowed for the ostensible vacation trip to make it less lonely. It was a sort of torture to have him along, since he carried thoughts of Bobby with him like biting fleas. But Henry loved Hobart as honestly as he had ever loved anything or anybody. And, in stark opposition to his master, the dog seemed to love Henry back. Henry was reasonably sure he would follow him, his paws fancy-stepping, through the black square. But he wasn't going to ask him to do that. He had hired an old lady to bring Hobart back to Cambridge at the end of the week.

He reached down and hugged the dog around the neck. Hobart craned his neck back and licked Henry's face. A little girl in enormous sunglasses, who'd skibbled over twice already since they'd left Hyannis, did it again, pausing before the dog and holding out her hand to him. "Good holding out your hand for the doggie to sniff!" her mother called out from a neighboring bench, and smiled at Henry. "What's his name?" the girl asked. She hadn't spoken the other two times she'd approached.

"Blackheart's Grievous Despair," Henry said. Hobart gave up licking her hand and started to work on her shoe, which was covered in the ice cream she'd been eating a short while before.

"That's stupid," the girl said. She was standing close enough that Henry could see her eyes through the sunglasses, and tell that she was staring directly into his face.

"So are you," he said. It was one of the advantages of his present state of mind, and one of the gifts of the black square, that he could say things like this now, in part because his long sadness had curdled his disposition, and in part because all his decisions had become essentially without consequence. He wasn't trying to be mean. It was just that there wasn't any reason anymore not to say the first thing that came into his mind.

The little girl didn't cry. She managed to look very serious, even in the ridiculously oversize sunglasses, biting on her lower lip while she petted the dog. "No," she said finally, "I'm not. *You* are. You are the *stupidest*." Then she walked away, calmly, back to her mother.

He got surprises like this all the time these days, ever since he had decided to give up his social filters. A measured response from a five-year-old girl to his little snipe, a gift of flowers from his neighbor when he'd told her he didn't give a flying fuck about the recycling, a confession of childhood abuse from his boss in response to his saying she was an unpleasant individual. The last was perhaps not so surprising—every unpleasant individual, himself included, had a bevy of such excuses that absolved them of nothing. But there was something different about the world ever since he had discovered the square and committed himself to it. *People go in,* someone had written on the Black Square Message Board, which Henry called up over his bed every night before he went to sleep, *but have you ever considered what comes OUT of it?* Most of those who wrote there were a different sort of freak from Henry, but he thought the writer might mean what he wanted him to mean, which was those sort of little daily surprises, and more than that a funny sense of carefree absolution. Once you had decided to go in (he didn't subscribe to the notion, so popular on the board, that the square called you or chose you) things just stopped mattering in the way that they used to. With the pressure suddenly lifted off of every aspect of his life, it had become much easier to appreciate things. *So many wonderful things have come to me since I accepted the call,* someone wrote. *It's too bad it can't last.* And someone replied, *You know that it can't.*

The girl's mother was glaring now, and looked to be getting ready to get up and scold him, which might possibly have led to an interesting conversation. But it didn't seem particularly likely, and one surprise a day was really enough. Henry got up and walked to the bow of the ferry. Hobart trotted ahead, put his paws up on the railing, and looked back at him. The island was just visible on the horizon. Henry sat down behind the dog, who stayed up on the rail, sniffing at the headwind and looking back every now and then. Henry laughed and said, "What?" They sat that way as the island drew nearer and nearer. The view was remotely familiar—he'd seen it countless times when he was a little boy—though it occurred to him as he stared ahead that he had the same feeling, coming up on the island, that he used to get facing the other way and approaching the mainland: he was approaching a place that was strange, exciting, and a little alien, though it was only the square that made it that way now. Nantucket in itself was ordinary, dull, and familiar. *You are especially chosen,* a board acquaintance named Martha had written, when he'd disclosed that he had grown up on the island. *Fuck that,* he had written back. But as they entered the harbor, he hunkered down next to the dog, who was going wild at the smells rolling out from the town and the docks. "Look, Hobart," he said. "Home."

Those who ascribed a will or a purpose to it thought it was odd that the square should have chosen to appear on Nantucket, one of the least important places on the planet, for all that the island was one of the richest. Those same people thought it might have demonstrated a sense of humor on the square's part to appear, of all the places it could have, in the middle of a summer-mansion bathroom, where some grotesquely rejuvenated old lady, clinging to her deluxe existence, might have stepped into it accidentally on her way out of the tub. But it had appeared on the small portion of the island that was still unincorporated, in a townie commune that had been turned subsequently into a government-sponsored science installation and an unofficial way station for the ever-dwindling and ever-renewing community of people who called themselves Black Squares.

Every now and then someone posted a picture of a skunk or a squirrel on the board, with a caption naming the creature Alpha or Primo or Columbus, and calling it the first pioneering Black Square. It was true that a number of small animals, cats and dogs and rabbits and even a few commune llamas, went missing in the days before the square was actually discovered by a ten-year-old boy who tried to send his little sister through it. Around her waist she wore a rope that led to her brother's hand; he wasn't trying to kill her. He had been throwing things in all day, rocks and sticks and one heavy cinder block, and finally a rabbit from the eating stock. His mother interrupted him before he could send his sister through. He had put a helmet on her, and given her a flashlight, sensing, as the story went on the board, that there was both danger and discovery on the other side.

There followed a predictable series of official investigations, largely muffled and hidden from the eyes of the public, though it seemed that from the first missing rodent there was mention of the square on the boards. The incorporated portion of the island wanted nothing to do with it. Once the government assured them that it would be a very closely supervised danger, they more or less forgot about it, except to bemoan the invasion of their island by a new species of undesirable, one that didn't serve them in their homes or clubs. The new arrivals had a wild, reckless air about them, these people who had nothing to lose, and they made one uncomfortable, even if they did spend wildly and never hung around for very long. The incorporated folks hardly noticed the scientists, who once the townies had been cleared out never left the compound until they departed for good within a year, leaving behind a skeleton crew of people not bothered by unsolvable mysteries.

By then it had become obvious that there was nothing to be learned from the square—at least nothing profitable in the eyes of the government. It just sat there, taking whatever was given to it. It refused nothing (*And isn't it because it loves everyone and everything perfectly, that it turns nothing and no one away?* Martha wrote), but it gave nothing back. It emitted no detectable energy. No probe ever returned from within it, or managed to hurl any signal back out. Tethers were neatly clipped, at various and unpredictable lengths. No official human explorer ever went through, though an even dozen German shepherds leaped in obediently, packs on their backs and cameras on their heads. The experiments degraded, from the construction of delicate listening devices that bent elegantly over the edge of the square to the government equivalent of what the boy had been doing: tossing things in. The station was funded eventually as a disposal unit, and the govern-

ment put out a discreet call across the globe for special and difficult garbage, not expecting, but not exactly turning away, the
human sort that inevitably showed up.

Henry had contracted with his psychiatrist not to think about
Bobby. "This is a condition of your survival," the man had told
him, and Henry had not been inclined to argue. There had been a
whole long run of better days, when he had been able to do it, but
it took a pretty serious and sustained effort, and exercised some
muscle in him that got weaker, instead of stronger, the more he
used it, until he succumbed to fatigue. Now it was a sort of pleasure not to bother resisting. It would have been impossible, anyway, to spend time with Bobby's dog and not think of him,
though he loved the dog quite separately from Bobby. It was a perfectly acceptable indulgence, in the long shadow of the square, to
imagine the dog sleeping between them on their bed, though
Hobart hadn't been around when they were actually together. And
it was acceptable to imagine himself and Bobby together again—
useless and agonizing, but as perfectly satisfying as worrying a
painful tooth. It was even acceptable to imagine that it was he and
Bobby, and not Bobby and his Brazilian bartender husband, who
were about to have a baby together, a little chimera bought for
them from beyond the grave by Bobby's fancy dead grandma.

Yet Bobby wasn't all he thought about. It wasn't exactly the
point of the trip to torture himself that way, and whether the
square represented a new beginning or merely an end to his suffering, he wasn't trying to spend his last days on the near side of
the thing in misery. He was home, after all, though Nantucket
Town did not feel much like home, and he didn't feel ready, at
first, for a trip to the old barn off Polpis Road. But there was
something—the character of the light and the way the heat
seemed to hang very lightly in the air—that though unremem-
bered, made the island feel familiar.

He showed the dog around. It was something to do; it had

never been his plan to go right to the square, though there were people who got off the ferry and made a beeline for it. Maybe they were worried that they might change their mind if they waited too long. Henry wasn't worried about changing his mind or chickening out. The truth was he had been traveling toward the thing all his life, in a way, and while the pressure that was driving him toward it had become more urgent since he came to the island, he still wasn't in any particular hurry to jump in. There were things to say good-bye to, after all; any number of things to be done for the last time. He had spent his last sleepless night in Cambridge in a bed-and-breakfast down the street from where Bobby lived with his bartender, lying on the bed with his hands behind his head, staring at the ceiling and enumerating all those things he'd like to do one last time. He wasn't organized enough to make a list, but he'd kept a few of them in his head. It turned out to be more pleasant to do them with the dog than to do them alone, and more pleasant, in some ways, to do them for the dog instead of for himself. Last meals were better enjoyed if Hobart shared them with him—they ate a good deal of fancy takeout in the hotel room, Henry sitting on the floor with his back against the bed, Hobart lying on his belly with his face in a bowl resting between his legs. Henry made a tour of some dimly remembered childhood haunts, rediscovering them and saying good-bye to them at the same time: a playground on the harbor, a pond that he thought was Miacomet but might have been Monomoy, and finally the beach at Surfside.

He had pictures of himself at that beach on his phone, taken by his father during Henry's very well-documented childhood. He was his father's last child, and the only one from his second marriage. His brothers were all much older than him, born when their father had been relatively poor, when he still made his living, despite his Haverford education and his well-received first book, playing piano in bars. Henry came in well after that, when there was money for cameras and camcorders and time, attention, and interest to take a picture of the baby every day. He had thumbed through them in bed the night before, showing them to Hobart, who somehow got conditioned to yawn every time he saw a picture of Henry at the beach with a bucket and a shovel. It was a less melancholy pastime, and less pathetic, to look at old pictures of himself, instead of pictures of himself and Bobby, though he did that, too, late into the night, with Hobart's sleeping head on his chest.

They spent the morning making their way slowly down the beach by throws of a rubber football the size of a child's fist. Henry had a reasonably good arm: once or twice he threw the ball far enough that Hobart disappeared around a dune to go in search of it. He daydreamed considerably as they went, and thought indulgently of Bobby as Hobart leaped and galumphed and face-planted into the sand. He had to be persuaded every time to give up the ball, running back as if to drop it at Henry's feet, then veering away and playing a prancing, high-stepping keep-away until Henry caught him around the neck and pulled open his jaws. It made him a defective sort of retriever, and it doubled the work of play with him, but Henry didn't mind it.

He laughed at the dog, and thought of his father laughing behind the camera at him, and thought of something Bobby had said to him more than once. He'd accused Henry of being unable to delight in him, and had said that this was part of the reason that Henry had never been properly able to love him, or anybody, really. Bobby had said deflating things like that all the time—he'd kept an arsenal of them always at hand and ready to spoil any occasion—and the Bobby in Henry's head still kept up a running commentary years after they broke up. But it had been fair, for Bobby to say he was delightless, a million years before, when Henry had been an entirely different person, selfish and self-loathing and more in love with his own misery than with the man who wanted to marry him.

All that had changed. It was far too late to make any difference with Bobby, but now he was the sort of person who couldn't help but take pleasure in the foolish exuberance of a clumsy black Lab. "Look, Bobby," he said quietly as Hobart raced after the football. "Look at him go." He shook his head at himself, and sat down, then lay down on his back with his knees bent and his arms thrown out at his sides, staring up at the sky for a while before he closed his eyes. "I'm tired, Hobart," he said, when the dog came back and started to lick his face. "Sit down and relax for a minute." But the cold nose kept pressing on his eyelids, and the rough tongue kept dragging across his cheek and nose and lips. He swatted at the dog's head, and grabbed his collar, and reached with his other hand to scratch the Lab's neck.

In another moment his face was being licked from the other side. When Henry opened his eyes he discovered that this was Hobart. The dog he had been petting was someone else entirely, another black Lab, but with a face that was much pointier (and frankly less handsome) than Hobart's. The owner came trotting up behind him. He was standing in front of the sun. Henry only registered his hairy chest and baseball cap before the man asked him, "Why are you making out with my dog?"

One heard various stories about Lenny. He was alternately from San Francisco, or Houston, or Pittsburgh, or Nantucket, or someplace no one had ever heard of. He was a teenager, or an old man, or in his middle age. He was perfectly healthy, or terminally ill. He was happily married, or heartbroken and bereft. He was a six-foot-eight black man or he was a diminutive honky. He might not even have been the first one to go through. It was only certain that he'd been the first to announce that he was going, and the founding poster on what became the Black Square Message Board. As the first official Black Square (the anonymous individuals who might have passed in before him, as well as the twelve German shepherds, together held that title unofficially) he had become something of a patron saint for everyone who proposed to go after him. *Lenny knows* was a fairly common way to preface a platitude on the board, and his post, *this is not a suicide,* had become a motto of sorts for the whole group. The post had a *ceci n'est pas une pipe* quality about it, but it was consistent with what became the general attitude on the board, that the square offered an opportunity to check into another universe as well as the opportunity to check out of this one. *He should have said, This is not MERELY a suicide,* Martha wrote. Not everything she wrote was stupid, and Henry was inclined to agree with her on this count. There was an element of protest to Lenny's leap into the square: it was a fuck-you to the ordinary universe the likes of which it had not previously been possible to utter. By entering into the square you could express your disdain for the declined world, so far fallen, to some people's minds, from its potential for justice and beauty, as effectively as you could by blowing your head off, but instead of just dying, you might end up someplace else, someplace different—indeed, someplace full of people just like you, people who had leaped away from their own declined, disappointing lives.

The pointy-nosed Lab's name was Dan; his master's name was Luke. Henry ought not to have talked to him beyond saying "Sorry!" Meeting yet another handsome, witty, accomplished fellow who was utterly uninteresting on account of his failure to be Bobby was not part of the plan for his last days on the near side of the square. Henry tried to walk away, but the dogs were already fast friends, and Hobart wouldn't come. The man was smiling and looking at Henry in a particular way as Henry tugged on Hobart's collar. He was short and muscled up and furry, and had a pleasant, open face. Henry was trying to think of something inappropriate to say, but nothing was coming to mind. The man stuck out his hand and introduced himself. Henry, his left hand still on Hobart's collar, stuck out his own, shifting his balance as he did, so when Hobart lunged at his new friend he pulled Henry over.

Henry ought to have let go of the stranger's small, rough, appealing palm—he thought as he squeezed it harder that it felt like a blacksmith's palm, and that it went along nicely with the man's blacksmith build—but he gripped it harder as he fell, and pulled the other man over on top of him. They were momentarily a pile of bodies, human and canine, Luke on Henry on Hobart, with Dan on top of all of them. Henry got a paw in his face, and a dog nail scratched his cheek, and his face was pressed hard into Luke's chest. Luke smelled like coffee and salt, and tasted salty too, when Henry thought he had accidentally tasted the sweat on the man's hairy chest, but it turned out that it was his own blood on his lip, trickling from the scratch.

The injury, though it wasn't totally clear which dog had inflicted it, prompted profuse apologies and an invitation to dinner. Henry felt sure he should have declined. All his plans aside, he knew that he wasn't going to be interested in this man as certainly as he knew that the sun got a little colder every day, or that eventually the whole island would be incorporated as surely as Hilton Head or Manhattan, and that the rich folk would have to ferry in their household help from Martha's Vineyard. It was inevitable. But he considered, as he wiped the blood off his face and listened to Luke apologize, that he might be overlooking another gift of the square, and that it didn't matter that loving Bobby had ruined him, and smothered in the cradle any possible relationship with any other man. He had no future with anyone, but he had no future at all. That took the pressure off dinner. And it was something else to say good-bye to, after all: dinner with a handsome man.

"Sometimes I kind of like being the only homo in a ten-mile radius," Luke said while they were eating. "Or almost the only one." Henry had asked what had possessed him to come to Nantucket for a vacation. When Henry cocked his head at that, Luke asked him the same question.

"Something similar," Henry said, reaching down to pet

Hobart's head, a gesture that was becoming his new nervous tic. They were sitting outside at a restaurant in 'Sconset, both dogs at their feet and a bowl of clams between them. Dan was just as well-behaved as Hobart was. They both sat staring up at the sky or at another table, or staring intently into each other's eyes, leaning forward occasionally to sniff closer and closer, touching noses and then touching tongues before going back to looking distracted and disinterested until they started it all over again with a sudden glance. Henry and Luke took turns saying, "I think they like each other."

"I was born here," Henry added. Luke was smiling at him—he seemed to be one of those continuous smilers, the sort of people that Henry generally disliked (Bobby, until he had left, had always appeared perpetually troubled), but there was something sad, or at least resigned, in Luke's smile that Henry found appealing.

"I didn't think anybody was born on Nantucket," Luke said. "I thought people just magically appeared here once they made enough money."

"They do," Henry said. "Sort of. There's a ceremony. You claw your way naked through a pool of coins and they drape you in a white robe and everyone chants, 'One of us! One of us!' But if you're poor you just get squeezed out of a vagina and they put your name on a plaque in the hospital."

"You have a plaque?"

"Sure. Henry David Conroy. May 22, 1986."

"I figured you were special," Luke said, managing to smile differently, more warmly and more engagingly and more attractively. Henry looked away. It was part of his problem that flattering attention from handsome men only made him more sad, and made him feel Bobby's rejection more achingly and acutely. The handsomer the man, and the more flattering the attention, the greater his sadness. To date, anybody else had only discovered in miserable degrees how thoroughly and hopelessly they were not Bobby. But there was always that homunculus in Henry, weakly resistant to the sadness, that protested in a meek little voice whenever he said good-bye early, or declined an invitation up to someone's apartment. Proximity to the square made it a little bolder, and Henry thought he could hear it shouting something about saying good-bye to sucking on a nice cock.

Henry took a clam and looked at the dogs. They were looking away from each other now, but he said it anyway. "Look at that. They really like each other, don't they?"

"They sure do," Luke said.

Because of my mother, somebody wrote. Half the messages on the farewell board were unsigned. You were only supposed to post your final notes there, but this was a rule that was impossible to enforce, since anybody could retire one ID and come back with a new one. And you were supposed to limit yourself to just one reason, either by prioritizing, or, more elegantly, by articulating a reason that contained all other possible reasons. While *Because of my mother* could be unpacked at length, there was something crude, or at least unsophisticated, about it. *Because of incorporation* was its political equivalent: it contained a multitude of reasons, all the accumulated disappointments of the past decade for the people who cared to mourn the dashed hopes of the early part of the century. But it was less subtle and less mysterious than *Because I believe,* into which one could read a richer sort of disappointment, one that was tempered with hope that something besides oblivion lay on the other side of the square. This sort of post could be crude as well: *Because I want to see Aslan* was its own common type. Still, there was something pleasing about these notes that looked forward through the square and saw something or someone waiting there, Aslan in Narnia, Dejah Thoris on Barsoom, or more private kings in more particular kingdoms. *Because I have suffered enough* was less appealing than *Because I wish to suffer differently.*

Most mysterious and most mundane of all were the last posts

of the lovelorn. They were neither necessarily hopeful nor despair-ing. *Because of Alice* could mean anything in a way that *Because of my mother* generally could not—Alice might be hero or villain, after all, but all mothers were villains on the board. *Because of Louise, Because of Juliet, Because of John, Because of Alan and Wanda and Bubbles*—that one seemed like cheating to Henry, though he liked it for the possibility that Bubbles might be a chimpanzee, and for the likelihood that the circumstances driving the poster through the square must be uniquely weird and horri-ble. *Because of George, Because of Althea, Because of you. Because I broke his heart, Because she broke my heart. Because of Bobby.*

Henry took Luke and the dogs out to the old barn. There were pictures of that, too, taken back when it had been Henry's home. Henry had called them up on the ceiling and they had all looked at them, even the dogs. It was hardly a first-date activity, to share your distant past this way, though he'd done it with Bobby, the two of them sitting in an overpriced café in Cambridge with their phones on the table, excitedly trading pictures of their dead brothers and fathers. That had felt like showing each other their scars, part of the process of recognition by which they came inde-pendently to understand that, while it was probably too early to say they were meant for each other, they were at least very lucky to have collided. It was a less intimate revelation to show pictures of himself at five years old, naked except for a little cowboy hat and boots, to a man he had fucked three times in the twelve hours he had known him, but it was still a startling bit of progress. He hadn't been interested in that sort of thing—the moving on that his friends and shrinks and Bobby himself had encouraged him to do—largely because it seemed both impossible and unnecessary. Trying to not be in love with Bobby was like trying to not be gay anymore, or like annulling the law of gravity by personal decree. It was ridiculous to try, and anyway gayness and gravity, for what-ever sadness or limitation they might generate, felt right. Henry still wasn't interested in moving on, but there was something about his pending encounter with the square that made it feel like this was something else, similar in form but not in substance to getting over it at last, since he was about to make a permanent attestation to his devotion to Bobby, and to his objection to the end of their relationship.

"This is okay," he said to Hobart, the only other one of the four still awake after the slide show. Luke and his dog had fallen asleep before it finished, and now the man's head was on Henry's chest. "This is okay," Henry said again, staring down his nose at Luke's face. He was doing a whistling sort of snore, in through the nose, out through the mouth. "I'm not making out with your dog," Henry said quietly. "He's throwing up into my mouth." He wondered why he couldn't have thought to say that two days before. Hobart crawled up the bed and added his head to the empty side of Henry's chest. It was a little hard to breathe, but he still fell asleep that way.

The barn was in as much of a state of ruin as the law would allow. No one had lived there for five years, and no one sanely inclined to keep it up had lived there for fifteen. A friend of his father's, a crazy cat lady who kept birds instead of cats, had moved in after his father had died, and after she died Henry had left it empty, never visiting and only paying now and then to have it painted when the nearest neighbor complained that it was starting to look shabby in a way that was no longer picturesque. All the nearest neighbors were eventually eaten up by incorporation, and there were mansions all around now in the near distance, but Henry had never sold the place in spite of offers that grew both more generous and more threatening. He'd left it to Bobby with instructions never to sell, which he probably wouldn't—Bobby was not exactly a friend of incorporation—but who knew. Maybe he and the Brazilian would want to make another baby together, and Bobby's grandma had only been good for one.

. . .

"You used to live here?" Luke asked in the morning. "All the time?"

"All the time," Henry said. "It's why my manners are so atrocious." They were standing in what remained of the living room. A pair of squirrels were staring at them from a rafter above. The dogs were staring back. "It was fine," Henry said. "It was great, actually. As much as I remember. It doesn't have anything to do with . . . it."

"Yeah. Mine neither," Luke said. They had started talking about the square during breakfast. Henry wasn't the one to bring it up. Out of nowhere and all of a sudden Luke had asked him what he was going to wear when he went through. "Shorts," Henry had said, not thinking to deny it, or even ask how Luke knew he was a Square.

"I brought a parka," Luke said.

"Because you think it will be cold?" Henry asked.

"Because I like the parka," Luke said. "It's my favorite piece of clothing. It's puffy but not too puffy." A silence followed, not entirely awkward. They were eating in the room, on the bed, and had just moved the plates to the floor for the dogs to finish up. Henry was still trying to decide what to say next when Luke reached over for his cock, and what followed felt like a sort of conversation. Henry had always thought that having someone's cock in your mouth ought to provide you with some kind of insight on them, though this hadn't ever been the case. Staring into someone's eyes while he pounded on their ass made him feel infinitely remote from them, except of course for Bobby, and maybe it was the extraordinary intimacy he had achieved doing such things with Bobby that spoiled it with everyone else. But there was something revealing in the exchange between him and Luke. Luke was holding on to him too tightly, and he was holding on too tightly to Luke, and Henry thought he heard notes of agonized sadness in both their voices when they cried out at each other as they came. By the end of it Henry felt as if they had communicated any number of wordless secrets, and that he had a deep, dumb understanding of why Luke was going through the square, and felt sure that Luke felt the same way, and it seemed all of a piece with the whole process that it would fuck things up by asking if this was true.

"I was such a happy kid," Luke said. "Not one single thing about my childhood was fucked up. I always wanted to put that on my gravestone, if I was going to have a gravestone."

"Mine would say . . ." Henry started, and then thought better of it.

"What?" He had been going to say, *He made bad choices.*

"Poodle," he said. "Just, *Poodle.* And let people wonder what that meant, except it wouldn't mean anything." Luke put an arm around him.

"I like you," he said. "I *like* you." The way he stressed the *like* made it sound as if he hadn't liked anybody for a while.

"I like you, too," Henry said, feeling stupid and exalted at the same time. It changed nothing, to like somebody. It didn't change anything at all about why he was here, or what he was going to do. He could like somebody, and say good-bye to liking somebody, in the same way he was saying good-bye to ice cream and ginger-snaps and blow jobs and the soft fur on the top of Hobart's head. It didn't change the past, or alter any of the choices he had made, or make him into a different person. It didn't change the fact that it was too late to do anything but proceed quietly and calmly through the square.

The dogs were taking turns leaping and barking uselessly at the squirrels. "I *like* you," Henry said again, trying to put the same charming emphasis on the word that Luke had, but it only came out funny, his voice breaking like he was thirteen, or like he was much sadder or more overcome than he actually was. Luke gathered him closer in his arms, and pressed his beard against Henry's beard, and Henry was sure this man was going to say something that would be awkward and delightful and terrifying, but after five minutes of squeezing him and rubbing their faces together but never quite kissing all he said was "You're *cuddly*."

Some days I'm INTO, Martha wrote, *and some days I'm THROUGH. But I'm never not going.* Everybody had those days, when the prospect of going into the square, with no expectation of anything but oblivion on the other side, was more appealing than the prospect of passing through it to discover a new world where pain was felt less acutely, or less urgently, or even just differently, although most people liked to pretend that they were only interested in the latter destination. These were not suicides, after all. But how many people would pass through, Henry wondered, if it were in fact a guaranteed passage to Narnia? He wasn't sure that nuzzling with Aslan would make him any less troubled over Bobby, or that topping Mr. Tumnus's hairy bottom would dispel any unwanted memories. Living beyond Bobby, beyond the pain and delight of remembering him, beyond the terrible ironies of their failed almost marriage, required something more than the promise of happiness or relief. It could only be done someplace farther away than Narnia, and maybe even someplace farther away than death, though death, according to the deep illogic that had governed all Henry's actions since he and Bobby had broken up beyond any hope of reconciling, was at least a step in the right direction. When he had made his drunken attempt to hang himself all Henry had been thinking about was getting away from Bobby, from loving him and hurting over him and from the guilt of having hurt him, but when he actually settled his weight down on the telephone cord around his neck and let himself begin to be suspended by it, some monstrously naive part of him felt like he was accelerating back toward his old lover. Killing himself, as he tried to kill himself, felt like both a way forward and a way back.

He blacked out ever so gently—he'd chosen to hang himself for the sheer painless ease of it—and he felt sure that he was traveling, felt a thrill at having made what seemed like a reportable discovery, that death was falling. This seemed like tremendously important news, the sort of thing that might have validated his short-lived and undistinguished scientific career. He thought how sad it was that he wasn't going to be able to tell Bobby—*It's all right after all*, he would have said, *that our brothers are dead and our fathers are dead because death is only falling.* And at the same time he thought, I'll tell him when I see him.

He woke up with a terrible headache, lying among the shoes on his closet floor, all his neatly pressed work clothes on top of him and splinters from the broken closet bar in his hair. He spent the night there because it seemed like this was the place he had been heading all his life, and the dreary destined comfort of it gave him the best night's sleep he'd had in months. When he woke again all the desperate intoxications of the night before had worn off, and he only felt pathetic, failed suicides being the worst sort of losers in anybody's book, his own included. He stayed in there through the morning—he'd wet himself as he lay unconscious, and did it again without much hesitation—feeling afraid to go out into what seemed now like a different world. It was early evening before growing boredom forced him to look at his phone. He'd sent a text to Bobby—*I'm so sorry*—and received no reply.

Henry went walking at dusk with Luke along the fence around the station where the square was housed. The dogs went quietly before them, sniffing at the grass that poked around the chain link but neither one ever finding a place to pee. When they came into view of the concrete shed, Dan barked softly at it, but Hobart only lay down and appeared to go to sleep. Henry and Luke stared silently for a while, holding hands.

"How did you know I came to Nantucket for this?" Henry asked.

"I don't know," Luke said. "Same way I knew you were gay, I guess. Squaredar."

"Huh," Henry said. "I didn't know with you until you asked. And then I knew." This seemed like a terribly lame thing to say. He was reminded of all his late conversations with Bobby, before Bobby had ended their long fruitless talk about whether or not they should try being together again by marrying the Brazilian, when hapless unrequited love of the man had kept Henry from making a single articulate point.

"And you didn't know I was gay until I came in your mouth."

"I'm slow," Henry said. "But that doesn't make you gay. Hundreds and hundreds of straight guys have come in my mouth. Hundreds and hundreds and hundreds." It suddenly occurred to him that holding hands they would be too big to fit through the square.

They were quiet for a little while, until Luke heaved a big sigh and said, "There it is." His tone was somehow both reverential and disappointed.

"You couldn't have thought it would be bigger," Henry said. "Everybody knows how big it is."

"No. I just thought I would feel something . . . different. If I close my eyes I can't even tell it's there."

"Well," Henry said. "Maybe it's just a hole."

Luke shook his head. "Look," he said, and pointed. Someone was approaching the shed. Luke raised a little pair of binoculars to his eyes and made an odd noise, a grunt and a laugh and also something sadder than either of those noises, and handed the glasses to Henry. It was a woman wearing a short, sparkling dress. "I don't think it's very practical to go through in heels," Henry said.

"Makes it difficult to leap properly," Luke said. "She's probably just going to fall in, which isn't right at all."

Henry put the binoculars down. "Why do you think she's going?"

Luke shrugged. " 'Cause she's too pretty for this world." He took the glasses back from Henry, who gave them up gladly, not wanting to watch her pass through the door.

"Let's go," Henry said.

"Hold on," Luke said, still watching. "She's stranded here from another dimension, and thinks this might be the way back."

"Or some dead person told her to do it," Henry said. "To be with them again. Let's go."

"Just a minute," Luke said, and lifted his head like Hobart sniffing at the harbor smells, cocking his head and listening. Henry turned and walked away, whistling for Hobart to follow him, but the dogs stayed together, sitting next to Luke, all of them sniffing and listening. Henry kept walking, and shortly they all came bounding up behind him. Luke caught him around the shoulders and pulled him close. "She's gone," he said matter-of-factly. "Did you feel it?"

All through dinner Henry wanted to ask the question that he knew he shouldn't, the question that probably didn't need to be answered, and the one that he felt intermittently sure would be ruinous to ask. But it wasn't until later, as Luke lay sweating on top of him, that he couldn't resist anymore, and he finally asked it. "How come?" he said into Luke's shoulder.

"What?"

"How come you're going through?"

"It's complicated," he said. "Why are you going?"

"It's complicated," Henry said.

"See?"

"Yeah. Dumb question," Henry said. Though in fact his reason for going through no longer seemed very complicated at all. If it was simple that didn't make it any less powerful, but crushing hopeless loneliness was something Henry suddenly felt able to wrap his arms around even as he wrapped his arms around Luke. "I'm lonely" did no sort of justice to what he'd suffered in the past two years, and yet he could have said it in answer and it would have been true. It seemed suddenly like it might be possible that loneliness did not have to be a crime punishable by more and more extreme loneliness, until a person was so isolated that he felt he was being pushed toward a hole in the world.

"Not dumb. Not dumb." Luke kissed the side of Henry's neck each time he said it. "You're *cuddly.*"

"I was going to go tomorrow," Henry said. "That was my date. That's what I paid for. But I was thinking of changing it."

"Really?"

"Really. It's not going anywhere, right? It'll be there next week. And the next week. It's kind of nice, you know, how it's always there, not going anywhere. Nice to know you could always just go in, whenever you want. But that you don't have to, yet, if you want to go to the beach tomorrow instead. Or if you want to play tennis, instead, or before. Tennis, and then in you go. Unless you want to make pancakes first."

"I don't think Hal gives refunds," Luke said. Hal was the guard who took semiofficial bribes to look the other way while people took one-way trips into the shed.

"I don't mind," Henry said. "It's just money. When were you going?"

A long silence followed. Henry was afraid to ask again, because he couldn't imagine that Luke hadn't heard him. But Luke only lay there, dripping less and less and breathing more and more deeply, until Henry decided that he was asleep. Henry was almost falling asleep himself, for all that the unanswer was a disappointment, when Luke spoke, not at all sleepily, into his shoulder. "Next week," he said. "Around then."

Then he really did fall asleep, and Henry stayed awake, thinking of the week to come, and the one after that, and the one after that, and of repairs to the barn, and sex among the power tools, and the dogs frolicking, and of Bobby wondering what happened to his wonderful fucking dog, and whether Hobart would be sad if he never went back to Cambridge. Henry fell asleep not any less sad, or any less in love with Bobby, but surprised in a way that did nothing to satisfy his cynicism. Nantucket, he thought before he slept, and two dogs, and a good man asleep on him. It was all relatively all right.

How a two-hundred-pound man could roll off of him and get dressed in the dark and take his parka out of a closet full of rattling wire hangers without waking him up Henry never could figure. He left a note. *You are lovely but the square is lovelier.* It was pinned to Dan's collar. Both dogs stared at Henry impatiently while he sat on the bed with the note in his hands, probably wondering when they were going to go out, or be fed, or be played with, or even acknowledged when they licked his hands or jumped up on the bed to nuzzle his chest. Dan eventually peed in the corner, and then joined Hobart to lie at Henry's feet, both of them wagging their tails, then staring up at him with plaintive eyes, then eventually falling asleep as the morning turned into the afternoon. Henry finally dozed himself, the note still in his hand, maintaining the posture of sad shock he felt sure he was going to maintain forever, and did not dream of Bobby or Luke or the square or his brother or his father or the frolicking dogs or of the isle of Nantucket sinking into the sea. When he woke up he stood and stretched and rustled up his phone from where it had got lost amid the sheets. Then he called the old lady, sure he was going to tell her there was an extra dog for her to bring to Cambridge until he left her a message saying he would bring Hobart back himself.

Jane Delury

Nothing of Consequence

THEY CAME to Madagascar—women, all educators—to train a group of French teachers from around the island. They were housed in the living quarters of an abandoned coconut plantation and conducted their classes in warehouses still dusty with copra. By the second week, the red soil had colored their soles and the sun their faces. Though in the classroom they were as rigorous as they were back home, their minds drifted. Lessons on the imperfect, discussions of Orientalism, were interrupted by thoughts of what would be served for lunch or whether a driver might be hired for an excursion to the rain forest. They returned to themselves when a student raised a hand.

One man in particular impressed the women from the start because he never made an error in construction or conjugation, and he listened to their explanations with a critical tilt to his head. Unlike the other students, who wrote in pencil, Rado took notes with a fountain pen. He was young, in his twenties, but he walked in his youthful body as if borrowing it on the way to an older one. A lycée teacher in the capital, he intended to live one day in France and pursue "his work in poetry."

At the first night's dinner, after punch coco and before fish curry, Rado sat down next to Bernadette, the Merry Widow, as the others had named her at the orientation in Paris, where she barely cracked a smile or revealed anything except that her husband had been dead a year and that she found Colette underrated. She was the most taciturn and the plainest among them. The boldness of her blunt chin and large mouth might have made for pretty ugliness during her youth but in late middle age made her look masculine. She wore collar shirts, buttoned just below her clavicle, the sleeves rolled over her elbows. Judging by the measure of her chignon, her brown hair would fall to her shoulders.

As Bernadette spoke to Rado, she fiddled with the corner of her napkin. Now and again she laughed, which the women had never heard her do, not even that afternoon when they'd attended a performance of a dance troupe in the nearby town and were all brought onstage for a lesson. Rado laughed with her. The solitary line that marked his brow deepened, and his teeth showed, as they did not in the classroom. Neither rose to help bring the dishes out from the kitchen until, the plates being cleared, Bernadette looked around apologetically and announced that she and Rado would fetch the pudding. The next evening, and the next, Bernadette and Rado seemed always to be leaving for the kitchen or talking over their untouched food. Their discussions could be overheard in snatches: Rimbaud's Catholicism, the lyrics of Prévert, nothing to raise suspicion in the Director, hunched over his plate at the other end of the table, necktie tucked into his shirt front. But the women interpreted what he ignored. In the communal bathroom, on the path to meals, and evenings, over herbal tea, Bernadette and Rado became the subject of hushed conversation.

The coconut, he told her, as she followed him into the plantation, can travel for hundreds of miles on the ocean, even washing up on the shores of Antarctica and Ireland.

"Really?" she asked.

He smiled. "There is no fooling you, is there?"

"Perhaps if you were a botanist. Instead of a poet."

She forced the last word from her mouth. At dinner the third night, he had shown her his notebooks of verse, which he hoped to publish in France, since on the island there was no press. She recognized the force of will it must have taken for him to go all the way to university, having grown up in a one-room house with eight brothers and sisters fated to repair cars and work plantations. Yet his writing was flat as a postcard, well-turned lines about waves on the ocean, the colors of the sunset. He chose obvious words for obvious subjects. He did not see past the surface of things.

"I hid in the fronds when I was supposed to be doing my chores," he said.

"You would have done better growing up in the Alps. Pines give good cover."

"You did so too?"

"Don't all children?"

He stopped to pull a frond blade from the heel of his sandal. She imagined him shirtless and barefoot while she, dressed in a school smock, walked with her mother through the square of her childhood village. But no, she realized, calculating the difference in their years, that was not right. When Rado was a boy, climbing trees, she was carrying babies and groceries up the steps of her apartment building. When Rado's voice was just starting to change, she was years into her fine but dull marriage, sitting at her kitchen table with a stack of papers to grade, ignorant of the affair her husband had just ended.

Only Bernadette's roommate protested the rumors. "Who knows what's going on in your room when you aren't there," one woman said, and the roommate said, "Reading." She saw what the others didn't see. How Bernadette tossed in her sleep. How she changed into her nightgown in the bathroom and slept with the sheets pulled up to her chin. If Bernadette got up at night, it was only to go down the hall to the bathroom. She was never gone long. And was it so terrible, anyway, that Bernadette had something she looked forward to in the morning, something that made her check her face in the mirror? The mirror was small and low on the wall, the light poor, and as the roommate walked into the room, Bernadette was bent toward the glass, cupping her cheeks as one might those of a child. This the roommate did not mention, but a few days later, when one of the women cornered her to let her know that Bernadette was now smoking Rado's cigarettes, the roommate said she was starting to be reminded of *The Crucible*.

"We are becoming the subject of gossip," Bernadette told Rado.

He laughed and took her hand to help her over a fallen tree, an unnecessary gesture that closed her throat. She could smell his body through his clothes: a stiff white shirt, a pair of creased pants, the apparel of a schoolboy. If she had been another kind of woman, she would have wanted to take him to the shops on the Avenue Montaigne, to pick out scarves and sweaters.

"It's the same for me," he said. "When I go back to my village, I am spurned for having left."

"But what do I have to envy?" The hope in her voice made her cringe.

"A university professorship."

"Not everyone wants that. And it's only part-time."

He understood nothing of the *education nationale*. She had told him that she taught at a lycée and a course in the continuing studies department of the university, so he imagined her a professor. She saw it happen the first night, the way his eyes stopped roaming, but she didn't correct him.

The ground turned from grass to sand. Ahead was the ocean. "The whales are migrating," Rado said. "You can see them from here."

"Really," she said flatly, then laughed. "I'm sorry. Animals have never been my thing."

"We will never own a dog together then."

Though she knew he was teasing, her chest collapsed. She had forgotten the physical yearning. The same symptoms her husband complained about in the early stage of his illness. Shortness of breath. Dizziness. Pain near the heart. Was that why he was brought back to his mistress in those days? Why he disclosed the affair?

Rado was telling her about the song of the indri lemur, which sounded like that of a humpback. He said that the lemur was magnificent and wise. Its cry was haunting. His embellishments irritated her, and she cut him off. "I saw a snake this morning. On the reef."

He lowered his hands—he had been charting the course of an invisible lemur through the canopy above—and fumbled in his shirt pocket for his cigarettes. "You're lucky," he said. "You wouldn't want a bite from one of those."

"Do you believe in omens?" she said.

"No," he said. "Nor in taboos."

Some of the women mentioned the situation, as they called it, to their husbands when they phoned home from the Director's office, left to them after he'd gone to bed. His quarters were on the floor above, and as they talked through the crackle of static, the women thought of the Director and kept their voices down for fear that he might be listening. The husbands barely reacted. Thirty years earlier, upon hearing about Bernadette, the husbands might have worried about their marriages. Thirty years earlier, at the airport in Paris and Lyon, the husbands would have kissed their wives longer. A few of the women became angry upon hanging up. Bernadette might have it right. What if they found a student of their own? Broke rules in all directions. Right there in the classroom, against the map of Europe, or, like Bernadette, on the beach, where they supposed she and Rado went.

From where Bernadette stood with Rado, the reef looked smooth as a rug, but up close it was a web of crags and holes. The water was layered, a crust of cold and warmth below, the reverse of the students, whose smiles hid gentle disdain. Four-eyes, old chicken, good girl. Rado had told her the nicknames that the students coined for their teachers. Back home, Bernadette had friends like the women, friends who held her hand at her husband's funeral, called daily in the following weeks, took her to the mountains, and, after a decent interval for her to grieve, would want to invite her to dinner with divorced and widowed men. Friends who worried about her, about the way she picked up and ran off, as they called it, giving them notice only a week before. She needed time alone, so from the first she kept her distance from the women, though she knew she'd be disliked.

Earlier, her roommate had asked her for the third time if she'd like to go snorkeling, and Bernadette agreed, not wanting to tip into rudeness. Also, this was something to fill the morning until Rado was free. Bernadette went right into the water, but the roommate, winded from the walk, said she would rest first with her book. When Bernadette kicked to the surface, having seen the snake coiled in a crevice, the roommate raised her eyes.

Looking down, Bernadette saw that in her escape, the knot of her bathing suit had come undone. She was naked to the waist. "Why not?" the roommate called, and untied her own halter. Bernadette covered herself back up with a quick knot to her bathing suit straps. "It was an accident," she told her roommate, "but yes, you're right, why not?"

Later, back at the compound, before they parted ways, the roommate said, "Do you really care for him?" Her voice was hard, but her face wasn't, and it occurred to Bernadette now, as she sat down in the sand next to Rado, that the roommate might not have been fishing at all but instead giving a warning.

If Bernadette hadn't held herself apart, hadn't taken on airs, the women might have felt sorry for her. Rado, in the end, would move on. He was interested only in Bernadette's connection to the university system, though he was mistaken, since she was, after all, a *vacataire,* not a real professor. He would have been better off with the one who came from Marseilles and ran a feminist press and had friends in the right places. Or with the prettiest one, whose skin and figure they all envied. If Bernadette and Rado ended up together, since these things sometimes happened (there was talk of the friend of a friend who after a stint with a medical nonprofit married a man from the Congo), Rado would expect Bernadette to wait on him like a slave. Seen in this light, they were victimizing each other.

"Show me where you live," Rado said as they shared a cigarette.

She drew a map of France in the air with her finger and pointed to the center. "It's not much of a town, more like a village."

"I thought you taught in the city."

She wondered if he knew what it was like for black men in the small villages. "Yes," she said. "It is only a short ride by train."

"I've always wanted to see it. The grave of Baudelaire."

Was that the beginning? The opening? Would he bring up not having enough for a ticket? Could she lend him the money? Was that how this kind of thing went? In the hospital she had interrupted her husband's deathbed confession and said, "You're cruel." He thought she meant the affair he was revealing, but she meant his telling her so many years later. If she had known at the time, when she was a young woman, perhaps she would have stayed with him. Perhaps she would have had her own affair. She did not know. But he had robbed her of the choice.

Rado looked up at the coconut tree over their heads. "Do you want one?"

She nodded. And then he was gone. Feet flat on the trunk, he climbed toward the fronds. His pink heels looked tender against the leathered trunk, and she felt a twinge of pity. Here, or in France, he would rise to become head of a school district. He would wear bow ties. A coconut thumped down beside her. "Too close?" he yelled.

She picked up the coconut and handed it to him when, breathing heavily, he returned to the ground. "You looked smaller from up there," he said. He husked the coconut, then slammed the point of a pocket knife into its eyes. He pressed the coconut to Bernadette's mouth, and the water spilled over her chin. She pushed the coconut away. He kissed her neck.

"Don't," she said.

He put the coconut to his own mouth and drank.

"I'm sorry," he said when he was done. "It's too soon for you. My father has been gone ten years, but my mother still can't look at his picture without weeping."

Bernadette was surprised by how his words stung. "It's not that," she said. "I'm not thirsty."

"So let's not drink." He threw the coconut down the beach and leaned into her again. She imagined how he would write about this moment: the crashing waves, the fluttering palms. But her heart was thumping. She unbuttoned her shirt.

Bernadette and Rado were seen walking back from the beach, without bags or towels, her hair down, her hand in his. That evening, at dinner, the women couldn't look down the table without imagining that elegant mouth on Bernadette's. Rado, too big for his chair, seemed to them dangerous and fragile. In Bernadette, as she passed the bowl of salad and salted her fish, the women watched for some sign of regret, but she was straight shouldered and quiet, her hair back in its chignon. Each of the women, for her own reasons, was resolute. They went to bed having decided what they must do.

The next morning as Bernadette left class, the Director called her into his office. When he was done talking, Bernadette said, "You patronize him. Is it his youth or his color?"

"It is the abuse of power," the Director said. "You are his instructor."

"We did nothing wrong," she said. That was all she would give him. She had decided so at dinner the previous night as she and Rado were bathed in sidelong stares. Or perhaps the preparation started earlier, when she walked away from her roommate without answering the woman's question. "I'll go," she said. "Leave him be."

Outside, she passed students reading under a baobab tree, playing a game of checkers on the grass. She thought of the papers being stacked, the blackboards being wiped, behind the cloudy classroom windows. What would they talk about now? She sat in her room, bags by the door, and read for a while, then looked out the window to watch the sky drift down into the trees. She recalled the softness of Rado's hand as they walked back from the beach. He started to let go as the trees thinned for the buildings, but she held on tighter. For the first time since his death, she felt tenderness toward her husband. He thought he was seeking her forgiveness, but he also wanted her rage.

"You shouldn't have come," she said after opening the door for Rado.

"They're too busy toasting their victory to notice." He sat on the edge of the bed. "I know you took the blame. Your roommate told me."

"She saw it coming," Bernadette said.

"What will happen to you?"

"Nothing of consequence."

"You threw yourself on the sword," he said. "Why?"

It was the first time he'd asked a real question, and for a moment she believed that they were what he seemed to think they were: tragic lovers. But then he smiled, and she wasn't sure what he thought. "I leave that to you," she said.

Some of the women sought the book. Others stumbled on it. He looked mostly the same despite the time that had passed, but there was less fierceness in his jaw. He was the first man from the island to win such a prestigious award. They flipped through the pages in bookstores, in bed, on the couch, looking for something they recognized. They didn't know where truth ended and poetry began. They didn't know if he climbed a tree to pick a coconut or if she punctured the eyes with her thumbs. Did she undress him like a mother? Did a thicket of palm fronds grow over the sky? They didn't know if the ocean claimed the empty shell, which floated around the Horn of Africa and past the icebergs of the north. They didn't know if the coconut still traveled, studded with barnacles and bleached by salt. There was so much they didn't know.

Adam Foulds

The Rules Are the Rules

H E WOULD HAVE to begin any minute now; everyone else was there: the half-dozen dads on each sideline, the boys shoaling up and down the pitch with a couple of practice balls. They were getting boisterous. He stood up tall and scanned beyond the field of play to the edges of the park. To his left, the low autumn sun shone heavily into his eyes. Elsewhere it made the colors rich, pulled long shadows from the trees. Nothing. Walkers with dogs. Mothers with pushchairs. A cyclist zoomed silently along a path, spokes glittering, and disappeared for an instant behind the back of one of the fathers, who held a baby astride his right hip. Maybe eighteen months old. It narrowed its eyes in the breeze, soft hair lifted from its forehead. It held one arm up and tried to grasp with its curling fingers the moving air.

"Rev, are we gonna start?"

"Yes, we are. I was just waiting for Jack. Let's get those balls off the pitch."

When Reverend Peter blew his whistle he saw a few shoulders in Jack's team drop with disappointment. The boys moved slowly into position. Peter carried the match ball to the spot on his fingertips and just as he placed it, rolling it precisely with his boot, he heard a shout. It was Jack running toward them. He had sprinted ahead of his father, whose tiny, bag-carrying form rose and fell far away, laboriously shrugging off the distance.

Peter didn't particularly like Jack. The boy had one of those innocent, insolent faces with an upturned nose and styled brown hair. He was ten and he had a hairstyle. He looked too much like the cinema's idea of a boy, too much like everybody's idea of a boy, and this made him vain. He was vain of his footballing skills in particular. Moreover, he had a professional's tendency to foul, to fake, and to celebrate his goals with excessive displays, running with his arms outstretched, his shirt pulled up over his head to reveal his white, muscled body, his blind mauve nipples. He was strong and pretty and cruel, at least in his careless mastery. Peter's sympathy was elsewhere. It was his natural Christianity perhaps; he felt himself with the boys who weren't as fit or as sure of themselves, the frightened ones. Those boys, however, lit up when Jack joined them.

"You're late."

"It was traffic. My dad . . ."

"People are getting annoyed. Just get into position. Right." He pulled a fifty-pence piece from his pocket and pointed at the opposing captain. "You."

"Heads."

He flipped it up in a spin, swatted it down onto the back of his hand. "Heads it is." He raised his arm, blew his whistle, and the game began.

The low sun was awkward, flashing uncomfortably whenever the game turned in its direction and heating one side of him. His neck sweated as he ran between the shouting fathers. With sharp blasts of his whistle he cut the game into sections until there was a long period of fluid play when it found its rhythm, the boys in midfield bustling back and forth quietly, the defense lines pulled forward, pushed back. After minutes of this the boys tired and the game degraded into a series of pointless long kicks, the ball lofted practically from goal mouth to goal mouth. At the end of one run up the pitch, at the end of the tether of his breath, Peter slowed to a standstill. He turned when he heard a baby crying. He saw the child rearing up on its father's hip, its face red and mouth wide. Clear globes of tears stood on its cheeks. Its small fists trembled. The man was doing a poor job of comforting the child. Surely if he spoke soothingly to it and stroked that soft hair it would quieten. Frustrated at his powerlessness to intervene and take the child, he heard another yelp on the pitch, turned again, and saw the game halted, a knot of arguing boys around one boy lying flat on his back, rocking from side to side, his forearm over his eyes. Peter blew again and ran over. Blood: a long streak of it down one boy's shin. It poured from a flap of startled white skin just below the knee. Jack was protesting. Of course he was. He reached for his cards. "Right, you, off." The boys swarmed around him when he pulled out the red card, tossing their heads and flinging their arms down in despair. Jack shouted at him, "It wasn't me! It wasn't me!" Peter bent down and asked the injured boy, grave-faced and silent amid the uproar. "Was it him?" The boy said nothing, nodded. "Thought so." He stood up again and felt a brief, cold dizziness of blood draining from his head. He saw Jack's father running on.

"He didn't do it."

"Off the field."

"But he didn't." Jack's father's ears were small, pink, and tightly curled.

Peter avoided his eyes. "He didn't."

"He did do it. The rules are the rules. He's off."

"You didn't even see it. You were looking at Mike's Janey. I saw you."

"You and your son, off now."

"But . . ."

"Off. Now!"

He raised the red card for everyone to see and blew as loudly as he could.

The bathroom was warm and heavy from Steve's use, the air scented with shower cream and deodorant and aftershave. Peter arrived trembling from the exercise, his mind marked with the argument. The shower cubicle was warmer and heavier still. A remnant of foam still stood over the plughole, whispering away to nothing. Steve wasn't always very tidy when he was excited to be going out on sermon night. After Peter had showered, watching the soil spiral away, he stood wrapped in a towel, pink and soft, and saw the gunpowder of Steve's beard still in the sink. The lid of his hair gel was off, its contents lashed up into a crest by his delving fingers. Peter dried himself, added his own blasts of deodorant to the funk, then dressed, stabbed the plastic of a ready meal, and put it in the microwave.

He ate in front of the television. He told himself it was to find a neat quirk of topicality to add to his sermon, something to remind the congregation that he lived in their world, but he watched quite mindlessly the celebrity dancers in their camp little outfits, taking their turns then awaiting judgment, chests throbbing, smiling crazily, sweating through their makeup. He thought of Steve, perfumed and pristine, sitting on the Tube or already at a bar chatting to someone. Steve, who had arrived like the spring, painfully, changing everything with his provoking warmth, his beauty, who stepped in and out of Peter's cage like it didn't exist, who argued that it didn't exist: *Half the bloody church, Peter.* All that. Steve who was getting bored, who was elsewhere.

Peter felt his rice and meat settling, looked down at his belly. He'd put on black jeans and a black top. Even when he wasn't working, that's what he would put on. He noticed that these two blacks didn't match. The jeans were older than the top; their dye had grayed in the wash. It made him think something, about dailiness, about time spent. The sadness of laundry. Clothes laboring through the wash week after week. *The sadness of laundry! Listen to yourself. Just write your sermon, pray, and go to bed.*

The phone rang, stalling him in his seat. He let it bleat and bleat until the answerphone came on. After his own voice apologizing for his absence: "Hello, this is Steve . . ." No, it wasn't. It was the wrong Steve, a non-Steve. "I'm Jack's father, from football. I thought I'd ring you because I'm not happy, really, with the way things went this afternoon. What you did wasn't . . . it just wasn't the right call. Jack wasn't guilty and I think you know that, more than you could let on at the time anyway. I sort of wanted to clear the air and just get things straight with you. I've got a very upset lad here and it'd be nice to tell him it'll be all right next time. Maybe you can call—" the machine cut him off with a long beep. In the silence afterward Peter said out loud, "Now go away."

Perhaps he had made his decision quickly and perhaps the evidence had been circumstantial, but a decision had to be made and he was the referee. Also, he'd sensed Jack's guilt; he knew it was there. If he hadn't been guilty at that precise moment, he had been at others and would be again. He was selfish and superb, a greedy player. The boy needed punishing.

Toilet, toothbrushing, prayers, and in. He read for a bit before turning the light out and wondered when he would feel the bed sink under Steve's satisfied weight—alcohol in his bloodstream, semen in his belly—if he would feel it or whether by then he'd be too far gone.

He woke with Steve's arm over him, Steve's mouth against the back of his neck, breathing warmly onto his spine. The back of Steve's hand was blotched with the stamp of a nightclub. He lifted the arm and exited as through a door. Steve rolled onto his back, chewing and murmuring in his sleep.

Peter left early. He liked to be the first person at his church. This was hard to do: his verger, Bill, also liked to be first with his keys, round-shouldered, busy, in possession of the place. Peter walked through a glorious autumn morning. The trees and cars were radiant, their edges haloed with soft sunlight. The fallen leaves were dry, skittering along the pavement in the breeze. Pigeons called from bright aerials, twanging them as they took flight.

St. John the Evangelist's was a thick-looking Edwardian church of polychrome brick. It was homely, not beautiful, heavy and earnest and suburban. If he could have chosen his parish church, Peter would have preferred something medieval, something with the ghost of its Catholic past hovering just under the whitewash, something with a hint of the monastic, maybe a preserved anchorite's cell. Still, St. John's greeted him with its solid familiarity as he approached.

Someone must have forgotten to put out the sand bucket for the alcoholics last night; the doorway was littered with cigarette butts. He knelt to pick them up. That felt good: a mild abasement. The butts were bent, dingy, sadly human. He filled his left palm with them and unlocked the door. First the bin in the vestry to throw them away, then to wash the ash and odor from his hands. Stepping into the church proper, he received the unfailing shock of the sight of the cross over the altar, that jolt delivered by its strong bare shape, by its meaning. He repeated the shape onto his chest with his fingertips, sinking to his knees. In an empty pew at the front of the church, with the noise of occasional cars beyond the glowing windows, he prayed. When Bill arrived, brisk and muttering, a crinkling carrier bag in his hand, banging on the lights, he heard him fall satisfyingly silent out of respect. He gave it a minute more then stood up, smiling. "Good morning, William."

His standard Sunday congregation was decent, about forty souls, including the three African ladies who sat in a row under their hats, smiling, and the Davises who sat at the front, either side of young Natalie. She remained placid and bored and pleased with herself, quite still under the arch of her Alice band and long, thoroughly brushed hair. Only her feet swung back and forth impatiently, counting the minutes away.

Peter had honestly tried for a while not to have a church voice but it proved impossible. His normal voice wouldn't carry. To be audible and dignified he needed that slow ceremonial sound. He heard himself go into it at the beginning of the liturgy and it ran like a machine. He could let it function, could feel the motions of his mouth, while up behind his eyes he looked around and thought. It was thus, entering the choreography of the service and delivering solid, meaningful words, that he watched the new couple enter. The man was nervous, tiptoeing with his hands raised, in a pink polo shirt and jacket. He grimaced, baring his teeth as he maneuvered into place. His wife looked pretty and was, as Peter's mother would have put it, "in full sail," decidedly pregnant, her face soft and round, tan with makeup. So that was why they were here. They'd be wanting to make use of Reverend Peter's services, arriving late enough in her pregnancy not to have to suffer too much church and soon enough to seem willing. They settled slowly at the back.

Peter spoke and sang. The rhythm of the ritual took hold, appeased him. He saw it take hold of the congregation also. Shaking hands with them at the door afterward they were clean and light, not quite tired, glazed with smiles as they were let out into the Sunday quiet. The new couple, having watched everything including the exit of all the others, were the last out.

"New faces. I'm delighted you joined us. I'm Reverend Peter."

The man smiled, but differently to the regulars, as though amused at the thought of meeting a vicar at all, as though this too were part of a show. His fingers were short and heavy, his grip tight. A builder, maybe. His head was set low over high, muscular shoulders. A small gold stud, caught by the sun, shone in one earlobe.

"Nice to meet you. I'm Rob. This is my wife, Cassie."

Cassie reached her small hand forward and smiled with a little scrunch of her nose. "Lovely to meet you, Vicar."

"I see you're expecting a happy event, the happiest event."

"That's right," Rob replied. "Fact, that's sort of why we came."

"Yes, I rather thought it might be."

"We want to get her started right. And we are local. We live just down by the Peugeot garage."

"Well, just call the number on the sign and we'll arrange to meet and talk about it. There are things to discuss for a christening."

"Ah, that's terrific. Thanks, Father."

"It is, indeed. Another soul saved."

Rob smiled, his head swaying slightly. "Exactly."

Peter watched them walk away. Rob hadn't gone five yards before he pulled a cigarette from his pocket and lit up, his smoke a lovely blue rising over his shoulder.

Peter stretched across the bed to turn the radio down. Rolling on his back, he shucked off both shoes and settled his hands behind his head to watch Steve dress.

"I've got a new congregant."

"Oh yes?"

"Think you'd like him, actually. Terribly butch."

"Is she now?"

Peter would never mention this, but sometimes Steve reminded him of his grandfather. It was the length and flatness of his back, perhaps stiffening now with middle age. That long plane made his proportions strange when he leaned forward from his waist to look through the drawer: it was straight all the way up the back of his neck.

"Are you trying to make me jealous?"

"Would I ever do that to you?"

Steve dropped his towel: brief, matter-of-fact nudity, determinedly unarousing. He kept his back to Peter. His buttocks twitched together, hollowing at their sides, when he pulled up his Y-fronts. He sat on the edge of the bed to put on his socks. Now, standing again in his underwear, he looked childish, like a sexy little boy.

"Do you have to go out tonight?"

"And what are you doing?"

"Youth mission."

"So you're out?"

"I'll be back by nine."

Steve raised his eyebrows, disbelieving.

"All right, nine-thirty. It shouldn't be later than that."

"Oh, I'm sure. So you want me to sit here and wait for you?"

"You know what I mean."

Steve chose a shirt from the wardrobe, unbuttoned the top, and angled it carefully off the hanger. He slid his arms into it.

"Fine, fine." Peter gave up. "Not tonight then. But we should do something one of these nights. I should come with you."

"No, you shouldn't."

"What do you mean?"

"Not exactly your scene, dear. And what if someone should see you?"

Peter hadn't apologized because he wasn't wrong so there was no need to. The ball flew high over his head. He always loved that moment, the purity and stillness of it, the ball in another element, silently traveling over the noise below. It sank toward the green. Jack blocked it down with the side of his boot, turned on the spot, and looped past the defender. Peter ran toward him, feeling Jack's father's gaze fastened on him. Jack ran three strides and struck the ball cleanly. It shot up, humming, into the top left corner of the goal and Jack stopped still with his arms raised as his teammates rushed toward him. When they'd gone, Peter patted him on the shoulder. Jack turned round startled, shrugged the vicar's hand from his shoulder, and ran away. Another boy shouted, "You taking sides now, ref?" Peter shook his head, back in the game. "Backchat. Don't make me warn you twice."

Rob waved as he and Cassie arrived. They sat at the back of the congregation as though still interlopers. Cassie pulled up her bra straps beneath her blouse, settling her heavy breasts. Rob murmured something to her and they both, simultaneously, turned their faces up to Peter. Through the ceremony they were calm and amiable but as if not quite getting the point. They looked continuously expectant, like children awaiting the end of a magic trick that never arrived. Every week they sat like that until they were released into the real world of air and cars and food and TV.

Rob was larger than Peter had remembered. Perhaps he went to the gym. Certainly he had the big cylindrical thighs of a bodybuilder. They held him up on the bulk of himself, as though he couldn't ever properly sit down. Briefly, Peter glanced at his crotch, at his trouser front clogged with his member. Cassie's ringed hand rested on her belly. They looked peaceful, animal, comfortably thoughtless. Rob caught Peter's eye for a hot moment and confused Peter by giving him an inappropriate encouraging nod.

The following week Peter thought that Rob looked hungover. He sat with his arms folded, his drained gray face tilted back, observing proceedings from under half-closed eyelids. At the door he excused himself. "Bit dicky today. Must've been the takeaway last night." He rubbed his stomach to illustrate but Peter wasn't having it.

"I'm sure it was. You can't always trust them, can you? Temperance. Temperance in all things." That was a foolish choice of word he'd heard himself say twice. Quite probably Rob didn't know what it meant.

. . .

He'd chosen the wrong moment to go to the shop. Peter was surrounded by schoolchildren in loud groups. They wandered erratically across the pavement in front of him, shrieking at each other, stepping off into the gutter, oblivious to oncoming cars. Before he could pay for his milk, bread, and baked beans, he had to wait behind a few of them as they bought the sugary drinks and sweets that shook their concentration into a useless noisy fizz. He rolled his eyes at the shopkeeper, who didn't respond, seemed confused, in fact.

As Peter was leaving the shop, a man entering greeted him. It took Peter a moment to recognize Rob because Rob was wearing a suit. He'd made the standard after-work adjustment: top shirt button undone, tie pulled a little loose. Peter hadn't thought of Rob as someone who would need to wear a suit for work.

"It's Rob, isn't it?"

"That's right."

Peter often ran into parishioners when he was out and actually quite liked to. It was contact that required only his fluent, professional self, and it made the world sometimes cheerful and friendly, familiar.

"How are you? How's . . ."

"Cassie?"

"Yes, I was going to say Cassie."

"She's diamond. Really well. Won't be long now."

"No, I suppose it can't be."

"It's a big relief, to be honest, Reverend. Cassie, she, um, she miscarried a couple of times."

"Oh. Oh, I'm sorry to hear that."

"Yeah. Well. So. So, we're properly excited."

"I'm sure you must be."

"Here, I've got a scan I carry around I can show you."

"Oh, don't worry."

"No, no, it's just here." Rob pulled a folded piece of paper from his wallet and handed it to Peter. "It's a little girl."

Peter looked at the faint white swirl, the luminous bones, the brighter white of its heart and spine. "A little girl, is it?"

"Yes. There." Rob pointed with the nail of his little finger. "That blob there is her heart beating away."

"Yes, I thought it was. You must be very happy."

"We are. Anyway, I'll let you get on. We're seeing you next week, aren't we, to talk through arrangements?"

"That's right."

"Great." Full of his fatherhood, full of his ordinary joy, Rob gave Peter a friendly pat on the shoulder as he left the shop. Peter looked back at him and tried to smile.

Peter walked slowly to football. It was no longer a release for him, a clearing onto which he stepped once a week to move in light and air. Now it was something else that opposed him, another place of solitude without freedom. Dimly he knew that it was his fault, that his personality had seeped out and somehow stained it all.

The day was chilly also, the pitch heavy and stiff. Wind hustled the trees. Cold rain flung across and stopped, started again. The ground was waterlogged near the center circle. Running through it, the boys' boots stamped up flashes of water that soaked their socks. They played slowly. Jack was impatient, working with more energy and will than the other boys. Peter watched his frustration and indulged the temptation to thwart him further. Three times when Jack had received the ball and was ready to start on one of his glorying flights toward goal, balanced and expert, his hair fetchingly lifted by the wind, Peter blew for offside. It was satisfying to snap the leash and watch him stop, letting the ball roll from his feet, unused. *You're not going anywhere.* He knew he was doing it, that the offsides were marginal at best, and he heard confirming voices of protest from the sidelines. So he wasn't surprised after the game when Jack's father, his face and voice by now so familiar, approached and said, "Look, I don't know what it is but you've got some sort of a problem."

"I'm not sure I know what you're talking about."

"Don't use your posh voice on me. If you don't know, that only makes it worse. I'm not saying you're funny with kids."

"You better not be. That would be, that would be."

"I'm not saying that. What I'm saying is that there's something about you and Jack. I've asked him. He said there's no funny business whatever. Point is, I've got a good lad here, a good player, and he's not getting a chance to develop. I've found somewhere else for him, a Sunday league game he can play in. So you won't be seeing us again."

Peter regarded the man with narrowed eyes, that face so familiar now, the small blue eyes, the sprouting chest hair at his collar. "I have to say I'm relieved," he said eventually.

"You what?"

"Jack's a little cheat, isn't he? Can't trust him to play properly at all. It'll be nice to get rid of him. The game will be much improved."

"Now, listen." Jack's father jabbed a pointing finger at Peter then shook his head, giving up. "If you weren't a man of the cloth, seriously . . ."

He turned and walked away.

Off the grid. That was how Peter thought of himself when he lost contact with God, when Jesus was a dead man and he was alone. Then the world was vast and contained nothing, nothing real, only his loneliness between hard surfaces. How long he spent like this was a secret kept between him and God, and of all his secrets this was the most private. Of course this all belonged in the category of "doubt," which was integral to faith and sounded strong and simple, even heroic, in the spiritual lives of others. But for Peter right now it meant sitting alone in his house with the radio on, the light coming down, leftover baked beans hardening on his plate, and his soul shriveling inside him like a slug on salt. It meant thinking of Steve out there, loose in the gusty evening city. It meant wanting Steve and Steve not wanting him back.

Sometimes Peter wished for ordinary things, ordinary thoughts. He could have had what the others were having, had he been born that way. But this, apparently, was not what was destined for him.

Peter was angry with loneliness the day Rob and Cassie came to his office to discuss the christening. He sat them down without offering drinks, watched their gazes travel nervously around his bookshelves and religious images, unable to settle.

"You see, this is something to be taken very seriously. Nothing more seriously in fact. Now, I know that I serve a function. I know that's what I do as far as some people are concerned."

"Sorry, I don't follow."

Peter stared. "People need me for this and that, to get their children into the good church schools, to visit the elderly relatives they can't be bothered to see and so on. But I have to insist, I am a servant of God, of Our Lord Jesus Christ, and He demands faith and respect—"

"I understand," Rob cut in. "It's a stressful job. You're stressed."

Cassie rolled forward over her belly. "Highly strung," she suggested, and lapsed back.

"That's not what I'm saying, actually."

"And I promise you," Rob went on, "we're not taking the mick in any way. We're here—aren't we, Cass?—because we want things done right for our little girl." Here he reached across and rested his hand lightly on his wife's belly.

"Well, good. That's good." Peter felt a stab of envy: that was what it was. Recognizing it, his anger gave way. He felt his body soften with contrition, humiliation. He could behave better toward them now he knew. "That's good. That's what we want to hear. So, I'll take you through the ceremony, what we'll be doing."

He made them a cup of tea and they talked on. A rain shower

rang against the window. It made the room they were in a hushed small shelter. Peter felt close to them. He felt kind.

He walked home under lit streetlights and a mildly exhilarating sky of cold silver and long colored clouds where the sun was setting. Water clucked in the drains. The small trees shone. When he got in and found that Steve wasn't in he didn't pause. He changed his shirt and jacket and went out after him, walking to the station against the flow of returning commuters, tired and grim but still moving at a tough city speed. He sat in an almost empty carriage through the long, rattling journey out of the suburbs and down under the ground.

He emerged in the West End and realized that he hadn't been into town for months. It was dark now. The place was full of entertainments. It had lost its daylight shape and now was structured by its fantasies, by the floating lit signs for different shows and shops, restaurants and bars. The people there all moved toward them or poured away around him down into the station. The traffic was loud. A bus shuddered in front of him. He walked to the street with all the gay bars, to one in particular he knew Steve visited. The street was already full, men everywhere, smoking outside the bars, talking into their phones, laughing, watching. Their hard bodies inside their T-shirts. He passed close to some to get inside once he'd found the place. He could smell them. He kept his gaze low. The music was horribly loud. Its bass thumped right through him like a new and panicking heartbeat, overruling his own. He walked around, couldn't find Steve, and realized he was relieved. What would he have said? He sat at the bar. He could see it all happening from there, could see the desire creeping out between the men. He ordered gin and tonic, wanting to be adult there, wanting to be strict and colonial.

He drank several with a few thoughts beating in his head, like: how different this place must look in the mornings, with the lights on when the cleaners arrive, or: look at that one. The lights in there were strips of blue. Skin looked violet. Cheekbones were sharply shadowed. All this alien beauty. He drank more, expecting Steve finally to walk in. The place filled with more men but Steve did not arrive. Someone materialized next to Peter, a man of about his own age. He wore a white shirt. He looked round at him, at the shape of his shaved head, then let him slide out of view again, but the man put his hand on Peter's. He brought his face close and shouted through the music.

"It's not that terrible, is it? Tell Auntie what's wrong."

"Nothing's wrong."

"If you say so. All alone, though. Gloomy."

"Why do we have to do this?"

"Don't know what you mean."

"All this. Why do we have to do this?"

"We don't have to, duckie. We like it. I bet you do too."

"Is that enough? Is that right?"

"Isn't it enough?"

"People don't care. They're not ashamed."

"Quite right. Absolutely shameless."

"Your hand's on my thigh."

"What?"

"Your hand's on my leg."

"Is that where I left it? Shameless of me."

"It's not . . . we don't have to."

"But we like it. Why don't you come with me a minute? I want to show you something."

Back at home in the bathroom, Peter took off his shirt, splashed cold water up into his armpits and over his face. He brushed his teeth, rinsed his mouth with mouthwash. He took his clothes off and left them on the floor. He went to bed. Steve was waiting for him.

"Hello," he said.

"Hello."

"Where've you been? Blimey, you actually smell of drink."

Peter pulled the quilt over his shoulder, lay on his side with Steve behind him. "I went looking for you."

"I see. Did you find me?"

"No."

"That's a bit sad. Did you have a good time, though?"

"No. Did you?"

"Not really. Awful, actually. Place is full, everywhere's full of just children really."

Peter reached behind him and took hold of Steve's wrist, lifted his arm over him, wanting to close that door again.

"Think of you. Out and about."

"Can't we just go to sleep?"

They weren't there. Natalie's feet ticked back and forth beneath the pew. They were gone, as they had said they would be, to have their baby. Imagine that, the lavish TV drama of it: hospital and pain and beeping monitors, the birth of their baby girl, the tears, the child wrapped in a soft blanket and placed in their trembling hands.

Rob and Cassie had filled the church for the christening. The pews creaked with that laden, seafaring sound that Peter liked. He looked out over the solid formation of their family and friends, the women tanned to varying shades, the men's hair glinting with gel. Rob and Cassie were meek and well behaved, perhaps because they knew Peter's moods and were nervous that all should go well. But for the rest of them, this was a day out, a souvenir experience, and he couldn't reasonably ask more of them. He reminded himself of that and his anger flared during the service only when, with the godparents, they smirked at having to repeat that they rejected the Devil. Christianity: good for horror films, good for a laugh. He stared them down.

The moment that he was waiting for, that he was dreading, arrived. Rob and Cassie's baby, to be named, with surprising good taste, Harriet Sarah, kicking her feet up inside the crisp white cotton of her gown, was placed carefully into his hands. A heaviness swelled in his stomach. It rolled up his spine, flooded his brain. He laid the beautiful small weight of her along his left forearm. Her eyes widened, struggling to focus, as her forehead rolled against his stole. The plush red triangle of her mouth opened as she breathed. The skin of her cheeks was glossy, her eyebrows faint and delicate. A baby. A baby in his arms. The Edwardian font swaying in front of him now seemed dangerously hard and massive. He placed his right hand gently on the soft throb of her belly. To have one, to be a father. He yearned as he stared down at her, feeling sweat run through his thin hair. He glanced up, and the sight of the people standing and waiting shocked the liturgy back into his mind. He said what he had to say. Then, his fingers wet with holy water, he saw a way to disrupt the sweetness of the moment, to release himself. He dipped his fingers again and painted as much water as he could carry onto her head. She looked confused and squirmed against him. He reached for more to apply the horizontal bar of the cross and did so with as heavy a touch as he dared. She rolled her eyes, shrank down into herself then expanded, screaming. Cassie took a step forward.

"Is she all right?"

"What? She's fine. This always happens." Peter felt sweat trickling down his right side from his armpit, cold at his waist. "Water's a bit cold."

"Here, I'll take her."

"She's fine. She's fine. Please."

Peter, with difficulty, with clumsy hands, opened his front door, stepped over an ugly splash of pizza leaflets, and went and made himself a cup of tea. He put on Radio 3. He took his cup to a chair by the window that he never normally sat in and waited for his pulse to slow. The music was orchestral, late Romantic, with a winding melody that rose to mild crises of percussion and brass. It did have a calming effect sitting there out of place, a little outside of himself, somewhere not soiled with familiarity. The day beyond the window was steady: parked cars, a width of road, the house fronts opposite.

Lying in bed he heard Steve's key in the door, the light metallic scraping. His stale anxiety woke again inside him; it felt as though Steve were fitting his key loosely into Peter's chest, turning him over. He switched on the light and sat up. He heard Steve's tread on the stairs. Then the strong reality of him entering the room—always sudden, always shocking, however long imagined and expected. But this time Steve looked miserable. His shoulders drooped. His gaze was low. He stood as if a bucket of something had been tipped over his head.

"What's wrong?"

"What's wrong?" Steve sighed. He wiped the side of his face as though clearing tears. "I'm old," he said. "I'm too old."

"Oh, baby. I'm sorry."

"Course you are. Are you? You shouldn't be."

"I am. I am. Come here."

Steve walked over and sat on the edge of the bed. Peter stroked his shoulders, gripped them, swayed him back and forth, and pulled him down so that his head lay in his lap.

"Sad old boy. Come here."

"Hmm."

"Are you sorry? Are you sorry for what you've done?" Peter took hold of his earlobe and pulled gently, increasingly.

"Look, if you're going to . . ." Steve started to get up but Peter pressed down on the side of his head, keeping him there.

"Ow. If you're gonna . . ."

"Shh. I'm sorry. I won't." He stroked the soft hair at his temple.

Steve stared, saying nothing, then: "Course, I'm bloody sorry."

"Shh. It's all right. Poor old boy. Don't worry. Don't worry. I'm here."

Peter stroked down Steve's cheek, following the line a razor would take, then over to his mouth, feeling the warm breath from his nostrils. With his forefinger he strummed Steve's lips. Steve didn't resist.

"We're all right, though, aren't we?"

Leslie Parry

The Vanishing American

THE BUFFALO arrived on the island at daybreak.

From where he stood, on the deck of a seaside hotel built by a chewing-gum baron, Indian #9 watched as crates were lowered from the ship by toady, copper-necked men in wool. Back inside, the other actors were still in bed, comatose and saddlesore, but Indian #9 had lain awake all night, listening to the waves sucking at the sand below. In a few hours he'd be in bronzer and a wig, mouthing his very first line of dialogue to the excited crank of the camera. He'd risen early and crept down to the washroom to practice his expressions in the shaving mirror, but the sight of his face had only made him more nervous, so he'd gone up to the deck to catch a glimpse of the animals instead. Pulleys lurched and squealed as the crates, each as big as an automobile, swung off the ship and rocked above the water. He saw blue snouts blossom between the planks and nuzzle the sunlight, twitching at the fetor of seaweed that lay scrapped on the beach in black, wormy festoons.

Soon, back home at the DeLuxe Theatre, everyone would see him speak again—his mother, his sister, the neighbors—all crowded onto those stained velveteen seats, squinting through the roiling dust at his face, two stories high. And here was his costar, ferried like a treasure through the rough and stinging surf, borne ashore in a box stamped PROPERTY OF PARAMOUNT STUDIOS.

Indian #9's voice was gassed out of him in a trench in the Argonne Forest. After the war he'd left Chicago and come to California; with no voice, he decided to seek work in the movies. Because of his bulk—broad shoulders, bullish jaw, fists as big as pumpkins—he'd spent the past few months playing bad guys, all scowls and grimaces and bared teeth. A wrinkle had formed between his eyes from looking mean all the time, and the burglar makeup had started to leave permanent raccoon stains around his eyes. He rented a little bachelor suite on McCadden, with a view of the Chinese laundry and a tattoo parlor. His day jobs were always a quick ride away, down in the flatlands of Hollywood or up the Cahuenga Pass. But this role was different. He'd traveled out to Catalina Island and stayed overnight with a millionaire's view of the sea. He'd nabbed his first line, and his very own intertitle. (His mother had seen everything he'd ever been in, but between the well-traveled prints and her runny, myopic eyes, she'd never managed to distinguish him among the gray swarm of bodies on-screen.) All night he'd flopped nervously on the hotel sheets, flexing his lips over his teeth, working his tongue over each syllable, imagining what the words would look like when they were projected—a giant, luminous stanza, so tall it would touch the toes of the griffins on the theater proscenium.

If he were in Chicago now, he'd be in his old fleece jacket and too-small hat, prying slabs of ice from the steps of the boarding-house, haggling with Zielke over their account at the delicatessen. But here the air was damp and fragrant, rich with brine and euca-lyptus and cactus flowers. Last night he'd begun a letter to Private Olivieu about his new role—how the buffalo had been shipped all the way from the Dakotas, how he'd even met a real Chumash

Indian on set, a mummy-faced old man who smelled like sage and tinned beef. That's the kind of stuff Olivieu would like—Olivieu, who used to keep him awake in the bivouac at night with stories about vigilante sharpshooters felling hot-air balloons from the sky, or an elephant that escaped from the Bronx Zoo and was found paddling merrily down the Hudson, all the way to the Statue of Liberty. It was hard to tell if anything Olivieu said was actually true or not, but when that lilting voice started up in the cot beside him, Indian #9 always listened in spite of himself, laughing softly into the grain of his rucksack. Private Olivieu could rattle off the name and caliber of every pistol fired at the O.K. Corral, and claimed to have had a short, spectacular career as a one-man band on the Cincinnati vaudeville circuit. It was Olivieu, more than anyone, who would love the idea of him masquerading in feathers in front of the camera. His sister had only written, *Why didn't they make you a cowboy instead?*

Inside, the other actors stirred; soon he'd walk back into a sweet-smelling fog of aftershave and cigarettes. But no matter how many pleasantries they shared during morning ablutions—a casual word while they mopped their chins and slicked their hair—this was not the army. They stood side by side, polite but distant. They gazed aloofly out the window and waited for telegrams from girls they would see the following week. They practiced calisthenics alone on the deck. They sipped coffee from monogrammed teacups and sniffed over the latest issue of *Screenland*. Sometimes Indian #9 wondered if their averted eyes, their bored, inward sighs, the habitual checking of their pocket watches, didn't somehow hinge on him—maybe the fact that he couldn't speak had, in a way, silenced everyone else.

On the esplanade below, the crew was starting to load the equipment into trucks. They took swigs from canteens and joked mildly in the early light. Indian #9 thought he heard the buffalo bleat in their cages—a stuttering, tuneless rumble, like a motor that wouldn't start.

Someone sidled up next to him and leaned over the balustrade. "I read somewhere that bison tongues were once used as hairbrushes."

He looked over to see a young man about his age, freshly awake, sipping a cup of coffee and staring out at the water. Indian #9 turned around to see whom he was talking to, but there was no one else there.

The man breathed in the steam from his coffee and sighed. "Their skin was made into factory belts, too."

Indian #9 stared at him—bathrobed, blond hair sleepily askew, bare feet turning pink on the cold granite. Now began the long, uneasy pause when he was supposed to answer. This man would expect gruffness from him, a baritone. Back before the war, Indian #9 had delivered newspapers to the stoops of Ashland Avenue, and his voice had echoed richly among the chatter of sewing machines and wash-line arias. But now he could only sigh and hiss and pop his lips, like a sputtering spigot someone forgot to turn off. (The last word he spoke, right before the gas, had been a retort to one of Olivieu's stories: *baloney.* That's it. Sometimes he woke up at night, stuttering and apoplectic. *Baloney?* He couldn't think of anything more than that?)

Delicately he cleared his throat, put on his "thoughtful" face, and offered the man an awestruck whistle, a rolling wheel of sound: *No kidding!*

"Did you know a baby bison can stand up just minutes after it's born?" The man turned and smiled at him. His eyes were gray and wet, like summer storm clouds. A stray curl stood up from his forehead. Indian #9 whistled again, this time ascending, a question: *Is that so?* But under the man's hot, dewy gaze, it came out warbling and thin.

"In a few hours they're able to walk. Then, a few hours later, they can run." He swirled his coffee and looked back to the sea. "From the day they're born, they're running."

Indian #9 drummed his fingers awkwardly on the balustrade.

He wished he could say something wry or profound at this point, but all he heard was the air rattling in and out of his throat. He dropped his hands and twisted them deep into his pockets. The water disappeared from view as he turned, red-faced, away. Before he knew it, he was loping back toward the terrace doors, staring at the granite passing underfoot. Everything seemed very bright and far away, as if he were watching the scene from a great height. He wanted to look back, but he couldn't; his body was stricken, his whole face alive with heat.

So he went back inside and finished his letter, in a firm hand on thick hotel stationery, then put it in his suitcase next to the others, all bundled and unsent, and thought about how the movie stars, who were waking, would really have tickled Olivieu, who was dead.

Indian #9 had only been on a horse once before, as a boy. Every year around Easter the gangsters would arrive on Ashland with gifts for the children: a morning of maple cakes, magic tricks, and pony rides. They even hired a real photographer to take portraits of the kids against a canvas backdrop, atop a horse named War Paint. As a boy, one gangster in particular had fascinated him—not the garlicky, potbellied giants who kissed the mothers' cheeks and slipped dollar bills into their aprons—but the reedy one who hung back near the photography booth, smoking perfumed ciga-rettes and blotting his eyes with a handkerchief. This man, ashen but handsome, helped Indian #9 into the saddle—those gentle hands hooked under his armpits; that silk suit flashed like water in the sun. Indian #9, mortified by his own cardboard shoes (made from a cereal box and tied with butcher string), refused to put his feet in the stirrups. He waited while the picture was snapped, the gangster's hand hovering behind him to keep him from falling, his mother smiling delightedly behind the camera. Then the gangster helped him down again, and their eyes met—a moment of frank, silent, unhurried recognition—until Indian #9, nauseous with a perplexing shame, broke away and ran into the crowd. When he looked back, the gangster was alone, standing apart from the revelry. He lit a cigarette, and his hands were so delicate and white they seemed to disappear in the sunlight, until only a disembodied bulb of tobacco glowed. The kids called him *il fantasma*.

Back then Indian #9 was teased constantly—for his strawlike arms and chicken legs, for shoes that turned to pulp in the rain, for a hand-me-down coat that had belonged to his sister, for trundling home from Mr. Zielke's with groceries too heavy to carry, his cheeks red and slimy with sweat. A long-lashed, leaky-nosed mama's boy. The only way to survive, he thought, was to change. So he started lifting paint cans in the dead scrub grass of the yard, swimming the canals during the summer, eating his bread with a pat of lard coaxed from the side of the frying pan. Whenever his father stumbled home, Indian #9 would earn a few pennies stashing empty gin bottles in the neighbors' trash, and with the money he bought strongman elixirs from hawkers on the street—a few spoonfuls were supposed to make him big enough to lift a horse. He thought it would make a difference, this new brawn, but instead the other kids steered away from him, their faces narrow and suspicious. And when he pushed his paper wagon through the soggy streets at dawn—bumping one hundred pounds of *Daily Trib*s through the gutters—he lobbed them so hard against the houses that they left ink stains on the wood, a row of black eyes to greet the morning.

After breakfast he went downstairs to be fitted for his costume. In the lobby he caught a glimpse of the director, holding court among the cigar smoke and potted palms, a straw hat throwing checkered shadows over his face. Indian #9 wondered if he should approach him and introduce himself, but his stomach felt tight and he decided not to. Some people seemed to think that because his tongue had stopped, his brain had, too. If they met his eyes, they'd smile bashfully, apologetically, then find an excuse to look away.

Until now his roles hadn't required much, just a certain thuggery. After takes, he'd grown used to slapping steaks against his eye, or wincing as slivers of glass were tweezed from his knuckles. Today there were no stunts, though. Just his face—and he wasn't sure what to do with it. He worried it would be obvious, fake— the audience would be able to tell he wasn't really speaking. If they could read the actors' lips, maybe they could read their muscles, too. In close-up, they'd be able to measure the roll of his jaw and swell of his chest. He couldn't quite remember how far he should open his mouth. He should show his teeth, perhaps—that would look natural and be a nice contrast to his dark bronzer—but he shouldn't gape so wide that the corners of his mouth were pulled clownishly back to his ears.

In the dressing room he stood in front of the mirror while two girls stitched him into his costume. They giggled and eyed him from beneath their pasted lashes. *You're the one in the buffalo scene?* He nodded and they turned pink, right up to the roots of their molded, antiseptic-smelling curls. *The hero,* they purred, cinching the pants tighter around his waist. He held his breath and stared ahead, avoiding their coy smiles and peals of laughter, the way they licked and bit the thread. These girls found his silence rugged and masculine, the wound of some mysterious hardscrabble life, and the less he said, the more they blushed. Their awkward attempts at sultriness, as their fingers slid over him, made him feel (even so many years later) embarrassed by his body and what it invited. He stared at his face in the mirror and tried to concentrate on his line. Returning to Chicago after the war, he'd had trouble sleeping, so in the middle of the night he'd take a few scraps of paper into the bathroom, scribble down the lines he'd seen at the movie house that week, and try to re-create the faces of John Gilbert or Lionel Barrymore in the mirror. It was the only time he had to himself, those nights, away from the nervous energy of his mother. She spent her days soft-shoeing through the rooms, drawing long ski-like tracks against the grain of the rug, and cooking him soft food—rice in cold milk, scrambled eggs—nothing to crack or grind, as if the noise in his head would torment him. She and his sister would confide in low tones in the back of the flat, out on the porch where the laundry flew—as though any sound at all would startle him, remind him just what he'd lost. Sometimes they would look at him—lean and wasting, smoking his cigarettes through the kitchen window—and turn their brimming eyes away.

The girls kept him late at the fitting, and when he motioned that he was getting a ride up to the set with the wrangler, one of them said, "I'll go with you—they need one of us up there," and began packing her sewing kit.

While she adjusted her eyelashes in the mirror, Indian #9 walked ahead, out to the bleached esplanade where the truck was waiting. The wrangler, shouldering coils of rope and costume harnesses, closed up the trailer and waved him into the cab. The air inside was pungent with horse sweat, leather, and grassy manure. The girl climbed in after him and pretended to slip; she pouted and sighed until he offered her a hand up. He'd met this kind of girl before—nice complexion but bad teeth, kittenish but sloppy—not poised enough to be in front of the camera; and too artless to know the difference between vanity and mystique. She smiled up at him, her eyes heavy and shy, one false lash already curling up at the end. He stared at the naked smear of glue on her lid.

From up the road someone whistled. "Hey, hold up!" Through the windshield he saw the blond man jogging toward them. Those gray eyes lifted to meet his, and suddenly the air in the cab seemed unbearably thick.

"Ooh! We better make room," the girl giggled, climbing into Indian #9's lap. A fake French perfume lifted from her skin. He turned his head away but wasn't sure where to look.

He felt the blond man ease into the seat next to him, and his stomach surged. Squeezed between the two men in their dusty khakis, with the girl nestled in his lap, he could only stare out the windshield as they sputtered up the hill. He gazed at the violet ice plant along the cliffs, out to the faraway scrim of the ocean, hoping for a glimpse of the buffalo. The Spanish-tiled roof of the hotel dropped away, and he remembered the Chumash man recounting how he'd sculpted many of those clay tiles over his knees, until his skin was stained a deep red. The girl chattered on, and even though she twisted subtly against Indian #9's groin, grabbing his thigh with every lurch and turn, he was all too aware of his knee knocking gently against the blond man's—just an accidental brush as the tires waddled and popped over the gravel. Every drop of blood flooded to the hollow of his kneecap. While the girl talked, the blond man turned to him and winked. Indian #9 swallowed drily and half smiled back, wondering what it meant. Was it that he approved of the girl, or disapproved? Or was it something else entirely? He folded his arms across his chest so no one could see how his veins jumped. On the next turn, he pulled his knee away.

The set was just a wild glen between the hills, standing in for the windswept plains of the Middle West. It was the biggest set he'd ever been on—there were no walls or backdrops, just the sky. Normally, back in the city, other movies would be shooting just a few yards away. The noise had always made him feel safe. But here there were no saws and hammers to drown out the directors at their megaphones. No moody violins or traffic rushing past or the cricketlike trill of cameras. He heard only the hiss of the ocean, the wind in the trees. His bronzer was starting to melt away. He stepped up to his mark, and told himself to focus.

Under a white tent, the girl had set to work mending a cigarette burn in another Indian's jacket. Behind the camera, the blond man consulted with the director, who fanned himself peevishly with his straw hat. This director was young, with an expensive

Princeton haircut and plump, inquisitive lips that he kneaded constantly with one knuckle. Beside him the blond man, with uprolled sleeves and well-thumbed suspenders, lifted a viewfinder to frame the scene.

The crew waited patiently in the rising island dust, their arms burned and folded. Indian #9 stood alone in front of the camera. Behind him, the herd of buffalo was hidden in the tall grass. He saw only their brown humps: musky, sun-warm shag tinseled with hay. One of the assistants jogged over and tried to shoo them apart, but they trod stubbornly together, snorting and churning up dirt. Then, nearby, the grasses snapped and flattened, and one of them nosed out into the glen. Indian #9 drew a breath. Instinctively he tried to cry out—his tongue slicked the roof of his mouth—but all he managed was a stupefied rasp. It wasn't the animal he recognized from the nickel, or the covers of Kit Carson dime novels. This buffalo was white, like a cloud, with drowsy, silver-flecked eyes that opened and closed in the warm December sun.

"Jesus Christ, look at that!" shouted the man in the straw hat. "Start it up!" From somewhere came the familiar chirp of the camera. "Now listen up, Number Nine! You're shell-shocked. Delusional. You've just returned home to your tepee. This is the land of your people, but it's not the way it used to be."

Indian #9 knew every twitch of his lips, every blink of his eyes would be magnified. He tried to focus. But still, he never imagined a buffalo to be white. He couldn't stop staring at it.

"You call out to the buffalo! You try to touch it! But it's only a mirage.".

The buffalo drew closer, head bobbing, and snuffled Indian #9's outstretched hand. A hot gust of air shot into his palm—he couldn't believe it. A white buffalo! And its gentleness, the way its frothy nose rooted tenderly around his fingers. He moved his hand up between the horns and sunk it into the thick, kinked mane, which was so bright in the sun he almost had to close his eyes. The buffalo made a noise like a happy sigh, and bowed its head to pull at the dandelions. Indian #9 felt a sharp ache in his heart, whether because it was full or empty he didn't know.

"It's the first time you've seen the homeland in such a state! Now remember, the buffalo is just a figment of your imagination. Make us feel for the old redskin, buddy."

He knew it was silly, but those nights in the tent together, listening to Olivieu's stories, he started to have ideas about where they would go together after the war. Not back to Cincinnati or Chicago. Olivieu had traveled; he spoke often of California, where he lived briefly as a boy. There was a cactus plant, he said, that grew not upright in the air, but sideways along the ground like a snake. *I'm serious! The Indians called it the Creeping Devil.*

Baloney.

"Now maybe put your hand over your heart! Lean forward a little! That's it."

Lately, Indian #9 had been having this dream. Not a dream, exactly, but more like an image—a snatch of film that played over and over in his mind whenever he found himself idle or alone. It was so startlingly clear that at times he was sure it must have happened in life. He was outside in a garden, smoking a pipe in a clean white linen shirt, and for some reason there was a typewriter on a table in front of him, its blank page stirring in the breeze. Beyond him, cantilevered on the hillside, stood Olivieu. He was in his old army pants and gloves, tending to the succulents, framed by their ribs and thorns, blossoms and paws. Birds singing, oranges ripe in the air, the golden sheen of sweat on his arms. As Indian #9 sat there with his pipe, he watched the simple movements of his friend—his concentration, the phantom smiles that crossed his face, the gentle dent in his shoulder that had been carved by a vaudeville kettle drum. Olivieu paused and looked up to the sky—at what? Indian #9 couldn't be sure, but it didn't matter. The shame and beauty of that little fantasy—it kept him going and it weighed him down. And when he finally saw the

Creeping Devil for himself, undulating down the canyons of Hollywood, the first vision he had was of the men in their uniforms, lying twisted on the ground together, a frozen wave of green.

"That's it, buddy! God-*damn*. Now let's see you call out!"

Indian #9 smiled sadly. The word he began to mouth—it wasn't even his line. It was something else entirely. *Olivieu*. And the relief of it made him nearly weep—a breath burned into silver, stored in the dark, hidden in a canister and carried away on the rails, where one day it would be exhaled across a thousand walls of light. It was a strange feeling—safe, but alone—knowing this was a word that could never be read.

And then it was over. They moved on to the next scene. Indian #9 walked in a daze to the tent. He poured himself some water and waited to react. What exactly had happened? His mind raced, struggling to re-create each pantomime, how he'd moved his eyebrows, his mouth, the muscles in his jaw. He couldn't be sure of anything. But then people started coming up to congratulate him. Even the director clapped him on the back: *Good work, pal!* They complimented him on his face, his size, his solemn, wondrous expression. He sat down on one of the benches, light-headed, while the seamstress cooed over him and sniffled unconvincingly into her handkerchief.

As he finished his water and peeled off his jacket, he saw the blond man approaching. Nervously he grabbed for the girl, who squealed and wriggled away. His sister had once sent him clippings of an actor who'd died young—there were accounts of women weeping, fainting, poisoning themselves with arsenic, even trying to climb into the casket. It made him laugh at first, queasily, trying to imagine a theater full of swooning females. *See, see?* he told himself as he caught the seamstress by the wrist and pulled her into his lap. *I can get used to this.*

That night they went down to the cantina on the waterfront.

There was a full moon, a five-piece band, and tequila brought over from Ensenada. He danced with the girl and drank, and for the first time since he moved from Chicago, he felt like he was part of the picture people—not some flat tire returning home at eight o'clock to down a cold pot of coffee and a cheese sandwich. He'd only been to one party before, in a producer's palatial backyard off Franklin, but the smell of chlorine in the swimming pool had sent him into heaves—he'd spent the evening retching uncontrollably in the bathroom, wiping his chin with a prim potpourri-scented hand towel. In the end he'd stumbled home, guided by street-lights, and lain shivering in bed till dawn, staring at the lights of the tattoo parlor and a band of sailors smoking on the sidewalk below.

In the moonlight the girl kissed him sloppily, and he assented. They stumbled back to the hotel together, into the dark dressing room, where they wrestled each other's clothes off between the headdresses and bandoliers. But once their bodies started knocking clumsily together, his bravado left him. The slap and peel of skin seemed base and common, and her moans so lonely and absurd. He shut his eyes and tried to concentrate. She squirmed and panted, her fingers clamping around the rung of a costume rack, but he was distracted by the squeak of the casters, the slosh of tequila in his stomach, her weird, hiccup-like yelps. He ground his teeth together and held his breath and finished with a mute, unsatisfying shudder. Afterward she tried to get him to go back up to her room, saying she had a nice bottle of gin, but he shook his head, miming exhaustion. She smiled and shrugged it off, like any big-city girl who longed for the appearance of sophistication, but he could see the disappointment in her eyes, the resolve clashing with the hurt, and he felt ashamed of what he had done.

He stole upstairs and took a long, hot bath, thinking he'd fall right into bed, but his heart was pounding and he couldn't lie still. He fished around the desk for some stationery and started writing a letter about the buffalo. But it seemed silly and boyish, like a grammar school report; the sentiment came out all wrong. He crumpled up the page and went out to the terrace to watch the sun rise over the island. Everything was good, he told himself—a posh hotel, a pretty girl, and a real step up as an actor.

Still, he couldn't help but think of the buffalo, how they had been left there in the glen overnight, how no one would be going back for them. He had a strange, childish fear that they would be cold, or frightened. But later that day, when the noon ferry, heavy with day players, pulled away from the harbor, he saw them there on the cliff between the flowers and fog, as if they had gathered to watch him go.

When the movie opened on Vine Street, he was first in line for the matinee. His heart swam up in his chest when he saw the title on the marquee: *The Vanishing American*.

In the balcony he sat alone. He barely paid attention to the pageantry, just cracked open peanuts with his teeth and spat the shells on the floor, until his mouth was raw and puckered with salt. He watched the horseback rides, the schoolhouse scenes, the drawn-out duel—all the while leaning forward with his elbows pinned to his knees, as if he could push his way into the next scene. When the music swelled and the final card dissolved, he felt the peanut oil churn in the back of his throat, the crumbs nagging under his tongue. He sat there, tremulous, disbelieving. So he sat through the next show, and the next, but his scene still wasn't there.

He left the theater. The sun was so bright his eyes began to throb. Half-blind, he got on the streetcar and rode it down to Paramount, where he passed a note to the secretary, an owlish woman who cracked her puffy knuckles and eyed him suspiciously before lifting the phone and whispering something into the mouthpiece.

Indian #9 waited, pacing the floor, ignoring the crowd of hopeful day players who craned their heads curiously over their trade papers. There was a strange pressure in his chest—he put his hand there to make sure his heart was still pumping. The secretary got up and shuffled through a door. When she emerged again, she was followed by the blond man. When he saw Indian #9, his eyes flickered almost imperceptibly. The secretary looked annoyed, but the blond man led Indian #9 back through the lot, down cloistered walkways shaded with sawtooth fronds and papery sprays of bougainvillea, into what looked like an editing room—a cramped, dark vault with spotted tiles and a smell that was inky and metallic, like typewriter ribbons. The man pulled a film can from the shelf. All at once he seemed shy, hushed, and wouldn't meet Indian #9's eyes. He pried off the lid and touched the whorl of celluloid, which was raised and fine as a fingerprint. Clearing his throat, he threaded it into the machine and said, "These are the rushes. From the scene in the glen."

On the small hooded screen, a scene flickered to life. Indian #9 saw himself among the grasses, his oiled body glowing in the sun, the buckskin textured and almost tangible, a husky pucker in the smooth and even scenery. He looked good. He looked like he was really speaking. But the buffalo was so white it hadn't even registered. The only thing discernible were its eyes, two damp blots, and the fairy-wing silhouette of its shag.

Something caught in Indian #9's throat. He motioned for the man to play it again. He squinted at the toy vision of himself, dwarfed and sputtering on the screen, his hand petting a milky bruise, calling out to something that wasn't there.

"What is it you're saying?" the blond man asked, leaning in, his breath smelling like cocoa and tobacco. "It looks like you said . . . I love you." He reached out and gently touched Indian #9's hand. Indian #9 stared at the fingers, soft and white against his scarred knuckles, and, trembling, drew his hand away.

The blond man dropped his eyes and turned back to the screen. Slowly, dazedly, he started winding the film back. Indian #9 saw himself move backward across the screen. If he could only keep rewinding. Back, back, back, his whole life in reverse. Back to Olivieu, dropping his hands from his throat and spitting out the gas like an elegant, phosphorous band of smoke. Back to the men in green, soaring up from the mud—a barbed thicket of limbs unraveling, snatching rifles from midair, and landing easily on their feet. Back until he was just a little boy again, the ponies trotting backward around the corner, the flash of the camera disappearing into the photographer's pan, maple cakes bubbling down into lumps of sugar and egg, his shoes restored to a box of corn flakes with a few swipes of his mother's scissors, the ink stains sucked from a neighborhood stoop by a *Tribune* vaulting its way to his outstretched hand—all the way back to the newsprint running tacky and flat up the belts at the mill, the plates lifting the letters from the pages and leaving them white and unblemished, the story yet unwritten.

He looked at the man's downturned head, at the tender divot pulsing behind his reddened ear. Now he knew the silence wasn't a sentence, but a gift. If he could speak again, who knows the things he might say?

Outside the California sun was bright, the sidewalk like glass. It was the height of the afternoon, dusty and busy and ordinary, the street full of people seeking a cool place to lunch. His sadness, as they passed, was something he knew he could never describe. When he returned from the war he had heard it again, in a whisper—but this time the children were looking at him, tall and gaunt, holding his box of relics like a saint (those personal effects and papers, entombed with Olivieu's broken pocket watch). *Look.* They pointed as he walked down the street, as he mounted the steps of his mother's house. Look, they'd said. *Il fantasma.*

Mark Slouka

Crossing

IT WAS RAINING as they drove out of Tacoma that morning. When the first car appeared he could see it from a long way off, dragging a cloud of mist like a parachute, and when it passed he touched the wipers to clear things up and his mind flashed to a scene of a black road, still wet, running toward mountains larded with snow like fatty meat. For some reason it made him happy, and he hadn't been happy in a while. By seven the rain was over. The line of open sky in the east was razor sharp.

He looked over at the miniature jeans, the sweatshirt bunched beneath the seat belt's strap, the hiking boots dangling off the floor like weights. "You okay?" he said. "You have to pee?" He slowed and drove the car onto the shoulder and the boy got out to pee. He looked at him standing on that rise in the brome and the bunchgrass, his little hips pushed forward. When the boy walked back to the car he swung the door open for him, then reached over and pulled the door shut and bumped out on the empty road.

Not much had changed, really. A half hour out of Hoquiam he began to see the clear-cuts through the firs: a strange, white light, as if the world dropped away fifty feet out from the pavement. He hoped the boy wouldn't notice. The two of them had been talking about what to do if you saw a mountain lion (don't run, never run), and what they'd have for lunch. Twenty minutes later they were past it, and the light behind the trees had disappeared.

He'd been at the house by dawn, as he'd promised. He sat in the driveway for a while looking at the yard, the azaleas he'd planted, the grass in the yard beaten flat by the rain. For a long time he hadn't wanted her back, hadn't wanted much of anything, really. He went inside, wiping his shoes and ducking his head like a visitor, and when the boy came running into the living room he threw him over his shoulder, careful not to hit his head on the corner of the TV, and at some point he saw her watching them, leaning against the kitchen counter in her bathrobe, and when he looked at her she shook her head and looked away and at that moment he thought, maybe—maybe he could make this right.

The forest-service road had grown over so much that only his memory of where it had been told him where to turn off. The last nine miles would take them an hour. This is it, kid, the old man would say whenever they turned off the main road, you excited? Every year. The car lurched and swayed, the grass hissing against the undercarriage. He could see him, standing in the river hacking his lungs out, laying out an eighty-foot line. "Almost there," he said to the little boy next to him. "You excited?"

He slowed under the trees to let his eyes adjust and when he rolled down the window the air shoved in and he could hear the white noise of the river. God, how he needed this place, the nests of vines like something scratched out, the furred trunks, soft with rot. He'd been waiting for this a long time. A low vine scraped against the roof. He smiled. Go ahead and scrape, you fucker, he thought, scrape it all.

Eight years. It didn't seem that long. Where the valley widened out he could see what the winter had left behind: the gouged-out pools, the sixty-foot trunks rammed into the deadfalls, the circles of upturned roots like giant blossoms of Queen Anne's lace. A gust of warmer air shoved in: vegetation, sunlight, the slow fire of decay. Sometimes it wasn't so easy to know how to go, how to keep things alive. Sometimes the vise got so tight you could forget there was anything good left in the world. But he'd been talking about this place—the rivers, the elk, the steelhead in the pools—since the boy was old enough to understand. And now it was here. He looked at the water, rushing slowly like flowing glass over car-size boulders nudged together like eggs.

He explained it all as they laid out their things in the mossy parking place at the road's end. The trail continued across the Quinault; they'd ford the river, then walk about three miles to an old settler's barn where they could spend the night. They'd set up their tent inside anyway because the roof was pretty well gone. Of course they'd have a campfire—there was a fire ring right there—and sometimes, if you were quiet, herds of elk would graze in the meadow at dusk.

When they came out of the trees and onto the stony beach he felt a small shock, as if he were looking at a house he'd grown up in but now barely recognized. The river was bigger than he remembered it, stronger; it moved like a swiftly flowing field. He didn't remember the opposite shore being so far off. He stood there, listening to it seething in its bed, to the inane chatter of the pebbles in the shallows, the hollow *tock* of the stones knocking against each other in the deeper water. Downstream, a branch caught in a deadfall reared up like something shot, then tore loose. For a moment he considered pulling out, explaining . . . but there was nowhere else to go. And he'd promised.

"Well there she is," he said.

They took off their packs and squatted down next to each other on the embankment. "You want to take your time, kiddo," he said. "People in a hurry get in trouble." The boy nodded, very serious. He'd bring their packs over and then come right back for him. It would take a little while, but he'd be able to see him the whole time. He'd wave when he got to the other side.

He took off his pants and socks and boots, stuffed the pants and socks into the top of the pack, then tied the boots back on over his bare feet. The boy's weightless blue backpack, fat with his sleeping bag and teddy bear, he strapped to the top as well, then swung the whole thing on his back. No belt. He looked at the boy. "First rule of river crossing—never buckle your waist belt. If you go down, you have to be able to get your pack off as quickly as possible, okay?" The boy nodded. "I'll be right back," he said.

It wasn't too bad. He took it slow, carefully planting the stick downstream with his right arm, resisting the urge to look back. Ten yards out the water rose above his knees and he slowed even more, feeling for the edges of the rocks with his boots, moving from security to security. The heavier current swept the stick before it touched the bottom, making it harder to control, and he began drawing it out and stabbing it down ahead of himself and slightly upstream to make up for the drift, and then he was on the long, gravelly flat and across. He threw down the packs and looked back. The boy was just where he'd left him, sitting on the rocks, hugging his knees. He waved quickly and started back. You just had to be careful. So what do you do if you fall? he remembered asking once—how old could he have been, seventeen?—and the old man calling back over his shoulder, "Don't fuckin' fall."

The second crossing, with the boy on his back, was actually easier. They talked the whole time, and he made his way carefully, steadily, feeling the skinny legs bouncing against his thighs, leaning into the hands buckled across his collarbone, and halfway across, with the hot smell of the pines coming from the shore and the sun strong on his face, he knew he'd made it out the other side. Where had it come from—this slide into weakness, this vision of death like a tunnel at the end of the road and no way to get off or turn around? It didn't matter. Whatever it was had passed. He and his son would be friends. Nothing mattered more.

. . .

The barn was just where he remembered it, standing against the trees like a rib cage. What could they have been thinking, building a barn, here, with ninety inches of rain a year? Its roof was half gone and its floor rotted through but there was something about pitching a tent inside that skeleton that was pretty neat, they agreed, and snapping the compression poles together—always a good trick—he remembered the two of them working together, quietly, easily, then his father crawling into the tent to lay out the sleeping bags. Something about rooms in rooms.

They set up the rain fly just in case, then shined the flashlight at the bats clustered under the peak of the roof, making them squeak like kittens, and went outside to the fire ring. It was a beautiful evening, still and perfect, the sky above the trees deepening to the blue of a butterfly wing he'd once found by the side of a trail in Guatemala, and they took turns eating the macaroni out of the pot (he let him pour in the orange cheese powder) and afterward they fenced with the marshmallow sticks and waved the torches they made against the darkness and when the marshmallows were black and sagging, they pulled out their uncooked hearts and ate them off the wood with their lips and teeth, delicate as horses. At some point it started to rain, and standing in the double door of the barn, the boy on a pile of boards, they could see the shapes of the elk coming into the meadow and they watched, staring into the dark, until the only way you could tell the herd was still there was that every few seconds one would shiver the rain out of its hide, making a small white cloud, like breath. He could hardly make out the boy next to him: now his hand against the dark wood, now the plane of his cheek. "Dad?" he heard him say. "Do the elk have to sleep in the rain?"

"I think they're pretty well used to it," he said.

"You think they're cold?"

"Hard to tell. Wet, anyway."

He put his arm around him—that tiny shoulder, tight as a nest—but, aware of the weight, didn't let it rest completely. And they were quiet. Thank you, he thought, then mouthed the words to himself in the dark.

The rain made sleep easy. The two of them lay side by side in their softly crackling sleeping bags like pods, identical but for size. When he crawled out of the tent in the middle of the night to pee, the rain had stopped and he could see stars through the missing places in the roof. Later he thought he heard the rain again, but he'd been dreaming something about rain, and with half the boy's rib cage cupped in his palm, he slept.

In the morning the ground was soaked but he managed to get up a fire anyway. There was a heavy mist on the meadow, and it rose and drifted across the sky in long smoky sweeps. He couldn't remember the last time he'd seen something so beautiful. After breakfast they left their packs in the barn and went exploring. He'd promised he'd have him back that night. They didn't have to leave till noon.

The morning went too quickly, but he didn't mind. Better not to overdo it the first time. There would be other trips. He wanted to leave things undone. They walked a mile up the trail to a tributary of the river where they found a big track pressed into the mud that looked like it might have been a cat's, and then it was time to go.

They were about a mile from the river when he realized that coming back he'd have to hold the stick in his left hand: the current would be coming from the other side now. It didn't matter; his right shoulder was a little stiffer maybe, so sitting the boy on his arm would be a little less comfortable, but that was all. It shouldn't matter much.

He had thought the river sounded louder even before they came out of the trees, and it did. He understood right away. It wasn't the rain—there hadn't been enough to make a difference. It was the afternoon melt: in the mountains, forty miles away, the snowfields were melting in the sun. They'd slow in the evening cold, and not pick up again until the following day. He knew this. He'd forgotten.

Still, it didn't amount to all that much. Looking at the river, you could hardly tell the difference. The boy had run ahead; he could see him throwing sticks into the current. He'd just have to take it slow, that's all. Anyway, it wasn't as though they could wait till the next morning; he'd promised to have him back. There was no way of letting her know. But it didn't matter. Slow down, fella, he said to himself, but the sound of his own voice made him uncomfortable, so he didn't say anything more.

He walked in over the wet stones and splashed some water on his face, then pointed out where the current ran clear and flat over fist-size rocks, thigh deep. He was thinking too much. He took off his shoes and socks and pants, retied his shoes, and slipped on the two packs, the belt dangling free.

"Okay, kiddo," he said, "same thing as yesterday. You just stay put right here, and I'll wave from the other side."

The current was stronger—he could tell right away from the pull on his calves, the sound it made—not much stronger, but stronger. He worked slowly, picking his path, lifting the stick completely clear of the water and jabbing it down, leaning into the current, avoiding any rocks larger than a plate. It was a good track. With a river of any size, there was only one way—straight across, maybe slightly quartering upstream. You had to pick your path and go. You had to plan ahead, never take a step you couldn't move from.

Halfway across he stopped and rested his arm. It felt strange to be standing there, the current wrapping itself hard around his thigh. He looked at his watch. It was taking a little longer. So what? He'd crossed this thing a dozen times. More. Eight years was nothing. Same man, same river.

When he made it to the beach he dumped the packs and waved quickly and started back across. It had gone well. Well enough. His left arm was a little tired but he could rest it on the way back—the current was from the other direction now—and not having the packs made a difference. He tried not to look at the boy sitting where he'd left him on the opposite shore because there was something about the smallness of him in his blue shorts against the bank of stones he didn't like and because he wanted to keep his eyes on the water, and yet when he slipped, the toe of his right boot catching on the edge of something then sliding over rock as slick as any ice, he was looking straight down into the water. He floundered awkwardly, stumbled, thrust the stick with both hands into the current as if lunging at something under the water, and felt it catch. He hadn't seen it—whatever it was. He breathed, feeling his heart thrashing in his ribs. You never see it, he thought.

There was no point in waiting, so less than a minute after he'd slopped out onto the rocks and flexed his arms like Mr. Universe ("You ready, kiddo?"), he squatted down and the boy crawled onto his back. "You see how I almost fell back there?" he said. "You have to be careful. I got a little sloppy."

"I saw an eagle," the boy said. "It was enormous, and it flew right over the river."

"Really?" he said, already walking into the water.

The boy felt a little heavier than he had before, and thirty feet in he hoisted him up and shifted the weight. "Okay?" he said. He continued on, feeling for edges, probing ahead like a snail testing the air, then stopped and readjusted him again. When he stopped the third time, he knew it was going to be a push. He should have brought the boy across first. He wished he could switch him to his left, hold the stick with his right. He had to stretch his arm for a second, he said. He dropped his arm and the boy dangled from his neck, and then he caught him up and the pressure eased from his windpipe and they continued on. He tried not to look downstream. "How you doin' back there?" he said. He was strong. He could do this.

They didn't go down when it happened, but they should have. How he managed to stay up in that current, already sliding four, five feet downstream, slipping on one algae-slick rock, then another, he didn't know. How he managed not to turn upstream or down, which would have been that, he didn't know either. All he knew was that they were still up and the boy was still on his back and he was straightening up, still facing the shore, no more than a broomstick's length from where they'd been a moment earlier. The current was midthigh and strong.

He could hear himself, breathing hard. "I'm okay, kiddo. I'm okay. That wasn't good, but we're fine."

They weren't fine. Ignoring the quivering in his shoulder he tried to take stock. The rocks were bigger here. He couldn't get back to where they'd been. He couldn't quarter upstream and intercept the path because there was a flat pale rock the size of a small table in the way, and the water below it was too deep. "Do me a favor, kid," he said. "See if you can feel where my eyes are. That's it, don't worry—I've got you. Now when I count to three, I'll close my left eye and you wipe the sweat out with your thumb, okay?" He could feel the boy's thumb slide gently over his eyelid. "Good, now do it again."

There had to be a way—something he couldn't see. There was nothing. A step behind him, the rocks were smaller. It didn't matter. He couldn't step back. Crossing a river meant moving forward, holding the weight on the back leg while the front foot felt for purchase. Turning around was impossible. At some point he'd have to take the full weight of the current with his legs perpendicular to the shore like a tennis player anticipating a serve; unbraced, he'd come off the bottom like nothing at all. A thin stream of panic started in his head, dulling the sound of water. He looked around stupidly, blinking back the sweat. The shore looked like it was behind a screen. He moved his right foot forward, felt it begin to slide, pulled back. Fuck you, he whispered. Fuck you.

They'd get out of this. They had to get out of this. My God, all his other fuckups were just preparations for this. This wasn't possible. He could feel the current—strong, insistent, pumping against his thigh like a drunken lover. Was this how it went? One stupid move? One stupid fucking move, and your son on your back? No. He could do this. He tried to remember the strength he'd felt, that rude, beautiful strength, felt it pushing back the curtain of fear. There was nowhere to go.

He could barely bring himself to speak. He couldn't move. The way ahead was impossible. Far below, he could hear the water sucking on the shallow cavity made by his hip. The river. It wanted to be whole, unbroken. It wanted him gone. He could see it, forming and re-forming, thick-walled jade, smoothing out its sides with its thumbs like a hypnotized potter. The water blurred. He wanted to scream for help. There was no one—just the rushing plain of the river, the trees. He couldn't move. A muscle in his shoulder was jerking like a poisoned animal. What combination of things? Everything had come together. He couldn't move. He was barely holding on. There was no way. The river ahead was smooth, deep, gliding over brown boulders trailing beards of moss in the deep wind. He wanted to laugh. For a second, he felt the hot, shameful fire of remorse and then unending pity—for himself, for the boy on his back, for the world—and at that moment he remembered hearing about a medieval priest who, personally taking the torch from the executioner, went down the line of victims tied to their stakes and kissed each one tenderly on the cheek before lighting the tinder.

"Dad, you okay?" he heard his son saying as if from some other place. There was nowhere to go. It didn't matter. They had to go.

And then he heard his own voice, answering. "I'm okay, buddy," it said. "You just hang on."

Lori Ostlund

Bed Death

W E MET MR. Mani because we paused on the footbridge
that spanned Jalan Munshi Abdullah, a busy street near
our hotel, for it was only from up there that the sign for his
school, the unobtrusively named English Institute, could be seen.
The school, which occupied the second floor of the decrepit
building just below us, did not look promising, and when we trotted back down the steps to the street and went inside, it seemed
even less so. Still, we presented our résumés to the young woman
at the front desk, and she, not knowing what to do with them or
us, summoned Mr. Mani from class.

Mr. Mani was a small Indian man in his sixties, no taller than
either Julia or I, which put us immediately at ease, and when he
smiled, he seemed at once boyish and ancient because he was
missing his top front teeth. He did not speak Malaysian English,
which we were still struggling to understand, but sounded in
every way British, to the point that when he heard our American
accents, he winced, which could have annoyed us but instead
made us laugh. He studied our résumés at length before explaining, apologetically, that the school provided only enough work for

him, though when we met him for dinner that evening, we learned that he rarely spent less than twelve hours a day at the school, teaching mornings and afternoons and then, at night, checking homework and attending to paperwork. The empty space created by his missing teeth accommodated perfectly the neck of a whiskey bottle, which spent more and more time there as the night wore on, and after he had consumed a fair amount, he revealed that he stayed late at the school also as a way of hiding from his wife, whom he referred to as "my Queen."

I do not think that it occurred to him, ever, that Julia and I were a couple, yet he spoke to us without nonsense or innuendo, mainly about his marriage, which had been arranged, stating repeatedly that he did not question the matchmaker's thinking in putting together a poor but educated man from Kuala Lumpur and an illiterate woman from the rubber plantation. "After all, we have produced eleven children," he pointed out proudly, confessing that, given his long hours, he saw them only when they brought his meals or attended their weekly English lessons. His favorite was the fifth child, a girl by the name of Suseelah, who loved Orwell as much as he did and loathed Dickens almost as much. In fact, he spoke of Dickens often, always with contempt, and I could not help but view it as a classic example of a man railing against his maker, for Mani was a character straight from Dickens, an affable, penniless fellow who bordered on being a caricature of himself.

When he had consumed the entire bottle of whiskey, he declared the evening complete and insisted on the minor gallantry of walking us back to our hotel, a seedy place that he promptly deemed "unsuitable for two ladies." At the door, he shook our hands sadly and said, as though the evening had been nothing more than an extended job interview, "My ladies, I am afraid that I cannot hire you."

"Thank you for meeting with us," I replied.

He turned to leave but stopped, saying, "I shall pass your

résumés to my old friend Narayanasamy at Raffles College. If there are no objections, of course. The school is newly opened here in Malacca, though quite established in other areas of Malaysia, I assure you." We thanked him for his kindness, but I am ashamed to admit that we dismissed his offer as drunken posturing.

So, of course, we were surprised to return to our hotel the next day to find a note from him informing us that Mr. Narayanasamy wished to meet us. We left early for the interview the following morning, half expecting the directions that Mani had included to be faulty, which is how we came to be sitting in the overly air-conditioned office of Mr. Narayanasamy, briefcases on our laps, waiting for him to finish a heated telephone discussion regarding funds for a copy machine.

I leaned toward Julia. "What do you make of the bed?" I whispered.

"What bed?" she whispered back.

"What bed?" I repeated, indignation adding to my volume, for, simply put, Julia often overlooked the obvious.

"Welcome to Raffles College," Mr. Narayanasamy announced, putting down the phone and rising, hand extended to greet us, inquiring in the next breath what had brought us to Malaysia and, more specifically, to his school. When I answered that what had brought us to his school was his friend Mr. Mani, he paused before replying, "Ah yes, Mani," the way that one would refer to laundry on the line several minutes after it has begun to rain. I knew then that I would not like this Mr. Narayanasamy. Still, we spent the next hour convincing him that we were indeed up to the task of teaching business communications, a subject we knew little about, for I was a writing teacher and Julia, ESL, and as we stood to leave, he offered us the jobs.

In the process of making myself desirable and friendly, I forgot entirely about the bed, but as we passed through the main lobby, there it was again—enormous and pristine, housed behind glass like a museum exhibit—and Julia had the good grace to look sheepish. We stood before it in silence, believing that it would not do to be overheard discussing any aspect of our new place of employment, but finally Julia could not contain herself.

"It's huge," she said authoritatively, as though the bed were her find, an oddity that she was deigning to share with me but did not trust me to fully appreciate.

"Yes," I agreed. "I don't know how you missed it." Then, to press my point, I added, "Julia, sometimes I think you could get into bed at night and not notice that a car had been parked at the foot of it." I said this in an intentionally exasperated tone, a tone so exaggerated that I knew I could dismiss it as playful if need be, but Julia, pleased by our employment, merely laughed.

We settled quickly into a routine, teaching from eight in the morning until that same hour of the evening, with blocks free for eating and preparation. Business communications was tedious but not complicated, and we soon developed a system for teaching it, which we modified slightly for each of the three departments that we served: marketing, business, and hospitality management. The bed, we learned, belonged to the latter department, and we often saw its students huddled around it, notebooks open, as an instructor made and remade it, stopping to gesture at folds and even, with the aid of a meter stick, measuring the distance from bedspread to floor. Students visiting the college with their parents stopped to gaze at the bed as well, the entire family standing with a quiet air of expectation as though watching an empty cage at the zoo, and I came to realize that not only did these families consider it perfectly normal to have a bed on display but they actually seemed impressed by it, impressed and reassured, as though the bed gave them a sense that the school was for real and not some place where one did nothing but stare at books. Never did I see a student touch the bed, however, and when I asked one of the hospitality instructors why this was, she explained that what the students needed to know was theoretical, information that could be quantified via a multiple-choice exam—which meant there was no reason for them to touch it.

The hospitality management students were, ironically, the most timid of the lot; I was hard-pressed to imagine any of them behind the desk of an actual hotel, greeting guests and making them feel at home. "Do you even understand what 'hospitality' means?" I blurted out one day, fed up with the way they sat in their stiff blue uniforms, red pocket kerchiefs peeking out with an almost obscene jauntiness, eyes turned downward whenever I asked a question. I turned and wrote "HOSPITALITY" across the board in large letters, and as I did, I heard behind me a low, scornful chuckle. I knew that it could only be coming from Shah, a corpulent young man who ignored the uniform policy and generally chose to wear purple, perhaps in keeping with the regal connotations of his name. Shah was an anomaly in the class—fat where the others were thin, the only Malay in a class full of Chinese, more often absent than present. He spent his days loitering around campus, attending classes sporadically, which was fine with me, for I had taken a thorough dislike to him and found it tiring to conceal the depth of my feelings. It bothered Julia greatly that I allowed myself to harbor such animosity toward a student, particularly one whom she saw as awkward and pathetic, one whose neediness, she claimed, was so wholly transparent that to respond to it as anything but neediness was to be purposely disingenuous. I mention this only so that one can see how it appeared from her perspective, for I believe (and have all along) that her position was the logical one, the one with which, in theory, I would have agreed had I never met Shah and discovered what it was like to be so utterly repelled by a student.

Already, I had been visited by his father, who was a *datuk,* a minor dignitary of the sort that made appearances at local events, speaking a few words to commemorate the occasion, generally after arriving late. He came unexpectedly during my lunch hour, and, to the horror of the colleague sent to find me, I insisted on finishing my noodles first. When I finally entered the room where Shah and the *datuk* waited, it was ripe with the smell of Shah, an oppressively musky odor that I suspected was caused by some sort of biological malfunction, but that did nothing to make me better disposed toward him. His father was visibly annoyed at being made to wait, and I could see that this would only make things worse for Shah, which struck me as unfair but did not particularly bother me, for Shah had already caused me an inordinate amount of work and worry, and that also struck me as unfair.

Shah's father did not speak English, but not trusting his son to translate, he had brought along a translator, through whom I explained that Shah rarely attended class and never turned in homework but that I often saw him lounging around the cafeteria. When I spoke to him about his absences, he replied, with an annoying lilt to his voice, that he had not been feeling well. "Upset stomach," he would say coyly, patting his very large stomach as though it were a kitten he had not yet tired of. Once I sent another student to fetch him, but the boy returned alone. "He says that he is feeling faint," the boy reported, and the others looked at me hopefully, for the students enjoyed being surprised by my behavior, which they attributed to my being American. I sensed that Shah wanted me to find him and demand his presence, and so, unwilling to give him that pleasure, I did nothing.

Throughout the course of our exchange, the *datuk* and I made no eye contact, and when the meeting was finished, we stood, but even in parting, he did not acknowledge me, instead averting his eyes until I realized that he was waiting for me to leave first. I did, and as I closed the door behind me, I could hear him yelling and then a sound like a pig snuffling at a trough, which I suspected was Shah crying.

That night as I passed through the dark lobby of the school, I was startled by what appeared to be a shape atop the bed, a shape not unlike that made by a supine body, albeit a very large one. I drew close to the glass, quite sure that once my eyes adjusted to the dim glow of the night lights, I would find nothing more than a hefty stack of linens awaiting the next day's lesson, but it was clearly a person and, judging from the size, I knew that it could only be Shah. Slowly, the details of his face grew more pronounced, and I could not help but feel that lying there with his eyes closed, hands clasped high atop the mound of his stomach, he looked defenseless, almost benign. I had never been that close to him, so close that I could have reached out and touched his brow were it not for the glass between us. His lids began to flutter, his eyes rolling slowly open, casting about nervously until they settled on my face, recognition hardening them into two bits of coal that burned with unmitigated contempt.

The next morning, the bed looked as it always did, neatly made, ready for service. I mentioned the encounter to no one, certainly not Julia, who would have pursued one of her usual melodramatic interpretations—bed as performance space or sacrificial altar—rather than simply a comfortable place to snooze.

Mr. Narayanasamy had warned that our work permits might take a week, even two, suggesting that we "stay put" at our hotel until they were issued. We agreed, though we had already been living at our seedy hotel for two weeks by then, two long weeks during which a man of indeterminate age, wearing only a pair of shorts, lay upon a plastic chaise longue in the hallway just outside our door, groaning day and night, no doubt from the pain caused by the gaping wound that ran from one of his nipples to his navel. Although we never saw anyone attending to him, we knew that somebody was because some days the wound was concealed by an unskillfully applied bandage, while other days it was exposed, flies gathering on it like poor people lined up along a river to bathe.

We had no idea what had happened to the man and did not ask, primarily because nobody had even acknowledged the man's presence to us, but the wound resembled a knife cut, approximately eight inches long and jagged with a suggestion of violence to it, though we understood that the shabbiness of the hotel, combined with the fact that blood still seeped from the wound, contributed to this effect. Since he was directly outside our door and prone to groaning, particularly at night, we often found it difficult to sleep, but it was unthinkable that we ask him to groan less, to keep his misery to himself. There was also the issue of whether to greet him as we paused to lock or unlock our door. Julia felt that we should, that a hello was in order; otherwise, it was like treating him as though he were invisible, dead in fact, but as I prefer to pass my own illnesses without interference, I maintained that we should not ask him to engage in unnecessary politenesses when he so obviously needed his energy for mending. Of course, this quickly became an argument not about the wounded man but about me, or, more specifically, about what Julia termed my stubborn disbelief in the world's ability to maintain a position at odds with my own, which I felt was overstating the case.

The day after we were hired, a Saturday, we walked out toward the sea along a road cramped with vehicles that blew sand and oily exhaust into our faces. We returned to our room filthy and went together into our little bathroom, which was equipped with a traditional *mandi,* a large, water-filled tank from which one scooped water for bathing. There, we stripped down, laughing and lathering ourselves and each other and then shrieking at the water's coolness, welcome but startling nonetheless. We felt amazingly clean afterward and lay on the bed, naked and wet, enjoying the flutter of the fan across our bodies, our hands touching.

We could hear the wounded man shifting repeatedly on his chaise longue, the fact that he was moving so much suggesting that he felt stronger, perhaps even bored, and while the possibility of this cheered us greatly, for we had actually pondered what to do if we rose one morning to find him dead, there was something unsettling about the sound of his skin ripping away from the vinyl each time he moved. The thought began to creep into each of our heads that he was not feeling better at all but was instead flailing out in desperation against the narrowly defined, joyless space he now occupied. Furthermore, we worried that we had caused his agitation, that the sounds of pleasure we made as we bathed had led to his sudden despair. For the first time, we felt that the man was aware of us—even worse, that he had been aware of us all along, an intimacy that was too much to bear. It was ironic, for we had put up with so much—the sight of him, bloody and damaged, as we came and went, the groaning throughout the night—but somehow this, the feeling that our pleasure intensified his pain, this had overwhelmed us, so we packed our bags and escaped down the street to the Kwee Hang Hotel, which was more expensive by far but did not involve a wounded man outside our door.

At the Kwee Hang Hotel, the long, sunny foyer was mopped twice daily, our toilet paper was monitored, and when we returned each night, the bathroom smelled pleasantly medicinal and the beds stood neatly made with sheets that bore the fresh smell of a dryer. The only thing that we had to complain about really was that the owner and his son sat for hours behind a desk at the end of this long, sunny foyer with their eyes glued to the television, across which ran the ticker-tape information for the Malaysian stock exchange during the day and international exchanges during the night, but even this we could not really form a complaint around, for they kept the sound muted, day and night, making, only occasionally, some sort of quiet comment to one another, a low chuckle of pleasure or a disgusted *ay-yoh* when things presumably had not gone their way. Of course, it made no sense for us to be paying by the day an amount that, each month, added up to half our salaries. Even the old man and his son began to tell us as much. "Find an apartment and stop paying like tourists," they said, but week after week, our visas were delayed, a state of affairs that we protested in only the most cursory fashion, for we were content.

Still, one feature of the room did bother us (though to call it a feature is misleading, for "feature" implies something added to make life more pleasant for hotel guests rather than less): there existed, on the inside of the wardrobe door, a crudely rendered drawing of two penises, both erect and facing one another as though, I could not help but think, they were about to duel. It had been made with a thick-tipped black marker, hastily so that one of the penises had unevenly sized scrota and black slashes of hair, while the other was symmetrical but hairless. Beneath the picture, in a more controlled hand, somebody, presumably the artist, had written: *I am waiting every night on the footbridge.* Since we generally opened only the left door and the drawing was on the right, we did not discover it for weeks, but once we had, we began to feel different about the room, which we now understood to have a history, a life that was separate from us, yet not entirely. It sounds naive to say that we had never considered this before, for it was a hotel after all, but until then, we had never stopped to imagine that things had been said and done in this room, upon these beds, prior to our arrival. Worse, I began to feel sheepish around the father and son, the drawing inserting itself into the conversation each time I spoke to them about something as ordinary as getting an extra towel or received a warning that the stairs were wet.

We knew the referred-to footbridge, of course. From it, we had first spotted Mr. Mani's school, and we crossed it often as we made our way to and from our favorite food stalls. But once we had learned of its secret, we found ourselves increasingly drawn there, particularly at night, when a handful of men gathered and spread out across it, maintaining their posts as vigilantly and nervously as sentries. Each time we climbed the stairs, they turned toward us, their faces momentarily hopeful, hungry for something that we could not provide. Still, we felt comfortable there among men who regarded us with so little interest, and as we crossed, I sometimes glanced surreptitiously at a face and wondered what the man was thinking, wondered whether he had ever been in love.

Descending the steps of the footbridge one evening, we noticed that the light in Mr. Mani's office was on and decided to pay him a visit, a long-overdue visit, for although we had been teaching at the school some two months, we had not yet thanked Mr. Mani for securing us the positions. It was after eight, but the outer door was unlocked, and we went in, calling his name. We found him reclining on an unmade cot that was wedged into one corner of his tiny office, whiskey bottle in hand.

"My American ladies," he announced, smiling his toothless smile and struggling like an overturned cockroach to sit up. "Kindly join me for a nightcap." He thrust the bottle toward us, tipping forward with the weight of it.

"Perhaps we should return another time," I said, but he looked hurt at the suggestion and, focusing deeply, stood and wobbled to his desk.

"Please, have a seat," he said, gesturing at the cot.

The room, I had noticed as we entered, possessed a rank odor, attributable, I thought, to its smallness and the fact that its one window was closed. It was the sort of smell to which one adjusted quickly, unlike the overwhelming stench that rose up, surrounding us, as we settled on the cot, its dominant feature sourness—sour in the way of sheets that have been sweated in for nights on end and never washed—and beneath this, a secondary stink, a unique blend that included but was not limited to the following: clove cigarettes, spices, whiskey, unwashed feet, urine, and moldy books. Next to me, Julia gagged, covering it with a cough, and I, holding my breath so that my voice came out nasally, said, "We've come to thank you for your help."

"I'm happy to be of service," said Mani, looking, in fact, about to cry.

"Mr. Mani, are you living here?" I asked.

"Yes," he replied mournfully. "My Queen has banned me from

our dwelling. My clothes and the bed were delivered two months ago, shortly after our splendid evening together. I have not seen her since. Of course, she still sends my meals twice daily, and while I know that her hands prepared them, it is not the same."

"But why?" I asked.

He shrugged. "I cannot explain to you the mind of a woman," he said, as though Julia and I were not women, and then he took a small sip from his bottle. "Ladies, do you know the story of the British man and the snake? It is a famous Malaysian tale." When we shook our heads, he gathered himself up and said, "Then I shall tell you, but be warned: it is a story about love." I acknowledged this with a nod.

"A British man," he began, "lived on his tea plantation up in the highlands, all alone save for the servants who attended to his fairly simple needs. Each afternoon, he took a lengthy walk, disappearing with his hat and walking stick for hours, going where and doing what, no one knew. This remained his habit for many years.

"Eventually, he became engaged, but just two days before the wedding was to transpire, the man went out for his walk and did not return. A search party was formed. He was found the next morning, his legs protruding from the mouth of a large snake, both man and snake dead by the time that this strange union was discovered. The snake had to be hacked apart with machetes in order to extricate the man's body. Later, it was determined that the man had died of asphyxiation, which meant that the snake had attempted to swallow him while he was still alive."

"Should we be worried about snakes, Mr. Mani?" asked Julia, speaking for the first time. She was afraid of snakes, even more so because a pair of paramedics with whom we had chatted soon after arriving told us that they spent an inordinate amount of time removing snakes from houses.

"No, ladies, you are missing the point. I mean, yes, the snake's behavior is the point, but only because it is highly unusual. And so there is no way to explain it, as any Malaysian will tell you, except that the snake was in love with the man, and—"

"In love?" I interrupted.

"Yes," Mr. Mani replied firmly. "They were in love with each other, and that day the man had finally come clean—he had informed the snake of his impending marriage. But the snake could not bear the news, and so . . ." He shrugged, brought his hands together as though to pray, and then thrust them outward, away from each other, away from himself. "That is jealousy, you see. Everything destroyed."

"And you believe this also, Mr. Mani?" I asked, though I could see that he did.

Mr. Mani regarded us for a moment. "Well," he said at last, "with love, there are always two: there is the snake who devours, and there is the one who cooperates by placing his head inside the snake's mouth."

The next afternoon as we were leaving the school, Miss Kumar, who handled payroll, approached us. "I hear that you require an apartment," she whispered. "I know one. Cheap. Not too big. It belongs to my sister-in-law."

This, we knew, was Mr. Mani's doing, for as we stood to leave the night before, he had requested our address and, upon learning that we still lived in a hotel, shook his head in horror. "It is not right, and it is not proper," he said repeatedly as I explained about the visas, and then, "I am surprised by my old friend Narayanasamy."

We recognized the building that Miss Kumar stopped in front of immediately—Nine-Story Building, which we had passed numerous times, commenting on how much taller it was than everything around it and how this made it seem awkward and defenseless, like a young girl who had shot up much faster than her classmates. We entered near the courtyard, a large asphalt area around which rose the four sections that collectively made up

Nine-Story Building and which Miss Kumar herded us past, saying, "Please, my sister-in-law is waiting." But she was not waiting, and we stood outside the apartment for ten minutes until she stepped off the elevator at a trot, speaking Tamil rapidly into a cell phone. She was, in every way, a hurried woman, and when she stooped to unlock the door—knees bent primly, phone wedged against her ear with an upraised shoulder—and wiggled her fingers impatiently, we took on her sense of urgency, which is to say that we found ourselves the tenants of a dark, one-bedroom, squat-toilet apartment on the fourth floor of Nine-Story Building, closer to the bottom than the top, which was apparently considered desirable, for she mentioned it repeatedly.

Our colleagues considered our move to Nine-Story Building strange, though perhaps no stranger than the fact that we had continued to live in a hotel for months, and in the weeks that followed, they inquired frequently about our new lodgings. When we answered, "Everything is fine," they appeared skeptical, and so we began complaining about the elevator, which smelled of urine masked by curry and made noises suggesting that it was not up to the task of carrying passengers up and down day after day. Soon we began using the stairs, which we generally had to ourselves because the other tenants seemed not to mind the elevator's strange noises, or minded more the certainty of the exertion that the stairs required than the mere possibilities suggested by the noise, and so we went back to answering that everything was fine, dismissing our colleagues' interest as yet another example of the unsolicited attention that we received in Malacca, where we were the only westerners in residence.

In fact, as we walked around town, people whom we had never met called out, "Hello, Miss Raffles College," greeting us both in this same way. We were regarded as the American spinsters, teachers so devoted to our work that it had rendered us sexless, left us married to the school, thought of in this way because we were strict with healthy expectations—that students study and not cheat, that they arrive on time, that they not take on the disaffected pose that teenagers find so appealing—but also, I suspect, because we were women without men.

As spinsters, we were thought to possess a certain prudishness, a notion that was clearly behind the request that Mr. Narayanasamy made of us one day after summoning us to his office. "We have a grave situation requiring our expeditious attention," he began, gesturing grandly at the produce market visible from the window to the left of his desk. "That is the produce market," he said, assuming that American spinsters would be unfamiliar with such a dirty, chaotic place, though, in fact, we stopped there often to buy vegetables and practice our Malay because the vendors rarely tried to cheat us.

"I have just this morning received an upsetting visit from several of the vendors. It seems that two of our students have been observed holding hands and even"—he cleared his throat—"kissing." He looked at us apologetically, as though explaining that we would not be receiving raises, and we nodded because we knew the couple to whom he referred.

"You must speak to them," he declared, slapping his hand down on his desk.

"And tell them what?" Julia asked.

"Tell them that they must stop," he explained in a reasonable tone. "Tell them that they are discrediting the school, their families, and themselves."

"But they're adults," Julia said.

"Very well," said Mr. Narayanasamy, looking back and forth between the two of us. "Then I shall speak to them, though I too am busy. Still, it is my duty to attend to the duties for which others lack time." He reached up as though to tighten his tie, but the knot already sat snugly against his throat, and Julia and I departed, allowing our refusal to stand as an issue of time constraints.

"You let me do all the talking," said Julia several minutes later as we sat outside a café, waiting for our orange juice to arrive. We had become a bit obsessed with orange juice, for no matter how carefully we stressed that we did not want sugar, we had yet to receive juice that met this simple specification. "You made me seem like the unreasonable one."

I knew that Julia hated to appear unreasonable, and so I considered apologizing. "Care to bet on the sugar," I said instead, hoping to redirect her ire, to remind her that I was an ally, at least when it came to sugar.

The waitress, a young Malay woman with a prominent black tooth, appeared, balancing two very full glasses of orange juice on a tray. As she drew near, she seemed to lose speed, as though she sensed the depth of our thirst and was overwhelmed by the power she held to alleviate it, finally stopping altogether, resting the tray on the back of a nearby chair. As we watched, she picked up one of the glasses and took a sip before placing it back on the tray and continuing toward us. Smiling, she set the sipped-from glass in front of me, the untouched one in front of Julia.

"Excuse me," I said politely. "I believe you drank from my glass."

She smiled at me. "Is fine," she replied, and departed gracefully.

"What did she mean by that?" I asked Julia. "Did she mean, 'Yes, I did drink from your glass and the fact that I did so is fine,' or did she simply mean that the juice is fine, as in 'I took a sip of your juice just to make sure, and it's fine.' "

We studied the juices for a moment. I knew that Julia wanted to drink hers, and why shouldn't she? Nobody had sipped from her glass.

"Well," I said peevishly. "Go ahead."

"Maybe she was just smelling it," she suggested, once she had taken two very long drinks.

"Smelling it?" I said.

"Yes, you know. Just sniffing it."

"You saw her drink from it."

"Yes, she definitely drank from it," she agreed, changing tack. "Though I don't see what the big deal is."

I considered the implications of this last statement, considered it, that is, within the context of our relationship. Julia and I had been together for two years, not a lifetime, granted, but it was, I believed, a *sufficient* length of time. She knew things about me: that I could not tolerate the smell of fish in the morning; that I felt suffocated at being told the details of other people's bodily functions; that I abhorred public nose picking, both the studied sort in which some of my students engaged as well as the fast poking at which I always seemed to catch people on buses or in line. Then, too, there was the matter of what she jokingly referred to as "the zones," which, simply put, are the areas of the body that I do not care to have touched nor to see touched on others nor, quite frankly, to even hear discussed. During my last checkup just before we left for Malaysia, my doctor nonchalantly pressed her hands to my abdomen, coming far too close to my navel, which, along with my neck, is a primary zone.

"Could you please not brush against my navel?" I had said, perhaps a bit sharply.

"Your navel?" she replied, pulling back as though I had accused her of biting.

"Yes," I said. "It unsettles me." I felt that "unsettles" was a perfectly appropriate word for the situation, precise enough in connotation to convey my displeasure but cryptic enough to save me from feeling foolish, assuming that she had the good manners not to press the issue, which she did not.

"How strange," she replied, pausing to regard me. Then, her hands drawn to her own navel, she began to massage it. "The navel, you know, is the final remaining symbol of our connection to our mothers, a reminder of our past dependence." Her rubbing intensified, and I suspected that she might be newly pregnant.

"Please," I said stiffly. "I would prefer that you not touch your navel in my presence. In fact, I would prefer that we not even discuss navels."

When I arrived home that afternoon, I told Julia about the encounter, huffily, in a way that suggested that the doctor had been intentionally trying to goad me. She had been sympathetic, but that night at dinner, she had tentatively broached the subject again, her tone suggesting that she found my reaction perplexing, even perturbing, and though I concealed my dismay, I could not help but recall the early days of our relationship, when she had stroked my brow encouragingly as I related the story of the wood tick that had worked its way deep into my navel when I was eight.

"The big deal," I replied, speaking loudly, which Julia hates. "The big deal is that this is my juice." That night, as I lay in bed, Julia asleep next to me, it occurred to me that I did not even know whether the juice had come with sugar or without.

The following Saturday, Julia and I encountered Shah on the footbridge. I was surprised to see him there, though not surprised at what his presence meant. He was wearing a pair of large white pants that flapped like sails in the evening breeze and, as usual, a purple shirt. As we passed him, he looked away, thus acknowledging my presence, and I, in deference to his wishes as well as bridge etiquette, said nothing.

"Poor fellow," Julia remarked as we descended the steps at the other end.

"It does not justify his behavior," I said vehemently, for I sensed something in her tone, particularly in her use of the word "fellow," which made Shah seem hapless, free of guile.

The next morning, Sunday, we were awakened early by the sounds of screaming, and when we dressed quickly and stepped out of our apartment, we found our neighbors gathered on the walkway outside, pressed against the railing that curved around the courtyard like theater patrons looking down from their box seats. As we wiggled our way in next to them, we saw that all around Nine-Story Building the tenants stood in similar rows, everyone peering downward at where a body lay in the courtyard below, face down, arms out, like a doll flung aside by a bored child.

"But this is becoming too much," complained our neighbor Prahkash. "Why must they always come here to do themselves in? I pay the rent, not they. We should begin charging admission." He spit over the rail, and I watched the drop fall and disappear.

The next day, we read in the newspaper that the victim was a Chinese man in his late forties who had just returned from a gambling trip to Australia, where he had lost fifty thousand dollars, a sum of money that it had taken his family five years to save. They were preparing to start a business, a karaoke restaurant, and the man, impatient to begin, had flown to Sydney, lost everything at the blackjack tables, and returned to Malaysia broke, taking a taxi from the airport in Kuala Lumpur back to Malacca. He was dropped at the night market, where he drank a cup of coffee at one of the stalls, leaving the suitcase behind when he departed. After seeing the man's picture in the paper the next day, the stall owner had announced that he had the man's suitcase, the suitcase that had, presumably, been used to tote the fifty thousand dollars on its one-way journey. The story of the abandoned suitcase had appeared as a separate article, next to a picture of the stall owner holding it aloft.

"Did you see the suitcase in the newspaper?" a neighbor inquired several days later as Julia and I passed her in the hall.

"Yes. The poor man," I replied sourly. "Misplaced his suitcase as well."

She paused and then, not unkindly, said, "Ours is the only building tall enough. It can't be helped, you see." She was trying to prepare me, letting me know that this was not an anomaly, but perhaps I looked puzzled or in need of further convincing, for she said it again, with the same air of resignation that tenants used to discuss the smell of urine in the elevator: ours was the only building tall enough—she paused—tall enough to ensure success. That was the word she used—*success*—from which I understood that somebody who jumped and lived would also have to suffer the humiliation of failure.

Julia said nothing during this exchange, but after we closed our door, she turned to me angrily and said, "Why do you have to act that way?"

"What way?" I asked, feigning innocence.

"Like you're the only one who cares what happened to that man. Like she's a jerk for even talking about him."

"She was not talking about him," I replied. "She was talking about his suitcase."

"People are never just talking about a suitcase," Julia said quietly.

That night, she did not come into our bedroom to sleep, which was fine with me as I found sleeping alone preferable in the tropical heat, though I had not mentioned this to Julia because it seemed imprudent to discuss anything related to our bed at that particular moment. There is a term that lesbians use—*bed death*—to describe what had already begun happening long before Julia took the bigger step of physically removing herself from our bed. In fact, at the risk of sounding confessional, a tendency that I despise, we had not actually touched since the afternoon that we bathed together at the seedy hotel. That this kind of thing occurred with enough frequency among lesbians to have acquired its own terminology in no way made me feel better. If anything, it made me feel worse, for I dislike contributing in any way to the affirmation of stereotypes.

Then, on the second Friday after she stopped sleeping in our bed, an arrangement that had continued without discussion, I was returning from Mahkota Parade with groceries when I ran into three students. "We saw Miss Julia at the bus station," announced Paul, an amiable boy with a slightly misshapen head. This happened often, people reporting to us on the other's activities, even on our own, as though we may have forgotten that we had eaten barbecued eel at a stall near the water the night before.

"Oh?" I replied, striving for a nonchalant "oh" rather than one that indicated surprise or begged for elaboration.

"Is she going back?" Paul asked, by which he meant leaving.

"Yes," I said without hesitation, knowing it to be true, for, as Paul spoke, I had the sense that I was simply being reminded of something that had already happened.

Her clothing and computer were gone, but so, too, were the smaller, everyday pieces of her life: the earplugs she kept beneath her pillow, the biography of Indira Gandhi that she was halfway through, the photo of her great-grandmother Ragnilde with her long hair puddled on the floor. In fact, their absence hurt more, for it suggested a plan, a methodical progression toward that moment when she boarded the bus with her carefully packed bags, leaving nothing behind—not even, it turned out, a note, which meant that she left without any sort of good-bye, that she had considered the silence that reigned between us those last few weeks a sufficient coda. I sat on the bed and tried to determine the exact moment her decision had been made, when she had thought to herself, "Enough," but I could not, for it seemed to me a bit like trying to pinpoint the exact sip with which one had become drunk.

Eventually—hours later, I suppose, for it had grown dark outside—I realized that I was hungry and, with no desire to cook the food that I had purchased for the two of us that afternoon, decided to visit our favorite stall, where we had often whiled away the cool evenings eating noodles and potato leaves and, occasionally, a few orders of dim sum. I knew, also, that the owner would ask about Julia's absence and that this would afford me the opportunity to begin adjusting to the question and perfecting a response.

Checking that I had money and keys, both of which were Julia's domain, I locked our apartment door, but as I turned toward the stairwell out of habit, I felt a heaviness in my legs and considered taking the elevator. If Julia had been there, she would have said, "We are *not* taking the elevator," and I would have felt obligated to make a small stand in favor of it, but Julia was not there, which meant that the decision was mine: if I took the stairs, it would be as though Julia still held sway, but if I took the elevator, it would seem too deliberate, a reaction against her, particularly as I hated the elevator as much as she. As I stood debating in the poorly lit doorway of the stairwell, there came from farther up the stairs a heavy thudding sound. I imagined some large, hungry beast making its way down the steps toward me, for boundaries between inside and out did not always exist there, and I shrank back, prepared to flee.

A moment later, Shah appeared, lumbering onto the landing where I stood. My first, naive reaction was to wonder whom he had been visiting there in Nine-Story Building, and my next, to marvel that he, whose body literally reeked of lethargy, had chosen the stairs. He paused on the landing, catching his breath in wet, heaving gasps, and then turned, looking back over his shoulder like a hunted creature. His face was streaked with tears and snot and displayed neither the coyness nor the mocking obsequiousness that I had come to expect; even his jowls, those quivering, disdainful jowls, sagged more than usual. In that instant, of course, I understood what had brought Shah to Nine-Story Building, the realization crashing down on me with all the weight of Shah himself. From my hiding place, I looked on as he removed a large, dirty handkerchief from his pocket and cleaned his face. Then, keeping a distance between us, I followed him down the four flights of stairs and out onto the busy night street. Julia would have insisted on something more, but Julia was no longer there, so I watched Shah shuffle off down the sidewalk before I turned in the opposite direction, joining the flow of people exhausted from being out in the world all day who were finally heading home to their beds.

Brian Evenson

Windeye

1.

They lived, when he was growing up, in a simple house, an old bungalow with a converted attic and sides covered in cedar shake. In the back, where an oak thrust its branches over the roof, the shake was light brown, almost honey. In the front, where the sun struck it full, it had weathered to a pale gray, like a dirty bone. There, the shingles were brittle, thinned by sun and rain, and if you were careful you could slip your fingers up behind some of them. Or at least his sister could. He was older and his fingers were thicker, so he could not.

Looking back on it, many years later, he often thought it had started with that, with her carefully working her fingers up under a shingle as he waited and watched to see if it would crack. That was one of his earliest memories of his sister, if not the earliest.

His sister would turn around and smile, her hand gone to knuckles, and say, "I feel something. What am I feeling?" And then he would ask questions. *Is it smooth?* he might ask. *Does it feel rough? Scaly? Is it cold-blooded or warm-blooded? Does it feel red? Does it feel like its claws are in or out? Can you feel its eye move?* He would keep on, watching the expression on her face change as she tried to make his words into a living, breathing thing, until it started to feel too real for her and, half-giggling, half-screaming, she whipped her hand free.

There were other things they did, other ways they tortured each other, things they both loved and feared. Their mother didn't know anything about it, or if she did she didn't care. One of them would shut the other into the toy chest and then pretend to leave the room, waiting there silently until the one in the toy chest couldn't stand it any longer and started to yell. That was a hard game for him because he was afraid of the dark, but he tried not to show that to his sister. Or one of them would wrap the other tight in blankets, and then the trapped one would have to break free. Why they had liked it, why they had done it, he had a hard time remembering later, once he was grown. But they *had* liked it, or at least *he* had liked it—there was no denying that—and he had done it. No denying that either.

So at first those games, if they were games, and then, later, something else, something worse, something decisive. What was it again? Why was it hard, now that he had grown, to remember? What was it called? Oh, yes, *Windeye*.

2.

How had it begun? And when? A few years later, when the house started to change for him, when he went from thinking about each bit and piece of it as a separate thing and started thinking of it as a *house*. His sister was still coming up close, entranced by the gap between shingle and wall, intrigued by the twist and curve of a crack in the concrete steps. It was not that she didn't know that there was a house, only that the smaller bits were more important than the whole. For him, though, it had begun to be the reverse.

So he began to step back, to move back in the yard far enough away to take the whole house in at once. His sister would give him a quizzical look and try to coax him in closer, to get him involved in something small. For a while, he'd play to her level, narrate to her what the surface she was touching or the shadow she was glimpsing might mean, so she could pretend. But over time he drifted out again. There was something about the house, the house as a whole, that troubled him. But why? Wasn't it just like any house?

His sister, he saw, was standing beside him, staring at him. He tried to explain it to her, tried to put a finger on what fascinated him. *This house,* he told her. *It's a little different. There's something about it . . .* But he saw, from the way she looked at him, that she thought it was a game, that he was making it up.

"What are you seeing?" she asked, with a grin.

Why not? he thought. *Why not make it a game?*

"What are *you* seeing?" he asked her.

Her grin faltered a little but she stopped staring at him and stared at the house.

"I see a house," she said.

"Is there something wrong with it?" he prompted.

She nodded, then looked to him for approval.

"What's wrong?" he asked.

Her brow tightened like a fist. "I don't know," she finally said. "The window?"

"What about the window?"

"I want you to do it," she said. "It's more fun."

He sighed, and then pretended to think. "Something wrong with the window," he said. "Or not the window exactly but the number of windows." She was smiling, waiting. "The problem is the number of windows. There's one more window on the outside than on the inside."

He covered his mouth with his hand. She was smiling and nodding, but he couldn't go on with the game. Because, yes, that was exactly the problem, there was one more window on the outside than on the inside. That, he knew, was what he'd been trying to see.

3.

But he had to make sure. He had his sister move from room to room in the house, waving to him from each window. The ground floor was all right, he saw her each time. But in the converted attic, just shy of the corner, there was a window at which she never appeared.

It was small and round, probably only a foot and a half in diameter. The glass was dark and wavery. It was held in place by a strip of metal about as thick as his finger, giving the whole of the circumference a dull, leaden rim.

He went inside and climbed the stairs, looking for the window himself, but it simply wasn't there. But when he went back outside, there it was.

For a time, it felt like he had brought the problem to life himself by stating it, that if he hadn't said anything the half window wouldn't be there. Was that possible? He didn't think so, that wasn't the way the world worked. But even later, once he was grown, he still found himself wondering sometimes if it was his fault, if it was something he had done. Or rather, said.

Staring up at the half window, he remembered a story his grandmother had told him, back when he was very young, just three or four, just after his father had left and just before his sister was born. Well, he didn't remember it exactly, but he remembered it had to do with windows. Where she came from, his grandmother said, they used to be called not windows but something else. He couldn't remember the word, but remembered that it started with a *v.* She had said the word and then had asked, *Do you know what this means?* He shook his head. She repeated the word, slower this time.

"This first part," she had said, "it means 'wind.' This second part, it means 'eye.' " She looked it him with her own pale, steady eye. "It is important to know that a window can be instead a *windeye.*"

So he and his sister called it that, *windeye.* It was, he told her, how the wind looked into the house and so was not a window at all. So of course they couldn't look out of it; it was not a window at all, but a windeye.

He was worried she was going to ask questions, but she didn't. And then they went into the house to look again, to make sure it wasn't a window after all. But it still wasn't there on the inside.

Then they decided to get a closer look. They had figured out what window was nearest to it and opened that and leaned out of it. There it was. If they leaned far enough, they could see it and almost touch it.

"I could reach it," his sister said. "If I stand on the sill and you hold my legs, I could lean out and touch it."

"No," he started to say, but, fearless, she had already clambered onto the sill and was leaning out. He wrapped his arms around her legs to keep her from falling. He was just about to pull her back and inside when she leaned further and he saw her finger touch the windeye. And then it was as if she had dissolved into smoke and been sucked into the windeye. She was gone.

4.

It took him a long time to find his mother. She was not inside the house, nor was she outside in the yard. He tried the house next door, the Jorgensens, and then the Allreds, then the Dunfords. She wasn't anywhere. So he ran back home, breathless, and somehow his mother was there now, lying on the couch, reading.

"What's wrong?" she asked.

He tried to explain it as best he could. *Who?* she asked at first and then said, *Slow down and tell it again,* and then, *But who do you mean?* And then, once he'd explained again, with an odd smile:

"But you don't have a sister."

But of course he had a sister. How could his mother have forgotten? What was wrong? He tried to describe her, to explain what she looked like, but his mother just kept shaking her head.

"No," she said firmly. "You don't have a sister. You never had one. Stop pretending. What's this really about?"

Which made him feel that he should hold himself very still, that he should be very careful about what he said, that if he breathed wrong more parts of the world would disappear.

After talking and talking, he tried to get his mother to come out and look at the windeye.

"Window, you mean," she said, voice rising.

"No," he said, beginning to grow hysterical as well. "Not window. *Windeye.*" And then he had her by the hand and was tugging her to the door. But no, that was wrong too, because no matter what window he pointed at she could tell him where it was in the house. The *windeye,* just like his sister, was no longer there.

But he kept insisting it had been there, kept insisting too that he had a sister.

And that was when the trouble really started.

5.

Over the years there were moments when he was almost convinced, moments when he almost began to think—and perhaps even did think for weeks or months at a time—that he never had a sister. It would have been easier to think this than to think she had been alive and then, perhaps partly because of him, not alive. Being not alive wasn't like being dead, he felt: it was much, much worse. There were years too when he simply didn't choose, when he saw her as both real and make-believe and sometimes neither of those things. But in the end what made him keep believing in her—despite the line of doctors that visited him as a child, despite the rift it made between him and his mother, despite years of forced treatment and various drugs that made him feel like his head had been filled with wet sand, despite years of having to pretend to be cured—was simply this: he was the only one who believed his sister was real. If he stopped believing, what hope would there be for her?

Thus he found himself, even when his mother was dead and gone and he himself was old and alone, brooding on his sister, wondering what had become of her. He wondered if one day she would simply reappear, young as ever, ready to continue with the games they had played. Maybe she would simply suddenly be there again, her tiny fingers worked up behind a shingle, staring expectantly at him, waiting for him to tell her what she was feeling, to make up words for what was pressed there between the house and its skin, lying in wait.

"What is it?" he would say in a hoarse voice, leaning on his cane.

"I feel something," she would say. "What am I feeling?"

And he would set about describing it. *Did it feel red? Did it feel warm-blooded or cold? Was it round? Was it smooth like glass?* All the while, he knew, he would be thinking not about what he was saying but about the wind at his back. If he turned around, he would be wondering, would he find the wind's strange baleful eye staring at him?

That wasn't much, but it was the best he could hope for. Chances were he wouldn't get even that. Chances were there would be no sister, no wind. Chances were that he'd be stuck with the life he was living now, just as it was, until the day when he was either dead or not living himself.

Lynn Freed

Sunshine

They told Grace they'd found her curled into a nest of leaves, that since dawn they'd been following a strange spoor through the bush, and then, just as they'd begun to smell her, there she was, staring up at them through a cloud of iridescent flies.

They peered through the mottled gloom. Flies were clustered on her nose and eyes and mouth, and yet she didn't move, didn't even blink. "It's dead," said one of them, stretching out a stick to prod her.

That's when she sprang, scattering the flies and baring all her teeth in a dreadful high-pitched screech. They leapt back, reaching for their knives. She was up on her haunches now, biting at the air between them with her jagged teeth. But with the leaves and flies swirling, and her furious, wild hair, it took some time before they understood that it was a girl raging before them, just a girl.

"Hau!" they whispered, and they lowered their knives. She was skinny as a stick—filthy and naked, and the nest smelled foul.

One of the men dug into his pocket for some nuts. "Mê," he said, holding them out to her, "Mê."

She lifted her chin, trying to sniff at the air. But her nose was swollen and bloody, one arm hung limp at her side.

"It will be easy to catch her," the older man said. "How do we know the Master won't pay? Even half?"

Julian de Jong stormed out into the midday sun. "What on earth's the matter out here, Grace?" he said. "Why've you locked the dogs away?"

One of the men held the girl up, the other lifted her hair so that the Master could see her face.

"They found her in the bush, Master," Grace said, not looking up. She never wanted to see the girls when they were brought in. "They say if they put her back, maybe the jackals will get her."

The girl writhed and twisted to free herself from the grasp of the men. She bared her teeth, screeching pitifully. All the way up the hill, she had screeched and struggled like this, and all the way baboons had come barking after her.

De Jong stepped out into the yard and the men dropped their eyes courteously. Everyone knew he was not to be looked at when he was inspecting a girl, even an ugly one like this, even their own daughters. The girl stopped her squirming when he walked up, as if she too knew what was good for her. She stared at him as he questioned the men, breathing lightly through her mouth like a dog.

He put his monocle to his eye and, for several minutes, examined the girl in silence. And then, at last, he stood up and said, "Grace, clean the creature up. Here," he said to the men, digging around in his pocket for change. "Take this and divide it between you."

. . .

"Bring me the scissors!" Grace said to Beauty. "Bring me the Dettol!"

Beauty held the girl down while Grace took the scissors to her hair. "Ag!" she said, handing the tangle of hair and grass and blood to the garden boy. "Burn that," she said. "And bring me the blade for shaving. And the big tin bath."

By the time the bath was filled with hot water, the girl was almost bald, her scalp as pale as dough, and bleeding here and there from the blade. When they tried to lift her in, she struggled even more, twisting and thrashing and working one leg free so that she slashed at the flesh of Grace's arm with a toenail.

"Be *still*, you devil!" Grace cried, giving her a hard slap on the flesh of her buttock. "You want to go back to the bush? You want the jackals to get you?"

But the creature would not be still. By the time she was clean, the kitchen floor was awash with dirty water and she was cowering against the side of the bath, shivering, the teeth chattering. Now that she was clean, they could see that the nose and arm had been badly broken, and that the skin was sallow where the sun had not caught it. It was covered in scratches—some old, some new—and her hands and feet were calloused as hooves.

"He'll send her back after all this trouble," Beauty said. She was standing in the kitchen doorway with an armful of clothes. They were the same clothes each time, flimsy things that the girls loved to wear. "They will only be spoiled," she said. "It's a big shame." She put them on the kitchen table.

Grace pulled a small chemise out of the pile. She didn't understand these clothes, she hadn't understood them when she'd had to wear them herself. "Hold up her arms," she said to Beauty.

But it was hopeless. One by one, the clothes were tried, torn, bitten, abandoned. The best Grace could do was to pin a dishcloth onto the girl as tightly as she could. And then once it was on, the creature only squatted on her haunches like a monkey and clawed at the cloth with her good hand, drawing blood in her madness to have it off.

"It's too cruel," said Grace. "Let's take it off."

And so the girl was carried onto the veranda, naked and bald, to be presented to the man who would decide what would become of her.

Over the years, there had been rumors in the local villages of children living with baboons in the forest—of children snatched by baboons if you left them outside unguarded. Some children the baboons ate, the rumor went, some they kept for themselves. But only the old women ever believed this.

"Look again," Julian de Jong said to the local administrator. "See if anyone reported a baby missing—six or seven years ago, white, half-breed, anything you can find. I don't want any trouble later."

But no one had reported such a thing, not in the whole province. No one would challenge his claim.

"She could have been thrown away as a newborn and left for dead," said Doctor McKenzie, leaning over to examine the arm. "Some desperate teenager, who knows? I suppose it's not out of the question that baboons could have taken her up. But it hardly seems plausible, does it? Mind you, these fractures could very well be the result of a fall from a tree. She could have grown too big, I suppose. And she's malnourished, which would make her prone to fractures. Anyway," he said, straightening up, "there it is, and something needs to be done about the teeth. Don't mind telling you, old boy, I'm glad *I'm* not the dentist. Oh, and here—don't leave without the worm powder. Sure you're up for this one, Julian?"

The first night, de Jong had Grace lock the girl into the storeroom in the servants' quarters. But all through the night, the creature screeched and wailed, keeping the servants awake. The next morning they found that the sling on her arm had been bitten away, the bandage torn from her nose. Even her calloused hands and feet were bloodied and raw from trying to climb to the small, barred window above the door.

"It's cruel to lock her in there, Master," said Grace. "She's like an animal. We must train her like a dog."

De Jong looked at the girl. All night she had visited him in dreams—more like presences, really, than dreams—but, when he woke up, he could still not put a face to the creature. Usually he knew just what he had. At first they'd cry and beg to be sent home. Sometimes it would go on for weeks, and then he'd have to punish them. But in the end Grace always managed to have them ready for him, cleaned and oiled and docile.

If there was a principle that drove Julian de Jong, it was never to obscure his motives. And so, from the outset, there'd never been a question of theft. He was doing the girls a favor, everyone knew that, even their families. How else could it be that old McIntyre the missionary had never got any of them to talk? They'd just shake their heads when he came calling, press their lips together. They knew that when he was finished with them, the girls would fetch a decent bride price regardless. There was the money, of course, but there were other things too, things they'd learned from Grace—how to lay the table and mend the sheets, and sometimes even how to make a pudding or a soup. And so, when he finally sent them home, they seemed not to know where they'd rather be. And who was the worse for it then?

He stretched out his hand to touch the rough skin of the creature's cheek. He wanted to stroke it as he would stroke one of the others when she was new, for the pleasure of the life under his hand—grateful, warm, blameless. But just as his fingers came near her, she whipped her head around and tore at the flesh of his thumb with her teeth.

"Good God!" he cried, watching the blood well into the wound. He grasped the wrist tightly with his other hand as if to restrain it from grabbing her by the throat. And all the while, she was staring at him, panting, waiting, ready.

Grace lowered her eyes. She had seen him take the riding crop to a girl for staring. She had seen him take the crop to a girl for doing nothing at all.

"I'll call Beauty to fetch the Gentian, Master," she said quickly.

He turned then, as if he had forgotten she was there. A breeze was up, playing with his frizzy gray hair. But there was nothing playful in his face, she knew. It was flushed with fury, ready for the Lord knew what.

"Grace," he said, "I want you to tell the rest of them that no hand is to be laid upon this girl, not even if she bites. You will treat her like any of the others. Do you hear me?"

"Yes, Master."

"De Jong," McKenzie said, smoothing down the last of the plaster of paris, "she will need to be restrained to a board if this is to do any good. And I'll have to fashion a bucket collar so that she can't get at the nose. No one come forward to claim her?"

"No one."

"Well, the word is out, you know. The papers are bound to dig it up sooner or later."

"Let them dig. I have Dunlop's word he'll fix things. Anyway, who'd want her? She's an animal—just look what she did to my hand this morning."

McKenzie took the hand and turned it over. "It'll need a stitch," he said, "and we should test her for rabies. Here, keep still."

Grace took the girl to the chair in the corner. She held her there by the wrists, securing the girl's hips between her own copious thighs. But still the girl strained forward, as if she wanted another go at de Jong's hand.

"How long till the bones knit?" de Jong said.

"Bring her back in four weeks, and we'll take a look."

For four weeks, the girl was kept strapped to a board on the sleeping porch of the upstairs veranda. There Grace fed and cleaned her, and there, every night, de Jong himself slept in the bed next to hers, talking softly to her, telling her things he wouldn't have told the others. The hot season was beginning to die down, but when he tried covering her with his knee rug, she gasped and gagged, straining against the straps that held her head in place. So he took it off again.

After a while, he began to sit at the edge of her bed, and then place a hand on her forehead, almost covering her eyes. He'd hold it there until she stopped struggling, and, when she did, he'd run his fingers around the coil of an ear and under her jaw, down into the curve of her neck and shoulders. And then, if she was quiet, he'd feed her a piece of raw liver, which she loved best of all.

And so, soon he had her suffering his touch without struggling. She would lie still, staring at him around the plaster on her nose. Once, as his hand slipped itself over her rump, she even closed her eyes and fell asleep; he could hear her breathing settle. But when he stood up to leave, she was instantly awake again, following him with her eyes through the fading light to his own bed.

As the fourth week approached, de Jong had a cage built and placed at the back of the sleeping porch. Inside, Grace placed a tin mug and bowl, his knee rug and a driving glove that had lost its mate. The girl was to be lifted so that she could see every stage of the preparations, and Grace was to hold the bowl for her to sniff before she put it inside, and then the rug, and then the glove.

"Master," Grace said, "maybe she's not so wild now. Maybe we can let her walk for herself when the arm is better."

But the minute the plaster was off and the girl was given the freedom of the cage, she began to rage and screech again as if she had just been caught. With both arms growing stronger, she began to climb and swing and leap as well. She bit and tore at the blanket until it lay in shreds on the floor of the cage. The glove she examined carefully, turning it this way and that way, and then testing it with her teeth. The teeth themselves had been drilled and cleaned before the plaster came off. But they were still brown, and a few had been pulled out, giving her an even wilder look.

No one could work out how old she really was. Certainly, she was the size of most of the girls they brought to him. But the dentist seemed to think she was a bit older, which made the whole thing a little more urgent. All night and much of the day, de Jong stayed up there, talking softly to her. The servants watched and listened. It was the voice that he used for the dogs, and for the girls when they were first brought in. Never for anyone else. After a while even the girl herself seemed to listen. She would stare at him through the bars of the cage, frowning her baboon frown. And then he would pour some water into her mug, showing her how to drink it without lapping.

Over the weeks, she became quiet for longer and longer stretches of time. Even when de Jong went away and Grace came up to sit with her, she would wait quietly for her water, for her food. It was Grace herself who found a way to stop the girl tearing up the newspaper that was placed there day after day for her mess. And then one day, when the girl messed on it by chance, Grace began to sing. "You are my sunshine," warbling in her high-pitched vibrato, and the girl cocked her head like a bird. She ran to the bars and hung on, waiting for more. But Grace just waited too. And the next time the girl messed on the newspaper, she sang the song again, adding a line or two. And so, with singing, Grace managed to coax the creature into a pair of pants and a vest, and by the time de Jong returned, she'd learned how to pull them off and put them on herself.

"Master," Grace said, "maybe we can unlock the dogs now."

And so the dogs were led one by one to the cage, ears back, straining at the leash. When the girl heard them coming, she ran wildly for the far corner of the cage, upsetting the bowl, climbing the bars and hanging there, screeching with all her teeth. The dog itself would jump up, wagging, barking wildly, only to be scolded, corrected, made to sit and stay.

Day after day the ritual was repeated until dog and girl could stare at each other without fright. After a while, de Jong could trust the dogs to approach the cage unleashed. And then, at last, when the girl was ready to be taken out, the dogs ran beside her without incident.

"Master," Grace said, "I can't make her stand straight like you said. She still wants to bend over like a baboon. I think she was living with the baboons over there. I think she can still be like them."

De Jong smiled down at the girl. Thick black curls were beginning to cover her head. And her face was beginning to reveal itself, the nose long and straight, a high forehead, small ears, olive skin and the wide black eyes of a gypsy. Considering only the head, she could be any child, any dark, silent girl, no breasts yet, no body hair either. If she still stooped, what difference would it make? She was ready, baboons or no baboons, he could see it in the way she looked at him. It was Grace who was trying to hold her back for some reason.

"You'll bring her to me tomorrow evening," he said, "the usual hour."

Grace bowed her head. Usually, she was only too glad to hand a girl over because then she'd have her two weeks off. When she did return, as often as not the girl would be over the first fright of it. So what had come over her this time? "Maybe a few more days?" she said.

He smiled at Grace. It was almost as if she'd known from the start how it would be with this girl. And now that he was taking pride—well, not so much pride in the girl herself as in the things she could do, the way he could make her obey him—now that he was waking each morning to the thought of what he might make the girl do for him next, now came Grace with her suggestions.

"She does not even have a name yet," Grace said.

They were walking down to the river, which the girl always liked to do. Once he'd thought he heard her laugh—laugh or bark, it was hard to tell which. The sun was shining brilliantly on the muddy water, and she'd looked up into his face, her mouth and eyes wide. And then, freeing her hand from his, she'd bounded down the hill with the dogs, down to the water's edge.

"Tomorrow evening. In the atrium. The usual time." .

Grace had dressed the girl in a simple silk shift. There was a pool in the middle of the atrium, with a fountain at its center. Most of the girls couldn't swim, but the pool was shallow, and he'd be sitting in it, naked, waiting for them with his glass of whiskey. The girls themselves always stopped at the sight of him there, the pink shoulders and small gray eyes. And then he'd rise out of the water like a sea monster and they'd make a run for it, every one of them, never mind how much Grace had told them there was no way out.

Men in the village liked to say they'd come to the house one night and cut off his manhood like a pawpaw. But Grace knew it was all talk. Without his money, where would they all be? Where would she be herself? The Master himself knew that, standing there, shameless, before her. But when he had finished with this one, where would she go? Usually, they'd run home with the money, and then, sooner or later, they'd be back at the kitchen door, wanting work. But what about this one? Where *could* she go except back to the baboons?

Quickly, Grace turned and walked out of the atrium.

He held his hand out to the girl, but she didn't take it. She was leaning over the low wall, splashing one hand into the water. He caught it in his own then, and took her under the arms and lifted her in. She didn't struggle, she was used to his lifting her here or there. But this time he was lifting her dress off her too, throwing it aside. She wasn't wearing any panties, he never wanted them wearing panties when they came to him. So now there was nothing but her smooth olive skin. He ran his hands down her sides and cupped one around each buttock—small and round and girlish, the rest of the body muscled like a boy's.

She let him coax her down into the water, lapping at it happily. And when he moved one hand between her legs, she just glanced down there through the water with the frown she always wore when Grace tried to show her how to wipe herself after she'd used the toilet. But he was stroking her, prodding into her with a finger so that she jumped away and stared hard at him. And still he came after her, taking her by the arms before she could scramble up onto the fountain. He was pushing her backward to the side of the pool and his smile was gone, he was holding her arms wide so that he could force his knee between her legs.

Caught like that, she slammed her head wildly then from side to side against the edge of the tiles, shrieking piteously. A trickle of blood ran down her neck, and when at last he had her legs apart and was thrusting himself into her, she was bleeding there too. He knew from her narrowness that she'd be bleeding properly when he'd finished with her, that her blood would cloud out beautifully into the pool, turning from red to pink. It was the moment he longed for with every new offering, first the front, then the back, and always the mouths open in astonishment like this, the eyes wild and pleading, and for what? For more? More?

By the time he was finished with her and resting his head against the side of the pool, she was moaning. They all moaned like this, and what did they expect? What did this one expect after all these months she'd kept him waiting with her grunts and squawks? He stretched out an arm to grab her neck. Usually that's all it took to shut them up. If it didn't, he'd duck them under the water until they were ready to listen. "Quiet," he'd croon in his deep, soft voice. And if that didn't work, he did it again, and for longer. "Do you hear me now?" he'd whisper. "I said quiet!"

But with this one words were useless. And just as he was about to push her under, she slipped free, twirling herself into the air, twisting, leaping, springing out of reach until, at last, he had caught her by an arm. But then she only doubled back, sinking her teeth into his wrist, and, when he'd let her go, into an ear, and, at last, as his hands flew to his head, she took his throat between her jaws. And there she hung on like a wild dog, only tightening her bite as he bucked and flailed for air. But the more he struggled the deeper she bit, never loosening her jaws until he was past the pain, past the panic. Only then, only after the last damp gurgling of breath had left him limp, did she rip away the flesh and gristle she'd got hold of, and, gulping it down as she ran, leap out through an open window.

When they came in with the tea things, the whole pool was pink, pinker than they'd ever seen it, even the fountain. At first they just stood there, staring at what was left of his throat. But then they remembered the girl, and they ran, one for a kitchen knife, another to lock the doors and windows of the house.

But she never returned. And the generations that followed were inclined to laugh at the whole idea of a baboon girl—of *any* girl killing that demon like a leopard or a lion. They were inclined to doubt the demon himself as well. Surely someone would have reported him to the authorities? they said. Surely one of his girls would have told her story to the papers?

Elizabeth Tallent

Never Come Back

THIS WAS his life now, his real life, the thing he thought about most: his boy was in and out of trouble and he didn't know what to do.

Friday night when he got home late from the mill Daisy made him shower before supper, and he twisted the dial to its hottest setting and turned his back to the expensive showerhead whose spray never pulsed hard enough to perform the virtual massage its advertising promised—or maybe at forty-three he'd used his body too hard, its aches and pains as much a part of him now as his heart or any other organ, and he had wasted good money on an illusion. Ah well. He rubbed at mirror fog and told the dark-browed frowner (his own father!) to get ready: she'd had her Victor look. Whatever this development was, it fell somewhere between failing grade in calculus and car wreck, either of which, he knows from experience, would have been announced as soon as he walked through the door. This news, while it wasn't life or death, was bad enough that she felt she needed to lay the ground-work and had already set their places at the table and poured his beer, a habit he disliked but had never objected to and never would. As a special treat Daisy's father had let her tilt the bottle over his glass while the bubbles churned and the foam puffed like a mushroom cap sidling up from dank earth, and if she enjoyed some echo of the bliss of being in her daddy's good graces while pouring *his* beer, Sean wasn't about to deprive her of that.

Daisy told him:

Neither girl seemed very brave, yet neither seemed willing to back down. Not their own wounds but a sturdy sense of each other's being wronged had driven them to this. They had a kind of punk bravado, there on the threshold, armored in motorcycle jackets whose sleeves fell past their chipped black fingernails. A flight of barrettes had attacked their heads and seized random tufts of dirty hair. Dressed for audacity, but their pointy-chinned faces—really the same face twice—wore the stiff little mime smiles of the easily intimidated, confronting her, the tigress mother, bracing their forlorn selves as best they could, which wasn't very well at all. There was nothing to do but ask them in. As she told it to Sean, Daisy wasn't about to let them guess that (a) she pitied them, and (b) she understood right away there was going to be some truth in what they said. Victor's favorite sweater, needing some mending, lay across the arm of the sofa, and when one of the twins took it into her lap, talisman, claim, Daisy hardly needed to be told that girl was pregnant. As the twins took turns explaining not just one of them was in trouble, both were, an evil radiance pulsed in the corner of Daisy's right eye, the onset of a migraine.

A joke, Sean said. *Because, twins? Somebody told these girls to go to V's house and freak out his parents.*

Drinking around a bonfire and they wander deeper into the woods and they came across this mattress and it's like a sign to them. Sign is what they said. Does that sound like a joke to you? They have a word for it. Threeway. They have a word for it. Ask yourself what these girls know, what they've ever taken care of in their lives. Who's ever taken them seriously? We will. We will, now. Across the table Sean shook

his head, his heavy disgust with his son failing, for once, to galva-
nize Daisy's defense of the boy. In the appalled harmony of their
anger they traded predictions. Victor would be made to marry a
twin, maybe the one whose dark eyes acquired a sheen of tears
when she petted his old sweater, because she seemed the more lost.
Victor would be dragged under.

"When's he get home?" Sean said.

"Away game. Not till two a.m." It was Daisy who would be
waiting in her SUV when the bus pulled up at the high school to
disgorge the sleepy jostling long-legged boys.

"We hold off on doing anything till we hear his side of the
story."

We hold off? If she hadn't loved him she would have laughed
when he said that. It wasn't going to be up to them to hold off or
not hold off, but if Sean was slower to accept that reality than she
was, it was because he hated decisions being out of his hands.

However disgusted he'd been the night before, in the morning
Sean was somber, concerned, protective, everything Daisy could
have wished when he sat Victor down at the kitchen table for
what he called *getting the facts straight.* The reeling daylong party
was true, and the bonfire, and the rain-sodden mattress in the
woods where a drunken Victor had sex with both girls, though
not at the same time, which was what *threeway* meant. They must
have claimed that for dramatic impact, as if this thing needed
more drama, or because they were so smashed events blurred
together in their minds. The next several evenings were taken up
with marathon phone calls—Sean asked most of the questions
and wouldn't hand the receiver to Daisy even when she could tell
he'd been told something especially troubling and mouthed *Give
it to me!* By the following weekend they knew for sure only one
twin was pregnant, though it seemed both had believed they were
telling the truth when they sat on Daisy's striped couch and said
the babies, plural, were due July fifth. The sweater-petting girl
told Sean she had liked Victor for a long time—*years*—and had

wanted to *be* with him, though not in the way it had finally happened, and when he heard this Sean coughed and his eyes got wet, but *who were those tears for?* Daisy wanted to know. *Not for his own kid, for those girls?* Questioned, Victor remembered only that they were twins. He knew it sounded bad but he wasn't sure what they looked like. Nobody was quote in love with him: that was crazy. And no, they hadn't tried to talk to him first, before coming to the house, and was that fair, that they'd assumed there was zero chance of his doing the right thing? And why was marriage the right thing if he didn't want it and whoever the girl was *she* didn't want it and it was only going to end in divorce? The twin who was pregnant had the ridiculous name of Esme, and what she asked for on the phone with Sean—patient, tolerant Sean—was not marriage but child support. If she had that she could get by, she insisted. She'd had a sonogram and she loved the alien-headed letter C curled up inside her. At their graduation dance she shed her high heels and flirted by bumping into the tuxes of various dance partners. Victor followed her into the parking lot. Below she was flat-footed and pumpkin-bellied, above she wore strapless satin, her collarbones stark as deer antlers when he backed her up against an anonymous SUV hard enough their first sober kiss began with shrieks and whistles.

In the hushed joyous days after the baby was born Sean made a serious mistake that he blamed partly on sleep deprivation; the narrow old two-story house had hardly any soundproofing, and because Victor and Esme's bedroom was below his and Daisy's, the baby's crying woke them all. He had stopped in the one jewelry store downtown and completely on impulse laid down his credit card for a delicate bracelet consisting of several strands of silver wound around and around each other. Though simple, the bracelet was a compelling object with a strong suggestion of narrative, as if the maker had been trying to fashion the twining, gleaming progress of several competing loves. He was the sort of husband who gets teased for not noticing new earrings even when his wife repeatedly tucks her hair behind her ears, and any kind of whimsical expenditure was unlike him, but he found he couldn't leave the store without it. He stopped for a beer at the Golden West, and when he got home the only light was from the kitchen, where Esme sat at the table licking the filling from Oreos and washing it down with chocolate milk. Her smile hoped he would empathize with the joke of her appetite rather than scold the late-night sugar extravaganza as, he supposed, Daisy would have done, but it was the white-trash forlornness of her feast that got to Sean—the cheapness and furtiveness and excessive, teeth-aching sweetness of this stab at self-consolation. With her china-doll hair and whiter-than-white skin she was hardly the menace to their peace they had feared, only an ignorant girl who trusted neither her baby's father nor her sneaky conviction that it was she and not the grandmother who ought to be making the big decisions about the baby's care. Esme wet a forefinger and dabbed the crumbs from Daisy's tablecloth as he set the shiny box down next to her dirty plate. She said, "What is this?" and, that fast, there were tears in her eyes. She didn't believe it was for her, but she'd just understood what it would feel like if the little box *had* been hers, and this disbelief was his undoing: until those tears he had honestly had no notion of giving Esme the bracelet. He heard himself say, "Just something for the new mama." As soon as she picked the ribbon apart, even before she tipped the bracelet from its mattress of cotton, he regretted his impulsiveness, but it was too late: she slid it onto her wrist and made it flash in the dim light, glancing to invite his admiration or maybe try to figure out, from his expression, what was going on. In the following days he was sorry to see that she never took it off. Luckily the household was agitated enough that nobody else noticed the bracelet, and he began to hope his mistake would have no ill consequences except for the change in Esme, whose corner-tilted eyes held his whenever he came into the room. Then, quick, she'd turn her head as if realizing this was the sort of thing that could give them away. Of course there was no *them* and not a fucking thing to give away. Sean began to blame her for his uneasiness: she had misconstrued an act of minor, impulsive charity, blown it up into something more, which had to be kept secret. The ridiculousness of her believing he was *interested* was not only troubling in its own right, it pointed to her readiness to immerse herself in fantasy, and this could be proof of some deeper instability. He didn't like being looked at like that in his own house, or keeping secrets. He was not a natural secret keeper, but a big-boned straightforward husband. Since he'd been nineteen, a husband. Daisy came from a rough background too, her father a part-time carpenter and full-time drunk who had once burned his kids' clothes in the backyard, the boys running back into the house for more armfuls of T-shirts and shorts, disenchanted only when their dad made them strip off their cowboy pajamas and throw those in too. The first volunteer fireman on the scene dressed the boys in slickers that reached to their ankles and bundled their naked teeth-chattering sister into an old sweater that stank of crankcase oil, and to this day when Sean changes the oil in his truck he has to scrub his hands outside or Daisy will run to the bathroom to throw up.

As Esme alternated between flirtation and sullenness he tried for kindness. This wasn't all her fault: he was helplessly responsive to vulnerability, and—he could admit it—he did have a tendency to rush in and try to fix whatever was wrong. Therefore he imitated Daisy's forbearance when Esme couldn't get even simple things right, like using hypoallergenic detergent instead of the regular kind that caused the baby to break out in a rash. The tender verbal scat of any mother cradling her baby was a language Esme didn't speak. Her hold was so tentative the baby went round-eyed and chafed his head this way and that wondering who would come to his aid. More than once Esme neglected to pick up dangerous buttons or coins from the floor. She had to be reminded to burp him after nursing and then, chastened, would sling him across her shoulder like a sack of rice. Could you even say she loved the baby? Breast-feeding might account for Esme's sleepy-eyed bedragglement and air of waiting for real life to begin, but, Daisy said, there was absolutely no justifying the girl's self-pity. Consider where she, Daisy, had come from: worse than anything this girl had gone through, but had Sean ever seen her spend whole days feeling sorry for herself, reading wedding magazines in dirty sheets, scarcely managing to crawl from bed when the baby cried? It wasn't as if she had no support. Victor was right there. Who would have believed it? He was attentive to Esme, touchingly proud of his son, and even after a long day at the mill would stay up walking the length of the downstairs hallway with the colicky child so Esme could sleep. For the first time Victor was as good as his word, and could be counted on to deal uncomplainingly with errands and show up when he'd said he would. Victor's changed ways should have mattered more to Esme, given the desolation of her childhood. Victor was *good to her.* Esme could not explain what was wrong or what she wanted, Daisy said after one conversation. She was always trying to talk to the girl, who was growing more and more restless. They could all see that, but not what was coming, because it was the kind of thing you didn't want to believe would happen in your family: Esme disappeared. Dylan was almost four and for whatever reason she had concluded that four was old enough to get by without a mother. That much they learned from her note but the rest they had to find out. She had hitchhiked to the used-car dealership on the south end of town and picked out a white Subaru station wagon; Wynn Handley, the salesman, said she negotiated pleasantly and as if she knew what she was doing and (somewhat to Wynn's surprise, you could tell) ended up with a good deal. Esme paid in cash—not that unusual in a county famed for its marijuana. She left alone—that is, there was no other man. Not as far as Wynn knew, and he was being completely forthcoming in light of the family's distress. The cash was impossible to explain, since after checking online Victor reported their joint account hadn't been touched, and they hadn't saved nearly that much anyway. Esme had no credit card, of course, making it hard to trace her. Discussion of whether they were in any way to blame and where Esme could have gone and whether she was likely to call and want to talk to her son and whether, if she called, there was any chance of convincing her to come back was carried on in hushed voices because no matter what she'd done the boy should not have to hear bad things about his mother.

With Esme gone, Victor began to talk about quitting the mill. The ceaseless roar was giving him tinnitus; his back hurt; there were nights he fell asleep without showering and woke already exhausted, doomed to another day just like the last, and how was he supposed to have any energy left for a four-year-old? Had Esme thought of that before she left, he wondered—that he might not be able to keep it together? No doubt his steadiness had misled her into thinking it was safe to leave, and when he remembered how reliable and fond and funny and tolerant he had been, anger slanted murderously through his body; and it was like anger practiced on him, got better and better at leaving him with shaking hands and a dilated sense of hatred with no nearby object; and he began to be very, very careful not to be alone with his little boy.

Dylan understood this. After nightmares he did not try his dad's room, right next to his, but padded his way through the dark house up the narrow flight of stairs to the bedroom, where he slid in between Sean and Daisy. More than once his cold bare feet made accidental contact with Sean's genitals, and Sean had to capture the feet and guide them away. This left him irritably awake, needing to make the long trip to the bathroom downstairs, and when he returned the boy was still restless and Sean watched him wind a hand into Daisy's long hair and rub it against his cheek until he could sleep. Worse than jealousy was the affront to Sean's self-regard in feeling so contemptible an emotion. This was a scared little boy, this was his tight hold on safety, this was his grandfather standing by the side of the bed looking meanly down. Protectiveness toward his own flesh and blood had always been Sean's ruling principle, and if that went wrong he didn't know who he was anymore. He rose to dress for work one chilly 6:00 a.m. and noticed the amateur tattoos running cruelly down the boy's arm. Had an older kid got hold of him somehow, was this some kind of weird abuse, why hadn't he come running to his grandfather? Sean bent close to decipher the trail of descending letters. I LOVE YOU. Not another kid, then. Not abuse. But wasn't that bad for him, wouldn't the ink's toxins be absorbed through his skin, didn't she think that was going a little too far, inscribing her love on the boy while he did what—held his arm out bravely? Time, past time, for Sean to try to talk to Daisy, to suggest that day care would be a good idea, or a playgroup where the boy could meet other kids. When Daisy was tired or wanted time to herself she left the boy alone with the remote, and once Sean walked in on the boy sitting cross-legged while on the screen a serial killer wrapped body parts in plastic, and how could you talk to a child after that, what could you tell him that could explain that away? All right, they could do better. He supposed most people could do better by their kids. Maybe her judgment in taking a pen to the boy's arm wasn't perfect, but was it such a bad thing to have love inscribed on your skin, whoever you were? Half the world was dying for want of that. If Daisy adored this boy Sean could live with that. More than live with it: he admired it. He admired her for being willing to begin again when she knew how it could end.

Maybe Victor's mood would have benefited from confrontation— a kitchen-table sit-down where, with cups of reheated coffee to warm their hands, father and son could try to get at the root of the problem—but envisioning his own well-meaning heavy-heartedness and guessing that Victor would take offense, Sean was inclined to ignore his son's depression. In most cases, within a family, there was wisdom in holding one's tongue. Except for one thing: Victor could, if he concluded his chances were better elsewhere, take the boy with him when he left. This gave a precarious tilt to their household, an instability whose source was, really, Victor's fondness for appearing wronged. He came home with elaborate tales of affronts he had suffered, but Sean knew the foreman and doubted any unfairness had been shown Victor. When Victor needed to vent, Sean steered clear and Daisy, rather than voicing her true opinion—that it was time he got over Esme—calmly heard him out. Victor could ruin his mother's peace of mind by ranting at the unbelievable fucking hopelessness of this fucking dead-end town, voice so peeved and fanatical in its recounting of injustice that Sean, frowning across the dinner table, thought he must know how ridiculous he sounded, how almost crazy, but Victor kept on: he was only waiting for the day when the mill closed down for good and he could pack up his kid and his shit and get out. What were they, blind? Couldn't they see he had no life? Did they think he could take this another fucking day? From his chair near his dad Dylan said, "Are we going away?" "No, baby boy, you're not going anywhere," said Sean, at which Victor did the unthinkable, pulling out the gun tucked into the back of his jeans and setting it with a chime on his dinner plate and saying, "Then maybe this is what I should eat." Daisy said, "Sean," wanting him to do something, but before he could Victor pushed the plate across the table to him and said, "No, no, no, all right, I'm sorry, that was in front of the kid, that's taking it too far, I know I know I know, don't ask me if I meant it because you know I don't but I swear to god, Dad, some days it crosses my mind. But I won't. I never will." Gently he cupped his boy's head. "I'm sorry to have scared you, Dyl. Daddy got carried away." "I want that gun out of the house," Daisy said. Sean had gone out into the starry night and folded the passenger seat of his truck forward and tucked the gun into the old parka he kept there. In bed that night

Daisy turned to him, maybe needing to feel that something was still right in their life, and while he understood the impulse and even shared it, he found he was picturing Esme's pointed chin, her head thrown back, her urchin hair fanned out across a filthy mattress in the woods, an image so wrong and *good* he couldn't stop breathing life into it, the visitation no longer blissfully involuntary but nursed along, fed with details; the childish lift of her upper lip as she picked at the gift-box ribbon came to him, the imagined grace of her pale body against the filthy mattress, her arms stretched overhead, her profile clean against the ropy twists of dirty hair, no she wouldn't look, she wouldn't look and he came without warning, Daisy far enough gone that momentum rocked her farther, Sean relieved when she managed the trick that mostly eluded her while also, in some far-back, disownable part of his mind, judging her climax too naked, too needful, and at the same time impersonal, since she had no idea where he was in his head, and this, her greedy solitary capacity, bothered him. In the slowed-down aftermath when their habit was to roll apart and stretch frankly and begin to talk about whatever came to mind, a brief spell, an island whose sanctity they understood, where they were truly, idly, themselves, their true selves, the secret selves only they recognized in each other, she didn't move or speak and he continued to lie on her worrying that he was growing heavier and heavier, her panting exaggerated as if to communicate the extremity of her pleasure, and for a sorry couple of minutes he hated her. There was something offensive in her unawareness of his faithlessness. If he was faithless even in his mind he wanted it to matter and it couldn't matter unless she could intuit it and hold him accountable and by exerting herself against him, as she had a right to, make him want to come all the way back to her. That was up to her. If she couldn't do it then he might continue to be bewilderingly alone and even slightly, weirdly in love with the lost girl Esme, indefensible as that was, and astounding. Daisy squirmed companionably out from under, turned on her side, a hand below her cheek, the crook of her other arm bracing her breasts, the light of her eyes, the creases at the corners of her smile confiding, genuine, her goodness obvious, the goodness at the heart of his world, the expression on his face god knows what, but by her considering stillness she was working up to a revelation. With Daisy sex sometimes turned the keys of the secretest locks and he could never guess what was coming, since years and decades of wrongs and sorrows awaited confession, and even now, having loved her for twenty years, he could be surprised by some small flatly told story of some terrible thing that had happened when she was a kid. Damage did that, went in so deep it took long years to surface. Tonight he had no inclination to be trusted, but could hardly stop her. "This thing's sort of been happening. Maybe four or five times? This thing of the phone ringing and no one being there. 'Hello.' " The *hello* was hers. "And no answer. And 'Hello.' And no answer. Somebody there, though. Somebody there."

Such a relief not to have to travel again through the charred landscape of her childhood that he almost yawned. "Kids. Messing around."

"No," she said. "Her." His frown must have been puzzled because she said, "Esme."

"Esme."

"Don't believe me then but I'm right, it was her and the last time she called I said, 'Listen to me. Are you listening?' and there was no answer and I said, 'Never come back.' I didn't know that was about to come out of my mouth, I was probably more surprised than she was. 'Never come back.' "

"And then what?"

"And then she hung up." She scratched one foot with the toes of the other. "And that's not like me. And I didn't have any right, did I?" Rueful smile. "If I'd said, 'Honey, where are you? Are you in trouble?' that would have been like me, right? And maybe she would have told me, maybe something is wrong and that girl has nowhere else to turn. She's the kind of girl there's not just one filthy mattress in the woods in her life, not just one fantastic fuckup, but last time she was lucky and found us, and we let her come live in our house, and we loved her, I think—did we love her?—and I think if things got bad enough for her she'd think of us and remember we were *good* to her, weren't we good to her?"

"Yes."

"Yes and now it's like I'm waiting for her to call again. Or turn up. I think that's next. She'll turn up. And I don't want her to. I never want to see that girl's face again."

He couldn't summon the energy for *I'm sure it wasn't her,* even if that was probably true. He could also have accepted Daisy's irrational conviction and addressed it with his usual calm. *Of course you're angry. Irresponsible, not just to her little boy, but to us who took her in, who cared about her—she left without a word. It's natural to be angry.*

He lay there withholding the consolation that was his part in this back-and-forth until she turned onto her back and stared at the ceiling.

I made a serious mistake with Esme once. Gave her a bracelet. If he could have said that. If he could have found a way to begin.

Dent Figueredo wasn't someone Sean thought of as a friend, but this sweet May evening they were alone in the Tip-Top, door open to the street alive with sparrow song and redolent of asphalt cooling in newly patched potholes, Dent behind the bar, Sean on his barstool thinking about taxes, paying no attention until he heard "I want your take on this."

"My take."

"You're smart about women."

Women? But Sean nodded, and when that didn't seem to be enough, he said, "Hit me."

"See first of all despite her quote flawless English she utters barely a word in the airport, just looks at me like I saved her life, which you'd think I would be a sucker for but no, I'm praying *get me out of this*, ready to turn the truck around and put her on the next flight home, and like she knows what I'm on the verge of she unbuckles and slides over and you know Highway Twenty twists and turns like a snake on glass, I never felt that trapped before in my life, just because this itty-bitty girl has hold of my dick through my trousers and you *know* she's never done that before and I should've known that at this late date I'm not good husband material, should have lived with that but no, I had to get melty when I seen her doe-eyed picture on the Internet. Shit."

"Husband material."

"What you got to promise if you want a nice Filipina girl," Dent said. "She's some kind of born-again. Dressed like a little nun, baggy skirt and these flat black worn-out shoes. No makeup. Won't hold your eye." When he catches Sean's eye he looks down and away, smiling, this imitation of girly freshness at odds with Dent's bald sunspotted pate and the patch of silvery whiskers he missed on his Adam's apple, and Sean can't help laughing.

"What happens to her now?"

"Stories she tells, shit, curl your hair." Dent used his glass to print circles of wet on the bar. "America still looks good to a lot of the world, I tell you." He crouched to the refrigerator with his crippled leg stuck out behind. "She's staying in my house till I can figure out what comes next, and you should see the place, neat as a picture in a magazine. Hard little worker, I give her that. If any of my boys was unmarried I'd drag him to the altar by the scruff of his neck." He levered open his beer, raising it politely. Sean shook his head. "Course before long," Dent continued, "one of them boys will shake loose."

"Meanwhile where does she sleep, this paragon?"

"Nah, Filipina."

"And you two, have you been—?"

"Ming. Cute, huh?" Dent drank from the bottle before pouring into his glass.

"Took the upstairs room for her own, cleared out years of boy shit. Jesus won't let nobody near her till there's a ring on her finger. Twenty-two and looks fifteen. That's the undernourishment."

When, sitting down to dinner that night, Sean told Daisy about the girl, she said, "You're kidding," and made him tell the entire story again, then said, amused, "Poor thing. You *know* he lied to her. And do you think he ever sent his picture? He's, what, a poorly preserved sixty, a drinker, a smoker, hobbling around on that leg and he talks this child into leaving her home and her family and now he won't do the right thing?"

"He'd never seen her till she got off the plane. I think his lack of any feeling for her came as a shock. And in his defense he is leaving her alone."

"Of course he's terrified of any constraint on his drinking. Dylan Raymond, we are waiting for your father."

Dylan put down the green bean he was trailing through his gravy and said, "Why?"

"Yeah, I think that's maybe more to the point. Because she's a born-again, and might start in on him."

"Is she pretty?"

"He says she has drawbacks." He bared his teeth. "Primitive dental care."

"Oh and he's George Clooney."

"But she's sweet, he says," Sean said, prolonging his bared-teeth smile. "Good-natured."

Victor came to the table then in his signature ragged black T-shirt and jeans, his pale workingman's feet—which never saw the sun—bare, dark hair still dripping wet, and he stood behind Dylan, kneading the boy's shoulders. "Who're we talking about?" he wanted to know.

"My mom is pretty," Dylan announced, then waited with an air of uncertainty and daring—the kid who's said something provocative in the hope the adults will get into the forbidden subject. Victor could conceivably say, "What mom?" He could conceivably say, "You wouldn't know your mom if you passed her in the street." He could conceivably say, "That bitch." Sean knew Victor to be capable of any or all of these remarks, and was relieved when Victor calmly continued to rub the boy's shoulders. Not answering was fine, given the alternatives. When Dylan began drawing in his gravy with the green bean again, his head down, he inscribed circles like those his dad was rubbing into his shoulders, in the same rhythm. How does he understand his mother's absence? Sean wondered. Surely it's hard for him that his father never mentions his mother, worrisome that nobody can say where she's gone. Daisy has not made up any tale justifying Esme's desertion. Sean understood the attraction of lying consolation; he felt it himself. The boy's relief would have been worth almost any falsehood, but Daisy had insisted that they stick with what they knew, which was virtually nothing. Daisy said, "Yes, your mother is pretty," with a sidelong glance at Victor to make sure this didn't prompt meanness from him.

Victor changed the subject: "Who were you saying was sweet?"

Ming had no demure, closed-mouth smile, as he'd expected from an Asian girl, but a wide, flashing laugh whose shamelessness disturbed Victor, for her small teeth were separated by touching gaps, the teeth themselves incongruously short, like pegs driven hastily into the ground. The decided sweetness of her manner almost countered the daredevilish, imbecile impression made by those teeth. Seated on a slab of rock at the beach, he peeled off his socks. Flatteringly, Ming had dressed for their date—not only a dress, stockings, and *high heels*—while he had worn jeans and his favorite frayed black T-shirt, but he figured this was all right, she would know from movies that American men complained about ties and jackets. Ming's poise as she stood one-legged, peeling the stocking from her sandy foot, was very pretty, and the wind wrapped her dress—navy blue printed with flying white petals— tightly around her thighs and little round butt. Her panty hose were rolled up and tucked into a shoe, her shoes wedged into a crevice of the rock. In the restaurant earlier Victor had observed her table manners and found them wanting. It wasn't so much that she made overt mistakes as that she wasn't allowing for the grace-note pauses and frequent diversions—a smile, a little conversation—with which food is properly addressed in public, but chewed steadily with her little fox teeth. Her style overall began to seem quick and unfastidious and he was curious about what that would translate to in bed. He had been trying not to think about that because he knew from what Dent had said—first to his dad and then, when Victor called, to Victor himself—that she was a virgin, and it seemed wrong to try to guess what she would be like, sexually, when the only right way of perceiving her was as a semi-sacred blank slate. Respect, protectiveness: he liked having these feelings as he slouched against the rock, the wind bothering his hair, the bare-legged woman turning to find him smiling, smiling in return. There: the unlucky teeth. Guess what, she's human. He jumped from the rock and took her hand and they walked down the beach.

For nearly a year Victor was happier than his parents had ever known him to be, even after he was laid off from the mill for the winter. Not the time you'd want to get pregnant, but Ming did, and when she miscarried at five months, they both took it hard. "She won't get out of bed, Dad," Victor confided in a late-night call. "Won't eat, either." After work the next day Sean decided to swing by their place, a one-story clapboard cottage that suited the newlyweds fine except that it didn't have much of a yard and lacked a second bedroom for Dylan; all agreed the boy should continue living at his grandparents'. *Two birds with one stone,* in Sean's view. Not only was the continuity good for Dylan, but once she saw she wasn't going to have to negotiate for control of the boy, Daisy was free to be a kind, unintrusive mother-in-law. Privately, Sean has all along believed he is better than the other two at relating to Ming. To Daisy, Ming was the odd small immigrant solution to the riddle of Victor, the girl who had supper waiting when he got home, who considered his paycheck a prince's ransom, who tugged off his boots for him when he was tired. The miscarriage was a blow but such things happened. Ming was sturdy and would get over it. Basically Daisy was only so interested in anyone other than Dylan, and Victor—well, could you count on Victor to bring a person flowers to cheer her up? Or ice cream? Even if Ming won't eat anything else she might try a little of the mint chocolate-chip she loves. Safeway is near their cottage, so Sean swings into the parking lot and strides in, wandering around in the slightly theatrical male confusion that says *My wife usually does all this* before finding what he wants, remembering Daisy had said they were out of greens, deciding on a six-pack of beer, too, craving a box of cigarettes when it was time to pay, that habit kicked decades ago, its urgency a symptom of his sadness about the lost baby, and bizarrely, ridiculously, he was standing in the checkout line with tears in his eyes, recognizing only then that the girl thrusting Ming's roses into the bag was Esme.

She seemed to have been trying not to catch his attention, and he wondered if she had been hoping against hope he would conclude his business and walk out without ever having noticed her. She could reasonably hope for that, he supposed: a job like hers could teach you that the vast majority of people walked through their lives unseeing. The checker was hastening the next lot of groceries down the conveyor belt, loaves of bread and boxes of cereal borne toward Esme as Sean hoisted his bags and said, "So you're back."

"Not for long."

"Not staying long, or you haven't been back long?"

Over his shoulder, to the next person: "Paper or plastic."

"You're staying with your sister?"

None of his business, her look said.

The woman behind squeezed past Sean to claim her bag, frowning at him for the inconvenience—no, he realized, she was frowning because she thought he was bothering Esme, who scratched at her wrist, then twisted a silver bracelet around, *the* bracelet, part of her repertoire of nervous gestures, because this was Esme, fidgeting, resentful, scared—smiling to cover it up but construing the mildest gestures or words as slights, taking offense with breathtaking swiftness and leaving you no way to remedy the situation. In the face of such fantastical touchiness, gracefulness became an implausible virtue—quaint, like chastity. Nonetheless he tried: "Come to see Dylan."

"Paper or plastic."

"He wonders about you, you know."

"Plastic."

To Sean, who had edged out of the aisle and stood holding his bags, she said wretchedly, "Does he?"

Sean said, though it was far from the case, "No one holds anything against you. He needs you. He's five years old."

"I know how old he is," she said. "I do."

"Or I could bring him by if that's easier."

Abruptly she stopped bagging groceries and pressed the heels of her hands to her eyelids. It was as if she'd temporarily broken with the world and was retreating to the deepest sanctuary possible in such a place. It was as if she despaired. He was sorry to have been a contributing factor, sorry to be among those she couldn't make disappear; at the same time he felt formidably in the right, and as if he was about to prevail—to cut through her fears and evasiveness and self-loathing heedlessness to the brilliant revelation, from Esme to herself, of mother love, a recognition she would never be able to go back on, which would steady her and bring her to her senses and leave her grateful for the change that had begun right here and now in the checkout line at Safeway. Because lives had to change unglamorously and for the better. Because he had found her.

"Would you really do that?" Esme said.

"Yeah, I'd do that."

She tore a scrap from the edge of the bag she was filling, reached past the glaring cashier for a pen from the cup by the register, scribbled, and handed Sean the leaf of brown paper, which he had to hunt for, the next day, when it came time to call her, worrying that he'd lost it, finding it, finally, tucked far down into the pocket of the work pants he'd been wearing, but Esme wasn't there and instead he got her sister, who told him Esme would be home from work at five. Sarah was this one's name, he remembered. "You know, she said you were really nice. Kind. So I want to thank you. She might not tell you this herself but I know she can't wait to see the little guy. Me, too." Fine, they would come by around six. Sean hadn't yet broken the news of Esme's return to Daisy, much less Victor, partly for his own sake, because he wanted to conserve the energy needed to deal with Daisy's inevitable fretting and Victor's righteous anger, partly for Dylan, because he wanted the boy to meet his mother again in a relatively quiet, relatively sane atmosphere, without a lot of fireworks going off, without anyone's suggesting maybe it wasn't the best thing for the boy to spend time with a mother so irresponsible. Was there, in this secrecy, the flicker of another motive? Something like wanting to keep her to himself. Sean, driving, shook his head at this insight, and beside him Dylan asked, "Am I going to live with her now?"

"Honey, no, this is just for a little while, for you guys to see each other. You know what a visit is, right? And how it's different from *live with*? You live with us. You are going to *visit* your mom for a couple of hours. Meaning you go home after. With me. I come get you."

"What color is her hair?"

"Don't you remember? Her hair is black. Like—." He felt foolish when all he could come up with was "—well, not like any of ours."

"Not like mine."

"No, yours is brown." Sean tried to think what else Dylan

wouldn't remember. "Your mom has a sister, a twin, meaning they look just alike and that'll be a little strange for you maybe, but you'll get used to it, and this sister, see, is your aunt Sarah, and this's your aunt's house I'm taking you to. Because your mom is staying there. With her sister."

Too much news for sure, and for the rest of the brief drive Dylan sucked his thumb as he hadn't for years, but Sean didn't reprimand him, just parked the truck so the two of them could study the one-story white clapboard house with the scruffy yard where a bicycle had lain on its side long enough that spears of iris had grown up through its spokes. If this had been an ordinary outing, Sean would have explained, "They built all these little houses on the west side for workers in the mill, and they don't look like much maybe but they're nice inside and the men were allowed to take home seconds from the mill and they made some beautiful cabinets in their kitchens," because he likes telling the boy bits of the history of his hometown, but he kept that lore to himself and when the boy seemed ready they climbed the front porch steps together and stood before the door. "You want to knock or should I?"

"You."

Sean used his knuckles, three light raps, and then Esme was saying through the screen to Dylan, "Hey you," smiling her pained childish smile, and Dylan couldn't help himself, he was hers, Sean saw, instantly, gloriously hers because she'd smiled and said two words. She held the door ajar and Dylan went past her into the house and he never did things like that—he was shy.

"Coming in?"

"I'll leave you two alone. To get—" *Reacquainted* would strike her as a reproach, maybe. "So you can have some time to yourselves. Just tell me when to come for him and I'll be back." He paused. "His bedtime's eight o'clock and it would be good if I got him home before that." In case he needs some settling down. Sean doesn't say that, or think about how he's going to keep the boy from telling his grandmother where he's been, but he'll find a way, some small bribe that will soothe the boy's need to tell all.

"Not even two hours," she said.

"It's not a great idea to feed him a lot of sugar or anything, 'cause then he gets kind of wired."

"I wasn't going to," she said. "I know how he is."

"It would only be natural if you wanted to give him a treat or something."

"To worm my way back into his affections."

"Not what I meant."

In her agitation she gave her wrist a punishing twist—no, she was fooling with the silver bracelet, and he suffered an emotion bruising but minor, too fleeting or odd, maybe, ever to have been named, nostalgia for a miserably wrongheaded sexual attraction. Not regret. He had repented for giving her the bracelet by bringing her kid to her. Had that really been his reason? He repeated, "Not what I meant."

"So maybe you won't believe this, I can see why you wouldn't, but I wanted to see him so bad. Only I thought you-all would for sure say no. Blame me. Not, you know, trust me. And instead you've made it easy for me and I never expected that and I don't know how to thank you, Sean, I don't, but this means everything to me, it's kind of saving my life. It's really basically saving my life." Running the sentences together, so unaccustomed was she to honesty, afraid, maybe, of the feeling of honesty, scary if you weren't used to it, and Sean reached out to lay a finger on her lips, ancient honorable gesture for *hush now,* no further explanation was necessary, he got it that to see your child again was like having your life saved, he would have felt the same way in her shoes but also chastened and rebellious confronting someone like him who was doing the real work, constantly and reliably there for the boy, and he wanted to convey the fact that none of this mattered if she was here and could give the boy a little of what he needed, a sense of his mother: but now it was Sean who was inarticulate, moved by the girl softness of her mouth, Sean whose finger rested against her lips until she jerked her head back and he was blistered by shame, the burden of impossible apology and regret shifting from her shoulders to his. He waited for her to say something direct and blaming, scathing, memorable, and when she did not he was relieved. But he wasn't fooled, either. She knew exactly what had happened and where it left them. This girl believed she now had the upper hand, but must use her leverage tactfully, however unlike her that was, if he was not to instantly deny what had taken place. What he understood was that he was in trouble here, but that she was going to collude with him because, basically, he could give her more of what she wanted. The child. His agreement was necessary for her to continue secretly seeing the child. And Sean did not know how to set any of this right, only that he needed to keep his voice down and not do any further harm—not scowl in dismay or do anything else she could construe as a sign of problems to come. He told her, "Seven-thirty then, okay? See you at seven-thirty," and she said in a voice in no way remarkable, "We'll be here."

But they were not. "She has rights," Sarah told Sean, who was in her kitchen, in a rickety chair she had pulled away from the table, saying, "She has rights," saying now, "It's wrong for him to be kept from his *mother* the way you-all have done."

For some reason, when she'd pulled the chair out for him, he'd taken it and turned it around and straddled it. Maybe he had needed to act, to take control of something, if only the chair. This is her sister—or closer than sister, twin—and he keeps his voice down. "Ask yourself why I brought him by. I'm her best friend in this mess, but what she's done is damage her own cause. This isn't gonna look good."

"To who?"

"Do you know where she's going?"

"To who won't it look good?"

Trailer trash, Daisy called the sisters once. "The thing is to make this right without having anybody else get involved."

"You're threatening me."

"I'm the opposite of threatening you. I'm saying let's work this out ourselves. You tell me where she's gone and I find her and we work it out like reasonable people and there's no need for anybody else to know she abducted a five-year-old child."

"*A* five-year-old. You-all opened your door and *what's in this basket? A cute little baby!* She wasn't in labor eighteen hours. She never chipped a tooth from clenching or left claw marks on my hand. Tell me you ever even really knew she was in the house. Tell me you ever once really talked to her. Victor hit her upside the head so hard the ringing in her ear lasted a week. Do you know he said he'd kill her if she tried to leave? It was my four thousand dollars. So she ran, you know, she took the money and she ran and there was never any phone call and it kept me up a lot of nights. It wasn't the money, it was not knowing she was all right—they say twins know that but I didn't, not till I saw her again. And I never saw her look at anyone like she looks at that little boy when he says *I want to stay with you* and it's not like she planned this but after that how was she going to let him go? I'm not saying she makes great choices but you were unrealistic thinking she could give him back."

The chair wobbled as he crossed his arms on its backrest. "Maybe so. She and I need to talk about that. Work out what's best for all concerned."

"It sounds so reasonable when you say it."

"I am reasonable." He smiles. "Families need to work these things out."

"Now you're family."

"Like it or not." Still smiling.

Sarah gave in. Esme was driving north toward Arcata to go to college there. "None of you thought she was good enough for college."

An outright lie but he let it go. "How long ago did they take off?"

"Not long. She had to get her stuff. She was just throwing things into the car. Dylan helped. Laughing like they were both little kids." He continued to look at her. "Mmm. Twenty minutes ago maybe."

"What kind of car?"

"I don't know kinds of cars." He won't look away. "Smallish. A Toyota maybe. Green maybe." Not smiling now: he needs her to get this right. "Yeah. Green. A bumper sticker. Stop fucking something up. That really narrows it down, hunh. Trees. 'Stop Killing Ancient Trees.' Trees are her thing."

"You're sure about Arcata."

"See, she's wanted that for years, an apartment and classes and her little boy with her. Botany. Redwoods, really. Did you know that about her? She loves redwoods and there's this guy there who's famous, like *the* guy if you want to study redwoods, and she met him, and she might be going to be his research assistant this summer. She said—" But she'd told him what he needed to know and he was out the door. Lucky that it was north, the two-lane highway looping through the woods without a single exit for sixty miles and few places to pull over, lucky that after dark nobody drives this road but locals and not many of those. As long as he checks every pull-off carefully and doesn't overshoot her then it comes down to how fast he can drive, each curve with its silver-gray monoliths stepping forward while their sudden shadows revolve through the woods behind, the ellipse of shadow-swerve the mirror image of his curve, evergreen air through the window, no oncoming lights, which is just as well given his recklessness, the rage he can admit now he's alone, the desire just to get his hands on her, the searing passage of his brights through the woods like the light of his mind gathered and concentrated into swift hunting intelligence that touches and assesses and passes on because its exclusive object is her. At this speed it's inevitable he will overtake her—nobody drives this road like this—but now he's bolted past a likely spot, a scruffy rutted crescent rimmed with trees tall enough to shade it from moonlight: there. He brakes and runs the truck backward onto the shoulder, passing an abandoned car whose color, in the darkness, can't be discerned, and pulling in behind he reads STOP KILLING ANCIENT TREES. Such fury, such concentration, and he almost missed it. An empty car. Here is his fear: that she has arranged to meet someone. That Sarah was lied to, and Arcata was a fable, and there's a guy in this somewhere, and she told him she would go away with him if she could get her kid. Nobody to be seen but when he gets out in the moonlight it was as if the air around Sean was sparkling, as if electricity flashed from his skin and glittered at the forest, as if he could convey menace even to a stone. When he checked in the backseat there was the boy curled up, sleeping in his little T-shirt and underpants with nothing over him, no blanket, not even an old sweater or jacket, and cracking the door open—its rusty hinges alarming the woods—Sean ducks into a cave of deepest oldest life-tenderness and takes the child in his arms and leans out loving the weight of him and the shampoo smell of his mussed hair. He sets him down barefoot and blinking, his underpants a triangular patch of whiteness in the moonlight, the boy as shy as if it was he who'd run away, keeping a fearful arm's length from Sean, and when Sean says, "Where's your mom?" blinking again, seeming not to trust Sean, confused and on the brink of tears and there's no time for that. That was for later. "Get in the truck," he tells the boy, "and I don't want you coming out no matter what. Your job is to stay in the truck and I don't want you getting out of that truck for any damn reason whatsoever, do you understand me?"

"I have to pee."

"Come on then."

Watching from behind Sean feels the usual solicitude at the boy's wide-legged stance. Dry weeds crackle.

"She had to go pee in the woods," he said. Solemnly: "My mom did, in the woods."

That was a new one to the boy.

Sean said, "What happened to your clothes?"

"I threw up and she made me take 'em off and throw 'em out the window cause the smell was making her sick too."

"All right, now you get in my truck and you *stay* in the truck. What did I just say?"

"*Stay* in the truck."

"What're you going to do?"

"*Stay* in the truck."

He has to boost the shivering boy up to the high seat. Sean takes the flashlight from the glove box and checks to make sure the keys are in his pocket. He gestures for Dylan to push the lock down, first on the passenger side, then, leaning across, on the driver's. Sean nods through the window but the boy only wraps his arms around himself and twists his bare legs together, and Sean remembers the old parka stuffed down behind his seat and gestures for the boy to unlock again and leans in and says, "Look behind the seat and there's a jacket you can put on," and his flash frames twigs and brambles in sliding ovals of ghost light, stroking the dark edge of the woods, finding the deer trail she must have followed. By now she had to be aware that he was coming in after her, and he took the shimmer of his own agitation to mean *she* was scared, and somehow this was intolerable, that she would be scared of him, that she would not simply walk out of the woods and face him. That he is in her mind not a good man, a kind man, but instead the punisher she has always believed would come after her, and whether he wanted to cause fear or didn't want to scarcely mattered since that role was carved out ahead of him, narrow as this trail: coming into the woods after her he can't be a good man. He can't remember the last time he felt this kindled and all-over passionate, supple and brilliant, murderously *good*, and when his flash discovered her she was already running, but it took only two long strides to catch her. She broke her fall with her hands but before she could twist over onto her back he had her pinned. If she could have turned and they could have seen each other it might have calmed them both down but this way, with her back under his chest, his mouth by her ear, he was talking right to her fear-lit brain and what he said would be permanent and he felt the exhilaration of being about to drive the truth home to her, and he said *What is the matter with you* and then *You took my kid* and she said *He's not your kid* and he said *My flesh and blood* and they both waited for what she would say next to find out whether she had come to the end of defiance but she hadn't. *If you take him away I'll just come back.* Even now she could have eased them back from this brink if she had shown a little remorse and he was sorry she hadn't and said *What do I need to do to get through to you.* She thrashed as he rolled her over and her fist caught the flashlight, sending light hopping away across the ground. In the refreshed darkness he reached for her neck and she was screaming his name as his hands tightened to shut off her voice. Where his flashlight had rolled to a halt a cluster of hooded mushrooms stood up in awed distinctness like tiny watchers. When she clawed at his face he seized her wrists and heard twigs breaking under her as she twisted. The twining silver bracelet imprinted itself on his palm: he could feel that, and it was enough to bring him to himself, but she did not let up, raking at his throat when he reared back, and now her despairing *Fuck you fuck you fuck you* assailed him, its echo bandied about through the woods until feeling her wrath slacken from exhaustion he rolled from her so she would know it was over and they fell quiet except for their ragged breathing, which made them what neither wanted to be, a pair, and as he sat up something nicked the back of his skull in its flight, frisking through his hair, an electrifying noncontact that sang through his skull to the roots of his teeth and the retort cracked through the woods and there was the boy, five feet away, holding the gun with his legs braced wide apart. Behind him rose a fountain of sword ferns taller than he was. "Don't shoot," she said. "Listen to me, Dyl, don't shoot the gun again, okay? You need to put it down now."

He turned to Sean then to see how bad it was, what he had done, and in staring back at him Sean could feel by the contracted tensions of his face that it was a wrecked mask of disbelief and no reassurance whatsoever to the boy.

"It was a accident," the boy said. "I'm sorry if I scared you."

"Just you kneel down and put it on the ground," she said. "In the leaves—yes, just like that. That was good."

"It was a accident."

"Sweetie, I know it was." She sat up. With her face averted she said to Sean, "It could have been either of us. Did it nick you? Are you bleeding?"

He felt through his hair and held his hand out and they both looked: a perfect unbloodied hand stared back at them.

"A fraction of an inch," he said in a voice soft as hers had been: conspirators. "I left the damn gun in the car. Fuck, I never even checked the safety, I was so sure it wasn't loaded. It would've been my fault and he'd've had to live with it forever."

"He doesn't have to live with it now," she said. "Or with you."

She was on her feet, collecting the flashlight, and playing through the sapling audience the light paused and she said, "Jesus," and he turned to look behind him at a young tan oak whose dove-gray bark was gashed in sharp white.

She turned from him. She told the boy, "It's okay. Look at my eyes, Dylan. Nobody's hurt. You see that, don't you? Nobody got hurt."

"You did," he said.

"Baby, I'm not hurt. Pawpaw didn't hurt me, and you know what? We're getting out of here. You're coming with me."

Dylan looked down at the gun and she said, "No, leave it." Then changed her mind. "I'm taking it," she told Sean, "because that's wisest, isn't it."

"You can't think that," Sean said.

"Tell me you're okay to be left," she said.

"A little stunned is all."

"That's three of us then."

Dylan was staring at him and Sean collected his wits to say clearly, "You know what a near-miss is, don't you, Dyl? Close but not quite? That bullet came pretty close but I'm what you call unscathed. Which means fine. Are you hearing me say it didn't hurt me? Nod your head so I'm sure you understand." The boy nodded. "We're good then, right? You can see I'm good." The boy nodded.

Esme said, "We need to go, Dylan. Look at you. You're shivering."

"Where are we going?"

"Far away from here, and don't worry, it's all right if we go. Tell him now that we can go."

This was meant for Sean, and they watched as he took the full measure of what he had done and how little chance there was of her heeding what he said now: "Don't disappear with him, Esme. Don't take him away forever because of tonight. From now on my life will be one long trying to make this right to you. For him, too. Don't keep him away. My life spent making up for this. I need you to believe me. I can make this right."

"I want to believe you," she said. "I almost want to believe you."

Before he could think how to begin to answer that the mother and child were gone.

He knew enough not to go after them. He knew enough not to go after them yet.

Matthew Neill Null

Something You Can't Live Without

THREADGILL HAD been one of them, or something like it. This part of the world hadn't been penetrated by the Company in four seasons, ever since they lost him, their ace drummer, on the Blackwater River, where he'd been shot off a farmer's wife by the farmer himself. While the man fumbled a fresh shell into the breach of his shotgun, Threadgill ran flopping out the back door and tumbled down the sheer cliff behind the cabin. There he came to rest in the arms of a mighty spruce. The tree held him like a babe till they rigged up a block and tackle to lift him out. They said he had nothing but socks on, argyle. The image bored into Cartwright's brain like a weevil. The week the Company hired Cartwright on as a drummer, he found the dead man's sucker list wrapped in oilskin and tacked under the wagon tongue. It was the secret of Cartwright's success. He grew flush off commission in no time.

Polishing a new gold tooth with his tongue, Cartwright clattered down the road in a buckboard wagon. He followed the split-rail fence worming along the trace. Ironweed and seven sisters grew between the ruts, tickling the horses—a gelded pair of blood bays. The farther he traveled, the more the roadbed degraded. The spring rains had gnawed small ravines into it all the way down to the shining black chert; he kept his horses to a low canter, should they come upon a slip. The tunnel of rain-lush forest gave way, finally, to cleared farmland around the bend.

The only thing Cartwright knew about McBride, today's prospect, was that the farmer was a sucker, though the few neighbors around there would have told Cartwright that no one knew the valley better than honest Sherman McBride—the creeks that bred trout, the caves that held flint—except for the two boys he raised off those mouthfuls of corn that rose from the fields and strained for the sun. Even so, honesty would be the man's downfall. Cartwright gazed up at the Allegheny Mountains that trotted saw-toothed across the horizon. This was long before the forests were scoured off the mountain and the coal cut from its belly, before blight withered the stands of chestnut. A dozen passenger pigeons trickled through the sky, the first Cartwright had seen that year despite all his travels. The cherry of his cigarette tumbled, and he jumped and slapped it out of his lap.

Ah! The passenger pigeons he remembered best of all. Every fall, his family had waited for the black shrieking cloud. Word was passed down from towns to the north—Anthem, Mouth of Seneca—and there they were, a pitch river of millions undulating in the sky. When they touched down to rest, they toppled the crowns from oaks. They plucked any living plant and then the roiling swarm fell to the ground and tore at the grass. Under them, no one could tell field from road.

"Whoever cut this grade," Cartwright said to the horses, "must have followed a snake up the hollow. Followed a damned snake!" He roomed near the courthouse in Anthem, but he hadn't been there in seven weeks. He was deep into the summer swing through the highland counties, all the way up to Job and Corinth, the old towns once called Salt Creek and Beartown until their rechristening in a religious fervor. Cartwright glanced at the crate jostling under the tarp. He said, "Damn, boys. I'd almost buy it myself to get shut of this situation."

He swabbed his face with his tie. Soon, the sun burned off the fog and hoisted itself into the sky. "Horses, it's hotter than two rats fucking in a wool sock. I tell you that much."

He took another little drink. Bottle flies turned their emerald carapaces in the sun. Young monarchs gathered to tongue the green horseshit and clap their wings.

Before the Company hired him, Cartwright had sold funeral insurance, apprenticed himself to a farrier, and, in his youth, worked his father's acres. To hear his father tell it, Anthem was a profane place, and they would do well to keep ground between their children and such ways. But a month after she buried her husband, Cartwright's mother closed the deed on their land and moved them to Anthem without debate. Her sister lived by the railroad depot.

Though it had been years since he'd swung a scythe or sheathed his arms in the hot blood of stock, Cartwright's boyhood helped him build a quick rapport, or so he said, with the farmers who bought his wares. Truthfully, he bullied them into buying the tools, or, if they would not be bullied, he casually insulted the farmers' methods in front of their wives. "That's one way of doing things," he said to the hard sells. "Gets it done sure as any other. Yessir. Hard labor! Of course, you don't see many men doing it that way anymore. Last season, I found bluegums down in Greenbrier County working like that."

"You don't say."

"No, excuse me. Season before last. And they might have been Melungeons. Ma'am, you spare some water for a wayfaring traveler?"

Cartwright would bid them good night and retreat to the

hayloft, and, as often as not, be greeted in the morning by the farmer with a fistful of wrinkled dollars and watery, red-rimmed eyes, having been flayed the night long for stubborn habits that clashed with the progressive spirit of the times.

Like his own father, the people Cartwright sold to worked rocky mountain acres, wresting little more than subsistence from the ground. None had owned slaves. Some abstained from the practice out of moral doctrine; all abstained for lack of money. They carded their own wool, cured their own tobacco, and died young or back-bent, withered and brown as ginseng roots twisted from the soil. A handful of affluent farmers in the river bottoms owned early Ford tractors, odd and exoskeletal, but most still worked mules and single-footed plows. Cartwright had seen acres of corn that grew on hillsides canting more than forty-five degrees. But even to the humblest farmers, Cartwright managed to sell a few harrow teeth or axheads.

It also ensnared him: the more success he found, the more desolate the places the Company sent him, and the higher the profits they came to expect. He was the rare man who could wring dollars from these scanty places, but he'd grown tired of the counties they cast him farther and farther into like a bass plug. A man couldn't even buy a fresh newspaper where he roamed. Cartwright brought them the first word of the laws and statutes that a young state government was trying to filigree over the backcountry. Cartwright should have said no, but the Company representative had appealed to his vanity: "I'll be straight with you. We're in the middle of a recession and"—the man was a veteran of the Spanish War—"we need our best on the ramparts. We know you can make quota, buddy. You've proved yourself." The praise flooded Cartwright's belly with a singing warmth, sure as a shot of clean bourbon. Only now did he realize the Company had taken advantage of his loyalty. As soon as he hit Anthem, he'd demand a promotion.

Cartwright took the last hit of whiskey and licked his lips. "My ass hurts," he said to the horses, with a sly sidelong grin. "Do your feet hurt? Huh now?"

Now there was the trouble of the last plow. He'd never returned with inventory and wasn't about to start. Had to make quota. Cartwright lobbed the jar into a roadside holly bush, where it left a quivering hole in the leaves. "Hup," he said, slapping the horses' haunches with the reins. The sweat went flying. A swarm of insects gathered to sup at the horses' soft eyes, nostrils, and assholes. He began to doze but a furry gray deerfly tagged him on the neck. He slapped it away and cursed softly, so as not to spook the horses. Blood formed, round and perfect as a one-carat ruby. Again, he lifted his tie.

McBride seemed to be getting up a small orchard of thorny apples along the road. The split rails of the fence became fresher till they gave out, for around the bend Cartwright found two boys planing and setting lengths of locust by the roadside. Fresh from the adz, the cut lumber gleamed silver in the sun, if marred in places by heart shakes and spalting. The boys wore a coarse homespun, bearing the scurvy look of those who live without women. Their long hair was cut severely, as if it had been chopped with a mattock.

Over the *chip-chop-thunk* of the adze, the twins spoke to each other in a fluttering brogue, the voice of orioles. They saw the wagon and fell dumb, tools gone limp in their hands. Cartwright reined his horses and said, "Hello there, fellows. You the men of the place?"

While one answered, the other spat on the blade of the scrub plane and ran it grating over a stone. The boy said, "English barn a quarter mile up. Ought to find him there. You a preacher?"

"No."

"Ah. That's too bad. We haven't heard good preaching in a while." Cartwright wouldn't have guessed it, but both of the boys could cipher well. The eldest had read the family Bible seven times through. The one on the left asked, "You play music?"

"No."

"Not the tax man, are you?"

"I'm a salesman."

The boy had no comment for this. Waving Cartwright on, he opened a mouthful of teeth so black and broken they looked serrated. He stuffed a rasher of tobacco inside. Cartwright thanked both boys and slapped his horses forward. The wagon went rattling on.

When the drummer was out of earshot, one asked, "What do you think?"

"I expect he'll expect us to feed him dinner."

His brother sighted down the scrub plane, eyeing it for flaws. "Need that like a hot nail in the foot."

"Least he's not here for taxes."

"At least."

The twins turned away, shouldered a rail in tandem, and set it atop another.

Catholic Irish, Cartwright thought, like his mother's father, who'd been converted to the Southern Methodist Church when the preacher said how the pope's Catholics was little better than cannibals, eating up the body of Christ and carving the thumbs off of saints. The body is profane, the spirit real! When Cartwright was young, he heard a Catholic in the infirmary praying to beads. They'd come here to dig railroad tunnels, but, like exotic flowers, had never quite taken to the place and died about as quickly as the land would take them.

Soon, he came upon a sharp-shouldered man plowing up earth with acres to go. The farmer's face was sallow and long-whiskered under a broad-brimmed felt hat, but his hands and arms were the color of leaf tobacco. His boots had been mended with baling twine. McBride, for sure. He whoa'd the mule to a stop. The animal was stout and gleamed wetly in the sun, like a doused ingot of iron. Waves of salt had dried on its shoulders.

"Hi there," the drummer said, lifting a hand from the reins. "Name's John Cartwright."

"Sherman McBride."

"Good-looking animal you got there."

"Ought to be," McBride said. He took off his crushed felt hat and swept it across his forehead like a bandanna. "We paid big on him at the auction. My last mule lived to be thirty-two years old. Hell, my neighbor just give him to me on trade and we worked him swaybacked. After the war, it was. Know how much the price on a mule goes up in thirty-two years?"

Cartwright wanted to say, It's called capital, old buddy. Instead, he politely inquired as to what the years could do to the price of a mule.

"Enough to take a belt of the good stuff before raising my bidding hand."

Cartwright shook his head knowingly. "It's an animal you can't do without."

"Indeed. Like I tell my boys, you can't do without a mule no more than you can do without legs. You're a cripple without one. Don't I, boys? Don't I say you can't do without a mule no more than legs?"

"Yes. He says it all the damn time."

The boys had stalked up from behind. Cartwright couldn't help but jump.

"I told you," McBride said. "All the damn time I say it."

Cartwright regained his composure. The pitch: "You speak with a lot of sense and experience. Fellows, a mule is important and so's a man's tools. I was a farmer for many years and indeed I know that a farmer is only good as his tools. Let the harness match the hide, as they say. You need something to equal that good mule."

McBride flinched. A less experienced drummer might think

this the wrong tack, but Cartwright knew his trade, and his trade was talk. In his mind's eye, he saw the contents of the Irishman's barn: cracked, broken harnesses and homemade harrows, antiquated briar hoes and other tools of the Old World. They might even shell corn by hand. "Yessir," he continued, "I got something here that will double, if not triple, a man's yield at harvest with only half the effort. Half the effort, twice the yield. Powerful math. Now how about that?"

McBride said nothing. The good mule stood in the furrow, radiating a potent silence. The best draft animals have no discernible personality, and this one seemed such a beast.

"Now me," Cartwright said, "I'd say you couldn't beat that with a stick. This tool a man can't afford to be without. Latest from Virginia Progressive Agriculture. Help me, boys."

The twins pitched forward. Cartwright dismounted, whispered into the horses' toggling ears, and walked around to the wagon bed. He peeled back a yellow oilskin, revealing a rectangular crate. He took out a small pry bar and removed a series of staples. The twins helped him lift the lid off a steel-pointed, double-footed plow packed in dry straw. It had been polished to a violent gleam, and the sun caught and danced like hooked minnows on every point and angle. McBride didn't dare look back, but he was imagining his own single-footed plow: crude, hand-forged, nicked, and dull as any kitchen blade. Wouldn't even break roots.

"Brand-new, our latest model. This here is the McCrory Reaper," Cartwright said, "but I call it the Miracle Plow. Our engineers have designed it to render a maximum harvest as far as crops go, clearing twice as much land in the same amount of hours and cutting a deeper furrow, turning up fresher soil and more nutrients. We guarantee better crops or your money back. It's been tested by a scientist at the state college for three years and the results have been proven,

"Look. I'm not the first drummer who's come down the road and won't be the last, but I sell no snake oil. I'm a farm boy myself, grew up on a spread about the size of this one. I know what it's like to rise with the last star and work under the light of the first. We lost that farm because we had two bad years running," Cartwright said, licking his mouth with the moisture of the lie. "That's all it took: two bad ones. I say with confidence, if we'd of had the McCrory Reaper, we'd still be farming my dad's acres. But my dad wasn't progressive. Wouldn't change with the times. Now another's working our land—successfully, with the Miracle Plow. Sold it to him myself. Broke my heart, too. Probably shouldn't be telling it, but I did. You got to get that dollar. Boys, help me move this thing. If you don't mind, Mr. McBride, let's unbuckle your old plow and hitch up this one. You got a singletree? No? That's okay. Let's run a couple furrows with it, free of charge, and see how it measures up. Break a half acre. Would you be averse?"

The question hung there. The twins looked to McBride for instruction, eyes black and hard. Cartwright saw that one boy had only nine fingers—the one way to tell them apart. McBride gave them a slight nod, and they harnessed the new plow.

Tucking his tie between the buttons of his shirt, Cartwright approached the mule as the Irishmen sat on their haunches in the shade of an outbuilding. It was awkward for them to watch another man work without falling in line behind him. They rebelled against their jittering tendons, forced themselves still.

Cupping the mule's nose, Cartwright said, "You got to get to know a mule, right? What's his name? Ronald? Is that right? Ronald, do I have a treat for you. This thing's going to feel light as a vest."

He moved behind the double-footed plow, leaned forward, and slapped the mule on its ass with a tack fitted on the inside of his ring. The mule surged forward, the leather harness yanked with such force it began to groan.

"Jesus," McBride whispered. "Look at Ronald pull."

. . .

"This way, you're working the ground, and *it* ain't working *you*," Cartwright said, chewing on the poor food. "I hate to say it, but it's true. These days a man can't hope to compete without one."

They took supper in the kitchen, the core of a three-room shotgun, dredging up beans and their white, watery gruel with a great circle of corn bread that McBride had cooked in a deep skillet, scooping the golden meal from a sack that stood open beside the woodstove. The meal had quite a grit to it, so the corn bread offered no flavor and the consistency of damp sawdust. Cartwright choked it down, thinking, Promotion, promotion. The sullen boys ate little, seeming to draw their fire from tobacco and wee hits of whiskey from a jug, which they didn't attempt to conceal but didn't offer to share, either, as they surely would to a neighbor.

McBride and Cartwright discussed the merits and dimensions of the new plow at length. Look how effortlessly it turned the earth. Like a knife through hot bread, McBride kept saying, shaking his head. It barely wears on the mule, barely at all.

Cartwright looked about the room. Why'd Threadgill even note these people? But the sucker list said SHERMAN MCBRIDE in its lovely, arching script. Jumping Jesus, McBride couldn't scrape together fifteen dollars if you held a straight razor to his turkey neck, even if he sold everything in the cabin and not a cent to the government. These people were prime candidates for Moses's jubilee. Perhaps there was a relation who could lend them the money, with interest.

Come nightfall, McBride scratched up some fodder for Cartwright's horses and showed him to the barn loft. McBride bid him good night and retreated to the cabin. A shining sliver of moon rested on the planks, and blue foxfire wafted on the hills. Shivering in the cool of the evening, Cartwright stood in the barn door and watched Orion wheel in his chase.

Cartwright saw the twins standing in the twilight. They draped ancient flintlocks over their shoulders, the heavy octagonal barrels tamped with cut nails and brass buttons. Not far away, a boar hog threw itself against the stall and bawled out, raking tusks against the wood. If a man fell in, it would leave nothing but a skull plate. He looked at the guns.

"They got a fox pinned on the mountain," the ten-fingered boy said. "Sometimes they cross the river here at the cut. Might get us a shot. Hear them hounds singing?"

Bound in a nimbus of light, the boys cocked their ears as if to a phonograph for music.

"There a bounty on it?" Cartwright asked.

Oh yeah, the boys said. They named a good figure. Maybe a piece of that plow, they hinted. They said it carefully, their green young minds grappling with the hard currency of commerce. "I see you looking at my hand," the maimed boy said, holding it up to the lantern.

Cartwright felt his stomach coil.

"Lost it baiting a jaw trap. Hand slipped." He looked Cartwright in the eye and said it bluntly, without threat; he hadn't lived in a civilized town yet. He hadn't learned shame.

"We put too much oil to it," the other said. "Got it slickery."

"Easy mistake to make," Cartwright said, relieved. "Do you cure them or bounty them?"

"Depends if the fur traders or the government men are coming around," the ten-fingered boy said. "Neighbors send word up the road."

"You know," Cartwright said, with a knowing shake of his head, "an animal has just enough brains to cure its own hide, be it deer, fox, or bear. Something to study on, I'd say."

The boys thought on it for a minute. "That is something," the nine-fingered boy said. "I'd never thought of it, but it's true. Wouldn't call it a puzzle, but it's something to note."

A grin tugging at the corners of his mouth, the ten-fingered boy said, "You *were* a farmer, weren't you?"

"Oh yeah," Cartwright said, smiling. "Those were good times."

"Hunh. We'll have to talk some more about that plow."

Before they left, they slipped him a twist of tobacco, as they would a neighbor. Cartwright snapped his fingers, twice. He was in with them now.

Cartwright climbed the rungs of the ladder. Out the window, he glanced up at Andromeda, chained to the rock. The drummer was careful with his cigarette, cleaning the boards with his shoe and killing the cinder on the wood. Then he heard a woman screaming on the mountain, but remembered that it was merely the cry of a gray fox, a dog that walks trees like a cat. He leaned back, breathing the ancient smell of cured apples and tobacco hanging from the rafters. Also, a whiff of swallow droppings.

The smell brought to mind his father, mother, brothers, and sisters. Cartwright's family took up pine stobs, brooms, and pokers, beating pigeons to death by the dozens, so numerous and stupid they were. His father lined them up on the ground, and his sister Audrey broke kindling to fire the kettle and scald feathers from the bodies. They gorged themselves, like every other hard-up family from Canada to Texas. It was nothing less than manna, and the bird-soil fell like flakes of lime, his mother and sisters holding umbrellas straining over their heads to keep it off their dresses. The birds they couldn't eat, they ground into fertilizer. Back and forth, his sisters carried the pailfuls of feathers and pulp. The flocks blotted the sun and spooked the horses, which tried to crop grass to the verge of foundering because they weren't ready, at midday, to return slack bellied to the barn and stand hungry in the darkness. The screaming clouds peeled back the green table of grass, and the horses chewed faster, faster.

Cartwright's brother Nige handed him a dead passenger pigeon to play with. He turned it over in his hands: the red eye set there like a hardened drop of blood, the slaty guard feathers the color of water churning over the bottom of rivers that hold trout. The body was limp in his hand, neck lolling about, and he stroked the saffron underbelly. In his trunk in Anthem, he now kept that mummified pair of wings, feathers still crisp as fletching against his thumb. Wrapped in black gauze and smelling sweetly of dry mold, they could have been torn from its back yesterday. He would wrap them back up and put them away under his winter clothes. There were damn few pigeons left now and someday the sky would be evacuated of everything but rain, airships, and stars.

Cartwright turned and felt a sharp corner dig into his kidneys. He plunged his arm into the straw and came up with a jar of corn. "Hallelujah," he said, grinning. He held the clear liquor up to the moon, which looked as hollow and weird as Thomas Jefferson's death mask. He turned the jar, and the geography of the moon warped and spilled to the corners. With luck like this, he'd be back in Anthem in no time. He unscrewed the two-piece lid with a grainy, skirling sound.

After taking a third of the jar, Cartwright made a nest in the straw and settled into a dream-sleep rife with women. He was a man of low station, a virgin at twenty-five. He wouldn't be Threadgill, though. Cartwright wanted a steady woman. Regional manager pay would get him one. Maybe she'd have earth to till, a few acres. Yes, she would. He cocked his ear. The gray fox screamed.

The nine-fingered boy said, "Here it comes, dollar bills on the foot," and his brother laughed a laugh dry as corn husks. The boys waited for the fox under a wash of stars. There were hunts, too, ciphered in the sky above: the hare, the dogs greater and lesser, and the Great Hunter whipping them on.

A square of sun teased Cartwright's face and chest in the morning. Blinking, he glanced about the loft, trying to remember where he was. Swallows peeked out of their mud nests and streaked blue and gold out the window. He woke to their piping, and McBride called him out of the barn. In the kitchen, a tray of sloppy eggs was laid out and a kettle whistled. The tea had the musty tang of roots, or the kettle had been used to make chicory coffee, one. Cartwright asked if the boys had shot themselves a fox. McBride said he supposed they had not.

"That's a shame," Cartwright said. "Bounty's a good way to turn a few dollars."

McBride flinched. Cartwright meant to spur a conversation of whether McBride wanted to buy or not—his back ached from sleeping strangely and a bouncing wagon might cure it—but like these mountain people do, McBride shunned talk of money and led the drummer in an elliptical conversation that touched upon foxes, what foxes eat, foxes and chickens, bounties, plows, planting by the signs, the Stations of the Cross, the months of the moon, the death of his wife in the winter, TB, washing handkerchiefs of red roses, foxes again, plows again, and, finally, the matter of money. McBride counted out quarters, wheat pennies, and paper bills, building them into a small pile.

Cartwright frowned, plucking off the Confederate note the man placed on top—a two-dollar Judah Benjamin—and setting it aside. He said, "This is only half, I'm afraid. Barely half." It was time to go. Experience told him that McBride was about to offer him goats and old boots to make up the difference.

"I know this," McBride said. "But you said it yourself, this is a tool a man can't do without. I got something to cover the rest. It's out where we get flints, just sitting in the ground. It can be sold back where you come from for great profit."

"If you're talking about ginseng or hides, I don't truck in that," Cartwright said, the tooth flickering as he spoke.

"The agent buys hides all the time."

"Look, you don't understand. *I* don't buy them. Too much bother. Town-people don't barter no more. The Company says I have to take federal money. Legal tender. I had a fellow wanted to give me a rarefied sidelock shotgun all the way from Italy and I couldn't take it."

"This goes beyond your typical deal. This is five shotguns. Cover the plow and more and you can have the rest for your troubles."

Cartwright looked about the room. No. If McBride had some silver buried about the place, it wouldn't be such a wreck. "Well," Cartwright said, standing up, not even bothering to hide his disgust, "I'll be taking my leave of you, Mr. McBride. Good luck with your yield. Got to find somebody who can actually buy this thing."

When Cartwright went out the door, it was the serene way that McBride said, "You'll regret it," that called him back. The Irishman took a folded piece of newspaper from his wallet and smoothed it out on the knife-scored table. "I had to go to Jephthah for court day. I was on the jury that hung that Brad fellow for jiggering his little niece and I got this off the corner man."

Cartwright read it once, and read it again. McBride said, "I know where you can get one of them, a great big one."

"Why haven't you got it out already?"

"Thought you said you was a farmer," McBride said, bristling. "Anthem's more than sixty mile. You can't go leaving."

"Hey now, settle down," said Cartwright. "I ain't casting aspersions." He read the notice a third time, a grin swelling on his face. "We'll split it sixty-forty," he said. "But that's a *solid* forty."

No one had been to the cave much since the war, when a few dozen men harvested saltpeter for the Confederacy, and then for the Union, when they were told they lived no longer in Old Virginia. They'd shrugged, saying, Makes no difference to us, we just want to eat. And avoid conscription, they might have added. When the war ended, their profits vanished and the cave was plunged back to obscurity. A scattering of people knew the place, but none knew it like McBride's boys: they crawled into the Sinks of Gandy to harvest flint and hide from downpours when they hunted spring turkeys.

Toting a bundle of tools, the nine-fingered boy led Cartwright on cattle paths to skirt their few neighbors, suspicious people loyal to no one but blood and that even questionable. They wandered into high meadows drowning in beaver dams and dropped into the next valley. A thin jade river fled north and drained with a sucking roar into the Sinks of Gandy, a hatchet wound grinning in the mountainside. The Sinks led to a lacework of caverns undergirding the farmlands. The river resurfaced four miles north by northwest.

Stubby stalactites drooped from the opening and a hush issued from the hole, exhaling the smell of wet rock. Cartwright held out a hand and found it too mild for hell. He glanced over his shoulder at the humpy valley land, beckoning him back. "Two miles in," the boy said, stuffing his belongings into a wetproof satchel made of stomach. "Long miles."

They were swallowed into the cold bowels of the mountain. Cartwright cursed, sinking his leg into a sump of cave mud as the boy lit a pine knot from his satchel. The torch spat glow on soapstone walls that glistened wet as a dog's mouth.

A frothy roar. Crotch-deep in the river, their flesh shriveled. All manner of beast erupted from the crevices—blind wormy salamanders, hare-eared bats whose wings were silk fans brushing their faces. They scrambled over rocks and hangs as the river dropped and narrowed, sluicing through a trough. Deeper they went. Walls closed and they squeezed through closets of stone, rooms within rooms. Cartwright felt his chest cave, his ribs compress. Each breath painful, space no more than a corncrib. His lungs burned. He cried out, casting echoes through the tunnel.

"Quit your wailing," the boy said, holding out his hand to the mud-smeared man who *still* wore a necktie. "Breathe deep. Scoot sideways."

Cartwright popped free into a chapel of stone. The boy pulled a fresh pine knot from his bag, touched it off, and handed the hissing lantern to the drummer. The room soared overhead, massive wet ribbons of rock dripping in folds from the ceiling. The chemical burn of waste in his nostrils, a roof of rodents screeching above. In the old days the men said, The bats sow shit and we reap gunpowder.

They came to an opening, a single slur of light on the floor. Cartwright stuck his head inside and drank the sweet air. Covered crown to boot in coffee-colored mud, he asked, "Won't that fire choke us in here?"

The boy ran his four fingers over the remains of abandoned saltpeter hoppers pegged to the wall, troughs of cucumber wood and oak. "Big window up top lets the fire out. Indian smoke-house. Funny thing, you walk through the field and a flock of bats just pop out the ground beneath you. You near piss yourself."

They felt the earth settle and creak, the animals shuddering in waves overhead. A few squeaking kits fell from the ceiling, and they couldn't help but tromp them under boot.

"What if the whole mountain falls down?"

"Been standing since Genesis," the boy said. "Look, here we are."

The ground was a carpet of fossilized dung. With their torches, they studied the wall scratchings of a lost people, charcoal men in positions of coupling and war. That's when Cartwright saw the face glaring back at him. The maw of a cave bear jutted from the rock, trapped by flood long ago. The greasy pine fire burned against it with a contained fury, illuminating the hollows of its face. It was clearly no mean bruin, its skull gargantuan, with black canines dripping down the jaw. Cartwright put his hand to the wall and soft shale flaked and fell away. He took the clipping from his shirt pocket and read it aloud, taking a second go at the longer words.

REPRESENTATIVE OF THE SMITHSONIAN INSTITUTE TO APPEAR AT ANTHEM CHAMBER OF COMMERCE—COMPENSATION FOR FOSSILS OF PREHISTORIC MEGAFAUNA. *One of the state's most famous visitors, Thomas Jefferson, found rare claw bones of a*

giant three-toed sloth in the Organ Cave, on the old Nat Hin-
kle farm in Greenbrier County in 1792. Dr. Charles Lands
Burke, a young scholar from Washington, D.C., seeks to follow
in his footsteps and is looking to local landowners for aid with
this government initiative—with generous compensation.

"Sounds right to me," the boy said. Could the boy have even read it? Did someone explain it to them? He took a hammer and a chisel from his bag and handed them to Cartwright. Turning his shoulder so the boy couldn't see, Cartwright folded the newspaper clipping back into the sucker list, marrying the two documents together, and tucked them into his jacket.

Stepping forward, Cartwright ran his thumb against the sharp ring of the occipital bone and the worn points of fang, tracing the fissures of the skull that rippled like stitches under his touch. It thrilled him. He couldn't wait to turn it over in his hands. He was amazed there were such things in the ground, waiting to be dug out like potatoes. Cupping them in his brown palm, Cartwright's father used to show off the arrowheads he tilled out of the fields.

The boy said, "Something, ain't it?"

A scene came drifting up from the lake bed of memory. When Cartwright was seven years old, his father had bought a gold locket for his wife's birthday from a drummer passing through. A smile they hadn't seen before took hold of her face, but a week later, his father stood clutching the doorframe, looking shamefully at where the false gold stained her pale skin, like gangrene. He tore it from her neck and threw it down the well. It was the one time his father cried in front of them. The frightened children fanned into the woods. That night, Cartwright's father had to come looking for him with a lantern to fetch him back home.

Cartwright grooved the chisel's tooth into the base of the skull, where the spine would fuse, and lifted the hammer. He let it fall. The chisel jumped in his hand and half the skull turned to silt. It cascaded down the rock wall with the faintest sigh. The boy let out a string of oaths so profane, so unparalleled, that surely they'd been inspired by a hell so near.

Cartwright was glad to have a hammer in hand.

Once again they waded the river, water sucking at their limbs. A pinprick of light appeared ahead. Neither spoke, even when a toothy rock tore Cartwright's jacket with a startling rip. Soon, a delicate sun and then a javelin of light struck the drummer's chest. They came to the mouth of the Sinks of Gandy. "I see them coming," the boy said.

Indeed, McBride and the ten-fingered boy stood there with guns in hand, laughing, each with a fox draped over his shoulder. McBride held a double-barrel sixteen-gauge loaded with pumpkin-ball slugs, a gun the drummer hadn't seen before. They lifted their bloody foxes to the sun. They were fresh, tongues still pink with the suggestion of life. The foxes couldn't be eaten, only sold, because like all predators they reeked of the flesh they'd consumed. One was a black-socked vixen with a sleek coat, the other a gray fox, its face and limbs streaked with red, which had obviously been living in a briar patch. It could use a currycomb and wouldn't bring as much, Cartwright mused miserably, but still a good price.

"You all get it?" McBride asked. "Them bones don't look like much, but they say it's money in the bank."

"Ask your drummer here," the nine-fingered boy said, cocking his head.

"That skull was too old! No one told me how old it was. That was damaged goods."

McBride colored. "Good what now?"

"It's in a thousand pieces," the boy said. "You couldn't broom it out of the dirt."

Cartwright opened his hands. "That skull wasn't worth a damn. You misled me. You violated our contract."

"Misled you?"

"That's the law. It's a contract."

"We shook hands," the farmer said, looking to his boys. "Drummer, you said a man can't do without it."

"It's the law. The legislature wrote it. We just got to live by it."

"What? What are we going to do about that plow?"

"Hey now," Cartwright said, "don't bounty those foxes. Tan the hides and sell them. You'll turn a better profit. You get a few more dozen and I'll come back in the fall."

"Know how long it'll take to cure these hides?"

Cartwright said nothing.

"That's right. You'll be off down the road and we won't see you for a year. Hell, two year. You'll come back when you feel like it. Where will we be? I'm tired of this ground working me, I'm ready to work *it*. You said it yourself."

The nine-fingered boy said, "What's this?"

The boy knelt and picked up a folded piece of paper. Cartwright felt the world turn on a pivot. He grew light-headed and loose-limbed, as if he'd just been bled with leeches. The boy peeled the sucker list away from the newspaper clipping. His eyes scanned the lines. Cartwright thought about running, but he didn't know the way back to the road.

The nine-fingered boy read the words aloud, which listed the name McBride among the county's daft, drunken, gullible, and insane.

"Says we got an eye for any piece of metal, long as it's shiny. Drills, reapers. Pine away for it, we will."

"No better than rooks," his brother said.

Cartwright opened his mouth, then let it shut with a click. He felt weary from the cave, and the years on the road, and his entire body was slick with mud, pant legs heavy as dragnets. He leaned against a sycamore lording over the Sinks of Gandy. He could retch. "Look," he cried, "I know what it's like! I'm from here!"

With a crack, the nine-fingered boy slapped a creeping armored caterpillar off his pant leg. "Jesus Christ," he said, looking down. It was a brilliant green, nearly five inches long. He looked back to Cartwright.

The slug punched Cartwright's side like a party ballot. The drummer fell against the slippery bark and the shot patch fluttered against his face, a sulfur burn in his nostrils. Once, when he was young, he'd tasted a bitter pinch of gunpowder and said it tasted like a chimney. His father laughed, clamping a loving paw on the boy's shoulder, his palm rough as a file. Cartwright threw up a hand and the second shot took his forearm in a hail of bone and the third struck his chin, unhinging the mouth.

When Cartwright fell, he did it watching the light play through clouds on the face of the mountain.

McBride laid the shotgun on the ground and reached for a pipe of tobacco, hand shaking.

The ten-fingered boy asked, "What was that on your leg?"

"Hell if I know."

The boys turned the dragon-like caterpillar on a stick, its orange spikes waving. They ran their thumbs across them. The spikes were hard as apple thorns. "That's called a hickory devil," McBride said, turning back to the drummer's body. "Digs into the ground and turns into a big old red moth."

"Kill it," one said. "It'll kill a dog if it eats it."

Tartly, McBride said, "Don't. That's a myth. It won't hurt nothing."

It was a lonely place, and they merely covered the drummer in pine boughs, confident that no one would find him and no one would care. They should have known better, for the bears and the foxes broke him apart and scattered him a good ways. Rodents gnawed his belt and boot leather for their share of salt. Five years later, a hunter found Cartwright's brass belt buckle in the leaves and slipped it into his pocket.

It says something of the quality of the buckle's manufacture, as well as the hunter's eye, for it was the fourth week of October and the leaves were a thousand shades of brown, mottled like the skin on a copperhead's back. Later, some lost boys from Moatstown found part of him but paid it little mind, calling him a deer because they failed to check the long lithe bones for hooves or fingers. In twenty years, a bear hunter pried the gold tooth from his jaw and threw the husk to the ground. An old woman of Palatine German stock gave his rib cage a Christian burial after a dog dragged it behind her springhouse. She chanted the verses, murmuring, "Thorns and thistles shall it bring forth to thee, and thou shalt eat the herb of the field. In the sweat of thy face shalt thou eat bread, till thou return unto the ground. For dust thou art, and unto dust shalt thou return." But she was fading herself, near death, and troubled in her mind. Is only his torso in heaven? she wondered. Do his legs dance in hell? But she was too frail to go searching for the rest, though his pelvic bone rested near a prominent fork in the road, gathering dry leaves like a crock.

The three Irishmen painted Cartwright's wagon black—"black as Mariah," the neighbors said—and set the smart new plow behind the mule in its traces. With a searing poker, they smeared the blood bays with their own brand. Cartwright would have recognized the sound of crackling flesh, because it sounded like the red-hot horseshoes he dropped hissing into a water barrel in his days as a farrier's apprentice.

After a day's excitement, McBride and his boys eased back into the rhythms of planting and sowed their corn. They enjoyed a typical harvest, green spears coming up straight and tasseled in mean if nourishing numbers. They chewed the lining of their cheeks in wonder, but, then again, they'd merely completed their task with the Miracle Plow, a quarter of the fields. Next year would be the true test. The earth turned and cooled and they waited out the long winter like denned bears, wagering on next year's harvest.

When next harvest came, they would have killed Cartwright all over again. The Miracle Plow had failed to increase their yield by any measure whatsoever, no better than the one it replaced. When

Cartwright's replacement came down the road three years later, they told him so. He urged on his horses with a grim flick of the traces.

As for the three men, they never roamed beyond the Sinks of Gandy, they waited each year for the trickle of passenger pigeons, they reposed in the ground with the cave bears. Leaning against the completed fence, each lit a clay pipe, savoring the ache of a day's labor. McBride and his sons watched a lone red fox jumping in the hayfield, pouncing for mice with devilish glee. The people came to call this place McBride's Slashings, after the acres they wrestled for dominion, but the names can be forgotten. Trees can reclaim the fields, maps can burn, courthouse deeds can be painted in the wondrous colors of mold.

In the distance, among the frailing waves of grain, the fox's red tail flickered like the birth of a field fire. The two young men rose from their haunches, taking up their guns to go out and make it worth something, for from their visitors, they took their lessons.

Reading *The PEN/O. Henry Prize Stories 2011*

The Jurors on Their Favorites

Our jurors read the PEN/O. Henry Prize Stories in a blind manuscript in which each story appears in the same type and format with no attribution of the magazine that published it or the author's name. The jurors write their essays without knowledge of the author's name or that of the magazine, but occasionally the name of the author is inserted into the essay later for the sake of clarity.   —LF

A. M. Homes on "Sunshine" by Lynn Freed

I read the *2011 PEN/O. Henry Prize Stories* while on a long train ride and then reread them again on the way back. I then left them in a suitcase for a week or two as if to "cure" or define themselves further—which they did.

The short story has always seemed to me the perfect medium, the manageable masterpiece, its compact canvas sized for the reader in motion, perfect for when one finds oneself with a few moments to savor something rare and curiously other—and interestingly, I have always thought of the short story itself as a thing in motion.

When asked to describe the difference between a novel and a story, I often use the metaphor of a train; the novel is a cross-country trip; one boards leisurely in Washington, D.C., prepared for the landscape to unfold as the train passes through Maryland, Ohio, Illinois, bound for Los Angeles's Union Station. The short story is like hopping onto that same train already in motion in Chicago and riding it into Albuquerque with no time to waste. What makes a successful story is very different from what makes a successful novel—characters that are not sustainable for the duration of a novel, styles of telling, tones, narrative constructions that are perfect for a story but crumble or bore the reader if carried on for too long.

With this in mind, I noticed something about this year's selection of stories—many expressed an outsider's point of view, a discomfort, a sense of being between places, on the verge of being lost, and were rendered from the point of view of not belonging. I was struck by this sense of "otherness."

The urge to be seen, identified, known to others as one is known to oneself seems to be a fundamental human urge—as though it takes another to confirm our experience of ourselves—i.e., we don't exist in a vacuum.

And so it was that one of these wonderful stories had a strange effect on me; it seemed to escape the zippered suitcase and come calling, tapping me on the shoulder in the dead of night, demanding attention, as if to say, I'm not quite sure you understand—read it again. For this, among many other excellent qualities including being extremely challenging and persistently haunting, I chose "Sunshine."

Initially one is deceived (or seduced) by the surface simplicity of "Sunshine," the way in which it "un-says" things. There is something unusual and exceptionally artful in the way the author manages the balance between what is said and what is left unsaid. Enormously complex information and emotion is invisibly conveyed; this works because what is being said carries the fullness and weight of collective archetypical imagery, classical themes of mythological root, literary references, albeit barely spoken, and psychological theories—all adding up to the very essence of one's moral life and responsibility. And in some ways I wish I were kidding, I wish I could go lighter here—after all, the story is called "Sunshine." And while I am loathe to describe the story, which you'll read for yourself, suffice to say, starts quite innocently: "They told Grace they'd found her curled into a nest of leaves." Hardly threatening, but that quickly and subtly changes; at first the hunter trackers don't speak English and when they first spot the girl they're not even sure what "it" is. The only named characters are Grace and Beauty whom one can assume were long ago "it" and Julian de Jong, the master, whom even the trackers don't look in the eye. "It" is a wild child, her animal nature described by her sitting on her haunches and "baring her teeth in a dreadful high-pitched screech." If the Master, Julian de Jong, simply tamed her it would be a rather pleasant echo of George Bernard Shaw's *Pygmalion* in which Professor Henry Higgins trains Eliza Doolittle, the cockney flower girl to speak "properly," or François Truffaut's brilliant 1970 film, *The Wild Child*. But in this case, the Master seeks to more than tame his prize; after he pays the trackers for her, Grace and Beauty work to civilize her enough so that he can then rape her. It is the rape which throws the story into the stuff of mythology, psychological theory, and honestly creepy fiction. And here is the moral challenge in that everyone from the trackers, the doctor, the dentists, the missionary, and the townspeople are complicit—this isn't the first time Julian de Jong has done this. The narrator notes, that in the past when the Master finally sent "them" home, "they seemed not to know where they'd rather be. And who was the worse for it then?"

The author's deft summoning of the complexity of slave/master relationships, the struggle of women for legitimacy beyond man's object or possession, and questions of economic power and domination—de Jong has more money than anyone else in the story—are part of what give this story its resonance. That and the added cruelty that the Master preys not just upon the very young, but the undefended abandoned "it" who lives outside of society.

In the end it is that "it" not bound by social convention, who is free to act independently and who powerfully and heroically stands up to Julian de Jong.

I read this story multiple times and was disturbed by it and quite honestly I went back to reread several of the other stories again because I wanted to select something more conventional, something less threatening, and yet each time I tried to walk away, "Sunshine" demanded that I return. And so it is for these qualities and the author's careful balance of presence and absence, location and timelessness, what is said and left unsaid, which leaves the reader's imagination to create a world familiar enough to enter and yet distant enough that the reader feels "other" that I chose "Sunshine."

In "Sunshine," a broken-winged girl, taken for a beast, triumphs and I am at once reminded of the necessity of moral and artistic challenge—of Dostoevsky and his murderous Raskolnikov, of Nabokov and the finely wrought Humbert Humbert and here I could go on, but suffice to say that it is with all that in mind—that I celebrate the dark art here, applaud the gruesome, the transgressive, the thing that does not let us escape from the side of ourselves that we would rather not see.

A. M. Homes was born in 1961 in Washington, D.C. She is a novelist, short-story writer, memoirist, journalist, and screenwriter. Her books include *This Book Will Save Your Life* (2006), and the story collections *The Safety of Objects* (1990) and *Things You Should Know* (2002). Homes has received fellowships from, among others, the Guggenheim Foundation, the National Endowment for the Arts, and the Cullman Center at the New York Public Library. She lives in New York City.

Manuel Muñoz on "Something You Can't Live Without" by Matthew Neill Null

For over ten years now, one of my favorite reading experiences has been to go through the two premier award anthologies that appear every year—*The PEN/O. Henry Prize Stories* and *The Best American Short Stories*—and attempt to rank the stories for myself. It's an effort to make myself read slowly, to measure why my enjoyment deepens with particular work. Often the exercise makes me aware of my own reading patterns, of the ways in which I've become more receptive to particular styles of storytelling, or even of my willingness to give a favorite writer a free pass on something that is clearly not his or her best. No matter what, it's nearly always the most deeply fun reading I do all year, a surprising story never failing to emerge.

I kept this little habit to myself until around the time of the 2004 National Book Award nominations for fiction. That was the year when the five-book slate named only women writers—Sarah Shun-lien Bynum, Christine Schutt, Joan Silber, Lily Tuck, and Kate Walbert—and the uproar around this unusual circumstance lead to all sorts of shoot-from-the-hip speculation. None was more cutting (at least to me) than from *The New York Times*, which sniffed that the list shared "a short-story aesthetic" and that none of the books boasted a scope that was "big and sprawling."

What the hell, I wondered, is wrong with such an aesthetic? Is there even such a thing? And since when are stories not "big"?

I went right out and got those books.

I still seethe over that article six years later, and can always turn to *The PEN/O. Henry Prize Stories* for any number of examples of stories that are more than just big and sprawling—they overwhelm the page. This year, I'm happy to wave "Something You Can't Live Without" as one such story that offers almost too much to fathom. Even its title seems to call out its essential nature.

It's rare that a story makes use of nearly every part of speech, reminding us as readers that every part of our language—from verbs to adjectives—can gather awesome weight when coupled together. Pay attention, the pages seem to say. All over this story spring words chosen with accuracy and care, from words deeply wedded to the Appalachian geography ("ironweed" and "seven sisters" and "chert") to the labor of the farm ("carded" and "planing" and "hand-forged"). Even the story's time frame feels slickly yet unobtrusively referenced, with a word like "cipher," with its faint hint of history, employed as a verb of literacy, or "conscription," with a register that the more modern "draft" could never achieve.

But these are just words. Cartwright's attempt to pass on a cheap piece of goods to the poor farmer McBride is as straightforward a plot as anyone could ask, and the surprise comes in the story's largely silent battle of pride and comeuppance, two men thinking of the single way to emerge the better in the bargain. The real pleasure—and certainly not the only one—is in the sentences, as complex, deliberately assured, and lethal as Flannery O'Connor's. What an authentic, confident story this is, soaked through with deceit and menace and the distinctly abrupt strain of American violence. Add in a startling ending—an unforgiving embrace of the nature of time and history, if not the devouring jaws of myth—and you've got a work ready to prove that short stories and short-story writers are the most sprawling and unruly of all mythmakers.

Manuel Muñoz was born in Dinuba, California, in 1972. He is the author of two short-story collections, *Zigzagger* and *The Faith Healer of Olive Avenue*, which was a finalist for the Frank O'Connor International Short Story Award. His first novel, *What You See in the Dark*, was published in early 2011. He is the recipient of a National Endowment for the Arts literature fellowship and a 2008 Whiting Writers' Award, and currently teaches creative writing at the University of Arizona in Tucson.

Christine Schutt on "Your Fate Hurtles Down at You" by Jim Shepard

A great story announces itself entirely to start; its terms are then rolled over and over again, and the story is made larger for what new associations adhere until, by the end, the terms are profound. Every reading reveals some new, impossibly smart gesture, surely intended and cumulatively significant. I lose my way, snow-blind. A great story is as heavy as wet snow, the kind that rolls up like carpet and grows bigger for the binding of its parts.

Halfway through "Your Fate Hurtles Down at You," the narrator of this story, Eckel—his first name is never given—explains in scientific language, then in easier, metaphoric terms, what might in fact account for avalanches: a degraded crystal, a stratum of which if slightly jarred can set tons of more recently fallen snow in motion. His mother calls such degraded crystal "sugar snow" because it will not bond. Even when compressed, the snow does not cohere, a phenomenon at odds with great story-making, in which the parts must cohere. And the parts. Sifted into this story are wondrous accounts of nature's brute force, anecdotes, histories, avalanche lore recalled by Eckel or his companions in the course of their freezing work.

They call themselves "the Frozen Idiots." They are four volunteers researching the complexities of snow; they conduct experiments on a viciously windy slope miles above Davos in efforts, all potentially deadly, to better understand and defend against avalanche. The year is 1939; they live in a hut; they have no heat and only kerosene for light. They *are* frozen idiots; they go about their work with reckless enthusiasm. They have started an avalanche and destroyed a church. Few of their fellows find their subject significant; nevertheless, they are close to finishing an important book on snow, and Eckel's tone at the start of this authentic story is confident and self-deprecatory. His voice is more matter-of-fact when he recounts the catastrophes that have contributed to the researchers' industry. An airborne avalanche, the most destructive category of all, killed the group leader's father, and another avalanche, less severe perhaps but lethal, killed Eckel's twin brother, Willi. The boys were sixteen.

Images of these assaults, the unnatural uprootings, flattened houses—a roof mistaken "for a terrazzo floor"—powerfully amass and add to the story's gravity. An unbroken teacup bewitches while a broken girl unsettles as does a boy "entombed in his bed." Napoleon's little drummer is lost in a gorge and drums for days before he falls silent. Avalanches, the seductive enormity of them! How helpless we are, slight as flies before it, but must we die alone? "Seventeen people were dug out of a meetinghouse the following spring, huddled together in a circle facing inward." A consolation, I think, companionship at the end.

Contrastively, Willi's death is horrible. He dies twice: First, under an immensity of snow, alone in the dark for hours, he loses consciousness. The second time, an avalanche of fear triggered by Eckel when he puts out the light kills Willi. He is dead by the time his mother reaches him. As for the survivors, buffeted by gusts of rage, self-rebuke, and loneliness, they endure by contraction.

Even before the catastrophe of Willi's death, the family terrain emerges as stark and severe as the slopes, dangerously unstable. An elder sister is dutiful but retreats to her room and her romance subscriptions. The father, an Alpine guide, claims to be "content only at altitudes over eleven thousand feet" although his sons know otherwise. They consider their father's "homemade medicines" his sole pleasure, yet Eckel attends to his father's every mood, negotiating the shifting terrain "even as disinterest emanated from him like a vapor."

To be loved, it seems, is as fateful as any experience. "Why does anyone choose one brother and not another? I wanted to ask." Significantly, Eckel does not ask this question aloud—not of his mother or of Ruth, the young woman to whom he is hopelessly devoted. He grudgingly accepts his mother's preferential treatment of his twin and Ruth's deception of him with Willi. Against the wintery heart there is no defense beyond contraction, a withdrawal from the world with a cruel, self-absorbed intention to endure. Contraction, silence. At the onset of an avalanche a survivor trick is to keep your mouth shut; this has been Eckel's strategy throughout his life.

I underestimated how difficult it would be to act as a juror for the PEN/O. Henry Prize Stories. Beyond the challenge of making a selection from the forgathered, there has been the trauma of writing about the choice; my choice makes me sick. All great stories make me sick with their muchness. The parallel actions and anecdotes, repeats and reversals, all made with pickax accuracy, add breadth and bulk. Everything connects. The alpine landscape, God-like, brooding and indifferent, gives contour to the characters' lives. The story of the old guide's devotion to the empress mirrors Eckel's devotion to Ruth; just so, the avalanche's "fractures . . . stress lines . . . fusillades of pops and cracks" apply to the human drama. And how better to represent our essential helplessness in the universe than with the image of a researcher inadequately dressed, awake in his hammock, hanging in the cold dark? The harrumph a boy makes with his skis to signal to his brother "We're so close" fatally severs and forever binds them. In Jim Shepard's story, the snow coheres; it coheres for now. The hammock creaks. Someday, maybe tomorrow, maybe the next, Eckel and his fellows will—we all will—be overtaken by that white ambush.

Christine Schutt is the author of two short-story collections and two novels. Her first, *Florida*, was a 2004 National Book Award finalist; her second, *All Souls*, a finalist for the 2009 Pulitzer Prize. Among other honors, Schutt's work has twice been included in *The PEN/O. Henry Prize Stories*. She is a recipient of fellowships from the New York Foundation for the Arts, Yaddo, and the Guggenheim Foundation. Schutt is a senior editor of the literary annual *NOON*. She lives and teaches in New York.

Writing *The PEN/O. Henry Prize Stories 2011*
The Writers on Their Work

Chris Adrian, "The Black Square"
This story was written for an issue of *McSweeney's* that endeavored to imagine what the world will be like in fifteen years. Each story was to be set in a different location all around the world. This meant that the magazine would have sent me more or less wherever I would have liked to go to research the setting for the story—Paris, Berlin, Ho Chi Minh City, Bali—by means of funding provided by mysterious South American filmmakers. For a reason that had a lot to do with stalking my ex-boyfriend, I chose to go to Nantucket and took his dog with me (with the ex's permission). I spent two days poking around the beaches and moors with the dog, but didn't start writing until many months after I returned. I threw out five or six drafts about Nantucket sinking into the ocean or being overwhelmed by intelligent shoes before I finally discovered what the story was about—me, the ex, and the dog. Which is often how it works for me: I put in a bunch of work on a decoy story while waiting for the real story to sneak up and announce itself.

Chris Adrian was born in Washington, D.C., in 1970. He is the author of three novels, *Gob's Grief, The Children's Hospital,* and *The Great Night,* and a collection of stories, *A Better Angel.* He lives in San Francisco.

Kenneth Calhoun, "Nightblooming"

"Nightblooming" was one of my many attempts to write about music. Throughout my high school and college years, music was my life. I worked in a music store and played drums for a variety of projects—punk and funk bands, theatrical productions, even a wedding band. As a drummer, I was especially interested in patterns and beats. At some point, I got it in my head that everything that was seemingly random could in fact be the articulation of a grand, overarching rhythm, but that the count hadn't yet been revealed because we hadn't reached the end of a measure. I realized while writing "Nightblooming" that this could be a comforting, religious sort of idea, not just a whimsical speculation.

Kenneth Calhoun was born in Upland, California, in 1966. He has published stories in journals such as *The Paris Review, Fence Magazine, Fiction International, St. Petersburg Review, Quick Fiction,* and others. He is a recipient of the Italo Calvino Prize in Fabulist Fiction and a winner of the Summer Literary Seminars/Fence Magazine Fiction Contest. He lives in Boston.

Jennine Capó Crucet, "How to Leave Hialeah"

Somewhere in the beginning of my thinking of this story, I made a list of all the people I hated. Then I strung together versions of a few of these people—along with versions of people I loved and who loved me—and unleashed this narrator on them. A lot of my stories come from a place of anger, which is probably not the healthiest place, but it's where I tend to start. Thankfully, because things so quickly become straight-up fiction once I'm actually writing, that's never, ever where I finish. In writing "How to Leave

Hialeah," it wasn't until the cousin showed up in my imagination and on the page that I knew this was a story I needed to hear.

Jennine Capó Crucet was born to Cuban parents in 1981 and raised in Miami, Florida. Her debut story collection, *How to Leave Hialeah*, won the Iowa Short Fiction Award, the John Gardner Memorial Prize, and the Devil's Kitchen Reading Award in Prose, and was named a Best Book of the Year by *The Miami Herald* and the *Miami New Times*. Her stories have been published in *Ploughshares, Epoch, Gulf Coast, The Southern Review, The Los Angeles Review,* and other magazines. A graduate of Cornell University and a former sketch comedian, she currently divides her time between Miami and Los Angeles.

Jane Delury, "Nothing of Consequence"

This story emerged from a description of sexual dynamics that I heard years ago from a French teacher who had volunteered in Senegal. But I recognize other elements from my lived experience as well: a snake that gave me a fright, an unfortunate episode with a bathing suit and a Pacific wave, and my recognition that for many, like Rado, writing is a long process of learning and refinement rather than a blazing ascension. Though each of the women making up the group of teachers has her own complexity, I was interested in the way that groups of people—especially those who find themselves outside of their familiar environment—can create a larger personality.

Jane Delury was born in 1972 in Sacramento, California. Her stories have appeared in journals including *The Southern Review, Narrative Magazine,* and *Prairie Schooner.* She has received an award from the Maryland State Arts Council and a fellowship from the Virginia Center for the Creative Arts. She teaches in the University of Baltimore's MFA in Creative Writing and Publishing Arts program, and lives in Baltimore.

Tamas Dobozy, "The Restoration of the Villa Where Tíbor Kálmán Once Lived"

The impulse to write is usually exactly that: an impulse. It starts for me in that need, experienced daily, a kind of negative drive, fueled by absence, that moves after something in the positive sense—a title, an image, an idea. For many, many years I've been mining material on the siege of Budapest, a particularly dark period in what is the general darkness of Hungarian history, in the hope of putting together a collection. This story comes out of that endless seam.

I have some relatives who own an old villa in a suburb east of Budapest, called Mátyásföld, that I have always loved. It seems to me a place that still somehow retains its Austro-Hungarian character despite the ravages of two world wars, revolution, Soviet takeover, land reapportioning, and the sudden and in many ways catastrophic shift into wild capitalism.

When I started writing this story the image of the villa came up for me, almost as it does for László, as a kind of golden lure, a place of security, a final goal. Of course, for me it was a way to tell the story, while for László it was salvation, though maybe in some way this is the same thing—the desire to engage with something that will save what we do from futility, that promises everything will come out all right in the end, that the sacrifices will be worth it, only to realize that it was only really important for what we did—good and bad—along the way.

I do wonder sometimes about this use—misuse some might say—of history in fiction, the way there's something both moral and amoral in it at the same time: a desire to write in a way that responsibly engages the world, and a desire to write about something simply because it makes for a marvelous story. Maybe this tension is productive and shouldn't be reconciled. It is, at any rate, a question that haunts the writing of this story, and leaks out in László's own uncertainties about what he's doing.

. . .

Tamas Dobozy was born in Nanaimo, British Columbia, in 1969. He has published two books of stories, *When X Equals Marylou* and *Last Notes and Other Stories,* whose French translation won the 2007 Governor General's Award. He is an associate professor of American literature in the Department of English and Film Studies at Wilfrid Laurier University. He lives in Kitchener, Canada.

Judy Doenges, "Melinda"

Soon after I moved to Colorado, my neighbor, who sells bail bonds, told me the story of methamphetamine use in the West. She knew all too well, she said, how the drug had damaged the infrastructure of towns and destroyed thousands of lives. Living with my neighbor at the time was the charismatic Mark, a recently paroled former meth chef and dealer. Mark introduced me, via interviews, to the practice of hijacking foreclosed farms for meth labs, the identity theft business that often accompanies a methamphetamine enterprise, and the particulars of meth production. A clerk in a local drugstore explained how the state polices sales of medicine containing ephedrine, which is a necessary ingredient in meth cooking. Now the name and address of anyone buying Sudafed, for example, enters a database of other cold sufferers—or meth users.

As is the case in many stories about drug or alcohol abuse, the addiction itself is a character, unavoidably yoked to the protagonist. In that way, Melinda not only humanized a social ill but also animated it. It was impossible for me to write about Melinda without meth and impossible to write about meth without Melinda.

"Melinda" is set several years in the past. Methamphetamine cooking is like any other kind of manufacturing: technological advances improve production. Now people can make meth in the back of a van or on a stove. It's a true American cottage industry.

. . .

Judy Doenges was born in Elmhurst, Illinois, in 1959. She is the author of a novel, *The Most Beautiful Girl in the World,* and a short-fiction collection, *What She Left Me.* Her stories and essays have appeared in many journals, among them *The Georgia Review, The Kenyon Review,* and *Western Humanities Review.* She has received fellowships and awards from many sources, including the National Endowment for the Arts, the Ohio Arts Council, and Artist Trust. She teaches at Colorado State University and lives in Fort Collins, Colorado.

Brian Evenson, "Windeye"

I owe a debt to Dan Machlin, since his poetry introduced me to the Old Norse word *vindauga* (*vindauge* in contemporary Norwegian), which translated literally means "wind-eye." That word worked on me, haunted me, and slowly took on for me a life of its own. Over a month or two it somehow subconsciously cross-pollinated with games my younger siblings and I used to play when we were little, with my own fascination with the difference between childrens' and adults' perceptions, with problems I was having with shingles warping and cracking on my house, and with my own basic distrust about the nature of reality. All of that secretly gestated for a long time, but when I finally sat down to write it, it came out all in a rush, something that rarely happens for me.

Brian Evenson was born in Ames, Iowa, in 1966. He is the author of ten books of fiction, most recently the limited-edition novella *Baby Leg,* and his work has been translated into French, Italian, Spanish, Japanese, and Slovenian. His novel *Last Days* won the American Library Association's award for Best Horror Novel of 2009. Other books include the story collection *Fugue State* and a new collection of stories, *Windeye,* that will be published in 2011. His work has been included in *The PEN/O. Henry Prize Stories* three times, and he has received a fellowship from the National Endowment for the Arts. Evenson lives and works in Providence, Rhode Island, where he directs Brown University's Literary Arts Program.

Adam Foulds, "The Rules Are the Rules"

The story began with a single image: a priest who longs to be a father holds an infant for baptism. It was this predicament, this public moment crowded with private feeling and detailed physical experience, that compelled my attention, and I wrote a few pages to try and get hold of it. This then was set aside, and it wasn't until *Granta* commissioned me to produce something for their "Sex" issue that I returned to it and the story became more than this fraught tableau. I thought about sex as an urgent, risky, and difficult kind of intimacy, as procreation, and as something that structures an individual's personality, determining what they notice and react to in the world. Peter's character and wider situation unfolded with these thoughts.

Adam Foulds was born in London in 1974. He is the author of two novels, *The Truth About These Strange Times* and *The Quickening Maze,* as well as a narrative poem set during the Mau Mau uprising in colonial Kenya in the 1950s, *The Broken Word.* In 2008 he was named the Sunday Times Young Writer of the Year, and he has won the Costa Poetry Prize and the Somerset Maugham Award, and was a finalist for the 2009 Man Booker Prize. In 2010 he was made a fellow of the Royal Society of Literature. He lives in London.

Lynn Freed, "Sunshine"

Perhaps it is the wildness itself of feral children that has always intrigued me. Or perhaps it is the very idea of life in a state of nature, beyond or before civilization. I don't know. What I do know is that the girl in this story, which was originally a failed attempt to begin a novel—several stories I have written have begun this way—has been with me always.

Lynn Freed was born in 1945 in Durban, South Africa. She came to New York as a graduate student, receiving her MA and PhD in English literature from Columbia University. She has published six novels *(Friends of the Family, Home Ground, The Bungalow, The Mirror, House of Women, The Servants' Quarters);* a collection of essays, *Reading, Writing & Leaving Home: Life on the Page*; and a collection of stories, *The Curse of the Appropriate Man.* Her short fiction, memoirs, and essays have appeared in *The New Yorker, Harper's Magazine, The Atlantic Monthly, Tin House,* and *Southwest Review,* among others. In 2002 she received the inaugural Katherine Anne Porter Award from the American Academy of Arts and Letters. She lives in Northern California.

David Means, "The Junction"

In order to write "The Junction" I had to write another story first. That story—still in a rough draft—was about a kindly Pittsburgh doctor, during the Depression, tending to a patient in a flophouse who mysteriously disappeared—against all medical odds—and took to the rails, ending up at State Line Junction, where he saves the day by falling across a switch mechanism. I put the Pittsburgh story aside and began to write a new story, using a little bit of the background material—i.e., when he tells the story at the dinner table—and some of the same energy of the other version. I didn't see the men in my story as drifters. They're looking for something, on a quest of sorts, trying to pin down exactly where they need to be to find solace and hope. Part of what inspired me to write this story was the image of a fresh-cut piece of pie on a windowsill waiting for someone. The ideal sense of home is something we'll never really find, but we keep wandering and changing our own stories in the hope that, at last, we'll find ourselves in the perfect place. Perhaps it's hard to write about the search for home right now, in this culture, because the Internet has provided all of us a hyperlink into what might or might not feel like safety: the safety of drifting from site to site, following one link to the next as if we're free. Setting the story back in the day before cell phones, before high-speed hookups, before Facebook and satellite hookups, back when all you had to do was take a few steps away from the campfire and find a complete solitude, allowed, I like to think, an access to a certain kind of situation, purified down, that allowed a certain pattern to be exposed. (The gibberish above is exactly why writers should, in most cases, avoid talking about their work. The truth is I just wanted to tell a good story and respect my characters and get the words right.) In any case, one other thing that informed this story was the fact that, when I was growing up in Michigan, my grandfather—a lovely man, a true self-made gentleman, who in many ways saved my life—often told me stories about surviving the Great Depression. He had a big cupboard in which he still stored canned goods in case the world crashed again and the food supply became short. Some of the cans actually dated back to the Depression, with labels that were so simple and beautiful and clear they seemed to be hand-painted. He vividly described the way men would come to the back door, knock, be invited in for dinner, and sit at the table with the entire family. There was an old coal yard up the road from his house, and it still had black mounds of coal left over from the days of steam. I paid careful attention to those old piles of coal—half-buried in the weeds, just glints of shiny dark coming through the green. Coal and steam engines weren't that far in the past in the late sixties.

David Means was born and raised in Michigan. He is the author of four story collections, including *Assorted Fire Events, The Secret Goldfish,* and, most recently, *The Spot.* Means lives in Nyack, New York.

Susan Minot, *"Pole, Pole"*

I began this story initially as a challenge to myself—to complete something. I'd not published a book—or a story for that matter—in a long time, and in the long years of working on what looked as if it was now turning out to be two novels, I wanted simply to finish something. So one winter I took a break from the book to write this story. I had spent some time in Kenya in the late '90s, and imagining a tryst there was a way of revisiting a place I'd been intrigued by. In the writing of the story I also began to envision a collection of intertwined stories set in east Africa of which *"Pole, Pole"* would be a part. So that's another book that now needs to be written, though I have its title already: *Fatina.*

Susan Minot was born in 1956 in Boston. She is the author of *Monkeys, Lust & Other Stories, Folly, Evening, Rapture,* and a poetry collection, *Poems 4 A.M.* Her nonfiction has appeared in *McSweeney's* and *The Paris Review,* among other publications. She wrote the screenplay for Bernardo Bertolucci's *Stealing Beauty.* The film *Evening* was the first adaptation of her fiction. Minot divides her time between New York City and an island in Maine.

Matthew Neill Null, "Something You Can't Live Without"

The drummer tale is a staple of storytelling. To be kind, you'd call it well-worn; to be cruel, cliché. So many have done it so well: Faulkner, Chekhov, Flannery O'Connor, Malamud. Breathing life into the form seemed an impossible task, so I had to try. Sitting down to the desk, I wanted to see if I could outdo the established demigods of fiction. An act of hubris for sure, but what isn't? I hope the reader judges me kindly.

The story, for me, always begins with an image. In college, my first love was geology. A group of us went down into a cave, and after what seemed like miles of dodging bats and slogging through mud, a professor showed us where the remains of an extinct bear—*Arctodus simus,* I think—had been discovered. I began with the vision of a skull, and then I had to dream the characters to find it. The story unspooled from there. Other stray images found a home: twin boys working fence posts by the roadside; a high meadow drowning in beaver dams; a pair of dead foxes, one red, one gray. Also, the story gave me an opportunity to write one of my favorite landscapes in West Virginia, where the karst lands meet the mountains.

Most of my work is a variation on one theme: the crisis of people who love the land, but are faced with the prospect of selling or destroying some aspect of it to translate the landscape into dollars. This is West Virginia's story. From timbering to coal mining to Marcellus shale fracturing, the ground has been sold again and again. Despite our common myths and party rhetoric, extractive industry has failed to improve the lot of West Virginians. For me, "Something You Can't Live Without" is a middle chapter in a long, fraught history.

Matthew Neill Null was born in Summersville, West Virginia, in 1984. He is a graduate of the Iowa Writers' Workshop, and his stories have appeared in *Oxford American* and *Gray's Sporting Journal*. He was the 2010–2011 Provost's Postgraduate Writing Fellow at the University of Iowa. Null lives in Iowa City.

Lori Ostlund, "Bed Death"

In 1996 my partner and I moved to Malaysia, where we taught business communications at a college very much like the one in the story. There was a bed, for example, behind glass in the lobby, and we looked at an apartment in Nine-Story Building, which, at least then, was the tallest building in our town and was thus, sadly, attractive to jumpers. We found an apartment elsewhere, but during our stay, several people committed suicide by jumping from the building's roof, and so we became familiar with the building through newspaper accounts and public lore as well as through a friend who lived there. What intrigued me was the way that people sometimes spoke of the jumpers, with a detachment that allowed them to view the suicides as an irritation, an occurrence whose salient feature was its ability to make less pleasant the lives of those who lived in the complex. Yet, on another level, I understood how and why the tenants came to feel this way, and this understanding—of the way that others' pain or suffering can become a minor and curious backdrop for the drama of our own lives—became the framework of my story.

Like the couple in the story, we stayed at a seedy hotel where the smoke alarms beeped every few minutes. After trying to explain that the batteries needed to be changed, to no avail, we spent an afternoon trying to buy replacement batteries—also to no avail. Finally, we were moved to the only beep-free room—outside of which lay a wounded, moaning man on a chaise longue. We never learned what had happened to him, which is ultimately for the best when it comes to writing fiction.

This story evolved slowly, over the course of ten years, beginning with images and scenes that I wrote down but did not necessarily regard as parts of the same story. Usually, especially with my first-person narrators, the narrator "arrives" first and starts telling the story, but this time the narrator came along later, a narrator who is nothing like me except for a shared navel phobia. As I recall, that narrator appeared one morning as I was reading through all these bits and pieces, wondering whether they would ever amount to anything; she began commenting on them, weaving these disparate parts together, and through her seemingly insightful and often cynical analysis, I began to see how ill-equipped she was for the world, how fragile her relationship was, and how incapable she was of extending compassion to another lost soul.

Lori Ostlund was born in 1965 in a town of 411 people in Minnesota. Her first collection of stories, *The Bigness of the World,* received the Flannery O'Connor Award for Short Fiction, the California Book Award for First Fiction, and the Edmund White Award for Debut Fiction, and was a Lambda Literary Award finalist and named a 2009 Notable Book by The Story Prize. Her stories have appeared in *The Best American Short Stories, The Kenyon Review, New England Review,* and *The Georgia Review,* among other publications. She was the recipient of a Rona Jaffe Foundation Writers' Award and a fellowship to the Bread Loaf Writers' Conference. She lives in San Francisco.

Leslie Parry, "The Vanishing American"

When I was a nerdy, Zoobooks-reading kid, my parents, tired of seeing me use their fancy ice tongs and expensive olive pitter to dissect my stuffed animals, sent me to a marine biology summer camp on Catalina Island. I learned many things there—how to breathe through a snorkel tube, the life cycle of a garibaldi—but what I remember most is shivering in my pup tent at night, listening to stories about the wild bison who'd been roaming the island since 1924. They'd been shipped out as "scenery" for a western movie, our counselor said, and afterward, when filming was done, they were—"Wait, what?" I sat up in my sleeping bag and blinked against the orange light of the mosquito lamp. "Just left there? Like . . . abandoned?" I wasn't sure what was more astonishing— that the movie people could be so extravagant and indifferent, or that the herd had managed, despite its new environment, to adapt, flourish, and survive. As an adult, I had tried a few times to write about a soldier who'd lost his voice in World War I. However, I just couldn't get any purchase on the character, so I put my notes away, frustrated and disappointed. A few days later I saw that *The Vanishing American* (hey, that buffalo movie!) was screening at the Silent Movie Theatre here in Los Angeles. I had a free night and so, perhaps nostalgic for the bygone days of peeing in my wet suit, I went. Afterward, as I emerged from the theater and crossed Fairfax Avenue, these two ideas—the bison and the soldier—joined serendipitously in my mind. I went home and began to write.

Leslie Parry was born in Los Angeles in 1979. She is a graduate of New York University and the Iowa Writers' Workshop, where she was a Truman Capote Fellow in Fiction. "The Vanishing American" is her first published story. She lives in Los Angeles.

Jim Shepard, "Your Fate Hurtles Down at You"

"Your Fate Hurtles Down at You" began as many of my stories begin lately—with my browsing around endlessly in an utterly nerdy and bizarre subject and then finding my imagination caught by a particular moment that resonates with me emotionally in unexpected ways. In this case I was reading about the history of the science of avalanches—I know, I know; imagine how my wife feels—and I was struck by the notion that a skier or hiker might cross a given area with no effect and then the next skier or hiker might, when doing the same thing, start an avalanche that carried away any number of those in his group. That desire that must follow to penetrate the capriciousness of such an event—as in, I *must* have done *something* different, *something* to cause such a catastrophe—seemed to me to have all sorts of crucially useful analogues, in emotional terms. I imagined someone at the very dawn of avalanche science who found himself wondering about his responsibility for the fate of someone he loved. And the story proceeded from there.

Jim Shepard was born in 1956 in Bridgeport, Connecticut, and is the author of six novels, including most recently *Project X,* and four story collections, including *You Think That's Bad.* His third collection, *Like You'd Understand, Anyway,* was a finalist for the National Book Award and won The Story Prize. *Project X* won the

2005 Library of Congress/Massachusetts Book Award for Fiction, as well as the Alex Award from the American Library Association. His short fiction has appeared in, among other magazines, *Harper's Magazine, McSweeney's, The Paris Review, The Atlantic Monthly, Esquire, DoubleTake, The New Yorker, Granta, Zoetrope: All-Story,* and *Playboy,* and he was a columnist on film for the magazine *The Believer.* Four of his stories have been chosen for *The Best American Short Stories* and one has been awarded a Pushcart Prize. He's won an Artist Fellowship from the Massachusetts Cultural Council and a Guggenheim Fellowship. He teaches at Williams College and lives in Williamstown, Massachusetts.

Helen Simpson, "Diary of an Interesting Year"

It's always fun when you're writing to zoom in on what's uncomfortable—on what causes a silence to fall—and one such touchy subject now is whether we ought to cut back on our rate of consumption for the sake of the future. This suggestion never fails to annoy. Anyway, I wanted to see if I could make interesting fiction from climate change. It's an undeniably important subject—it's the elephant on the horizon—but it's also undeniably difficult, boring (for the nonscientists among us), and horrifying to contemplate. Yes, I thought, that would be really difficult to do, make climate change interesting. Still, I like a challenge, and I went at it from different angles for my fifth story collection, *In-Flight Entertainment,* treating it as a love story, a dramatic monologue, a satirical comedy, a sales pitch and—the story included here—a dystopian diary. Having said this, I ought to add that I'm not interested in writing polemic. As a reader, I resent fiction that has designs on me. I think the only duty of a writer is to resist writing about what they think they ought to write about—and to write about what stimulates their imagination. Oddly, the subject of climate change did this for me. I sensed dark rich comic pickings, and I wasn't wrong.

· · ·

Helen Simpson was born in Bristol, England, in 1956 and grew up near Croydon. The first in her family to go to college, she graduated from Oxford with two degrees. She is the author of five collections of stories and a recipient of the Hawthornden Prize and the American Academy of Arts and Letters E. M. Forster Award. Her collection *In-Flight Entertainment* will be published in the United States in 2012. She lives in London.

Mark Slouka, "Crossing"

"Crossing" emerged, after a fifteen-year dormancy period, from an act of near-biblical stupidity on my part: in 1994, while crossing a river in the Pacific Northwest with my five-year-old son on my back, I found myself, very quickly, in serious trouble. It didn't matter that I'd forded the same river many times before without incident; this time, for whatever reason, was different. Even now I don't like to think about it. There are few things more excruciating than realizing you've put your child's life in danger.

Over the years that followed, I thought about the incident more than once; I knew I wanted to write about it, but I couldn't find the release, the spring, the image or phrase or note—often dissonant, almost always unexpected—that brings a story to life. Though the organic symbolism of the thing appealed to me, it felt too easy, too finished, inert. So I let it be.

It wasn't until I came across the anecdote about the medieval priest that flashes through the father's mind on the story's last page that I felt the tumblers fall. Of course! I had to leave him midstream, tricked by life, prey once again to his old fears and insecurities. A man poised between his past and his future, between the impossibility of going on and the necessity of it.

On some level, it feels almost ungrateful; I made it out, after all, and today my son could carry me across that river a good deal more easily than I could him. But fiction, I remind myself, is an act of trespass on the territory of the past, and those who have no stomach for it, whose reverence for apparent truths, as opposed to created ones, is too great, probably shouldn't play.

Both are equally true: We made it. And we're still, all of us, hip-deep in the current.

Mark Slouka was born in New York City in 1958. He is the author of a collection of stories, *Lost Lake;* two novels, *God's Fool* and *The Visible World,* which have been translated into sixteen languages; and *Essays from the Nick of Time.* He is a recipient of National Endowment for the Arts and Guggenheim fellowships and is a contributing editor at *Harper's Magazine.* His short fiction has appeared there as well as in *The Paris Review* and *Granta,* among other publications, and his essays and stories have been anthologized in *The Best American Essays* and *The Best American Short Stories.* He has taught at Columbia, Harvard, and the University of Chicago, and lives outside New York City.

Elizabeth Tallent, "Never Come Back"

The deep background of this story—which may not make itself felt very much in this final draft—are the changes confronting my hometown on the Mendocino coast: old ways of making a living have vanished, and with them the certainties they fostered, so there's a sense in which people are free to start from scratch but also bewildered by the prevailing scriptlessness. In "Never Come Back" I wanted to write about a young mother who leaves her child and how the grandparents left to care for the child handle an absence they can't understand but which they inevitably judge. My secret ambition in this story was to kindle empathy for characters whose actions are, on the face of it, indefensible, but which make the deepest kind of sense to them.

Elizabeth Tallent was born in Washington, D.C., in 1954. Her work includes the story collections *Honey* and *Time with Children* and the novel *Museum Pieces*. She teaches in Stanford's Creative Writing Program and lives in California.

Lily Tuck, "Ice"

My husband and I did take a cruise to Antarctica, and since I am both a pessimist and a contrarian, I imagined the worst: the boat hitting an iceberg, sinking, my husband falling overboard, drowning. As it turned out we had a very happy time and, except for the books, the clock, the bottle of sleeping pills, everything that was neatly stacked on our nightstand falling pell-mell to the cabin floor and the obnoxious fellow passenger whose goal it was to drive a golf ball in every country of the world, nothing bad happened. Antarctica is stark and desolate, and despite the presence of birds, penguins, and seals as well as the unexpected beautiful blues of the icebergs, one cannot help but be struck by how insignificant and intrusive the appearance of human beings is in that predominantly white landscape, and I wanted to try to describe how this strange and vaguely hostile environment might affect a long-married couple.

Lily Tuck was born in France in 1939 and lived in South America as a child. She is the author of four novels—*Interviewing Matisse or The Woman Who Died Standing Up, The Woman Who Walked on Water, Siam* (a PEN/Faulkner Award finalist), and *The News from Paraguay* (winner of the 2004 National Book Award)—a collection of stories, *Limbo and Other Places I Have Lived,* and a biography, *Woman of Rome: A Life of Elsa Morante.* Her essay "Group Grief" was included in *The Best American Essays 2006.* Her novel *Probability or I Married You for Happiness* will be published in fall 2011. She lives in New York City.

Brad Watson, "Alamo Plaza"

During my family's leanest years, when I was growing up, we spent our summer vacations (if we got one; sometimes we didn't, and sometimes they were as brief as three days) on the Mississippi Gulf Coast. It was always a boy's disappointment, compared to the Alabama and north Florida coasts, with their natural white sand beaches and comparatively huge waves rolling in. And their much clearer water, very clear and green in north Florida. The real beaches in Mississippi are offshore, on the barrier islands, accessible by private boat or ferry, but we never went out there. We got the Mississippi Sound, which in those days was polluted by bad stuff from plants upriver, by waste from the fishing industry, and I don't know what-all else. But it did have a charm about it. The whole place seemed calmer, more still, less corrupted by the glitzier and cheaper elements of upscale tourism. The smell—at first alarming and repulsive, then kind of wonderfully rich, a smell you realized was the rank richness of marine life and death—was one I experienced nowhere else, on no other coast, and not in New Orleans or any other coastal city. Except for a grand old hotel or two, most of the lodging was either run-down or modest. And the clientele was pretty much entirely local, Mississippi, with some Louisiana tourists mixed in. So I have fond memories of the place, even though I despised it at the time. These memories, mixed with memories of an imaginatively reclusive childhood, of often feeling like the odd boy out in my own family, were things I tried for a long time to combine in this story. It went into and back out of the desk drawer for many years, as I'd write a draft and fail, put it away, write it again a year or a few later, until it finally felt right. It feels highly personal, anyway, a story that comes from pretty deep inside. Putting it together, finally, felt like a great and pleasant relief. There was a kind of joyous sadness about it, which I guess is what I often experience when I recall that childhood, that family, mostly gone now.

Brad Watson was born in 1955 in Meridian, Mississippi. His stories have been published in *Ecotone, The New Yorker, Granta, The Idaho Review, Oxford American, Narrative Magazine, The Greens-*

boro Review, and *The Yalobusha Review,* as well as anthologies including *The PEN/O. Henry Prize Stories, The Best American Mystery Stories,* and *The Story and Its Writer.* His story collection *Last Days of the Dog-Men* received the Sue Kaufman Prize for First Fiction from the American Academy of Arts and Letters. His novel, *The Heaven of Mercury,* received the Southern Book Critics Circle Fiction Award (shared with Lee Smith), and was a finalist for the National Book Award. His most recent collection is *Aliens in the Prime of Their Lives.* He teaches in the MFA program at the University of Wyoming and lives in Laramie, Wyoming.

Recommended Story 2011

The task of picking the twenty PEN/O. Henry Prize stories each year is at its most difficult at the end, when there are more than twenty admirable and interesting stories. Once the final choice is made, those remaining are our Recommended Stories, listed, along with the place of publication, in the hope that our readers will seek them out and enjoy them. Please go to our website, www.penohenryprizestories.com, for excerpts from each year's recommended stories and information about the writers.

Adam Atlas, "New Year's Weekend on the Hand Surgery Ward, Old Pilgrims' Hospital, Naples, Italy," *Narrative Magazine.*

Publications Submitted

Stories published in American and Canadian magazines are eligible for consideration for inclusion in *The PEN/O. Henry Prize Stories*. Only print editions are considered; that is, online-only publications are not eligible.

Stories must be written originally in the English language. No translations are considered.

Stories may not be submitted by agents or writers. Editors are asked to send the entire issue and not to nominate individual stories.

Because of production deadlines for the 2012 collection, it is essential that stories reach the series editor by May 1, 2011. If a finished magazine is unavailable before the deadline, magazine editors are welcome to submit scheduled stories in proof or manuscript. Publications received after May 1, 2011, will automatically be considered for *The PEN/O. Henry Prize Stories 2013*.

Please see our website, www.penohenryprizestories.com, for more information about submission to *The PEN/O. Henry Prize Stories*.

The address for submission is:

Laura Furman, *The PEN/O. Henry Prize Stories*
The University of Texas at Austin
English Department, B5000
1 University Station
Austin, TX 78712

The information listed below was up-to-date when *The PEN/O. Henry Prize Stories 2011* went to press. Inclusion in this listing does not constitute endorsement or recommendation by *The PEN/O. Henry Prize Stories* or Anchor Books.

African American Review
Saint Louis University
Humanities 317
3800 Lindell Boulevard
St. Louis, MO 63108
Nathan Grant, editor
aar.slu.edu
quarterly

Agni Magazine
Boston University
236 Bay State Road
Boston, MA 02215
Sven Birkerts
agni@bu.edu
agnimagazine.org
semiannual

Alaska Quarterly Review
University of Alaska Anchorage
3211 Providence Drive
Anchorage, AK 99508
Ronald Spatz, editor
uaa.alaska.edu/aqr
semiannual

Alimentum
PO Box 776
New York, NY 10163
Paulette Licitra and Peter Selgin,
    editors
editor@alimentumjournal.com
alimentumjournal.com
semiannual

**American Letters &
    Commentary**
Department of English
University of Texas at San
    Antonio
One UTSA Circle
San Antonio, TX 78249-0643
Catherine Kasper and David Ray
    Vance, editors
AmerLetters@satx.rr.com
amletters.org
annual

American Literary Review
PO Box 311307
University of North Texas
Denton, TX 76203-1307
John Tait, editor
engl.unt.edu/alr/
semiannual

The American Scholar
1606 New Hampshire Avenue
    NW
Washington, DC 20009
Robert Wilson, editor
scholar@pbk.org
theamericanscholar.org
quarterly

American Short Fiction
PO Box 301209
Austin, TX 78703
Stacey Swann, Editor

americanshortfiction.org
quarterly

ANNALEMMA
Chris Heavener, editor
info@annalemma.net
annalemma.net
semiannual

Another Chicago Magazine
PO Box 408439
Chicago, IL 60640
Jacob Knabb, Michael Meinhardt,
    Joris Soeding, editors
anotherchicagomagazine.net
semiannual

The Antioch Review
PO Box 148
Yellow Springs, Ohio 45387-0148
Robert S. Fogarty, editor
antiochreview.org
quarterly

Apalachee Review
PO Box 10469
Tallahassee, FL 32302
Michael Trammell, editor
apalacheereview.org
semiannual

Arkansas Review: A Journal of Delta Studies
Department of English and
    Philosophy
PO Box 1890
Arkansas State University, AR
    72467
Janelle Collins, general editor
arkansasreview@astate.edu
altweb.astate.edu/arkreview

Arts & Letters
Campus Box 89
Georgia College and State
    University
Milledgeville, GA 31061-0490
Martin Lammon, editor
al@gcsu.edu
al.gcsu.edu
semiannual

The Atlantic Monthly
600 New Hampshire Avenue NW
Washington, DC 20037
Felix DiFilippo, literary editor
theatlantic.com
monthly

Avery
Stephanie Fiorelli, Adam Koehler,
    Nicolette Kittinger, editors
submissions@averyanthology.org
averyanthology.org
biannual

The Baltimore Review
PO Box 36418
Towson, MD 21286
 Susan Muaddi Darraj,
 senior editor
baltimorereview.org
semiannual

Bellevue Literary Review
Department of Medicine
NYU Langone Medical Center
550 First Avenue, OBV-A612
New York, NY 10016
Ronna Wineberg, JD, senior
 fiction editor
blr.med.nyu.edu
semiannual

Berkeley Fiction Review
10B Eshleman Hall
University of California
Berkeley, CA 94720-4500
Caitlin McGuire and Jennifer
 Brown, managing editors
bfictionreview@yahoo.com
ocf.berkeley.edu/~bfr

Black Clock
California Institute of the
 Arts
24700 McBean Parkway
Valencia, CA 91355
Steve Erickson, editor
info@blackclock.org

www.blackclock.org
semiannual

Black Warrior Review
Box 862936
Tuscaloosa, AL 35486
Stephen Gropp-Hess, fiction
 editor
bwr@ua.edu
blackwarrior.webdelsol.com
semiannual

Bloodroot Literary Magazine
PO Box 322
Thetford Center, VT 05075
"Do" Roberts, editor
bloodroot@wildblue.net
bloodrootlm.com
annual

BOMB
New Art Publications
80 Hanson Place
Suite 703
Brooklyn, NY 11217
Betsy Sussler, editor in chief
generalinquiries@bombsite.com
bombsite.com

Boston Review
PO Box 425786
Cambridge, MA 02142
Deborah Chasman and Joshua
 Cohen, editors

review@bostonreview.net
bostonreview.net
published six times per year

Boulevard
6614 Clayton Road, Box 325
Richmond Heights, MO 63117
Richard Burgin, editor
boulevardmagazine.org
triannual

Brain, Child: The Magazine for Thinking Mothers
PO Box 714
Lexington, VA 24450
Stephanie Wilkinson and Jennifer
  Niesslein, editors
editor@brainchildmag.com
brainchildmag.com/
quarterly

The Briar Cliff Review
3303 Rebecca Street
Sioux City, IA 51104-2100
Tricia Currans-Sheehen, editor
currans@briarcliff.edu
briarcliff.edu/bcreview
annual

Callaloo
4212 TAMU
Texas A&M University
College Station, TX 77843-4227
Charles Henry Rowell, editor

callaloo@tamu.edu
callaloo.tamu.edu

Calyx
PO Box B
Corvallis, OR 97339
Beverly McFarland, senior editor
info@calyxpress.org
calyxpress.org
semiannual

Canteen
96 Pierrepont Street, #4
Brooklyn, NY 11201
Sean Finney, editor in chief
info@canteenmag.com
canteenmag.com
quarterly

The Carolina Quarterly
Greenlaw Hall, CB 3520
University of North Carolina
Chapel Hill, NC 27599-3520
Matthew Luter and Ricky
  Werner, fiction editors
thecarolinaquarterly.com
triannual

Chicago Review
5801 South Kenwood Avenue
Chicago, IL 60637
V. Joshua Adams, editor
humanities.uchicago.edu/review
quarterly

Cimarron Review
205 Morrill Hall
English Department
Oklahoma State University
Stillwater, OK 74078-4069
E. P. Walkiewicz, editor
cimarronreview.okstate.edu
quarterly

The Cincinnati Review
University of Cincinnati
McMicken Hall, Room 369
PO Box 210069
Cincinnati, OH 45221-0069
Brock Clarke, fiction editor
cincinnatireview.com
semiannual

Colorado Review
Department of English
Colorado State University
Fort Collins, CO 80523
Stephanie G'Schwind, editor
creview@colostate.edu
coloradoreview.colostate.edu/cr.htm

Columbia
622 West 113th Street, MC4521
New York, NY 10025
Michael B. Shavelson, editor in
  chief
magazine@columbia.edu
magazine.columbia.edu/
quarterly

Commentary
165 East 56th Street
New York, NY 10022
John Podhoretz, editor
editorial@commentarymagazine.com
commentarymagazine.com
monthly

**Conclave: A Journal of
  Character**
7144 North Harlem Avenue,
  #325
Chicago, IL 60631
Valya Dudycz Lupescu, editor
editor@conclavejournal.com
conclavejournal.com
annual

Confrontation
English Department
C. W. Post of Long Island
  University
Brookville, NY 11548
Martin Tucker, editor in chief
confrontationmag@gmail.com
confrontationmagazine.org
semiannual

Conjunctions
21 East 10th Street
New York, NY 10003
Bradford Morrow, editor
conjunctions.com
semiannual

Crab Orchard Review
Southern Illinois University
    Carbondale
1000 Faner Drive
Faner Hall 2380—Mail Code
    4503
Carbondale, IL 62901
Allison Joseph, editor
craborchardreview.siuc.edu
semiannual

Crazyhorse
Department of English
College of Charleston
66 George Street
Charleston, SC 29424
Garrett Doherty, editor
crazyhorse@cofc.edu
crazyhorsejournal.org

Cream City Review
Department of English
University of Wisconsin—
    Milwaukee
Box 413
Milwaukee, WI 53201
Jay Johnson, editor in chief
creamcityreview.org
semiannual

Daedalus
American Academy of Arts and
    Sciences
Norton's Woods

136 Irving Street
Cambridge, MA 02138
Phyllis Bendell, managing editor
daedalus@amacad.org
mitpressjournals.org/loi/daed
quarterly (publication by
    invitation only)

Dappled Things
Mary Angelita Ruiz, editor in
    chief
dappledthings.editor@gmail.com
dappledthings.org
quarterly

Denver Quarterly
Department of English
University of Denver
2000 East Asbury
Denver, CO 80208
Bin Ramke, editor
denverquarterly.com
quarterly

descant
Department of English
Texas Christian University
TCU Box 297270
Fort Worth, TX 76129
Dave Kuhne, editor
descant.tcu.edu
annual

Ecotone
Department of Creative Writing
University of North Carolina
    Wilmington
601 South College Road
Wilmington, NC 28403-5938
Ben George, editor
ecotonejournal.com
semiannual

Electric Literature
325 Gold Street, Suite 303
Brooklyn, NY 11201
Andy Hunter and Scott
    Lindenbaum, editors
editors@electricliterature.com
electricliterature.com
quarterly

Epiphany: A Literary Journal
Willard Cook, editor in chief
epiphanyzine.com
semiannual

Epoch
251 Goldwin Smith Hall
Cornell University
Ithaca, NY 14853-3201
Michael Koch, editor
arts.cornell.edu/english/
    publications/epoch
triannual

Event
Douglas College
PO Box 2503
New Westminster, BC V3L 5B2
Canada
Rick Maddocks, editor
event.douglas.bc.ca
triannual

Exile
134 Eastbourne Avenue
Toronto, ON M5P 2G6
Canada
Barry Callaghan, editor in chief
exilequarterly.com
quarterly

Fantasy & Science Fiction
PO Box 3447
Hoboken, NJ 07030
Gordon Van Gelder, editor
fandsf.com
bimonthly

The Farallon Review
1017 L Street
Number 348
Sacramento, CA 95814
Tim Foley, editor
Editor@farallonreview.com
farallonreview.com
annual

Fence
Science Library 320
University at Albany
1400 Washington Avenue
Albany, NY 12222
Lynne Tillman, fiction editor
fence@albany.edu
fenceportal.org

Fiction
Department of English
The City College of New York
Convent Avenue at 138th Street
New York, NY 10031
Mark Jay Mirsky, editor in chief
fictionmagazine@yahoo.com
fictioninc.com

The Fiddlehead
Campus House
11 Garland Court
PO Box 4400
University of New Brunswick
Fredericton, NB E3B 5A3
Canada
Ross Leckie, editor
fiddlehd@unb.ca
thefiddlehead.ca
quarterly

Fifth Wednesday Journal
PO Box 4033
Lisle, IL 60532-9033
Vern Miller, editor

fifthwednesdayjournal.org
biannual

The First Line
PO Box 250382
Plano, TX 75025-0382
David LaBounty, editor
info@thefirstline.com
thefirstline.com
quarterly

Five Points
Georgia State University
PO Box 3999
Atlanta, GA 30302-3999
David Bottoms and Megan
    Sexton, editors
fivepoints.gsu.edu
triannual

The Florida Review
Department of English
PO Box 161346
University of Central Florida
Orlando, FL 32816
Jocelyn Bartkevicius, editor in
    chief
flreview@mail.ucf.edu
flreview.com

Fourteen Hills
Department of Creative Writing
San Francisco State University
1600 Holloway Avenue

San Francisco, CA 94132-1722
Lori Savageau and Michael
    Urquidez, fiction editors
14hills.net
semiannual

Fugue

University of Idaho
200 Brink Hall
PO Box 441102
Moscow, ID 83844-1102
Chase Colton, fiction editor
fugue@uidaho.edu
uidaho.edu/fugue

Gargoyle

3819 North 13th Street
Arlington, VA 22201
Lucinda Ebersole and Richard
    Peabody, editors
gargoyle@gargoylemagazine.com
gargoylemagazine.com
annual

The Georgia Review

The University of Georgia
Athens, GA 30602-9009
Stephen Corey, editor
thegeorgiareview.com
quarterly

The Gettysburg Review

Gettysburg College
Gettysburg, PA 17325-1491

Peter Stitt, editor
gettysburgreview.com
quarterly

Gigantic

Ann DeWitt, Rozalia Jovanovic,
    Lincoln Michel, James Yeh,
    editors
giganticmag@gmail.com
thegiganticmag.com
semiannual

Glimmer Train

1211 NW Glisan Street, Suite
    207
Portland, OR 97209-3054
Susan Burmeister-Brown and
    Linda B. Swanson-Davies,
    editors
editors@glimmertrain.org
glimmertrain.org
quarterly

Good Housekeeping

Hearst Communications
300 West 57th Street
New York, NY 10019
Laura Mathews, literary editor
goodhousekeeping.com
monthly

Grain

Box 67
Saskatoon, SK S7K 3K1

Canada
Sylvia Legris, editor
grainmag@sasktel.net
grainmagazine.ca
quarterly

Granta
12 Addison Avenue
London W11 4QR
United Kingdom
John Freeman, editor
editorial@granta.com
granta.com
quarterly

The Greensboro Review
MFA Writing Program
3302 HHRA Building
University of North Carolina at
    Greensboro
Greensboro, NC 27402-6170
Jim Clark, editor
greensbororeview.org
biannual

Grey Sparrow Journal
812 Hilltop Road
Mendota Heights, MN 55118
Diane Smith, editor in chief
greysparrowpress.net
quarterly

Gulf Coast
Department of English
University of Houston
Houston, TX 77204-3013
Nick Flynn, faculty editor
gulfcoastmag.org
biannual

H.O.W. Journal
12 Desbrosses Street
New York, NY 10013
Alison Weaver and Natasha
    Radojcic, editors
info@howjournal.com
howjournal.com
biannual

Harper's Magazine
666 Broadway
New York, NY 10012
Ben Metcalf, literary editor
harpers.org
monthly

Harpur Palate
English Department
Binghamton University
PO Box 6000
Binghamton, NY 13902-6000
Matthew Burns and James
    Capozzi, editors
harpurpalate.binghamton.edu
biannual

Harvard Review
Lamont Library
Harvard University
Cambridge, MA 02138
Christina Thompson, editor
harvrev@fas.harvard.edu
hcl.harvard.edu/harvardreview
biannual

Hayden's Ferry Review
Box 875002
Arizona State University
Tempe, AZ 85287-5002
Beth Staples, managing editor
HFR@asu.edu
asu.edu/piper/publications/
    haydensferryreview
biannual

The Hudson Review
684 Park Avenue
New York, NY 10065
Paula Deitz, editor
hudsonreview.com
quarterly

Idaho Review
Department of English
Boise State University
1910 University Drive
Boise, ID 83725
Mitch Wieland, editor in chief
idahoreview.org
annual

Image
3307 Third Avenue West
Seattle, WA 98119
Mary Kenagy, managing editor
image@imagejournal.org
imagejournal.org
quarterly

Indiana Review
Indiana University
Ballantine Hall 465
1020 East Kirkwood Avenue
Bloomington, IN 47405-7103
Alessandra Simmons, editor
inreview@indiana.edu
indianareview.org

Iowa Review
308 EPB
University of Iowa
Iowa City, IA 52242-1408
Russell Scott Valentino, editor
iowareview.org
triannual

Iron Horse Literary Review
Department of English
Texas Tech University
Mail Stop 43091
Lubbock, TX 79409-3091
Leslie Jill Patterson, editor
ironhorsereview.com
published six times per year

Jabberwock Review
Drawer E
Department of English
Mississippi State University
Mississippi State, MS 39762
Michael P. Kardos, editor
msstate.edu/org/jabberwock
semiannual

The Journal
The Ohio State University
Department of English
164 West 17th Avenue
Columbus, OH 43210
Michelle Herman, prose editor
thejournalmag@gmail.com
english.osu.edu/research/journals/
thejournal

Juked
110 Westridge Drive
Tallahassee, FL 32304
J. W. Wang, editor
info@juked.com
juked.com
annual

The Kenyon Review
Kenyon College
Finn House
102 West Wiggin Street
Gambier, OH 43022
Geeta Kothari, fiction editor

kenyonreview@kenyon.edu
kenyonreview.org

**Lady Churchill's Rosebud
   Wristlet**
150 Pleasant Street, #306
Easthampton, MA 01027
Kelly Link and Gavin Grant,
   editors
smallbeerpress@gmail.com
smallbeerpress.com/lcrw
semiannual

Lake Effect
School of Humanities and Social
   Sciences
Penn State Erie
4951 College Drive
Erie, PA 16563-1501
George Looney, editor in chief
behrend.psu.edu/lakeeffect
annual

The Laurel Review
English Department
Northwest Missouri State
   University
800 University Drive
Maryville, MO 64468-6001
John Gallaher and Richard
   Sonnenmoser, editors
catpages.nwmissouri.edu/m/tlr/
semiannual

Literary Imagination
Peter Campion, editor
litimag.oxfordjournals.org
triannual

The Literary Review
285 Madison Avenue
Madison, NJ 07940
Minna Proctor, editor
editorial@theliteraryreview.org
theliteraryreview.org
quarterly

The Long Story
18 Eaton Street
Lawrence, MA 01843
R. P. Burnham, editor
rpburnham@mac.com
web.me.com/rpburnham/Site/
    LongStory.html
annual

Louisiana Literature
SLU Box 10792
Southeastern Louisiana University
Hammond, LA 70402
Jack Bedell, editor
lalit@selu.edu
louisianaliterature.org
semiannual

The Louisville Review
851 South Fourth Street

Spalding University
Louisville, KY 40203
Sena Jeter Naslund, editor
louisvillereview@spalding.edu
louisvillereview.org
semiannual

The Lowbrow Reader
PO Box 65
Cooper Station
New York, NY 10276
Jay Ruttenberg, editor
editor@lowbrowreader.com
lowbrowreader.com
annual

Low Rent
Robert Liddell, fiction editor
lowrentmagazine.com
six issues per year

**Make: A Chicago Literary
    Magazine**
Sarah Dodson, managing editor
makemag.com
semiannual

The Malahat Review
University of Victoria
PO Box 1700
STN CSC
Victoria, BC V8W 2Y2
Canada

John Barton, editor
malahat@uvic.ca
malahatreview.ca

Manoa
English Department
University of Hawai'i
1733 Donaghho Road
Honolulu, HI 96822
Frank Stewart, editor
mjournal-l@lists.hawaii.edu
manoajournal.hawaii.edu

**McSweeney's Quarterly
    Concern**
849 Valencia Street
San Francisco, CA 94110
Dave Eggers, editor
printsubs@mcsweeneys.net
mcsweeneys.net
quarterly

Meridian
University of Virginia
PO Box 400145
Charlottesville, VA 22904-4145
Hannah Holtzman, editor
meridianuva@yahoo.com
readmeridian.org
semiannual

Michigan Quarterly Review
University of Michigan

0576 Rackham Building
915 East Washington Street
Ann Arbor, MI 48109-1070
Jonathan Freedman, editor
michiganquarterlyreview.com
quarterly

The Minnesota Review
Virginia Tech
ASPECT
202 Major Williams Hall (0192)
Blacksburg, VA 24061
Janell Watson, editor
editors@theminnesotareview.org
theminnesotareview.org
semiannual

Minnetonka Review
PO Box 386
Spring Park, MN 55384
Troy Ehlers, editor in chief
minnetonkareview.com
semiannual

Mississippi Review
The University of Southern
    Mississippi
118 College Drive
Box 5144
Hattiesburg, MS 39406-0001
Julia Johnson, editor
mississippireview.com
semiannual

The Missouri Review
357 McReynolds Hall
University of Missouri-Columbia
Columbia, MO 65211
Speer Morgan, editor
missourireview.com
quarterly

n+1
68 Jay Street, #405
Brooklyn, NY 11201
Keith Gessen and Mark Greif,
    editors
nplusonemag.com
semiannual

Nameless Magazine
namelessmagazine.com
annual

Narrative Magazine
Carol Edgarian and Tom Jenks,
    editors
Editor@NarrativeMagazine.com
narrativemagazine.com
triannual

New Delta Review
English Department
15 Allen Hall
Louisiana State University
Baton Rouge, LA 70803-5001
Lauren C. Tussing-White, editor

lsu.edu/newdeltareview
semiannual

New England Review
Middlebury College
Middlebury, VT 05753
Stephen Donadio, editor
nereview@middlebury.edu
nereview.com
quarterly

New Letters
University of Missouri-Kansas
    City
University House
5101 Rockhill Road
Kansas City, MO 64110
Robert Stewart, editor
newletters@umkc.edu
newletters.org
quarterly

New Millennium Writings
PO Box 2463
Knoxville, TN 37901
Don Williams, editor
newmillenniumwritings.com
annual

New Ohio Review
English Department
360 Ellis Hall
Ohio University

Athens, OH 45701
Jill Allyn Rosser, editor
noreditors@ohio.edu
ohiou.edu/nor

New Orleans Review
Box 195
Loyola University
New Orleans, LA 70118
Christopher Chambers, editor
neworleansreview.org
semiannual

The New Yorker
4 Times Square
New York, NY 10036
Deborah Treisman, fiction editor
fiction@newyorker.com
newyorker.com
weekly

Nimrod International Journal
University of Tulsa
800 South Tucker Drive
Tulsa, OK 74104
Francine Ringold, editor in chief
nimrod@utulsa.edu
utulsa.edu/nimrod
semiannual

Ninth Letter
Department of English
University of Illinois, Urbana-
    Champaign

608 South Wright Street
Urbana, IL 61801
Jodee Stanley, editor
ninthletter.com
semiannual

Noon
1324 Lexington Avenue
PMB 298
New York, NY 10128
Diane Williams, editor
noonannual.com/
annual

North American Review
University of Northern Iowa
1222 West 27th Street
Cedar Falls, Iowa 50614-0516
Grant Tracey, fiction editor
nar@uni.edu
webdelsol.com/NorthAmReview/
    NAR
published five times per year

North Carolina Literary Review
Department of English
East Carolina University
2134 Bate Building
Greenville, NC 27858-4353
Margaret Bauer, editor
BauerM@ecu.edu
ecu.edu/nclr

Northern New England Review
ATTN: Humanities Department
Franklin Pierce University
Rindge, NH 03461
Edie Clark, managing editor
nner@franklinpierce.edu
semiannual

Northwest Review
5243 University of Oregon
Eugene, OR 97403-5243
nwr.uoregon.edu
semiannual

Notre Dame Review
804 Flanner Hall
University of Notre Dame
Notre Dame, IN 46556
John Matthias and William
   O'Rourke, editors
nd.edu/~ndr/review.htm
semiannual

Noun Versus Verb
Burning River
169 South Main Street, #4
Rittman, OH 44270
Christopher Bowen, editor
editor@burningriver.info
annual

One Story
232 Third Street, #E106
Brooklyn, NY 11215

Hannah Tinti, editor in chief
one-story.com
published about every three weeks

Open City
270 Lafayette Street, Suite 1412
New York, NY 10012
Thomas Beller and Joanna Yas,
   editors
editors@opencity.org
opencity.org
triannual

Overtime
PO Box 250382
Plano, TX 75025-0382
workerswritejournal.com/
   overtime.htm
published six times per year

The Oxford American
201 Donaghey Avenue, Main 107
Conway, AR 72035
Marc Smirnoff, editor
oxfordamerican.org
quarterly

Pakn Treger
National Yiddish Book Center
Harry and Jeanette Weinberg
   Building
1021 West Street
Amherst, MA 01002-3375
Nancy Sherman, editor

pt2009@bikher.org
yiddishbookcenter.org/
  pakn-treger

The Paris Review
62 White Street
New York, NY 10013
Nicole Rudick, managing editor
theparisreview.org
quarterly

Parting Gifts
3413 Wilshire Drive
Greensboro, NC 27408-2923
Robert Bixby, editor
rbixby@earthlink.net
marchstreetpress.com
semiannual

PEN America
PEN American Center
588 Broadway, Suite 303
New York, NY 10012
M. Mark, editor
journal@pen.org
pen.org/journal
semiannual

Pilot
PO Box 161, Station B
119 Spadina Avenue
Toronto, ON M5T 2T3
Canada

Reuben McLaughlin and Lee
  Sheppard, editors
editor@thepilotproject.ca
thepilotproject.ca
semiannual

The Pinch
Department of English
University of Memphis
Memphis, TN 38512-6176
Kristen Iversen, editor in chief
thepinchjournal.com
semiannual

Pleiades
Department of English,
  Martin 336
University of Central Missouri
Warrensburg, MO 64093
Wayne Miller and Phong
  Nguyen, editors
ucmo.edu/englphil/pleiades
semiannual

Ploughshares
Emerson College
120 Boylston Street
Boston, MA 02116-4624
Ladette Randolph, editor in chief
pshares@emerson.edu
pshares.org
triannual

PMS poemmemoirstory
HB 217
1530 Third Avenue South
Birmingham, AL 35294-1260
Kerry Madden, editor in chief
pms-journal.org
annual

Post Road
Ricco Siasoco, managing editor
postroadmag.com
semiannual

Potomac Review
Montgomery College
Paul Peck Humanities Institute
51 Mannakee Street
Rockville, MD 20850
Julie Wakeman-Linn, editor
montgomerycollege.edu/potomac
review
semiannual

Prairie Fire
423-100 Arthur Street
Winnipeg, MB R3B 1H3
Canada
Andris Taskans, editor
prfire@mts.net
prairiefire.ca
quarterly

Prairie Schooner
201 Andrews Hall

University of Nebraska
Lincoln, NE 68588-0334
James Engelhardt, managing
editor
prairieschooner.unl.edu
quarterly

Prism International
University of British Columbia
Buchanan E-462
1866 Main Mall
Vancouver, BC V6T 1Z1
Canada
Jeff Stautz, fiction editor
prismmagazine.ca

A Public Space
323 Dean Street
Brooklyn, New York 11217
Brigid Hughes, editor
general@apublicspace.org
apublicspace.org
quarterly

Puerto del Sol
New Mexico State University
PO Box 30001, MSC 3E
Las Cruces, NM 88003-8001
Carmen Giménez Smith, editor
in chief
puertodelsol.org
semiannual

Raritan: A Quarterly Review
Rutgers University
31 Mine Street
New Brunswick, NJ 08901
Jackson Lears, editor in chief
raritanquarterly.rutgers.edu
quarterly

**REAL: Regarding Arts and
   Letters**
Stephen F. Austin State
   University
PO Box 13007, SFA Station
Nacogdoches, TX 75962-3007
Christine Butterworth-
   McDermott, editor in chief
real.sfasu.edu
semiannual

Red Rock Review
English Department, J2A
College of Southern Nevada
3200 East Cheyenne Avenue
North Las Vegas, NV 89030
Richard Logsdon, senior editor
RedRockReview@csn.edu
sites.csn.edu/english/redrockreview/
   issue.htm

Redivider
Emerson College
120 Boylston Street
Boston, MA 02116

Amber Lee, editor in chief
redividerjournal.org
semiannual

**Relief: A Christian Literary
   Expression**
60 West Terra Cotta
Suite B, Unit 156
Crystal Lake, IL 60014-3548
Christopher Fisher, editor in chief
reliefjournal.com
semiannual

River Styx
3547 Olive Street, Suite 107
St. Louis, MO 63103
Richard Newman, editor
riverstyx.org
triannual

Rosebud
N3310 Asje Road
Cambridge, WI 53523
Roderick Clark, managing editor
rsbd.net
triannual

Ruminate
140 North Roosevelt Avenue
Fort Collins, CO 80521
Brianna Van Dyke, editor in chief
ruminatemagazine.org
quarterly

Salamander
English Department
Suffolk University
41 Temple Street
Boston, MA 02114-4280
Jennifer Barber, editor
salamandermag.org
semiannual

Salmagundi
Skidmore College
815 North Broadway
Saratoga Springs, NY 12866
Robert Boyers, editor in chief
cms.skidmore.edu/salmagundi
quarterly

Santa Monica Review
Santa Monica College
1900 Pico Boulevard
Santa Monica, CA 90405
Andrew Tonkovich, editor
antonkovi@uci.edu
smc.edu/sm_review
semiannual

Saranac Review
CVH
SUNY Plattsburgh
101 Broad Street
Plattsburgh, NY 12901
Matt Bondurant, fiction
    editor
research.plattsburgh.edu/
    saranacreview
annual

Sensations Magazine
PO Box 132
Lafayette, NJ 07848-0132
David Messineo, publisher
sensationsmag.com
semiannual

Seven Days
PO Box 1164
Burlington, VT 05402-1164
Pamela Polston and Paula Routly,
    editors
sevendaysvt.com
weekly

Sewanee Review
University of the South
735 University Avenue
Sewanee, TN 37383-1000
George Core, editor
sewanee.edu/sewanee_review
quarterly

Shenandoah
Mattingly House
2 Lee Avenue
Washington and Lee University
Lexington, VA 24450-2116
R. T. Smith, editor

shenandoah@wlu.edu
shenandoah.wlu.edu

Silk Road
Gregory Belliveau, senior fiction
    editor
silkroad.pacific@gmail.com
silkroad.pacificu.edu/index.htm/
annual

Sonora Review
English Department
University of Arizona
Tucson, AZ 85721
Patti Hadad, fiction editor
sonora@email.arizona.edu
sonorareview.com
semiannual

South Carolina Review
Center for Electronic and Digital
    Publishing
Clemson University
Strode Tower, Box 340522
Clemson, SC 29634-0522
Wayne Chapman, editor
clemson.edu/cedp/cudp/scr/
    about.htm
semiannual

South Dakota Review
Department of English
University of South Dakota
414 East Clark Street

Vermillion, SD 57069
Brian Bedard, editor
sdreview@usd.edu
orgs.usd.edu/sdreview

Southern Humanities Review
9088 Haley Center
Auburn University
Auburn, AL 36849
Dan Latimer and Chantel
    Acevedo, editors
auburn.edu/shr
quarterly

Southern Indiana Review
College of Liberal Arts
University of Southern Indiana
8600 University Boulevard
Evansville, IN 47712
Nicole Louise Reid, fiction editor
usi.edu/sir/
semiannual

The Southern Review
Louisiana State University
Old President's House
Baton Rouge, LA 70803-0001
Jeanne Leiby, editor
lsu.edu/thesouthernreview
quarterly

Southwest Review
Southern Methodist University
PO Box 750374

Dallas, TX 75275-0374
Willard Spiegelman, editor in
 chief
smu.edu/southwestreview
quarterly

Spot Literary Magazine

Spot Write Literary Corporation
4729 East Sunrise Road, Box 254
Tucson, AZ 85718-4535
Susan Hansell, editor
susan.hansell@gmail.com
spotlitmagazine.net
semiannual

St. Anthony Messenger

28 West Liberty Street
Cincinnati, OH 45202-6498
Pat McCloskey, OFM, editor
mageditors@americancatholic.org
americancatholic.org
monthly

Subtropics

PO Box 112075
4008 Turlington Hall
University of Florida
Gainesville, FL 32611-2075
David Leavitt, editor
english.ufl.edu/subtropics
triannual

The Sun

107 North Roberson Street

Chapel Hill, NC 27516
Sy Safransky, editor
thesunmagazine.org
monthly

Sycamore Review

Purdue University
Department of English
500 Oval Drive
West Lafayette, IN 47907-2038
Anthony Cook, editor in chief
sycamore@purdue.edu
sycamorereview.com

Third Coast

English Department
Western Michigan University
Kalamazoo, MI 49008-5331
Emily J. Stinson, editor
editors@thirdcoastmagazine
 .com
thirdcoastmagazine.com
semiannual

The Threepenny Review

PO Box 9131
Berkeley, CA 94709
Wendy Lesser, editor
threepennyreview.com
quarterly

Timber Creek Review

8969 UNCG Station
Greensboro, NC 27413

John M. Freiermuth, editor
quarterly

Tin House
PO Box 10500
Portland, OR 97296-0500
Win McCormack, editor in chief
tinhouse.com
quarterly

upstreet
PO Box 105
Richmond, MA 01254-0105
Vivian Dorsel, editor
upstreet-mag.org
annual

Virginia Quarterly Review
1 West Range
PO Box 400223
Charlottesville, VA 22904
Ted Genoways, editor
vqr@vqronline.org
vqronline.org
quarterly

Water-Stone Review
Graduate School of Liberal
    Studies
Hamline University, MS-A1730
1536 Hewitt Avenue
Saint Paul, MN 55104-1284
water-stone@hamline.edu

waterstonereview.com
annual

**Weber: The Contemporary
    West**
Weber State University
1405 University Circle
Ogden, UT 84408-1405
Michael Wutz, editor
weberjournal@weber.edu
weber.edu/weberjournal
semiannual

West Branch
Bucknell Hall
Bucknell University
Lewisburg, PA 17837
Paula Closson Buck, editor
westbranch@bucknell.edu
bucknell.edu/x10858.xm
semiannual

West Marin Review
Tomales Bay Library Association
PO Box 984
Point Reyes Station, CA 94956
info@westmarinreview.com
westmarinreview.org
annual

Western Humanities Review
University of Utah
English Department

255 South Central Campus
Drive, LNCO 3500
Salt Lake City, UT 84112-0494
Barry Weller, editor
hum.utah.edu/whr
triannual

Whistling Shade
PO Box 7084
Saint Paul, MN 55107
Anthony Telschow, executive
editor
editor@whistlingshade.com
whistlingshade.com
semiannual

Witness
Black Mountain Institute
University of Nevada, Las Vegas
Box 455085
Las Vegas, NV 89154-5085
Amber Withycombe, editor
witness@unlv.edu
witness.blackmountaininstitute
.org

WLA: War, Literature & the Arts
Department of English and Fine
Arts
2354 Fairchild Drive, Suite
6D-149
USAF Academy

Colorado Springs, CO 80840-
6242
Donald Anderson, editor
editor@wlajournal.com
wlajournal.com

The Worcester Review
1 Ekman Street
Worcester, MA 01607
Rodger Martin, managing editor
wreview.homestead.com
annual

Workers Write!
PO Box 250382
Plano, TX 75025-0382
David LaBounty, editor
workerswritejournal.com
annual

The Yale Review
Box 208243
Yale University
New Haven, CT 06520-8243
J. D. McClatchy, editor
yale.edu/yalereview/
quarterly

Zoetrope: All-Story
916 Kearny Street
San Francisco, CA 94133
Michael Ray, editor
info@all-story.com

all-story.com
quarterly

Zone 3
Box 4565
Austin Peay State University
Clarksville, TN 37044
SusanWallace, managing editor
apsu.edu/zone3
semiannual

Permissions

JOIN PEN!

ASSOCIATE MEMBERSHIP IN PEN AMERICAN CENTER IS OPEN TO EVERYONE WHO SUPPORTS PEN'S MISSION. MEMBERS PLAY A VITAL ROLE IN SUPPORTING AND FURTHERING PEN'S EFFORTS ON BEHALF OF WRITERS AND READERS BOTH AT HOME AND ABROAD. BENEFITS INCLUDE:

► A SUBSCRIPTION TO *PEN AMERICA*, OUR AWARD-WINNING SEMI-ANNUAL JOURNAL

► DISCOUNTED ACCESS TO THE ONLINE DATABASE *GRANTS AND AWARDS AVAILABLE TO AMERICAN WRITERS*, THE MOST COMPREHENSIVE DIRECTORY OF ITS KIND

► SELECT INVITATIONS TO MEMBER-ONLY RECEPTIONS

► DISCOUNTS TO PUBLIC PROGRAMS, INCLUDING PEN WORLD VOICES: THE NEW YORK FESTIVAL OF INTERNATIONAL LITERATURE

► FREE WEB PAGE AND BLOG ON PEN.ORG

ANNUAL DUES ARE $40 ($20 FOR STUDENTS). TO JOIN, FILL OUT THE REGISTRATION FORM ON THE OPPOSITE PAGE, AND MAIL THE FORM AND PAYMENT TO:

PEN AMERICAN CENTER
MEMBERSHIP DEPT.
588 BROADWAY, 303
NEW YORK, NY 10012

YOU CAN ALSO JOIN ONLINE:
WWW.PEN.ORG/JOIN

Associate Member Registration

NAME: _____

ADDRESS: _____

CITY/STATE/ZIP: _____

TELEPHONE: _____

E-MAIL ADDRESS: _____

I AM A(N): ❑ WRITER ❑ ACADEMIC ❑ BOOKSELLER ❑ EDITOR
❑ JOURNALIST ❑ LIBRARIAN ❑ PUBLISHER ❑ TRANSLATOR ❑ OTHER_____

❑ I AM INTERESTED IN VOLUNTEER OPPORTUNITIES WITH PEN.

❑ I ENCLOSE $40, MY ANNUAL ASSOCIATE MEMBERSHIP DUES.
　　　-- OR --
❑ I ENCLOSE $20, MY ANNUAL STUDENT ASSOCIATE MEMBERSHIP DUES.

❑ I ALSO ENCLOSE A TAX-DEDUCTIBLE CONTRIBUTION IN ADDITION TO MY DUES TO PROVIDE MUCH-NEEDED SUPPORT FOR THE *READERS AND WRITERS* PROGRAM AT PEN, WHICH ENCOURAGES LITERARY CULTURE THROUGH OUTREACH PROGRAMS AND LITERARY EVENTS, INCLUDING AUTHOR PANELS, WRITING AND READING WORKSHOPS FOR HIGH SCHOOL STUDENTS, AND THE WRITING INSTITUTE, WHICH INVITES TEENS TO INTERACT DIRECTLY WITH PROFESSIONAL WRITERS IN A SERIES OF WORKSHOPS. FOR MORE INFO, VISIT: WWW.PEN.ORG/READERSANDWRITERS.

❑ $50 ❑ $100 ❑ $500 ❑ $1,000 PRESIDENT'S CIRCLE
❑ OTHER $_____

TOTAL: $_____

(ALL CONTRIBUTIONS ABOVE THE BASIC DUES OF $40/$20 ARE TAX DEDUCTIBLE TO THE FULLEST EXTENT ALLOWED BY THE LAW.)

PLEASE MAKE YOUR CHECK PAYABLE TO **PEN AMERICAN CENTER.**

MAIL FORM AND CHECK TO:
PEN AMERICAN CENTER, MEMBERSHIP DEPARTMENT
588 BROADWAY, 303, NEW YORK, NY 10012.

TO PAY BY CREDIT CARD PLEASE VISIT **www.pen.org/join.**